GERTRUDE BELLAMY-
HOMICIDE DETECTIVE

GERTRUDE BELLAMY- HOMICIDE DETECTIVE

A DETECTIVE HOMICIDE SERIES- BOOK 1 "DISCOVERY"

T. M. Morris

For information about special discounts for bulk purchases or appearances by the Author, please contact the Author or The Morris Legacy Group.

Morris Legacy Group
42103 50th Street Unit 3605
Lancaster, California 93586
www.morrislegacygroup.com
TiaMPublishing@gmail.com

Cover Design: by Natalia "Tai French" Edwards
Cover Photo: Courtesy of Natalia "Tai French" Edwards
Cover Model: LAPD Detective Cheryl Nalls (Retired)

I dedicate this Gertrude Bellamy Crime Series to my daughter, **Sergeant Britt A. Morris**, for she is the future of the Los Angeles Police Department and a strong leader amongst her peers, and in the Community. I owe a debt of gratitude to those whose shoulders I stood on, who forged a path for me, and so many others in my profession. Thank you **Georgia Ann Hill Robinson, Vivian Strange, Roberta Reddick; Marion Helenkamp, Marie Thomas,** and last but not least to all of my sisters in law enforcement from my generation who have rocked with me over the years, I thank you all immensely for your love and support. Secondly I dedicate this book to my husband Pjai, who is the inspiration behind one of the main characters in the series. I could not have brought this story to life without his incredible stories! KMA367… KJC625

TABLE OF CONTENTS

CHAPTER 1

"MESSY BOOTS"

———◆———

1980- "9-1-1 what's your emergency?"

"Can you please send an ambulance, my wife is in labor and I can see the baby's head coming out. Please hurry!"

"Ok sir, I see your address here on Dobbs Ferry Road. An ambulance is enroute and should be there very soon. I'll stay on the phone with you until paramedics arrive ok? *Please* try to stay calm."

IT APPEARED THAT CELESTE WAS two weeks early, but she probably gave the doctor the wrong date of her last period when she went for her first neonatal visit, which might have accounted for the baby's early arrival. The ambulance arrived quickly in spite of the falling snow. Thank God the ride to the hospital was very short. She yelled and panted while the Paramedics attended to her every need while Robert followed a safe distance behind in his car. By the time they reached the hospital she was rushed right into Labor and Delivery and within minutes gave birth to her one and only child.

"Mr. Bellamy, you have a beautiful baby girl." Doctor Richards said as she removed her protective mask.

"Congratulations! Mommy and baby are well."

Dr. Richards was Celeste's gynecologist for about 16 years. She liked her but wasn't fond of her ongoing antics of consistently arriving late for appointments, and being rude to her office staff for no damn reason. She was not happy about leaving her husband's birthday dinner in order to respond to the hospital for Celeste, but she was bound by the Hippocratic oath, so she decided to keep her attitude in check.

"So, it's a girl, for real? I sure hope she won't be like her mama." Robert said under his breath.

Dr. Richards realized that he was obviously disappointed. She smirked and walked away shaking her head. She understood his sentiment about Celeste all too well.

"Can I see my wife now?" He asked catching up to Dr. Richards.

"Soon." She replied looking back to face him with a growing smile suddenly appearing on her face. She felt bad that she had such a bad attitude. "She's in recovery right now, so give us about 45 minutes and we will have her and your baby girl ready for you to visit. Your wife will be in her room, but the little Miss will be in the Nursery ok?"

"Ok, thanks and I apologize for my attitude."

"Oh no problem." She said walking away.

Celeste was Dean of Students at her alma mater, Sarah Lawrence College, and Robert was a Grad student there when they met. After finishing his Degree he became an Adjunct Professor at the college. Celeste's big city upbringing made her an unlikely match for Robert, whose southern Mississippi roots sometimes embarrassed her in their social circle, however his model good looks and southern charm got the best of her *and* her uppity friends and colleagues. She was overbearing from day one, but he was okay with that because she reminded him of Grandma Rose, his Nanny, whom he loved and respected dearly. He was a country boy and didn't have a huge ego so he was ok with her taking the lead in their relationship just as his Nanny headed their household growing up.

Celeste was 10 years older than Robert and she wanted a baby badly before her biological clock timed out. They were married for about two years when she conceived as a last ditch effort to save their failing marriage. Robert was leery about starting a family with her, as he figured their future together was bleak but he was prepared to go along for the ride because he was too much of a coward to spar with her, or so *she* thought. Neither of them took the initiative to end their short marriage, and having a baby was no remedy, as they remained at odds throughout the pregnancy over a variety of issues.

"Hey you." Robert said as he tiptoed into the cold private hospital room at White Plains Hospital.

"Oh hey." Celeste responded dryly as she sat up in bed with the remote control in hand flipping through the TV channels. "Have you seen her? I know you were hoping for a boy. Sorry about that." She was being sarcastic.

"Oh, it's totally ok. I got a peek at her through the window. She's a little chocolate drop with huge brown eyes."

"Yeah and she has a head full of *course* hair just like Grandma Rose's side of the family. I didn't detect a curl or wave pattern like *my* side of the family." She commented turning the TV off and picking up a magazine.

"There you go. You are so damn superficial. She's a beautiful baby, *and* most importantly she's *healthy*. Did you detect that?" He was tired *and* annoyed. "You know what? I'm really hoping for a fresh start with you but I can see that you aren't going to let that happen, so I'm going to go visit my baby before I head home. Oh yeah, have you thought about a name for our little nappy headed princess?"

"Oh Robert. Come on. I'm not being critical of my own child. I was just making an observation. But you're absolutely right she is beautiful *and* she has keen features like *your* side of the family. Anyway, I want something traditional, like Harriett or Gertrude, a name that she can grow into as a woman."

"Ok yeah those are *real* traditional names. *Very* old fashion actually. Let's think about it overnight and I'll see you tomorrow." He said as he bent down and pecked her on her forehead before turning to leave.

———◆———

Celeste was two days into her 5-day hospital stay following her C-Section. She was anxious to get home and start her mommy duties. In spite of her bad attitude she was happy to finally have a child, as there had definitely been a void in her life.

Robert went to the hospital everyday after work to see her and the baby. He couldn't wait to bring them home.

"Your husband is here Mrs. Bellamy." The nurse said walking into the room.

She was happy that she was being discharged because she could get back to waiting on less demanding patients.

"Oh. Ok. Where's my baby? I thought you all were bringing her to me a couple of hours ago."

"Ma'am since you opted out of breast feeding, *and* you said you were too tired to feed her, they kept her in the Nursery to feed her before the two of you were discharged. Is that ok?"

"Well, I guess it's going to have to be. I'm ready to go now." She was rather indignant.

"I'll bring your bundle of joy to the room." The nurse said as she smirked and turned to walk away.

A couple of minutes later a male nurse showed up at the door pushing a nice new wheelchair. Robert was walking close behind him carrying a bouquet of flowers.

"Robert, what are you doing? You know I don't like flowers."

"These are for my little princess, not *you*. Where is she?" He had really brought the flowers for *her* but since she was being such a bitch he flipped the script and said he brought them for the baby.

"Mrs. Bellamy, we still need for you and your husband to sign the Birth Certificate." The nurse said pushing the baby's bed into the room. She picked up a clipboard attached to the foot of the bed and handed it to Robert.

"Sure. Hey *babe*. Have we decided on a name for her yet?" Robert asked taking the clipboard from the nurse.

"Yes, *babe*." She responded mimicking him and playing nice in front of company. "I like *Gertrude*. Gertrude Sheree Bellamy. It has a nice ring to it in case she grows up to be an Author or Playwright. I know she *is* going to be someone important one day."

"*Gertrude*? Ok I guess that's cool. I wasn't sold on it when you first mentioned it but I kind of like the sound of *Gertrude Sheree*. As a matter of fact I would call her *Gertie*." Robert handed the clipboard to Celeste for her to sign the Birth Certificate first, and then he signed and returned it to the nurse while she got settled into the awaiting wheelchair with Gertie resting in her arms.

The ride home was quiet with Celeste and the baby seated in the back of Robert's 7 Series BMW. He peered up at the rearview mirror periodically and watched her cooing with Gertie. She actually looked happy. Unbeknownst to her, he had asked her best friend Beatrice to come to the house to help ensure that everything was ready in the nursery when they arrived at home.

Bea was a pretty shapely blonde who befriended Celeste when the two were undergrads in college. She had dated only black men during their college years, which didn't sit well with Celeste because she felt it was unwanted competition, but she liked Bea's bubbly disposition and genuine helpful nature.

In spite of her dating history, Bea ended up marrying Larry, an older white Wall Street banker, in order to appease her parents. She was a full-time housewife and a *kept* woman who did absolutely nothing with her Journalism Degree. She and Larry had no children, and quite frankly she didn't want any to Larry's dismay. When she wasn't shopping or getting massages she volunteered her time with various social organizations in their community. She and Celeste remained close after college; they lived in close proximity to one another and attended many of the same social events.

"What's *she* doing here?" Celeste asked when Bea appeared from the doorway as the car slowly pulled into the dimly lit garage.

"Uh…well… she volunteered to come and help me get the nursery set up for you." He said rolling his eyes. At that moment he said a quick prayer. *Lord, please help me Jesus. I want to do the right thing here but I don't know how much more I can stand with this woman.*

"I wish you had told me. I'm really not in the mood for company, and you know Bea don't have shit to do so she is going to want to stay for a while and ask me a bunch of dumb ass questions about my delivery and why I'm not breast feeding and shit like that."

"I will have her help get you and the baby settled into the nursery really quickly and then I will have her leave. Let her help you." Robert said.

Just as the car came to a stop Bea rushed and opened the rear door. She held her hands out to help pull Celeste out of the car as Robert went to the other side to unlatch the car seat. The two women hugged and then they slowly walked arm in arm towards the house. Robert allowed them to enter before he closed the garage door. Just as he stepped inside the house he placed the baby's carrier on the kitchen island and then unlatched her and picked her up. Celeste went to a nearby couch in the adjoining den and kicked off her Ugg boots as Bea went to get a good look at the baby in Robert's arms.

"Oh my fucking God. She is gorgeous!" Bea squealed as she pulled the thin blanket from Gertie's pretty little face. "What did you name her?"

"*Gertrude.*" Celeste and Robert said in unison.

"What the fuck! That's like some old white lady name. She's going to hate you guys for that. Why not Brittany or Debra or even Sarah?"

Bea was not one to mince words. She said exactly what was on her mind. She was blond but not dumb, which is why Larry was ok with her running their household and being in charge of their finances and his accounting business. She was witty and smart and got along well in any environment, *and* she was *not* intimidated by Celeste. In fact she was the only one in their circle who Celeste did not bully. She *never* sweated the small stuff and had a zest for life that most of her friends loved about her, even Robert. Celeste had become increasingly jealous of Bea over the years when she thought Robert paid her too much attention. He wasn't the least bit interested in her romantically but he *loved* her personality.

"Bea, if that ain't the pot calling the kettle black. *Beatrice* is an old ass white lady name. Oh, but wait. You *are* a white lady, you're just not old *yet!*" Celeste said laughing and holding her stomach. Her belly was still in pain from the C-section incision. "I'm tired, and I'm taking my baby, with her white lady name and we are going to go lie down. Bea, I will call you later." She said as she walked towards the kitchen to get Gertie from Robert.

"I will come and check on you and the baby in a little
bit." Robert said as she walked away.

Celeste went to the nursery cradling Gertie in her arms leaving
Bea and Robert standing in the kitchen. The nursery was set up
in the downstairs bedroom, close to the laundry room, kitchen
and Master Suite. The 3 other bedrooms were upstairs in the spacious 3800 square foot home. Celeste got settled into the nursery
where there was a queen size bed, a white crib with a canopy, a
lovely wicker bassinet, a 50 inch flat screen TV on top of an oversized dresser; and a changing table stocked with cloth diapers,
hand towels, baby wipes and enough lotions and potions to fill
the cosmetic area of a Rite Aid drug store.

"Bea, I'll see you out." Robert said opening the door for
her to leave.

———◆———

It was late in November, and Celeste was happy to be on
Bonding Leave for the rest of the year. Gertie's 1st Christmas
was coming up and they looked forward to celebrating with
their new bundle of joy. Robert had planned to send for his
Nanny to come to New York for the Christmas holiday as he had
done every Christmas since he lived in New York, but that year
on Thanksgiving Day she suffered a fall and broke her ankle
so Celeste suggested that he go to Mississippi and spend the
Christmas holiday with Nanny.

Celeste didn't want to go to Mississippi with him because she
didn't want to travel with the baby so soon after giving birth so she
arranged for *her* parents to spend the holiday with her and Gertie
at her house while he was away. He readily agreed to go because
he realized that he needed to go check on Nanny anyway.

Christmas fell on a Thursday that year so Robert called his
personal contact, Ms. Wanda at American Airlines and booked
an early morning flight for the Sunday before Christmas so

he could spend the entire week with Nanny. He hated leaving Gertie but he was happy he didn't have to deal with Celeste's mood swings or *her* self-righteous pretentious parents during the holidays.

"It's going to be weird not having you home for Christmas." Celeste was having second thoughts about him leaving.

"I know, but what can I do? I don't want to leave Nanny there to celebrate alone. She looks forward to seeing me at Christmas time every year."

"Well she won't be alone. Your sister and her boys are there so on second thought you really could just send for her to come here *after* the holidays when she's all better."

"Yeah, but she looks forward to spending the holidays *with* me, so I *need* to at least go and be with *her* like you suggested. Gertie won't miss me because she's still so young."

"Yeah but you won't be here for *me.*" She said toying with him.

"Come on now you will have *your* parents with you so don't be selfish. Besides, Nanny's getting up there in age and I would never forgive myself if I don't go check on her and then something happens to her. I'm sure Bea will be hanging out with you as well, so you won't be alone and I'll just be gone a week."

"Ok. You're right." Celeste conceded.

———◆———

It was bright and sunny when Robert arrived at JFK Airport for the 2 hour and 34 minute flight to Mississippi. He was relaxed eating a Biscotti treat and drinking hot chocolate in the American Airlines Admiral's Club. He was glad to be going *home.*

Robert was looking forward to his brief escape from New York and all the pomp and circumstance, and formality of his big city life. He couldn't wait to lay eyes on his big ol' Nanny. She cooked a lot, and she ate even more. She ate very unhealthy, which was partly why he worried about her so much.

The plane arrived in Mississippi on time and as soon as he deplaned he headed to the nearest pay phone and called his sister who was already close by. Just as he stepped away from the pay phone and turned back towards the street he saw Nanny's gold fronts all exposed just as Jocelyn's station wagon pulled up to the curb.

"Hey baby! How you?" Nanny yelled over the noisy traffic as she poked her head out of the passenger window. Her head hit the doorframe as the vehicle came to an abrupt stop.

"Hi Nanny! Oh, it's so good to see you guys!" Robert said joyfully as he opened the door and placed his suitcase on the back seat.

He climbed into the station wagon and immediately leaned forward and kissed Nanny on her left cheek, and then Jocelyn, his older sister, and only sibling on her right cheek as she slowly pulled away from the curb.

"You got pictures of my little Angel?" Nanny asked.

"I got them already framed for you in my suitcase woman."

"How's Celeste?" She asked facetiously under her breath.

"Oh, you know. She's Celeste."

"Yeah I know. Just thought I'd ask. Anyway, guess who can't wait to see you?"

"Who even knows I'm home?" Robert really had no idea.

"That pretty little Clara. You know her husband died a few months ago. He had that *penis cancer...*"

"Nanny, you mean *Prostate* Cancer."

"Yeah whatever it's called. Well she here tryin' to settle his estate. I seed her in tha store yesterday, and I told her you was comin' to visit *me* this Christmas. She got excited when I told her you was comin' alone, so I invited her to come on over for dinner on Christmas Day."

"Nanny, why would you do that? I'm here to see *you and Jocelyn*, and besides I am married whether you like Celeste or not. You know you are wrong for that."

"But you and Clara was friends long before you met yo wife. Just 'cause you married don't mean you can't have friends. I'm sure she got friends, *and* she got her uppity ass mama and daddy too. So it's all good."

Nanny *was* being messy because she couldn't stand Celeste. Robert knew she always wanted him to marry Clara, his high school sweetheart, but they regretfully ended their relationship when they went away to separate colleges. He went to Morehouse and she went across the Country to Stanford. Clara had no family left in Mississippi. She was an only child and after she and Harold, her college sweetheart married, her parents *quit claimed* the family's Mississippi home to them to use as rental property and they relocated to Northern California to be close to Clara. Now that Harold was dead, Clara thought it was the perfect time to sell the property. She hated Mississippi and couldn't wait to get back home to California. Robert being home for the holidays was certainly going to make her trip more palatable she thought.

A sense of calm came over Robert as he rode through his hometown taking in all the sights. A lot had changed in the10 years since he moved away except in the area where all the black folks lived and congregated. He had fond memories of his childhood in Mississippi frequenting the Gulf Coast and going on fishing expeditions during the summer months with his Grandpa Moe and Uncle Charlie. He watched them use their best Moonshine to barter with fishermen for shrimp and oysters. That is why he was accustomed to the best of seafood dishes. Celeste thought that he just had champagne taste on a beer wallet whenever he expressed a liking for the finest of seafood, as she didn't understand his southern upbringing along the Gulf Coast.

Robert was lost in thought as Jocelyn made a sharp right turn into his old neighborhood. He swayed with the jerky motion of the car as he tried to keep his suitcase from slamming against the already battered door.

"Damn girl! You *still* can't drive and you need some shocks in this monster." He said bracing himself.

"Shut the hell up. You know I gotta go to work tonight so you lucky I didn't make you take a taxi-cab." Jocelyn laughed revealing her gold encrusted grill that matched Nanny's fronts. "Nanny, you know what I want for lunch right?" Robert asked touching her shoulder. "Some of your famous shrimp and grits. Oooh I can taste it right now!" He said smacking his lips and rubbing his hands together.

"Yeah, I know boy." Nanny said as she nodded her head to the beat of the gospel music playing on the radio. "Whew. We are finally here. I'm car sick from all those dangerous turns and bumps in the road." He said teasing Jocelyn.

"Yeah. Whatever. Get out!" Jocelyn was giddy. She was happy her brother was home.

Nanny's house looked exactly the same with the small screened in porch and worn cushions on the mix matched tan and army green aluminum patio furniture.

"I see not much has changed. Nanny you need to tell me about all of the little things that you want me to do while I'm here. I can't do much in a week but at least I can get *some* things done for you." Robert said looking around.

When he stepped inside the small modest three-bedroom house walking behind Nanny sadness suddenly crept over his spirit. He saw that she had slowed down quite a bit primarily due to her poor health. She had Diabetes *and* High Blood Pressure, and was walking with a slight limp due to her recent ankle injury. She had just celebrated her 70th birthday but walked like she was about 90. He felt bad that he wasn't there to help her maintain the property and Jocelyn was no help. She had her own issues raising her family as a single parent on a meager salary as a night manager at the local Walmart. All she was able to do in her spare time was drive Nanny around once a week to run her errands.

Robert retreated to his old bedroom, a small addition that his Grandpa Moe and Uncle Charlie built themselves at the back of the house. He sat his suitcase down on a rocking chair beside the twin bed as he glanced up at the dusty pictures scattered across the top of his old chest of drawers. He picked up the framed picture of his mother. She was a beauty. She took mostly after Grandpa Moe's creole side of the family, which largely accounted for his model good looks as well. Tears welled up in his eyes as he ran his fingers across the framed obituary. It had been 18 years since his mother and Grandpa Moe was killed in a head on collision on the way home from their family reunion in Louisiana. Nanny, Jocelyn and Robert were spared as they were seated in the back of the family's newer model Chevy Impala. Grandpa Moe's death left a huge void in Robert's life as his dad and mom split up when he was only six and he hadn't seen his dad since then.

"You gettin' settled in?" Nanny asked poking her head into the doorway of the room. "I got yo shrimp and grits ready."

"Ok Nanny." Robert said turning towards the door and quickly wiping the lone tear from his face.

"I knew I shoulda took that picture down befo' you got here." She said biting her bottom lip.

"No. You're good Nanny. I'm not sad. You always told me that *Mama's in a better place.* Anyway how you get that food ready so fast?" He asked joyfully changing the subject as the doorbell rang in the distance.

"Oh shoot, that must be Clara."

"Nanny! Come on! Why did you call her? I *just* got here. You said you invited her for *Christmas* dinner. That ain't until Thursday."

"I just called to let her know that I made some shrimp and grits that's all."

"Ok. I'll be out after I call home and check on Celeste and Gertie. Give me a few minutes." He said dialing his home number.

"Hey!" Robert acted happy to hear Celeste's voice. He didn't like her most of the time but he had a different kind of *love* for her since she had his child.

"It's about time you called me." She scolded. "Your plane got in a couple of hours ago."

"I really meant to touch bases with you before now but I was busy talking to Nanny and Jocelyn. I'm sorry woman."

"No problem." Celeste noted the somber tone of his voice.

"The flight was great; short and sweet, but that damn Jocelyn's driving wore me out. How's everything there?"

"Everything is good. The baby is sleeping and Bea *just* left. How's Grandma Rose? Did you give her the pictures I sent?" Celeste was firing off questions left and right not really giving him a chance to answer any of them.

"Nanny is good and yes I gave her the pictures. She loves them. Anyway, I'm about to go eat and then get some sleep." He said forcing a yawn. "I don't know why I'm so sleepy." He was ready to get off the phone.

"Well, get some rest and call me later ok? I love you." She said in a genuine tone.

"Alright. I love you too." He was surprised by the drastic change in her attitude. "Kiss my angel for me."

Robert removed a small bottle of Binaca from his toiletry bag and sprayed his mouth generously with the peppermint flavored breath spray, and then he walked out of the room with some pep in his step. Within seconds he was face to face with Clara, who was still as pretty as the last time he saw her 10 years before when they took off for college.

"Well hello there!" Robert felt a warm sensation all over his body the moment he laid eyes on her. The two embraced while Nanny slipped out of the living room and back into the kitchen where she put the finishing touches on the shrimp and grits dish she prepared for them.

"Oh Robert, it is so good to see you! If you feel up to it later maybe we can go out and have dinner and cocktails and catch up." She wasted no time.
Clara was hopeful he would agree to hanging out with her for a bit. They had tried to stay in touch by writing letters but that activity waned by their sophomore year in college. After getting settled in at the table Robert and Clara ventured off into a conversation about what they didn't miss about living in Mississippi.

"I remember when we were only about 7 and that doctor... what was his name? Oh yeah. Dr. Mason, Gilbert Mason. Remember when he went swimming at the beach with his friends and they were ordered by the police to leave? The police told them that *'Negroes don't come to the sand beach.'*" Clara recalled.

"Oh yeah. I remember my Nanny talking about that. Because of that incident my grandfather would not allow us to go to the beach without him." He said reminiscing about the past. "You know what's sad though? Not much has changed in the world. We are *still* fighting for equality."

"Yeah, I know. But we still got some of the best seafood cuisine in the Country right here in Biloxi." Clara said with a bolt of excitement.

"Yeah you are so right." Robert was grinning from ear to ear. He was glad he was there.

It was clear that Clara was no longer that shy little schoolgirl Robert once dated. She had a grown and sexiness about her that snapped him right out of his temporary funk. They ate the shrimp and grits and continued to reminisce about other aspects of their childhood.

"Well alright. I'm down for dinner *and* drinks later." Robert was intrigued by his impending date that he initially tried to avoid.

"I'm going to go home and shower and change, and I'll pick you up at about 8."

"Where are you taking me?" Robert asked.

"Remember Green's Café at the edge of town? Well now it's a small seafood restaurant called Green's Seafood Shack." Clara said walking backwards towards the door to exit. "It's the same owners, and the food and drinks are really good. I'll see you a little later Nanny." She yelled as she walked through the door.

"Ok baby. You gone already?" Nanny responded just as the heavy screen door closed.

"She's gone Nanny but she will be back to get me for dinner later."

Robert still had a couple of hours to catch a nap before Clara returned. He showered quickly and then lay down. The twin bed seemed as though it had shrunk over the years and the mattress was just as lumpy as he remembered, nevertheless he fell right off to sleep for a couple of hours before being awakened by a loud thud on the hallow bedroom door.

"Son." Nanny said as she slightly opened the door and poked her head into the room. "Clara's here."

"Whew, I was sleeping good." Robert sat up quickly, and swiveled around on the bed until his feet hit the floor. "Ok, tell her I'll be right there."

"Don't take all day boy." Nanny pushed the door all the way open and then walked away with her hefty hips swaying from wall to wall.

Robert closed the door and hurried and changed into fresh clothes. He left the bedroom and ran into the one and only bathroom at the front of the house. He waved as he passed Nanny and Clara who were sitting in the living room talking. He washed his handsome face, brushed his teeth and gargled with Scope before he reemerged.

"Clara, you looking good girl." Robert said as he ran his thumbs along his waistband straightening out his Gig line. He was wearing a neatly pressed dress shirt, dress slacks, and black leather Ralph Lauren belt that matched his soft black leather Ferragamo loafers. He was dressed conservatively and classy, and Celeste would have him dress no other way.

"You don't look so bad yourself. But you may want to grab a sweater or jacket because it's a little cold outside." Clara said inspecting him from head to toe.

"Ok. I'll be right back." Robert left the two women cackling in the living room and went to get his leather jacket. He decided to check in with Celeste one last time before he headed out.

"Hello. It's me." Robert was acting demure.

"I was hoping you would call me again before you went to bed. I just rocked Gertie back to sleep and now I am just looking at news reports about some post election stuff regarding President Reagan's staff selections, and wrapping some last minute gifts."

"That's cool. Well Nanny's ankle is healing nicely. She says it swells when she stands on her feet for too long but other than that it's looking pretty good." He was unusually chipper.

"How can she tell?" Celeste asked chuckling. "Her ankles always look swollen from all that pork she eats."

"Ok, you better stop talking about my Nanny." He warned. But he laughed too because he knew she was right.

"You sure are in a good mood." Celeste was surprised by his lightheartedness. She felt his mood was *odd,* but just figured he was happy to see that his Nanny was okay.

"I'm always in a good mood when I see my family. Anyway I just wanted to call before you turn in." He said.

"Is Grandma Rose asleep already?"

"Oh no. She's in the living room reading her bible."

"Ok. Well tell her I said hello, and I will talk to you in the morning."

"Ok. Talk to you then." He said ending the call. Celeste's antenna was up but she shook it off and went on to bed. Robert had never told her about his high school sweetheart Clara because there was no need.

Robert was excited about going out on the town with Clara, and glad that he was done with Celeste for the night. He grabbed his leather jacket from the doorknob and finally joined the ladies in the kitchen.

"I'm ready *and* I'm hungry." He said putting on his jacket

and motioning for Clara to walk ahead of him to the door.

Robert and Clara's time together was refreshing. They both had some life's experiences under their belts so it was almost as if they were meeting for the very first time. Clara clearly was starting over following her husband's death. She was married for five years after experiencing many failed relationships so it was back to the drawing board for her. Her parents were aging and relied on her for help so she didn't know which direction she was headed in her personal life at that moment.

Clara had tried getting pregnant for a few years before her husband was diagnosed with cancer. Unfortunately, due to the aggressive chemo treatments he had erectile dysfunction so it was pretty much impossible for Clara to conceive at that point, which was why they never had children. She felt very awkward during her evening out with Robert but her demeanor was refreshing as he thought she was genuinely sweet and very much unlike his wife's bossy ass.

"So, how are you handling Harold's death?" He asked leaning into the table sipping on Crown Royal Reserve on the rocks.

"I guess I'm ok. Harold battled cancer for a few years so I kind of prepared myself for his demise when he started to decline. I know this may sound bad but it was actually a relief when he passed away because I didn't like seeing him suffer." She said tearing up.

"I'm so sorry. We don't have to talk about it."

"I'm just so happy that you are here." She said holding back tears. She had worked hard to get her face beat just right so she didn't want any tears to ruin her image.

"Yeah, me too." Robert reached across the table and covered Clara's hand with his in a comforting gesture. "You know I would *love* to see your old house before I leave. We had so much fun in that house growing up."

"Ok. Sure. We can stop by there tonight on our way back to Grandma Rose's house." She said slowly pulling her hand from beneath his. "Are you ready to go?"

"Yes. Dinner was great." Robert said.

They laughed and talked on the ride to Clara's house. Robert almost didn't recognize the house as they approached. There were weeds sprouting up between the cracks in the driveway and the house appeared much smaller, and raggedier than he remembered.

"Where's the *For Sale* sign?"

"I didn't want one in the yard because I didn't want people in the neighborhood to know it was vacant. As you can see the neighborhood has changed quite a bit. I hired a property management company to maintain the yard and check on it weekly after the last tenants moved out. An investment company just bought it. I'm so happy it sold so quickly."

Robert thought the interior of the house actually looked pretty good as Clara had staged it hoping to help with a quick sell of the property and it worked. Her parents' furniture was still in the house, and she had kept the utilities on until the close of escrow.

"How about a nightcap before I take you home?"

"You trying to get me drunk?" Robert chuckled.

"Maybe." She said pouring him a glass of Old Grand Dad. "Sorry, but all I have is this Whiskey."

"That's fine it's still in the brown family so I shouldn't get sick. Crown Royal, Old Grand Dad, they are about what and what."

Robert and Clara sat in the living room and talked and sipped on their drinks for a couple of hours before Clara made her move. She walked behind his chair and began to gently massage his shoulders. He grabbed a hold of one of her hands and gently pulled her around to the front of the chair and down into his lap as the two began to kiss. Before long they were in her bed and after pleasuring each other for a little while they fell off to sleep. His snoring as driving Clara crazy so in the middle of the night she sneaked out of bed and went into the living room where she fell back off to sleep on the couch.

"Oh shit!" Robert exclaimed when the sun shining bright through the bedroom blinds awakened him. "Clara!" He yelled. "Why did you let me fall asleep?" He sat up on the side of the bed with his head hanging low. He had a major hangover.

Robert cupped his hands over his face just as Clara appeared in the doorway wearing a robe loosely draping her body while a cup of hot coffee warmed her hands.

"Thank you." She said smiling.

"For what?"

"For last night."

Robert jumped up and recovered his clothing piece by piece from the bedroom floor as Clara walked back to the kitchen. He dressed in a hurry as she sat at the dining room table. He became annoyed watching her thumbing aimlessly through the morning paper while still in her robe.

"I need to use your phone." He said as Clara nonchalantly pointed to the phone on the kitchen wall.

"I'm so sorry. Don't be mad but I fell asleep too." She said reflecting on the previous night. "I only left the room because you were snoring so damn loud. I tried to wake you up but you did not budge. You were drunk. You better call Nanny so she knows you are ok."

"Yeah, *and* I need to call *my wife* too." He declared boldly.

"Oh. You weren't thinking about *your wife* last night when you were in bed with me; screaming and sucking your thumb and shit." Clara said teasing Robert.

"Whatever. Take me home."

Robert was regretful that he had slept with Clara and mad at himself for cheating on his wretched wife.

"Hey son, I see you musta had a good time last night."

"Nanny that was *not* supposed to happen."

"*What* was not supposed to happen?"

"I did not mean to stay out all night that's *what*. We had too much to drink so Clara decided to bring me home first thing this morning." He explained trying to sound innocent. "I'll be home in a few. Did Celeste call the house?"

"Boy, ain't nothing wrong with you spending the night with Clara. It ain't like she a stranger and no Celeste ain't called here today."

"Ok Nanny, you are trippin'. I need to call home before it gets too late. I'll see you in a few."

Robert dreaded calling Celeste. It was still very early but he knew she was probably up with Gertie. He hoped that she wouldn't suspect anything was awry. Actually nothing was *awry*, he just thought things got a little out of hand as he had no intention of sleeping with Clara or anyone else for that matter. He couldn't believe what he had done.

"Hey, how are you?"

"I'm good. Your child had me up *all* night. She's acting colicky. Mom came over and stayed with me so I could get some sleep. I just woke up."

"I just wanted to check in before I get my day started." Robert said watching Clara out of the corner of his eye. She walked into the bathroom with her clothes draped over her arm and mouthed that she was about to shower. He nodded in acknowledgement.

"What are *you* doing?" Celeste asked.

"Oh, just getting up. About to go see what Nanny wants to do today. I'm sure she's going to want to go Christmas shopping." He could hear water running so he talked more freely believing Clara was in the shower.

"Well tell Grandma Rose I said *hi* and I'll talk to you later."

"Ok. Later." He said relieved that their conversation was so brief.

Robert was sitting in the living room twiddling his thumbs while anxiously waiting for Clara to finish dressing. He still had six days to go and was not looking forward to the rest of the week. He pondered over whether he should avoid Clara altogether or just show better restraint when she was around. Regardless of his intent for the rest of the week he allowed himself to be sucked into her trap everyday and sometimes twice a day. He was so weak around her.

Robert and Clara had hot steamy sex whenever they had any alone time. By the weeks end he said goodbye to her one last time on that Saturday night as he was scheduled to fly home bright and early on Sunday morning. It was good while it lasted but he knew that he would probably never see or hear from her again so he didn't worry about Celeste ever finding out about the affair. His initial tinge of guilt turned into sheer pleasure at the thought of Clara. He was very much attracted to her and hadn't felt like that about anyone in a very long time.

Likewise Clara had butterflies in her stomach when she thought of having sex with Robert because she thought he was so handsome. She wished there was a way to see him again but knew that was not going to happen since he was still married so she was prepared to move on. She couldn't wait to return to California.

"Are you ready?" She asked as she emerged from the bedroom dressed casually.

"Yeah, I've been ready. It was really great spending time with you but I have to admit I feel so guilty." Robert said.

"Guilty about *what?* That we *saw* each other, or that we had *sex?* Listen, I don't expect anything from you. Clearly you are married and have a life, which I don't plan on interrupting. We connected. We're good, and now we're moving on. Right?"

"Right." Robert said nodding his head affirming all that she said.

The look on Clara's face hinted at a sophistication that Robert was not accustomed to seeing in her. He liked her west coast swag. She was classy in a casual California pretty girl way, and not at all formal like Celeste and Bea. She had definitely lost her country girl mannerisms she had while growing up in the south.

Clara drove Robert the short distance to Nanny's house.

"You coming in?" He felt obligated to ask.

"No. I need to get back to the house because the Salvation Army is coming to pick up the remaining furniture, so I need to strip the bed and finish packing my things. Please tell Grandma Rose I will stop by before I leave on Monday. You have a safe flight home." She reached over and embraced Robert one last time before he got out of the car.

"Ok, you have a safe trip back home as well, and *please* tell your parents I said hello." He got out of the car and watched Clara slowly drive away. She never looked back.

"Hey!" Nanny yelled waving at the car from the screen door.

"She didn't hear you. She said she's going to stop by to see you before she leaves on Monday."

"You alright boy?" Nanny asked.

"Yeah. I'm just ready to get back home. I mean I'm going to miss you and Jocelyn, but you know I can't stay here too long before I get antsy *and* I need to see my baby."

"I know. Well, I'm glad you and Clara got to spend some time catchin' up."

Robert was happy he had gone to visit Nanny. He saw that she was recovering well so he didn't think he would worry about her that much when he left. His last night there was spent with her,

Jocelyn and her boys. They ate and drank, and planned for his transport to the airport early on Sunday morning.

"I sho' wish you was leavin' *after* church." Nanny said on the ride to the airport. "Pastor always askin' 'bout you."

"Well, tell Pastor freak 'em I said *hey*, but I am *not* sorry I missed seeing his old crusty butt." Robert remarked laughing.

"Whew ain't that the truth!" Jocelyn said laughing and nodding her head in agreement.

"Boy hursh!" Nanny laughed heartily. "I know Pastor ain't no saint. He just a man first, so I ain't judgin' him." She said as they pulled up in front of the American Airlines terminal.

"Thanks for the ride woman. I appreciates ya." Robert said jokingly as he exited the car.

He was thrilled to be going home. Jocelyn and Nanny got out of the car and met him at curbside where they hugged and kissed him goodbye.

Robert was elated to see Celeste and Gertie and happy to be back in his comfy surroundings. He stayed off work until just past the New Year, whereas Celeste remained off on Bonding Leave for the full four-month period, which was scheduled to end in late March. Bea loved that Celeste was home for a while because it gave her some place to go during the day when she was bored out of her mind at home attending to Larry's accounting business. It wouldn't be long before Robert would regret being back at home.

CHAPTER 2

"Surprise, Surprise"

———◆———

When Gertie started kindergarten, Celeste got rid of their part time nanny. She and Robert took turns dropping their princess off and picking her up from school; and taking her to Mommy and Me classes and gymnastics. They were thoroughly enjoying being parents but *their* relationship for the most part did not improve. He had transitioned into a full time professor so they fought over such things as who was going to take off from work when Gertie was ill. When neither of them could take off nor change their schedule, they called on Bea to help. Robert hated working on campus with Celeste so he looked for job opportunities at other universities in the area. He seriously considered an offer for a professorship at Cornell University in Ithaca New York.

"That's four hours away Robert, and I'm not relocating. I *love* my job and I don't know why you are not content with yours." Celeste said firmly. "I also want to stay close to my folks so they can spend time with their *only* grandchild *and* I can watch out for *them.*"

"It's *always* about *you.* I'm so sick of living in your shadow." He said. "I'm not happy."

Robert was growing more and more impatient and was quick to argue with Celeste more than ever before. He had not had any extramarital affairs before or since his rendezvous with Clara but he was open to the possibility. He and Celeste were not intimate that much, and he was ok with that. He could barely stand her so during their rare intimate moments he fantasized about having sex with the pretty young college students he locked eyes with during his lectures. Many of the young women in his classes thought he was very handsome and they crushed on him and some even asked him out but he always refused. He was frustrated with his relationship but he didn't know what he wanted to do to rectify it.

———◆———

1990-Gertie was identified as gifted in English at 10 years old. She *loved* creative writing. She was a precocious child with a knack for installing computer programs into the boxy desktop computer Grandma Rose bought her for her 10th birthday. She was obsessed with computer games, which consumed most of her time at home.

"What are you doing in here?" Robert asked playfully bursting into Gertie's bedroom after school one day.

"Daddy! You need to knock." She said laughing as she reached up to hug him around his neck. "I'm just playing Police Quest. Where's mommy?"

"Oh she's in there." Robert responded rolling his eyes.

"Please tell her that I did my homework already." She said waving her school papers in the air.

Gertie loved her mom but thought she was *mean,* and Robert totally understood her sentiment. Celeste *was* constantly nagging. *Brush your hair 100 strokes. Why do you want to wear that? Do this. Do that. Say this. Don't say that.* It was too much for Gertie, so on most days after school she retreated to her well-appointed bedroom and solved fake crimes on her computer.

On some evenings, Robert, Celeste and Gertie spent time together watching *The Cosby Show* and *The Fresh Prince of Bel-Air* after dinner, and once Gertie went off to bed they curled up on opposite ends of the over stuffed sectional and watched *Murder She Wrote, Columbo,* and a new variety show called *In Living Color.*

"Whew, that James Carey is hilarious and those Wayans are so talented. They have created a great show." Robert said.

"Yeah, that Keenan is fine. Almost as fine as you." Celeste said flirting with Robert in a rare moment of frivolity.

Gertie's 5th grade school year was in full swing as she looked forward to the upcoming holidays and her school's festive events. Robert's job search was still in full effect as the new year approached while Celeste spent her time fostering friendships with several of her Grad students who were on edge due to their impending midterms, and relied on her for advice.

It was a cold winter evening about 8pm when Robert and Celeste settled in to watch *A Different World* while Gertie played in her room. The phone rang and they looked at each other as neither felt like getting up to answer it.

"I'll get it." Robert said reluctantly as he slid his feet into the fluffy slippers next to the coffee table. He walked in a hurry towards the kitchen to catch the phone before it stopped ringing while Celeste kept watching TV.

"Hello."

"Hello. *Robert?*

"Yes, this is Robert." He thought he recognized the woman's voice but he wasn't sure.

"This is Clara."

"Oh, hey." He said in a soft tone as he peered over at Celeste who was intently watching TV and laughing at

Whitley's antics on *A Different World*. "What's going on? Are you ok?"

Robert was careful not to say her name and he tried his best to sound officious in case Celeste *was* listening. He was taken aback when it sunk in that it was actually *Clara* on the phone. The two had not seen each other nor talked to one another in a good 10 years.

"Who's on the phone Rob?" Celeste asked when he didn't come back to the den right away.

"It's one of my students in need of assistance." Robert said cupping the receiver with one hand. "I'll take the call in the study." He said as he walked hurriedly towards his home office.

"Ok. Hurry back. This shit is too funny." Celeste said digging her hips deeper into the couch.

"Yes, I'm fine Robert." Clara said. "I'm so sorry to bother you at home but I *need* to see you. We need to talk."

"Where are you? Are you here in New York?" He couldn't understand why Clara of all people was calling him.

"Yes, I'm here...here in New York City."

"Ok, but *why* do you *need* to see *me*? What do *we need* to talk about?"

"Trust me on this. We *need to talk* and in person."

"Where are you staying, and how long will you be here?"

"I'm at the Marquis Hotel in Times Square; Room 720 and I will be here for a couple of days."

"Marquis, Room 720 right?"

"Yes. That's correct."

"Ok. I will be in touch first thing tomorrow."

"Ok. I cannot leave here until we meet." She said ending the call.

Robert was suddenly nervous. His mind went into overdrive. *Oh shit, this bitch had better not be calling to tell me she has AIDS.* He thought as he reflected back on their brief connection years ago. He returned to the den and sat on the edge of the couch wringing his hands while deep in thought as Celeste laughed heartily at the TV. She attempted to catch him up on what was going on with Whitley and Dwayne Wayne but he was suddenly not interested in TV any longer. He was stumped by the voice from his past.

"So, what's going on with your student?"

"Oh, he just needs some advice about several of his midterms. I told him we could talk more tomorrow."

"What can be that important for him to call you at home?"

"People handle stress differently I guess. It's no problem. I have told all of my students that I have an open door policy so I have to adhere to that. Anyway I'm going to turn in because he wants to meet me early tomorrow and I have a full day." He was anxious for the next morning to hurry up and come.

Robert went to Gertie's room followed closely by Celeste. They hugged and kissed her goodnight in tandem and then went to bed. He tossed and turned all night and arose earlier than usual on the next morning to get his day started. When he arrived at his office he made arrangements for someone to cover his morning classes. It was late notice but he managed to get the coverage he needed so that he could be free for his impending meeting across town.

"Room 720 please."

"Hello." Clara answered the phone on the first ring.

"Hey, Clara?" Robert was wincing. He had hoped that she was gone.

"Yes Robert it's me. Are you *here* already?"

"No. I'm calling first to make sure you still want to meet."

"Yes. We *need* to meet. What time can you come here today?" She asked. "The earlier the better."

"Ok. Well I have already cleared my schedule and can be there within the hour. Shall we meet at Junior's Deli across the street and maybe have some breakfast?"

"No. I'm not hungry. We can meet right here in my Suite."

"Uh. I don't know about that…"

"I *promise* you I'm not trying to seduce you but it's imperative that we have some privacy." Clara said in a low and pleasant voice.

"Oh ok. You are scaring me."

"I'm not trying to scare you."

"Ok. I'll come to your room but can you please give me a hint as to what is going on?" He asked.

"I'm not going to kill you." Clara chuckled. "I just *need* to talk to you in person."

"Shit, I don't know *what* to expect. I mean I haven't heard from you in years then you call my house in the middle of the damn night. Luckily my wife didn't answer the phone. *Please* tell me what in the hell is going on?"

"There is something very important that we need to discuss *in person*." She really didn't like stringing him along but in her opinion she had no option. She needed to *see* him.

"I don't like this, whatever *this* is but I'll see you in a little bit." He said when he saw that she was not budging. Robert took the 30-minute ride on the Express Train from White Plains to Times Square. He was anxious. The early morning hustle and bustle in Times Square felt cozy as the snow lined the sidewalk; and surrounded the crowds of walkers who filled the busy corridor. He navigated his way down Broadway through the Theatre District towards the hotel. Once inside the plush five star hotel, he felt more and more anxious the closer he got to room 720.

Clara was expecting the knock on the door and when it came she slivered out the small opening she created in the doorway from her spacious suite, and into the hallway letting the heavy door close slowly behind her. Robert instantly became angry when he saw her sneaky antics, but his anger dissipated when he saw that she was just as beautiful as the last time he saw her.

"What's going on?" He asked calmly standing in the quiet hallway. "You call me after 10 years and demand that I meet you here in your *hotel* room for *privacy*, but then you slide out of the room and into this hallway like some old ass Call Girl. Why are we out here in this damn hallway? What do you want with me?" He asked with vertical furrows forming between his brows.

"I have someone in the room I want you to meet." Clara said looking all around the hallway rather than making eye contact with him.

"You want me to meet *someone*? Who Clara?" Robert asked as he grabbed her wrist and gently pulled her close to him. "What kind of game are you playing?" He asked under his breath.

"Please let go of me." She sternly whispered as she yanked her arm away from his grasp and abruptly turned towards the door. She walked back into the room and motioned for him to follow her.

Robert entered the room right on her heels when he spotted a precious little girl sitting Indian style on a chaise lounge playing with a Barbie doll. He then looked quickly at Clara with questioning eyes, and then back at the child.

"What is going on here?" He asked staring at Clara.

"Meet your *daughter* Savannah. Savannah, meet your *father,* Robert." Clara said in a meek voice while looking down at the paisley print hotel carpeting.

"Whoa. Are you serious?" He asked in disbelief as he spoke to her while periodically looking at the child.

"Hi Mr. Robert." Savannah said as a huge grin shone on her little angelic face. She jumped from the chaise and stood behind Clara facing Robert, who was still standing just inside the door.

He was confused but the fog in his head cleared as he quickly did the calculation in his head. Savannah looked to be about 9 or 10, and he pondered and shook his head as he thought about the week he spent sexing Clara up during his Christmas visit with Nanny in 1980.

"Hi baby." Robert responded as he looked around Clara in Savannah's direction.

"Oh, this is no game Robert. Savannah *is* yours, and after many years of counseling my therapist thought it was time that she know *who* her father is."

"I prefer not talking in front of her." Robert nodded towards the door and then turned and stormed out of the room motioning for Clara to follow him.

"I want a paternity test." Robert demanded.

"I do too that's why I already scheduled a test for tomorrow."

She and Savannah were scheduled to return to California on the next evening so they needed to get it done. There were so many unanswered questions Robert had but he was so angry and confused when he left the hotel he couldn't think straight. *This bitch.* He thought to himself as he walked up 7th Avenue towards the subway. His emotions were all over the place. He was no deadbeat dad and he didn't know how to handle the information that had been thrust his way with no warning whatsoever. He could not fathom explaining this situation to Celeste or worst of all to Gertie. *This is a real fucking boomerang.* He thought. The ride back to campus was too quick. He had no time to come up with a game plan.

"Where have you been?" Celeste asked gripping the phone tightly. She had been calling his office for a couple of hours. She had forgotten about the meeting he had with his *student.*

"We need to talk." He said nonchalantly. Celeste didn't know what to make of his tone but somehow she sensed he was not in a good mood. His tone didn't emit an emergent nature, but it was clear that *something* was wrong.

"Ok. What is wrong my dear?" Celeste asked playfully. "I'll drop what I'm doing and run over to your office."

"No. Just meet me at home. Please." Robert cancelled his afternoon classes and headed for the door. He was nervous and thought about how he would break the news of his possible love child to his family. *What in the hell have I done?* He asked himself repeatedly all the way home. He wasn't convinced that he was Savannah's father at that point but he knew there was a strong probability based on her age, and considering his hot steamy affair with Clara. Gertie was still in school when Robert arrived at home that afternoon so he knew he would have some alone time with Celeste. His heart skipped a few beats when he heard the garage door open.

"Robert." Celeste yelled. She rushed into the kitchen stopping in her tracks when she saw him sitting on the couch cradling his face with his hands. He jumped up as she approached.

"Whew...uh...I...uh...we gotta talk." He said as he started to pace between the couch and the coffee table.

"Yeah, I know. That's what you said on the phone. What's going on?" She was eager to hear what he had to say.

"Sit down. Please." He suggested as he motioned for her to sit on the couch and then he started right in. "You remember about 10 years ago when I went to visit Nanny for Christmas right?" Robert was seated on the edge of the coffee table facing Celeste who was seated on the edge of the couch.

"Ok, you are scaring me..." She said reaching out to touch his forearm.

"Listen to me." He pulled his arm away from her and cut to the chase, as there was just no easy way to break the news. "I may have fathered a child with someone else and she is here in New York." Robert muttered really quickly.

"*What?*" Celeste asked as she abruptly stood to her feet sidestepping away from him. "What do you mean you *may have fathered a child?*" She asked in utter disbelief.

"Well *she* has scheduled a paternity test..."

"*She?* Who the fuck is *she?*" Celeste was confused. Tears welled up in her eyes as if she was told a family member just died. In fact at that very moment, her life as she knew it had changed and her marriage died right then and there, but she hadn't fully grasped the totality of the situation not just yet.

Robert stepped towards Celeste and pushed her back down on the couch and continued to explain the details of the week he spent at home that Christmas, and how it came to be that he was just learning about Savannah. Celeste cried uncontrollably as he told her about Clara, his childhood friend and high school sweetheart a little fact he shared when Celeste demanded to know *all* the details about his relationship with the child's mother.

"She said she waited so long to tell me about Savannah out of respect for my marriage."

"I really don't give a fuck about this bitch. Where was her *respect* when she was fucking my husband?" She said screaming at the top of her lungs.

"She only came forward *now* because her Therapist supposedly told her that she and I need to accept full responsibility for our actions in Savannah's best interest."

"I want you *and* her out of my life, and I want nothing to do with your bastard child." Celeste said.

"Oh so Savannah has to suffer because of my actions?"

"You need to go be with that bitch." Celeste said angrily. "Then you can spend as much time as you want with *Savannah* or whatever her name is."

Celeste pushed past Robert and stormed out of the room leaving him standing there speechless. He understood how she might have felt and he was definitely at her mercy. He was wrong for the affair and he had to suffer the consequences. He and Celeste hadn't been happy in years and his indiscretion was sure to destroy what little bit of civility they had left between the two of them.

"I'll tell you what." Celeste said rushing back into the room. "I don't want my family, my friends or my baby to know about this shit or that little girl so you need to get the paternity test done and *if* that child is yours, and *if* we stay together, we are going to pay that woman child support and that's it and that's all." She said pacing and talking.

"It's not that easy. If the child...if *Savannah* is mine, I *need* to develop a *relationship* with her. I understand you are embarrassed. I am too but what's done is done." He said as Celeste walked away from him and towards the door to the garage.

"I'm going to go get *my baby* from school." She said opening the door wildly. Robert stood there looking defeated.

———◆———

On the following day Robert met with Clara and accompanied her and Savannah to a local lab accredited by the American

Association of Blood Banks, where cheek swabs were collected from the three of them. They were told that between 5 and 10 days they would receive the results in the mail. Clara and Savannah returned to Northern California immediately after leaving the blood bank and Robert returned home to his sham of a marriage.

Robert spent the next several days trying to act as if nothing was wrong while anxiously awaiting the news. The results came back in exactly10 days. He was seated at the kitchen island sorting through the mail when he came across the dreaded envelope. Celeste stood over his shoulder when he alerted her that the results were in. He slowly unfolded the neatly creased notice and read the bold print at the top of the page, which indicated in part that he was *99.9999 percent, the father* of Savannah. He instantly felt sick to his stomach as tears welled up in his eyes. Celeste gasped and walked away with her hand over her mouth as tears ran down her face. She couldn't think of anything but his infidelity, and worst of all his fathering a child with another woman; his high school sweetheart of all people.

"So, what are *you* going to do now?" Celeste asked through her tears. They were trying not to be heard by Gertie.

"I told you what *I'm* going to do. I'm going to accept responsibility for my child. I have to be a *father* to her just as I am to Gertie." He said as he paced the room holding the results in his hands.

"I don't know how you are going to do that. Your family is *here* and I am so serious, I don't want my parents or Gertie, or any of our friends to know about this situation. We will rightfully pay *that woman* child support and that's all *I* am willing to do." She said through her gritted teeth. "I will *not* have this child or her mother be a part of our lives. That's not going to happen."

"Yes, I made a huge mistake but you don't get to call the shots as to how *I* proceed with my life based on this indiscretion." He said checking Celeste. "*I* will tell Gertie when I feel she is old enough to understand, and I am going to tell Nanny now. She knows Clara and Savannah is her great grandchild and she deserves the right to have a relationship with her just as she has with Gertie."

"Well then you may as well tell the whole damn world if you tell Grandma Rose." She exclaimed and then stormed off towards her bedroom.

Robert immediately called Clara and acknowledged the paternity results; vowed to set up child support payments and told her that he wanted to see Savannah as much as possible, as time and opportunity permitted. He also made it very clear that Savannah was not welcome at the home he shared with his wife because *she* was not accepting, and he didn't think it was the right time for them to forge a relationship between the two girls mainly because Celeste was unwilling.

Clara agreed and apologized profusely for her part in possibly ruining his marriage. He assured her that his marriage was over long before they reunited but that this revelation probably sealed the deal for their inevitable split.

———◆———

Robert and Celeste went about their business at work and at home and only communicated when absolutely necessary. They slept in separate bedrooms for months following the discovery of his love child. Gertie was very intuitive and she sensed that things at home were very different but she did not understand why everything had changed. She spent time with both of her parents but never with them together anymore. Celeste and Robert always made up excuses as to why they spent so much time apart and Gertie was careful not to pry inappropriately.

After the dust settled Robert called Nanny and broke the news to her. She was angry that he and Clara had been so careless. Yes she loved Clara and she wanted nothing more than for her and Robert to be together but she thought it was ridiculous that Clara did not tell Robert about Savannah sooner.

"Robert, you mean to tell me Clara deprived that child of her father for all those years?" Nanny was genuinely upset.

"Nanny, she was torn about ruining my marriage. And I appreciate her for that. No matter what, *we* made a huge mistake and we are both regretting it so don't be mad at her. We should have used protection."

"Well, what Celeste and Gertie say when they found out?" Nanny asked.

"Well, Celeste ain't doing too well. She refuses to let anyone know about Savannah, and she forbade me from telling her folks or Gertie, but we both agreed on rightfully paying Clara child support."

"That woman is crazy as hell." Nanny said shaking her head. "I don't know how you put up with her ass for all these years. She the one drove you into Clara's arms."

"Nanny, you are too funny. Yeah she is crazy and I'm pretty much done with her ass. We are sleeping in separate bedrooms and we barely talk anymore." He shared. "Gertie is the one suffering and that's the only reason I feel so bad. Anyway, I want you to meet Savannah, so Clara and I will bring her down there soon." He said ending their conversation.

Clara was happy that Savannah was finally going to have an opportunity to develop a relationship with her father and Grandma Rose. Grandma Rose was 80 years old and not in the best of health so Robert knew he needed to take her to visit sooner rather than later.

———•———

1993- The tension between Celeste and Robert had risen to an all time high as they never could get it together after finding out about Savannah so they mutually agreed to a legal separation. Robert rented a nice apartment near the College prompting Celeste to take in a couple of roommates. She posted a *Room for Rent* Ad in the Student Union and hoped for the best. Michelle a 30 year-old Grad Student from DC and Ryan, a 28 year old Grad Student from Atlanta both responded to the Ad. Celeste felt that Michelle and Ryan both met her roommate qualifications, however she still hired a management company to have them vetted before agreeing to let them move in.

Michelle was an average looking white girl with somewhat of a tomboy vibe and Ryan was a very conservative scholar desirous of becoming an Attorney. Michelle and Ryan thought that Celeste was cool and very classy, and Celeste thought they were both very nice and welcoming.

After living apart for a few months Robert and Celeste both seemed much happier. Michelle and Ryan fell in love with Gertie from the start. Michelle played basketball as an undergrad in college so when she saw how tall and athletic Gertie was she talked Celeste and Robert into signing her up for club basketball at the local YMCA. Gertie loved playing basketball, and she was a pretty good shooter. She was very versatile, which is why she was groomed to play the Small Forward position. She didn't like that position because she wanted to play the Point Guard position but her ball handling skills were not good enough for her to perform well as a Point Guard, and she wasn't tall enough to dominate in the Post Position so Small Forward it was.

Gertie loved the game and she had *heart* according to Michelle. Whenever Celeste and Robert were unavailable to take her to basketball practice, Michelle was more than willing. Robert and Celeste oftentimes stopped in to watch her at practice but they *always* made time to attend her games.

Robert didn't want Gertie's life affected by the split so he spent a lot of time at the house where he, Celeste, Michelle, Ryan and Gertie watched movies, cooked gourmet meals, baked goodies and played board games like they were one big happy family. Sometimes Gertie was allowed to invite her school friends and teammates over for game night. Bea took it upon herself to stop by more frequently after Robert moved out so she could make sure that her best friend and her *niece* were ok living with *those strangers* as she referred to Michelle and Ryan.

Celeste didn't date after separating from Robert. She was about to turn 51 and very much menopausal. Her hot flashes were driving her crazy and her mood swings caused her to be an emotional mess most of the time so she welcomed her alone time. Robert on the other hand was in his prime. He was only 41 and appeared to be going through a mid life crisis; but in reality he was just enjoying his freedom from Celeste. He was in and out of short-term relationships with women his age and younger. He loved the change in his lifestyle and was happy to have the freedom to travel back and forth to California to visit with Savannah. During those visits he cozied up under Clara, who looked forward to his visits. Clara was hopeful that she and Robert would one day be together again especially since he was headed for divorce.

———◆———

It was Gertie's 13th birthday and Celeste allowed her to have a slumber party at the house. It was the weekend before her actual birthday, which fell mid-week. The party started at noon on that Saturday afternoon and was slated to end the next morning after breakfast. Bea went to the house to help prepare food for the party, and to help chaperone. It was a fun time for the girls, and Celeste and Bea made sure they had wine and snacks for themselves. The girls were loud and truly enjoying each other as well as the gourmet popcorn and other specialty treats.

"Ok girls I got some great movies for you all to pick from." Celeste was extremely animated while communicating with the girls. "I have *Hocus Pocus*; *Free Willy*; *Mrs. Doubtfire*; *Addams Family Values*; *What's Eating Gilbert Grape* with that cute little blonde boy Leonardo Di Caprio, and *Sister Act II* with that crazy Whoopi Goldberg. You all think about it and let me know what you want to watch first." She said while stacking the movies on the floor by the TV.

"Mom, where's daddy?"

"He's on a business trip in California." Celeste responded. She knew Robert was really in California visiting with Savannah.

"He sure goes to California a lot. Oh well, hopefully he will make it back before my birthday."

"Trust me, he won't miss your birthday Gertie." Celeste saw the angst in her eyes.

———◆———

At the end of Robert's trip that year he and Clara stopped for breakfast before he caught his early morning flight home.

"Guess what?" Robert asked.

"What hun?"

"I have some great news."

"Oh yeah? What you got?"

"I have been offered a professorship at USC." He proudly reported.

"Get out of here!" Clara exclaimed as a wide grin appeared on her face. "So, are you going to accept the job?" She crossed her fingers under the table.

"Absolutely." He said as a matter of fact. "I have filed for divorce and I'm so ready for a fresh start. I mean I'm going to miss seeing Gertie but she can come visit me in California anytime she wants and maybe, just maybe, she will even consider going to college here in California." He said happy about his new opportunity. "I need to get to the airport. I can't miss this flight because I *have* to make it back before Gertie's birthday celebration is over."

"Ok. Let's go." Clara said taking the last big gulp of her coffee. "She needs you to be there."

Robert had Ms. Wanda plan his flight from Northern California to make it into New York by 4pm, which allowed him enough time to get to Gertie's party long before the day was over. The flight landed on time and he went directly to the house.

"Well, hello there." Celeste said as she opened the door drying her hands on her apron. She was genuinely happy to see that Robert made it back in time for Gertie's birthday.

"Hi daddy!" Gertie said when she saw Robert walk into the den. She flew into his arms as if she hadn't seen him in months.

Gertie missed Robert living at home but she saw that everyone was happier with her mom and dad living their separate lives. She spent quality time with both of them so she had the best of both worlds. Celeste and Robert did a great job keeping Savannah a secret from Gertie. It helped that Savannah lived across the country, and the lucrative child support payments were perfect hush money for Ms. Clara. Robert hung out at the party for a few hours before he decided to call it a night.

"Ok, goodnight baby girl." He told Gertie as he prepared to leave. "I hope you liked your gifts I got you, *and* I hope you all have a great time tonight at your sleepover. Daddy's tired." He said. "I will pick you up tomorrow so we can have our private daddy-daughter birthday celebration ok?" He confirmed as he backed out of the front door yawning almost tripping over the threshold.

"Ok. Goodnight daddy. I'll see you tomorrow!" Gertie said giggling at her dad's falter.
The squealing teenagers in the next room distracted her so she hurriedly pecked her dad on his cheek and ran back into the den and plopped down on the floor as he gently closed the front door and walked away towards his car.

Robert returned the next day after all the girls had left.
"I need to talk to your mom *alone* before you and I leave." He said. "Can you get her for me?" Robert tiptoed into the kitchen and casually looked around while waiting for Celeste to join him.

"Hey Rob. How are you babe?" Celeste asked walking into the room. She was such a different spirit since their separation.

"I want you to hear it from me." Robert said.

"Oh Lord. What now? I don't want any more surprises from you. Savannah was enough of a surprise for a lifetime."

"*Oh Lord* nothing. I just want you to know that I accepted a job in California, so I will be moving at the top of the year."

"*Oh.* I guess that's good huh?" All of a sudden she had knots in her stomach.

"Yes. I think it's great."

"So, it looks like you will finally be able to be with your *whore*, oh I'm sorry your *baby's mother*, full time huh?" Celeste remarked. Her mood changed rather quickly.

"You know what? You are a trip."

"What about Gertie?" She asked. "What about *me*?"

"What about you? *Our relationship* hasn't worked for years, and you know that. I am still Gertie's father, aka *your* baby's daddy and nothing will ever change my love for *her*. No matter what the distance or who else is in my life I will always be here for my daughter."

"Yeah we will see."

"Why are you so fucking bitter?" He asked. "You are living *your* life, so why shouldn't I live mine? This is an incredible opportunity for me and I have already accepted the job, so you might as well get over it." He said gritting his teeth in an effort to keep his voice down. He didn't want to cause a scene with Gertie and Celeste's room-mates in the house. "We will work out all of the custody details during our divorce proceedings."

"Oh. So, *now* all of a sudden you want to move forward with the *divorce*?" She was becoming increasingly more and more angry and irrational but like Robert she didn't want to alert Gertie *or* her roommates so she maintained her cool as best she could.

Celeste didn't want Robert anymore but she felt like she *lost* him to a woman she knew his heart belonged to *first*, and besides she didn't like losing at *anything*. It was an, *I don't want you but I don't want nobody else to have you* moment she was experiencing as she stood there seething.

"Gertie!" Robert called as he turned to walk away from Celeste's angry chatter. "I'm ready to go baby."

"Coming daddy." She responded as she ran cheerfully into the room.

"We will talk later." Robert said to Celeste as he followed Gertie out of the house.

Robert playfully ran from Gertie towards his car as she tried to get him to carry her duffle bag. He opened the trunk and she tossed it on top of his clutter before she got into the car. As Robert was backing out of the driveway he nodded at a man seated in a commercial type van that was parked at the curb in front of Celeste's house. The process server Robert hired exited the van and approached Celeste, who was walking down the driveway to retrieve the newspaper.

"Mrs. *Celeste Bellamy?*" The young man asked as he cautiously approached her with his hands behind his back.

"Yes. How can I help you?" She did not recognize the young man so she backed away slowly as he approached. She wasn't too alarmed because he looked clean cut and was in a courier type uniform.

"I have a parcel for you." The man uttered as he flung the legal sized manila envelope from behind his back and shoved it into her abdomen. "You have been served." He said as he backed away then jogged the rest of the way back to his van.

Celeste was already stung by the news that Robert was relocating, but the service of divorce papers was the Coup De Grace. She stood there in amazement for a few seconds before she ran back to the house.

"That dirty bastard!" She screamed slamming the door behind her.

The tears were uncontrollable as she fumbled to open the sealed envelope. There it was a *Petition For Dissolution of Marriage* that she held in her trembling hands. She briefly read the Document Information Packet and angrily threw the papers onto the kitchen island as Michelle walked into the room. She had been watching the service from her upstairs bedroom window that overlooked the front of the house.

"What's going on? Are you and Robert ok? Where's Gertie?" Michelle asked as she approached Celeste who had collapsed to the floor with her back against the kitchen island and her knees drawn to her chest.

"That bastard just had me served. *Petitioner Robert Bellamy* it says. I don't deserve this. After all that I did for his country ass. We could have talked about this. He didn't have to do me this way."

"Do you *what* way?" Michelle asked looking at Celeste confused.

"He didn't have to have me served for the whole world to see!"

"Please forgive me but aren't you the one who wanted the separation *and* divorce?"

"Yes! But, it's the *way* he had me served." She responded as she wiped the tears from her face and angrily peered up at Michelle. "Well it's done now." She said struggling to get up off the kitchen floor. "I'm not even mad at him though because I don't really want his ass." Celeste said as she started laughing hysterically. '*You have been served*'! Wow!" She said mimicking the process server as she finally stood to her feet. "This is some shit you see on TV. Where's Ryan?" She asked as her laughter waned.

"He's scared to come out of his room. We heard you and Robert arguing and then we were watching from my bedroom window when you got served." Michelle said as she ran towards Celeste and embraced her in a bear hug pinning her arms down by her side. The two began to laugh hysterically in unison. "You are going to be just fine." She said shaking Celeste. "Robert is a sensible man and a great dad, and he needed to find the best way to serve your crazy butt." Michelle said as she loosened her hold on Celeste.

The two women laughed and hugged and then went to their respective rooms without saying another word. Ryan opted to stay put in his room. He was not into drama especially not Celeste's drama. He really liked and admired her, and was grateful to share in her beautiful home but he stayed out of *grown folks business* as he regarded the drama between Robert and Celeste. Celeste needed a moment to digest what had just occurred and she couldn't wait to tell Bea all about it.

———————

Celeste wasn't sure if Robert had broken the divorce news to Gertie after they left the house but she hoped they would be able to talk to her *together.* She spent the rest of the evening in her room talking on the phone to her parents about the latest developments with Robert. They were not surprised but they were concerned about Celeste and Gertie being in the house alone now that Robert was planning to relocate. Celeste assured them that they were not alone because she had Michelle and Ryan there, and Bea was close by. Her parents weren't fond of the idea of her running a *hostel* as they referred to her roommate situation. They just wanted her to be happy and vowed to be there for her during the entire divorce proceedings. Celeste ended her call with her parents by agreeing upon a top-notch Attorney to represent her. After the call Celeste fell off to sleep comforted by the thought of her sweet parents' undying support.

Celeste got up early on the next morning and called her office to tell them she would not be in. She was in a foul mood and anxious to see Robert that evening when he brought Gertie home. He called ahead when he was on his way and he also called Bea and asked her to meet him at the house so she could act as a buffer while he was there with Celeste.

"What's going on Robert? Is everything ok?" Bea asked with one eyebrow raised. She knew him well but she had not heard from him since he and Celeste split up months before.

"Everything is *fine*, it's just that Celeste and I had an issue yesterday when I picked Gertie up so I don't want any drama when I get to the house today." He explained. "I'm on my way there now to drop Gertie off and she and I need to talk to Gertie about an important matter together. I really need you to be there."

Bea obliged without prying further but she thought it was a good idea for her to call ahead so that Celeste wouldn't be surprised by her presence.

"Hey woman what are you doing?" Bea asked glad that Celeste picked up the phone instead of Michelle.

"I'm just waiting on Robert's ass to bring my child home. What's up?" Celeste replied coldly.

"Nothing's *up*. I was just going to stop by and hang out for a little bit. Larry is meeting with a client tonight and I'm bored as fuck." Bea was lying. She had plenty of work to do as she was behind with her end of year bookkeeping.

Celeste encouraged her to visit, as she wanted her there when Robert arrived. Bea got to the house within minutes and made herself comfortable on the sofa with a big cup of hot chocolate warming her hands. The first snow of the season was starting to fall and she was happy about that. She loved the winter months and especially her Christmas vacations in Cabo San Lucas. Larry owned a timeshare in the exclusive Pedregal section of Los Cabos and she loved hanging out there and on the Marina, and she loved eating at the local dives like the Crazy Sleepless Lobster where she enjoyed her lobster omelet and *two for one* cocktails all day long. That year she was hoping that Celeste and Gertie would join her in Cabo since Larry wasn't able due to his work schedule. Bea felt bad for Gertie when Celeste and Robert split so she wanted to treat her and Celeste to an all expense paid trip to the tip of the Baja Peninsula.

"I'm so glad you made it here before this *asshole* gets here." Celeste said when she met Bea at the couch with her Herbal Green Tea.

"Who? *Robert?*" Bea was surprised that Celeste still sounded so angry and even more surprised that she looked a hot ass mess with her thick curls all matted in the back of her head as if she had not combed her hair in a couple of days.

"No Wesley Snipes. Yes, of course *Robert!* That punk had me served when he picked Gertie up yesterday. The dickhead didn't even have the decency to *tell* me his intentions."

"Ok. So, now he's an *asshole* and a *dickhead* because he had *you* served? You know I love Robert too *and* you aren't the easiest person to get along with, *and* if I am not mistaken you were the one who wanted the separation right? So, surely you knew a divorce would follow. As you say, *'I'm just gonna keep it real'.*"

"What the fuck! So, now you are on his side?" Celeste said sitting her cup on the coffee table.

"Uh no. I'm not on anyone's *side*. I just want to be here for the both of you, *and* Gertie if ya'll need me." Bea was taken aback by Celeste's immature attitude. "Where are your *roommates?*" She asked sarcastically.

"Michelle is on her way home from work and Ryan has a night class so he will be home later if he doesn't hook up with one of his women for the night." She said picking her cup up again.

Bea wasn't fond of Michelle but she *loved* Ryan's chocolate self. She thought Michelle was weird and an opportunist. She noticed how well Michelle and Celeste bonded and saw how Michelle inserted herself into Gertie's life by always taking her to basketball practice. Celeste thought Bea was a tad bit envious whenever she complained but Bea tried to convince her that it was deeper than just some petty jealousy. She just could not put her finger on what she didn't like about Michelle so it was hard to get Celeste to understand her problem with Michelle.

Just as the women finished warming their bellies with their favorite winter drinks, Michelle walked in. They all exchanged pleasantries then Michelle disappeared into her bedroom as she respected Celeste's privacy whenever she had guests. Just as her bedroom door closed Celeste and Bea were alerted by the sound of the garage door opening.

"They're here." Celeste uttered as Bea sat quietly gazing at the TV. Celeste had no idea that Robert had called Bea to join them at the house.

"Mom. I'm home!" Gertie announced. "Daddy is coming in too." She said joyfully as Robert followed her into the kitchen.

"Hey Celeste. Hey what's up Bea?" Robert said as he nodded in Bea's direction. "Gertie can you go to your room please just for a minute so I can talk to your mom?" Robert asked as he sat on the edge of the coffee table looking nervously between Bea and Celeste who were sitting on the couch facing him. Gertie left the room without question. She didn't sense anything was wrong.

"First of all Celeste I want to apologize for having you served the way I did but there was no easier way and you know it. I didn't want to have you served at work, so this was the only place to ensure that you were available for service. I asked Bea to come over here so that you would have someone here to support you."

"Oh!" Celeste exclaimed cutting Robert off and looking at Bea. "So you two were conniving behind my back?" She was angry at the thought of her best friend plotting against her with her new nemesis.

"No!" Bea said throwing her hands in the air as she sat straight up with her feet firmly planted. "He just called and told me it was *important* that I be here, but he did *not* tell me *what* was going on. *You* told me what was going on when I got here. I have never pried or interfered in your personal business, so please do not go there. I'm here to support the both of you so calm the fuck down and listen to what the man has to say. Gee whiz woman."

"*Gee whiz* my black ass." Celeste tried to control her emotions but she could not hold back the tears.

"Oh come on stop fucking crying Celeste. I thought it was best that we talk to Gertie *together*, which is the *only* reason I am here right now. I want us to be able to co-parent amicably in the best interest of our child."

"Gertie!" Celeste yelled as she walked quickly towards the hallway leading to the stairs. "Gertie! Can you please come down here?" She wanted to get this shit over with.

Gertie was startled by her mother's sharp tone. Michelle appeared at the top of the stairs and looked down at Celeste's angry face. Celeste motioned for her to stay put, and assured her that they would talk later. Gertie walked hurriedly down the stairs as Michelle slowly walked back into her room and softly closed the door behind her. Michelle turned on her TV a little louder than usual to avoid being able to hear what was going on downstairs. Robert ushered Gertie into the room to join him, Celeste and Bea at the dining room table.

Gertie sat gingerly on the edge of Robert's chair cozied up right next to him. He reached for her hand and rubbed it as he led the conversation about the divorce and his impending move to California. Gertie hung on his every word. She was accepting of the split but she was *not* expecting to hear that he was moving across the Country. She cried aloud as she studied his eyes for further confirmation as Celeste moved into the seat on the other side of her.

Bea remained across the table from the trio and watched lovingly as Gertie occasionally wiped her falling tears with the sleeve of her thermal t-shirt. Celeste rubbed her shoulder in a comforting gesture and peered up angrily at Robert over her fallen head. She made angry faces at him doing all she could to keep from striking out at him physically. She wanted badly to disclose that he was actually moving closer to his *whore and love child* and he saw that spiteful look in her eyes. His body language told her that she had better not even go there. Then she remembered they had an agreement, and even though they were divorcing, the embarrassment was still the same if she were to divulge so she abandoned her angry thoughts. As far as Celeste was concerned Gertie didn't need to know about Savannah until she was older so she maintained her composure.

"Whoa. Hold up. This is too much." Bea blurted out as all heads sharply turned in her direction. I mean I figured the divorce was imminent but I had no idea you were relocating too Robert." Bea was surprised by the news. "Celeste and Gertie *need* you *here.*"

"Yes Daddy! Please don't leave me!" Gertie began to sob again uncontrollably. Robert pulled her closer into his arms and hugged her stifling her cry.

"Bea, I really appreciate your concern but this is *my* decision. I asked you to come here to offer support for *Celeste* but I am not asking for nor in need of your advice about moving forward with *my* life." He was stern and direct in his response to Bea. She was Celeste's best friend and he felt he didn't owe her any explanation. "I will always be here for my daughter *and* Celeste as long as they need me or welcome my help."

"Bea. Robert is right." Celeste said. "It's not for you to judge him. I am happy that you are *here,* as *my* friend, and I love you for that. Robert and I will find a way to co-parent as best we can, but I owe him the opportunity to live *his* life on *his* terms."

Celeste's demeanor changed noticeably when she saw how affected Gertie was by the news. She needed to be strong for her. Bea sat back in her chair with her arms folded across her chest and her legs crossed at the ankle and didn't utter another word. Robert and Gertie left the table and went into Gertie's room where they continued their conversation in a private setting. Celeste remained calm as she and Bea returned to the couch. She offered Bea a drink and she accepted. Within a few minutes they were sipping on Mimosas and making small talk about current events while waiting for Robert to leave. He stayed with Gertie for a good hour before he returned to the den.

"Celeste, I will be in touch to finalize the details of the divorce and custody arrangement. I will maintain our current routine with Gertie until I leave in January. I'm sorry it had to come to this but I believe that we will all be happier. At least I hope so." He said apologetically.

"Ok. No problem. It will all work out. I'll see you to the door." She was so ready for him to leave.

"No need. I'll leave through the garage like I came." Robert walked towards the door to the garage. "Bea thanks for your help. I hope I didn't offend you."

Bea looked at him but didn't respond verbally she just lifted her champagne glass in his direction as if she was toasting to his departure. After he exited she turned to Celeste and whispered *bye bye asshole.* The two women laughed heartily as they searched for a movie to watch.

CHAPTER 3

"Growing Pains"

———◆———

1994-Robert was happy to start his new job at USC. During his last trip to California before he moved, he bought a house in the upscale community of Ladera Heights where affluent black athletes, doctors, lawyers and other professionals resided. His commute to and from the university was a meager 6.9 miles from his new home. Clara knowing that he was relocating decided to move from Northern California to a spacious, three-bedroom townhouse in the nearby community of Fox Hills close to him so he could spend more time with Savannah. Clara was Vice President at a Wells Fargo Bank branch in Northern California and easily transferred to Southern California.

It was a bright sunny day early one Monday morning when Robert arrived on campus in South Los Angeles. He was amazed at the beauty of Los Angeles in general, but a 6.5 Earthquake, which didn't sit well with him, rocked southern California a week into his stay. He thought that maybe God was telling him he had made a big mistake by leaving New York *and* his baby girl.

"Oh my God! I was worried sick about you." Celeste said holding the house phone between her and Gertie's ears so they could both hear. "How is everything out there?"

"Oh hey Celeste. I'm good."

"That's a damn shame. You haven't been there a week and California has one of the biggest earthquakes in their history."

"Ain't that some shit?" Robert asked. "The earthquake destroyed an area out here called the San Fernando Valley, but where *I* live was not affected too badly. I already had cracks in these damn walls because you know I bought a fixer upper so a few more cracks ain't gonna hurt nothing." He was upbeat and happy to finally be able to get a call out with all the circuits being busy. "Gertie how's daddy's baby?"

"Here talk to your dad." Celeste said as she handed Gertie the phone, and excused herself from the call. "Talk to you later Robert. Glad you are ok." She walked out of Gertie's room and back to the den where Michelle was watching TV.

Gertie was ecstatic to hear from her dad and happy to make tentative plans to visit him for the upcoming summer as soon as school let out. The divorce and custody agreement would be finalized by then as Robert and Celeste had resolved pretty much everything that was in contention with the divorce. The biggest consideration was custody of Gertie and the agreement was that she would spend every summer with him in California, as well as every other Christmas and New Years Day for the next four years until Gertie turned 18. It had only been a couple of months since Celeste was served with divorce papers but Robert noticed that after all of her drama queen antics she bounced back from her temporary breakdown relatively quickly. He thought it was odd that she was taking it so well but on the other hand it was confirmation that the divorce was what needed to happen for the both of them.

———◆———

Robert was adjusting to his new environment and trying to learn his way around Los Angeles. He spent many evenings and weekends getting to know Clara all over again but he was most happy about developing a closer relationship with Savannah, which was long overdue. He still had no immediate plans to tell Gertie and Savannah about each other and he had no idea how that meet would ever come about. He just knew that it was not happening anytime soon if he could help it.

Clara was aging gracefully and still a very desirable woman but Robert was a *single* man and exercised his freedom as often as he could. He dated other women whenever he could break away from his bottom lady and baby mama. He had already made a huge mistake when he had Savannah outside of his marriage and he still had unfinished business with that situation so he didn't want to complicate his life with a steady new woman. Not just yet.

Robert never took the women he dated to his home because he didn't want any of them claiming ownership of him or his property. Clara had hinted that they could live together when his divorce was final and he strongly objected. He needed time to get his life together and needed time alone with Gertie whenever she visited.

The summer was quickly approaching and Robert was look-ing into a summer basketball program for Gertie to participate in. The YMCA was the first place he looked since he was already familiar with their program back east. Gertie was happy to have Robert to herself and looking forward to the break from Celeste, whom she loved dearly but didn't see eye to eye with most of the time.

As soon as school let out for the summer Gertie had her bags packed and she was ready to go. She reminded Celeste that she needed her hair braided before she left for California but Celeste dragged her feet for as long as she could. She hated that *fake syn-thetic hair* all up in her child's head.

"I haven't forgotten little girl. Lord knows if I leave it to you to do your hair everyday it will be all broken off by the time you return home and I know your dad doesn't know anyone in California to do your hair so I will get your hair braided before you leave next week. No worries."

"Mom, are you going to be ok here by yourself?"

"Gertie, you know I am not going to be *alone*. Michelle and Ryan are here, and Bea is right up the street." She said cutting her eyes at her little darling. She was surely going to miss Gertie but she was looking forward to the break from parenting. "You just go out there to California and have fun with your dad."

Gertie was up bright and early to catch her flight to Los Angeles. Her head was throbbing from the freshly done long individual braids, which she loved. She was excited about her trip but tried not to act like it for fear it would hurt Celeste's feelings. Things had not been great between her parents in the recent past and Gertie and Celeste had become closer by default since the divorce. Gertie felt that Celeste was distracted at times, by their roommates because whenever the opportunity arose for the two of them to spend some quality time together Celeste always invited Michelle and/or Ryan to join them for dinner and/or a movie.

Gertie was 13 and her hormones were raging, and her bad attitude was reflective of that change in her physiology. She was totally into boys and didn't care what color or creed they were as her parents had friends across the spectrum, black, white and other so Gertie, like her parents did not discriminate. She was raised a Christian but didn't attend church unless Celeste's parents were visiting on a Sunday and shamed them into going to church.

Playing club basketball as a teen exposed Gertie to girls who were *tomboys*, and girls who liked other girls, which was ok with her as long as the girls didn't hit on her. She wanted a *boyfriend*. She found herself crushing on some of the boys on her co-ed teams in the YMCA league, but she had an even bigger crush on Ryan. Whenever the topic of her having a boyfriend came up Celeste just jokingly warned her to keep her *dress down and panties up*, or keep a *dime between her knees*; two old wives tales. Regardless of the tactic employed to stifle her urges her mom validated her feelings about boys as *normal*. Celeste was sensitive to how her break up with Robert might have affected Gertie's ideology about relationships so she was always willing to talk to her about boys and sex.

Robert was just as easy to talk to about relationships because he wanted to make sure that he kept the lines of communication open during Gertie's adolescence especially since he was reduced to being a part time dad. The last thing he wanted was to have her figuring things out for herself and making bad decisions when he could have helped her. So, although she saw the worst in her parents' relationship while they were married, she regarded them as amazing parents individually when it came to her physical and mental well being.

The flight out of New York was delayed, which heightened Gertie's fears about travelling alone for the very first time but Ms. Wanda made sure that she was taken care of in the *Admiral's Club* until she was ready to board her flight. Wanda hooked her up with treats and drinks, and magazines to keep her busy.

Once she boarded the plane she realized that she was *very* claustrophobic. She found herself hyperventilating as more and more people boarded the plane. She reached up a few times and adjusted and re-adjusted the air flow before finally settling into her First Class window seat for the 5 1/2 hour flight to the West Coast.

"Would you like a blanket and pillow?" The pretty flight attendant asked.

"Yes please. Thank you Ms. *Foster.* " Gertie said squinting up at the woman's nametag. "I will take a pillow *and* a blanket." She said as she reclined her seat. She was the only young person in First Class, and the only one in her row and she was hoping it would stay that way.

"Here you go young lady. We are about to prepare for take off so you can't recline your seat just yet ok?" Ms. Foster warned as she handed Gertie the pillow and blanket.

"All right." Gertie said returning her seat to an upright position as required.

"After take off I will be serving refreshments." Ms. Foster advised as she stood by ensuring Gertie's seat was upright.

"Ok. Thank you." Gertie looked nervously around the cabin as the Flight Attendants prepared for take off.

———◆———

Celeste hurried back home to put the finishing touches on the décor for the celebration she and Bea planned for Michelle's graduation. Michelle had finally finished her Master's program and was set to teach at White Plains Senior High School where in addition to her counseling job she would also be the head coach for the girls' basketball team. Michelle was prepared to move into a place of her own after finishing Grad School but Celeste would not hear of it.

"You are more than welcome to just stay *here*. I have plenty of room. Pretty soon it will only be me and Gertie here."

"Nope, you can't leave." Ryan said. "What's Celeste going to do here without *both* of us? I'm definitely moving back to Atlanta for Law School so she and Gertie *need* you to stay here with them."

Ryan was sincerely worried about Celeste and Gertie being there alone especially since Robert had moved to California. They had all developed a real close relationship.

"Okie Dokey, then I guess I'll stay as long as I am wel-come." Michelle said beaming. Of course I will pay my fair share of the expenses since I will be a semi permanent fixture around here and not just renting a room."

Michelle was happy to be staying in the house versus being alone in an apartment. She wasn't close to her family in DC and had not been in a serious dating relationship for a few years so staying there with Celeste and Gertie was perfect as she regarded them as her family.

———————

Gertie was awakened by the Flight Attendant's soft poke against her shoulder just as the pilot announced their impending arrival at LAX.

"We are about to land sweetie so I need you to return your seat to an upright position and put your tray table away please." Ms. Foster said.

"Yes ma'am." Gertie felt around underneath the seat in front of her, with her feet searching for her shoes.

After locating her shoes she slid open the shade and peered out of the window taking in the aerial view of Southern California as the pilot announced the various landmarks they passed, while descending towards LAX.

The traffic around the airport was heavy as Robert made his way to the parking structure closest to American Airlines. He parked and jogged towards the terminal. He was excited to see his baby girl. Just as he ran into the crosswalk he spotted Gertie standing across the street at curbside nervously looking around with her luggage at her feet. Actually they spotted each other simultaneously.

"Daddy!" She yelled flailing her arms in the air. She was relieved to see him.

"Hey, baby girl!" He said waving. He tripped over a crack in the uneven pavement but regained his footing while keeping his eyes stayed on Gertie. "Damn, I almost fell." He said looking back at the crack in the street. "Welcome to California baby!"

"Daddy, I'm hungry." Gertie said without so much as a salutation.

"Ok girl, dang. Can I get a *hello* or somethin'? He asked pulling away from hugging her. "Come on I have the perfect place for you." He said as he grabbed the handles on her two bulging suitcases.

They loaded up the car quickly and headed towards the In N Out Burger Stand on Sepulveda Boulevard. It was the home of the best hamburgers in Southern California. They ate in the car and chatted and caught up a little bit.

"How's yo crazy ass mama?" Robert asked playfully taking a big bite of his Double-Double cheeseburger.

"She's good. When I left she and Auntie Bea were getting things ready for Michelle's party."

"Oh, like a going away party or something?"

"No. She's not going anywhere it's a *graduation* party." Gertie said. "Ryan talked Michelle into staying at the house so me and mom won't be there alone after he goes off to Law School."

"Is your mom dating anyone? She really needs to get back out there and date."

"Naw. She hasn't mentioned anyone. She's perfectly happy with Ryan and Michelle and Auntie Bea."

"Ok, well as long as she is happy. So what do you want to do for the summer? I have been looking for some summer basketball leagues for you to play in. Are you down?"

"Yes! That sounds like fun. That's why mom had my hair braided before I left so I can play ball and not worry about my hair at all." She said cheesing and inspecting the ends of her human hair braids.

Robert was anxious to get to the house and get her settled into her room. He had described his house as a *fixer upper* because it needed work when he purchased it but there were merely cosmetic changes that needed to be made, like removing the old paneling and shag carpeting for more updated options or a more contemporary feel. He had fared well in the divorce settlement so he had the funds to make all the necessary changes he wanted and needed right away, and Clara was on hand to lend a woman's touch with selecting furniture and providing decorating tips. Robert looked forward to having Gertie around. He had been spending a lot of time with Savannah, and the two were developing a great rapport but he missed his baby number one terribly.

Robert loved his neighborhood and hoped Gertie would too. He had befriended his neighbor John David who preferred to be called JD. He was a plumber who grew up in the neighborhood and had recently moved back into his childhood home with his mother, Ms. Pearl, following a horrible divorce. He had a teenage boy about Gertie's age so he couldn't wait for the kids to meet. Robert and JD spent a lot of time together on the weekends working on various projects at their respective homes. They shared dating stories and Robert even confided in JD about his love child Savannah and all the drama that came along with that.

───────◆───────

When Nanny finally met Savannah, she made Clara and Robert promise to let her spend every summer in Mississippi so she could get to know her and Jocelyn and the boys better. Robert told her and Jocelyn about keeping Savannah a secret from Gertie. The plan for Savannah to visit Nanny every summer worked out great because Robert didn't have to worry about the girls ever meeting during Gertie's summer months in Cali. When school let out for the summer the girls were like two ships passing in the night. When Gertie arrived in Los Angeles on the lower deck of American Airlines, Savannah departed from the upper deck. It was well orchestrated by Robert, and Clara went along.

Gertie was ecstatic about how close her dad lived to the Fox Hills Mall. She would surely be shopping *there* throughout the summer. She thought as they passed the Mall on their way to the house.

"Daddy who's that?" Gertie asked as Robert drove into his driveway.

"Oh, hey J.R."

J.R. was John David Jr. whom everyone referred to as J.R. He was an only child and lived with his dad and his grandmother Ms. Pearl. JD worked long hours in his plumbing business, so J.R. looked forward to companionship during the summer months while his dad worked.

"Hi Gertie!" J.R. exclaimed.

"Oh, hi." Gertie responded tentatively. He seemed a little too animated for her taste but *ok* she thought.

"I've been waiting for you all day." He said as he grabbed the suitcases from the trunk before Robert could get them. "Your daddy told me you were coming today."

He pranced away rolling the suitcases behind him.

J.R. was lonely and hated his mom for running off with a younger man and starting a new family. She insisted that he live with his dad so he felt abandoned by her. J.R. was a very respectful kid. He was a big awkward boy but he was friendly and always happy. He had never met Savannah as Robert visited Clara and Savannah at *their* house in nearby Fox Hills. Robert never brought Savannah to *his* home. Gertie evaded J.R. just long enough to go to her room and call home.

"Hi Mom. I made it here safely," She said as she closed the door to her bedroom and kicked off her shoes. "Can you believe I met a friend already?"

"Oh yeah? What's her name?" Celeste asked stopping in her tracks. "What's your *friend's* name?" She asked again urgently. She wanted to make sure her new *friend* wasn't *Savannah.*

"*His* name is J.R. and *he* lives right across the street." Gertie said. "I think he's gay mom."

"Why would you say that Gertie?" Celeste was not expecting this commentary from her.

"Well, I think I know what a gay boy looks like mom. My friend Troy is gay remember?"

"Yeah, well I don't like you judging people without getting to know them first." Celeste scolded.

"I'm not *judging* mom, I'm just telling you, ugh. Ok, I better go back out there with Daddy and J.R."

"Ok. I'm glad you called to let me know you got there safely. Tell your dad I'll talk to him tomorrow. I Love you."

"I Love you too. Later." Gertie ended her call and returned to the living room of Robert's plush ranch style home where he and J.R. were having a lively conversation.

———◆———

After J.R. left for the evening Gertie got settled into her room. She loved how it was decorated. She decided to leave most of her belongings she brought from New York right there at her dad's house rather than schlep them back and forth between homes especially since she would be spending her summers and other holidays there with her dad.

Robert worked throughout the summer on the campus at USC and made it a point to introduce Gertie to the head women's basketball coach during an inner city tournament they attended. Gertie found herself on campus frequently picking up games with club ball teams when she wasn't travelling with her own YMCA team.

That first summer in California set the stage for Gertie's future summers with her dad. When she wasn't playing ball she and J.R. shopped at the mall, ate tons of fast food, and on occasion J.R. travelled around the city with her and Robert to watch her play ball. They were each other's biggest fan and protector. They had the most fun hanging out in J.R.'s room where he used her to model his homemade designer fashions that he constructed from some of Ms. Pearl's old clothes.

"Boy, don't you get tired of being in this room all the time?" She asked lying across J.R.'s bed flipping through the tons of fashion magazines he had all over the place.

"You do what you do, I do what I do." He said flipping his imaginary hair over his shoulder. "Ain't nobody got time to be wearin' those baggy shorts runnin' 'round playin' with no big ass rubber balls." He scoffed.

The two bantered back and forth and laughed hysterically at J.R.'s antics. They cliqued. They bonded like brother and sister.

J.R.'s fashion sense was right on point as far as Gertie was concerned. He was stylish whether in jeans and a t-shirt, or in his Sunday's best, a 3 piece suit. They were too young to hang out at parties so his stylish fashions were mostly shone off weekly at First Baptist church where Ms. Pearl insisted they go with her on Sundays. Before long Ms. Pearl had the two participating in all sorts of youth programs at the church. The *Lock-Ins* sponsored by the church's women's organization, were regarded as more fun than any secular teen party. There was always plenty of good food, and talent shows and board games for everyone to enjoy.

Throughout the summer Ms. Pearl dropped J.R. and Gertie off at the church for the weekend *Lock-Ins*. They dragged their belongings to the basement where the boys and girls prayed and ate together and had good *clean* fun. When it was time to go to sleep the boys and girls went to opposite sides of the room where they curled up in their individual sleeping bags for the night.

It was at one of those sleepovers that Gertie got up in the middle of the night and went to the bathroom and when she passed the stairwell she heard voices. She didn't think much about the activity so she walked on past and into the restroom but on her way back her curiosity got the best of her so she investigated. She slowly pushed open the door to the stairwell and peered into the darkness where she saw a boy's profile in a stream of light illuminating from a window. The street light outside the window shone bright enough for her to see J.R. on his knees orally copulating the youth choir director, who everybody in the church *suspected* was gay.

Gertie backed away from the door quickly without being detected and ran on her tippy toes from the doorway, and slithered back into her sleeping bag. She closed her eyes tight and tried to forget what she had just seen. She was a virgin and had only seen some minor sex acts on TV but she knew exactly what she saw take place between J.R. and the choir director. She had heard little white girls at her school brag about giving boys *blow-jobs* but she had never heard of any black kids who engaged in that kind of sexual activity so she was stunned by what she saw. She was so tickled that she covered her mouth and giggled to herself until she finally fell off to sleep.

Gertie was a late bloomer. She was 14 and still had not started menstruating. Celeste was a little concerned because *she* had started her menstrual cycle at 11. She felt something might be wrong with Gertie but she was up to date with all of her doctor appointments and immunizations, and didn't complain of any ailments so Celeste didn't worry too much about her menstrual cycle starting later into puberty. Celeste had already talked to her about the birds and the bees and she hoped that Gertie remembered how important that talk was. After Gertie witnessed J.R.'s sexual activity she wondered if anyone had the *birds and the bees* talk with him. She didn't know what if anything she would say to him when she saw him the next morning.

"Ok. Listen up! Everybody make sure you have all of your belongings. Throw your trash away and stay inside the church until your parents sign you out. I hope you all had fun and we will see you in two weeks." The Chaperone said ending the *Lock-In.*

Gertie gathered her things and hurriedly walked to the edge of the stage to sit and wait for Ms. Pearl to come to take them home. She saw J.R. in the distance standing by the door being loud and playful with a group of kids. She didn't know anyone and hoped that no one noticed her sitting there alone. She didn't want to come off as a loser.

"Gertie! Gertie!" J.R. yelled.

"What!" She yelled back startled by his loud booming voice.

"Let's go. Your Dad is here."

Gertie was pleasantly surprised to see her dad. He offered to pick them up since Ms. Pearl dropped them off. She couldn't wait to get home and sleep in her comfy bed.

J.R. was his usual animated self on the ride home and Gertie laughed at his mannerisms and lingo. She and Robert were quite amused by his flamboyance but she never openly acknowledged his gayness after her mom scolded her when she mentioned J.R. being gay.

"Boy, you need to be playing basketball with Gertie this summer with your big ol' tall self."

"Daddy you know J.R. is not interested in playin' no ball."

"Uh no thank you Mr. Robert. I don't like sports like that. I'm going to be a fashion designer."

"He's a good designer too." Gertie chimed in. "I'm going to be modeling all of his fashions one day."

"Ok well it's a shame that all that height is going to waste." On many summer evenings when Gertie hung out with J.R. at his house, Robert visited with Clara at *her* place while Savannah hung out in Mississippi with Grandma Rose, Jocelyn and her boys. Savannah and the boys got along famously. The older Savannah got, the more resistant she was to spending her summers in country ass Mississippi. She loved her family and they loved having her there but she was bored in the small community.

Robert's double life was becoming an issue. Clara didn't like the deal that he made with the devil, Celeste, when they decided to keep Savannah a secret and she often complained to Robert about it. She told him on several occasions that they needed to plan how the girls' introduction would come to pass. Their avoidance tactics became more problematic as the girls got older. Robert repeatedly told Clara he didn't want to think about it.

———◆———

1998- Throughout Gertie's high school years she struggled to stay competitive playing basketball. It was her senior year, and her last semester in high school was fast approaching. She wanted desperately to play ball in college but she wasn't getting any looks from Division I school scouts in spite of her private lessons with Michelle and other club ball coaches. Ryan was one of her biggest cheerleaders but at the start of her senior year he moved to Atlanta to pursue his Law Degree. She missed his support terribly.

"Gertie, I'm serious you need to decide what you want to do about college. I know you want to play ball but it doesn't look like you are being recruited by the schools that you want to attend." Celeste said.

"I know mom but I really want to play ball." Gertie pouted.

"Your dad was telling me that since he is on staff at USC you could go there for free. That's an excellent university, and it would offer you great all around opportunities if you went there."

"Yeah he told me that too but I don't know if I want to move that far away from you."

"Girl, please. You better take advantage of that opportunity and save us some money."

"Oh so that's why you really want me to go there huh?" Gertie laughed teasing her mom.

"Hell yeah. I'm not shy about that. Why should we pay when you have a great opportunity to attend a prestigious university *and* for free?"

"You sound like you are trying to get rid of me."

"Just think about it ok? Don't worry about leaving me. I have mama, Auntie Bea and Michelle here and we will be more than happy to visit you in California and besides you will be close to your dad."

"Ok well I will think about it since you put it that way." Gertie and Celeste were having the same conversation about college ever since Gertie returned from her last summer trip to California. It was already January of her senior year and time for her to complete her FAFSA forms and college applications. Although she was not being considered for any basketball scholarships at Division I universities she was recruited to play for a variety of DII schools, and less prestigious State colleges and universities but she was not interested in any of those schools.

Celeste and Robert were prepared to pay for college but hoped they could talk Gertie into going to USC. She sulked as she completed her college applications because after all of the considerations she came right back around to USC being her best option. She loved the summers she spent with her dad, and the time she spent on the USC campus during those visits so she was open to the possibilities that might lie ahead at USC.

Gertie ended her senior school year with a 3.8 GPA, which was not stellar by USC standards but that's what she was working with. She was not a sports scholarship candidate so her admittance into a prime university had to be based on merit alone. She was a minority woman with a *good* GPA and financial means to go pretty much wherever she wanted so she applied everywhere and received acceptance letters from all over and to her surprise USC was amongst the *yesses*. She was prepared to *walk on* to a team wherever she decided to go but *USC* and *free* were music to her ears.

"I know daddy lives close to campus but I still want to live *on* campus." Gertie said.

"I'm good with that especially since your dad is close by. I'm sure you will be happy there so it sounds like a win win to me." Celeste was happy. "Let's call your dad and tell him the good news." She said as she dialed Robert's number.

"Hey Celeste. How's it going? Is everything ok?" Robert wasn't used to Celeste calling him.

"Gertie has some good news for you. Hold on." She said handing the phone to Gertie.

"What's up girl?" Robert asked.

"You'll be happy to know that *I* got accepted to USC." She said proudly.

"Yeah I just found out from the admittance staff that you were accepted and I'm so happy about that."

"Dang it they spoiled my surprise." Gertie proclaimed.

"Congratulations little mama. After your graduation we are going to Mississippi to get Nanny and fly with her back to California so she can spend some time with us this summer."

"Oh nice daddy. She's going to be so happy about that."

"Yeah she's getting up there in age and coming to California is on her bucket list. It's too much for her to make it to your graduation in New York *and* then come to Cali so she won't be attending your graduation ok?"

"I totally understand that." Gertie said.

Robert couldn't believe that both of his *babies* were graduating from high school. He had high hopes for them, as they were both very smart. In fact, although Savannah was a year younger than Gertie she was advanced from the 4th grade to the 5th grade due to her high test scores and maturity for her age. Clara was torn about whether she should allow the advancement but Savannah was bored in the lower grade and was acting out so the school psychologist echoed the teacher's sentiment by strongly encouraging the more challenging work for her. In spite of her outstanding elementary school performance her grades slipped significantly in high school primarily due to her ongoing rebellious nature.

Following Savannah's high school graduation, for the first time in several years she did *not* spend the summer with Nanny, as she was working part time and preparing to go to college. Robert and Clara talked about finally having the two girls meet however he was still not ready.

Robert looked forward to Gertie joining him in California. He had fallen in love with the City of Angels; loved his upscale community, and his job was amazing so he hoped she would be similarly affected once she lived there full time. Robert was thankful that she was going to attend USC but he was concerned about her living in the South L.A. neighborhood where the school was nestled amidst an old crime laden neighborhood, which housed the most notorious gangs in California, as well as some of the most raucous frat houses where criminals preyed on the naïve college students. He would have preferred that she live at home with him however she had her heart set on living on campus so he didn't want to rob her of that invaluable experience.

Gertie was busy rounding out her senior year with her Prom, graduation and Grad Night. She couldn't wait to see her dad at her graduation. He had been gone from New York for 4 years and Celeste hadn't seen him since he left. Robert was glad he'd be returning to NYC during the spring because he didn't miss those harsh winters at all. Savannah and Gertie's graduations fell on two different days, so there was no issue with him attending both ceremonies on opposite coasts.

———◆———

Robert had booked a room at the Renaissance Hotel in White Plains, New York and rented a car when he got there. Following Gertie's graduation ceremony he went to the house for her farewell party. He felt weird visiting the home he and Celeste established together. He noted some changes in furnishings but basically the place looked the same. It was still amazing inside and out. The minor changes were more contemporary than he expected but *hey* he thought *change is good*. The grounds were immaculate so it was obvious Celeste had not skipped a beat since he left.

"Hey Robert, how is Grandma Rose?" Celeste asked. "I'm so glad she is healthy enough to travel to visit you guys in California this summer."

"Yeah she's doing pretty well. She's dropped a lot of weight so she should feel up to travelling. Of course Jocelyn is mad she can't come with her but she's scared to leave her bad ass kids at home alone, and I definitely don't want them at my house for any length of time." Robert chuckled.

"Boy you are crazy." Celeste and Robert realized they were in a good place leading their separate lives.
"So how are your *roommates* working out?"

"Well, Ryan moved to Atlanta after school let out last semester and Michelle, well she's still living here." Celeste said as she moved about the kitchen.

"That's cool I guess. She's done with school right?" Robert asked.

"Oh yeah, yeah she's done. Actually I'm happy she's still living here especially now that my baby is headed off to college and Ryan's gone. I really don't like living alone. Michelle just got a coaching job *and* she'll be teaching." Celeste studied Robert's face wondering where he was going with his line of questioning. "She helps out a lot around here so my *roommate* is just fine thank you. I might have to move my mom to an Assisted Living facility though."

"Really? Why? Is anything going on besides old age?" Robert asked.

"She's pretty good health wise but she's not adjusting well to living alone since dad died and she doesn't want to move in with me. She thinks she will be a burden *and* she wants her own *space* as she puts it. Anyway, that's what's going on here." Celeste then turned her attention to the growing crowd in the back yard.

Robert felt good knowing that Celeste was in a good place. They enjoyed the post graduation festivities for the rest of the evening before he headed back to his hotel.

"Gertie!" Robert yelled out of the door into the back yard. She ran in his direction at the sound of his voice. "I'll be by here in the morning to get you so please have your things ready so that we won't be late to the airport." Robert said as he bent down to kiss her on the cheek.

"Ok daddy but I don't have much to pack because mom already shipped most of my clothes to your house yesterday. They should be there shortly after we get home." Gertie responded.

"Ok cool beans. Congratulations for graduating with honors. I'm one proud papa. Enjoy the rest of the evening with your friends and I'll see you tomorrow."

Robert headed out after exchanging pleasantries with Bea and Celeste. On his way to the hotel he drove through his old neighborhood to see what if anything had changed. He was happy to see that everything pretty much looked the same.

Robert got up bright and early on the next morning and drove to get Gertie for their flight to Mississippi where they would spend a few days with Nanny before the three of them headed to California. Nanny was uncomfortable on the plane ride to Cali but those cute little bottles of liquor calmed her nerves real quick. Once they arrived in California it didn't take long for her to start rearranging furniture and getting familiar with the kitchen while Gertie got her things put away in her room and got ready for club ball. She was intent on *walking on* to the team at USC so she needed to be in a summer league to help hone her skills.

Gertie and Nanny had a blast throughout the summer hanging out at all the usual tourist locations such as Universal Studios, Disneyland and the Wax Museum on wacky Hollywood Boulevard. Nanny got around pretty well for her age but she still moved slowly, so they mostly just sat at those places and ate junk food and people watched. When the summer came to an end Nanny was ready to go back home. She missed Jocelyn and the boys. The summer had flown by and it was time for Gertie to move onto campus. She was nervous and excited at the same time. She had hung out with Robert on campus during all of her summers in California but that summer was different because she was there in California for good.

———◆———

Gertie attended Freshman Orientation and had secured all of her requisite items for school. Savannah on the other hand was registered at Santa Monica City College. She had barely clung to a low "B" average in high school so she wasn't prepared for university life just yet. Robert assured Clara that the offer for Savannah to attend USC was still open to her if she did her part by getting good grades there at Santa Monica.

Robert accepted *some* responsibility for Savannah's less than stellar academics in high school. He wasn't living with either of his girls during their high school years and he regretted that because he couldn't offer them consistent help with their academics. Nevertheless he was a strong advocate for higher education and always expressed his expectations whenever they were with him. For selfish reasons he was relieved that Savannah was not eligible to attend USC at that time because it allowed him to keep the girls apart for a little while longer. After Orientation he and Gertie walked the campus ending with a walk through of Gertie's dorm room. It was pretty small but she still couldn't wait to move in.

CHAPTER 4

"NEW NORMAL"

———◆———

GERTIE MISSED HER MOM BUT she didn't worry about her because Michelle was still living with her. She talked to Celeste several times a week throughout the summer and she understood when her mom said she could not travel to California to help her move into her dorm room. At least she had her dad there.

"Baby girl are you good?" Robert walked in on Gertie organizing her room.

"Oh hi Daddy." She was surprised by his sudden presence in her doorway. "I'm great. I'm really happy that I don't have a roommate and I *love* my décor. Mom did a great job picking out my bedding. I just wish she was here to help me organize but I'll see her at Christmastime." She said sorting through her things.

"Yeah. Your mama did good. Now remember you need to leave that space over there available in case you get a roommate. You have shit all over the place." Robert said pointing to the other twin bed. "Keep all of your junk in *your* space girl."

"Whatever." She said rolling her eyes in Robert's direction.

"Ok, well I will let you get settled in. I'll be in my office until about 5 in case you need anything." He said backing out of the room.

Gertie was excited by all of the hustle and bustle on campus and she made a mental note of the cute guys and student athletes she saw roaming around. She had worked hard over the summer at refining her ball handling skills and the time had come to test them out. She was hell bent on joining the women's basketball team.

Gertie plopped down on her bed after she stuffed some clothes in the tiny closet and lined the dresser drawers with the contact paper her mom sent with the bedding. Just as she lay back and exhaled an imposing figure appeared in the open doorway.

"Knock. Knock." The young woman with freshly done cornrows said as she squeezed through the doorway holding a long duffle bag in one hand and a *Bed In A Bag* comforter set in the other.

"Can, I help you?" Gertie was caught off guard by her presence.

"Not really." The young woman said looking up at the door to make sure she was in the right room. "I guess we are room mates. I'm Taylor and you must be Gertrude." She said as she dropped the duffle bag on the floor next to the unmade extra long twin sized bed.

"Yes. I'm Gertrude." She said squinting in Taylor's direction. They locked eyes briefly before Gertie nervously turned away. "Excuse me." She said grabbing her wallet.

She hurriedly walked past Taylor and right out of the door. Gertie walked down the hall to the community bathroom even though she didn't have to *use* the bathroom. She just needed to go to a private setting, a place where she could gather her thoughts so she sat on the toilet fuming about the *stranger* who just invaded what she thought was *her* space. She had hoped she would not have a roommate.

Taylor was clearly an athlete; she was tall and lanky and looked a little rough around the edges. Gertie didn't know anyone on campus besides her dad, so she had no one to talk to. The last thing she wanted to do was run to her dad to complain so she pulled herself together and returned to her room.

The chatter in the hallway was loud and consistent as she made her way back to her room. The door was still open as was every other door in the building. The open doors allowed the students to easily come and go while moving into their rooms. She was nervous about being in such close quarters with a perfect stranger so she paused before she reached the threshold and then she slowly walked in.

"So do you have a TV?" Taylor asked as soon as Gertie walked in.

"I don't know yet. I mean I don't know if I'm going to *get* one." Gertie refused to make eye contact and started folding her t-shirts and filling her remaining dresser drawers.

"Ok then, well I'm only asking because I have one I can bring from home."

"Ok, but only if *you* want to."

"You look familiar. Did you play basketball this past summer?" Taylor asked.

"Yeah. I played in high school in New York *and* during the summers here in LA when I visited my dad. I was on one of the YMCA teams."

"I knew it! I have a pretty good memory." Taylor boasted. "You that girl who can shoot really good."

"I try." Gertie said relaxing her stance a little bit.

"Why you not on the team then?" Taylor asked shaking her bedding out of the plastic bag.

"I wasn't recruited but hopefully I'll be able to still try out for the team." Gertie totally let her guard down when she saw they had something in common.

Taylor grew up in Lynwood, California and was in and out of foster care from the age of 5. She started playing basketball at 10 when her foster dad was a club ball coach for a girls' league in Lynwood. Taylor went on to play ball in high school and was at USC on a full athletic scholarship.

The girls talked for a while and set ground rules for their dorm room and when they finally finished putting their things away Taylor invited Gertie to go with her to the Student Union to meet up with some of her team mates. Gertie was super excited knowing that her roommate was on the team so she kindly accepted her invite.

Although Gertie was thrilled to be in the company of Taylor's team mates she felt very intimidated by most of the girls, so she politely excused herself and returned to her dorm room after only hanging out for just a short while. The small room was stuffy, so she decided to leave the door open as many of the students did on a regular basis throughout Dexter Hall. She was lying facedown on her bed flipping through a magazine when she was startled by a knock on the door.

"Can I help you?" Gertie sat up abruptly and turned towards the door.

"Uh, is this Taylor's room?" The young man asked.

"Yes, but she's not here." Gertie recognized the handsome young man as USC track star Reginald "Jaxon" Atwater.

"Hey fool! Here I am." Taylor said as she rushed him from behind and embraced him in a bear hug. The two tussled playfully as they entered the room while Gertie sat watching from the side of her bed.

"Did ya'll meet?" Taylor asked as she looked back and forth between the two faces.

"Not really. He knocked on the door and asked if you lived here and then you showed up." Gertie was extra pleasant because she wanted to make a good first impression on Jaxon with his cute self she thought.

"Jaxon meet Gertrude. Gertrude meet my *best friend* Jaxon."

"Nice to meet you Jaxon, and you can call me Gertie." She exclaimed as she extended her hand with a big grin on her face.

Jaxon was born and raised in Compton, California and had attended Lynwood High School with Taylor, which is where they bonded as star athletes. He was tall and handsome and quite the ladies man.

———————

The semester was off to a great start academically *and* socially for Gertie. Taylor's vote of confidence resulted in the women's basketball coach inviting Gertie to tryout for the team. Her shooting skills impressed the coaches so much that they decided to add her to their roster especially since they didn't have to use one of their scholarships on her. She was already there courtesy of her dad.

Gertie got along well with her teammates but she felt uncomfortable with the open display of girl on girl affection. She sensed early on that Taylor was gay too but she still openly expressed her disdain.

"Man, you are a homophobe." Taylor exclaimed as they walked back to their dorm from practice one evening.

"No I'm not. *They* just need to do that PDA shit behind closed doors that's all. Don't nobody wanna see all that."

"All of what? Hugging? Kissing? Do you hug and kiss your boyfriend? Oh wait, you ain't got no boyfriend." Taylor laughed out loud.

"And *you* don't *want* no boyfriend because you are just like *them*." Gertie retorted.

"Girl you don't know nothin' about me so you need to chill." Taylor's laughing quickly subsided. "Why don't you go run to yo daddy and tell him you don't wanna room with no dyke because you know I'm just like *them*? Yeah I know your daddy is the Dean but don't think you are special because I will still beat yo ass if you keep talking reckless to me." Taylor followed close on Gertie's heels as they entered their dorm room.

"I don't care about your manly ways or ideals but you better not put your hands on me and I don't need my daddy to fight my battles." She proclaimed as she turned and stood chest to chest with Taylor. She was scared as hell but didn't dare show it.

Taylor lightly pushed Gertie in her chest causing her to fall back onto her bed as Gertie delivered a light kick to Taylor's thigh on her way down. The girls left it at that as they went their separate ways for the remainder of the evening without any further dialogue or contact.

Gertie didn't tell her dad about her issue with Taylor and the girls learned to coexist in their tiny environment as well as on their team excursions during the season. Gertie gravitated towards her teammates who were *not* openly gay, and she literally stayed out of her room on most days until bedtime in order to avoid Taylor. She only spoke to her when absolutely necessary and they were cordial to one another when they did communicate. As the girls maintained their distance, Gertie and Jaxon found themselves becoming friends in spite of Taylor's objection to them dating.

"She's an uppity little bitch and she thinks her shit don't stink because her daddy is the Dean." Taylor told Jaxon.

"So why ya'll still roommates then? Gertie *is* fine as hell, so why you cock blocking?" Jaxon asked.

"I mean yeah she is pretty but she's such a homophobe. *And* for the record I tried to change roommates but I can't until next school year so I'm stuck with this little bitch for another semester." Taylor and Gertie did a good job of avoiding each other in their spare time outside of their basketball activities.

———◆———

The Christmas holiday was fast approaching and Gertie was happy to be going home to New York to visit her mom and even happier to get away from school and Taylor's ass. She missed her mom like crazy.

"Ok mom. I get out of school in early December. I will let you know the exact date so you can call Ms. Wanda and book my flight. I can't wait to see you."

"I can't wait to see you either! So tell me, did you put on that *freshman 15*?"

"*Freshman 15*? Mom what's that?"

"*Freshman 15* refers to the amount of weight gained during a student's first year in college." Celeste said in a playful tone.

"Uh...I don't think so. But I'm sure you will tell me when you see me."

Gertie welcomed the winter break after what she considered to be a grueling first semester. She started out doing well until her social life heated up. She was upset at her Dean when he told her that she was very close to being on academic probation and needed to step up her academic game significantly if she planned on staying at USC. Robert was also on her case when he learned that her grades weren't quite up to par. Her basketball season was also pretty uneventful with the minimal playing time she received so needless to say she was happy to get away from

Cali for a little bit, however she worried that the winter break period would derail her new budding relationship with Jaxon.

"So how long you gonna be gone?" Jaxon asked as he chomped on a big bite of his Big Mac.

"I don't think you are supposed to be eating that junk food are you?"

"What are you? The food police?"

"Whatever. Anyway, I'll be back on January 2nd. What are you doing during winter break?"

"I'm gonna go see my Moms and Pops, and hang out with my homies and wait for you to get back."

Jaxon was lighthearted and charming for a boy from the 'hood but he really liked Gertie in spite of Taylor's expressed dislike for her. He hoped that Taylor and Gertie would rekindle their friendship so they could all hang out together.

Gertie was not looking forward to facing her mom. She knew she would be extremely disappointed with her less than stellar grades. All that Gertie could think about was what a travesty it would be if she blew an opportunity for a free college education.

"Are you all packed?" Robert asked walking into the dorm room. "You better be ready to talk to your mama about your grades when you see her. You know she is *not* going to be happy."

"Yes Daddy, I'm ready and I know. I know. I'm sorry. I guess I just wasn't focused this past semester."

"You damn right you were not focused but I bet you were focused on getting on that damn team and hanging out with that Negro from Lynwood though. Huh?"

"Daddy, he's from *Compton,* and I said I'm sorry."

"Lynwood. Compton. Same damn thang."

"What did Mom say when you told her about my grades?"

"I didn't tell her shit. That's *your* job to keep your mom up to speed with what's going on with *your* grades." He said. "Is this it? This all you taking?"

"Yup that's all I need." She had purposely packed light in anticipation of a shopping spree when she got home.

"Ok I'll be here bright and early to get you tomorrow to take you to the airport."

"Ok great I'm on my way now to meet J.R. for lunch."

"Alright. Tell him I said hello."

Gertie knew that her dad was still very upset with her, which is why she decided not to stay at his house for the few days before leaving. She didn't want to hear his mouth. On the other hand Savannah had a great first semester at Santa Monica. Robert had planned on spending some quality time with her during the winter break while Gertie was gone. She would have his undivided attention.

Gertie met up with J.R. as planned. He had a great first semester at the Fashion Institute of Design and Merchandising (FIDM) where he was creating and whipping up amazing sample designer clothes for some of the local up and coming recording artists. He was disappointed that he wasn't going to be able to hang out with Gertie during the break but he understood that she wanted to go and see her mom.

"Girl, do you remember those fun ass sleep overs we used to have at the church?" J.R. asked as they travelled down memory lane.

"Yeah I remember. That's when I found out for sure your ass was gay. I saw you in that stairwell making out with the choir director."

"Oh No! Bitch you saw me? Why didn't you say something back then? Girl I was handlin' my business." J.R. broke out into uncontrollable laughter.

"First of all I was shocked seeing you going down on dude." She said laughing. "I didn't know what to say to you afterwards. But for real though J.R., you need to be careful out there. I mean Magic Johnson is HIV positive and he ain't even gay so your chances of getting AIDS is even more likely than someone like him. Your ass better be careful."

Gertie suspected from day one that J.R. was gay but she accepted him for who he was without reservation versus how she responded to Taylor and her teammates right away. J.R. and Gertie laughed and kee kee'd for the better part of the afternoon before she headed back to campus. She caught the bus to and from FIDM because Robert and Celeste agreed that she did not need a car her freshman year, and with her suffering grades she certainly didn't deserve one.

Gertie's ride to the airport was quiet and awkward with her dad so it was good that it was a short distance. She breathed a sigh of relief when he pulled to the curb in front of the terminal. She always flew First Class on American at her mom's insistence. She looked forward to the extra leg room, comfort and gourmet meals. She hadn't slept well since her final grades were posted so she thought she'd be able to get some sleep on the long flight home. Unfortunately, the inclement weather along the route made for a turbulent ride so sleep was not an option.

Gertie settled in and watched *The Matrix* in lieu of napping. As the movie ended the Captain's voice advised that the landing would be delayed due to heavy air traffic with so many planes trying to land during the busy holiday season. The delay afforded her extra time to work on her excuse for having such a dismal start in college because she knew her mom was sure to ask about it. The weather was a cool crisp 41 degrees in New York City, which was quite a contrast to the warm California temperature she had just left. As soon as she deplaned she saw Celeste standing amongst the crowd of people eager to greet their respective family members all coming in from sunny California. Celeste searched eagerly until she spotted Gertie's gorgeousness in the crowd.

"Hi baby!" She exclaimed as she walked hurriedly towards Gertie with her arms extended outward. "You lookin' good lil mama!" She said as she quickly inspected Gertie from head to toe.

"Mommy! It's only been a few months and you look amazing but oh so different." Gertie inspected Celeste in return. "I missed you." She said excitedly as the two embraced and she buried her face in her mom's ample bosom.

Celeste then abruptly pushed Gertie away and held onto her at arms length as she inspected her again.

"I guess the *freshman 15* didn't get ya after all. You are as fit as a fiddle! I suppose playing basketball is really paying off for you?" Celeste noted. "Come on. Let's go get your bag and hit the road. I can't wait to hear all about school, and the boys, and California and all that shit." She said as she released her grasp and walked away holding hands with Gertie.

"Yeah. Ok." Gertie was not looking forward to the ride home but was prepared to accept responsibility for her poor performance in school if the subject came up.

The baggage claim area was ridiculously crowded but understandably so. Every kid in America was going home for the holidays, well, except for Taylor who had no home to go to. Her foster parents had divorced and both had left her childhood home where she had lived since the age of 5. She was closer to her foster dad, who had moved in with a friend so when the holidays rolled around Taylor literally had nowhere to go because her foster mother had moved to Vegas with family members. Of course Taylor did not tell Gertie she had nowhere to go because for one they didn't talk much; and two, she was embarrassed about her new homeless status so she asked a couple of team mates if she could bunk with them in their apartment for the winter break. They welcomed her with open arms because she was a neat freak *and* loved to cook so they thought she was sure to earn her keep by cooking and cleaning.

Celeste and Gertie walked quickly to the car, as it was cold; *and* they were hungry. New York style pizza was at the top of Gertie's list for food choices and Celeste was more than willing to oblige. On the ride to their favorite pizza restaurant Gertie noticed that Celeste was pretty mellow and the topic of school did not come up. *Hallelujah* she thought.

"Mom, I can't believe you cut *all* of your hair off *and* you got your nose pierced. What's up with that?" Gertie reached up and stroked the nape of Celeste's neck where her fresh pixie cut hair lay against her smooth golden skin.

"I have been wanting to cut my hair for a long time *and* wanted to get a nose piercing for a while too and Michelle convinced me to just do it. So I did. Do you like it?"

"Yeah, it's so pretty and I really *love* the piercing. Your new look makes you look a lot younger and hip."

Celeste was happy that Gertie approved of her makeover. By the time they reached the restaurant they both acted nervous as they sat and pondered over the familiar menu. Celeste kept wringing her hands and looking down at the menu while Gertie made small talk about living in California, Grandma Rose, her dad and any and everything other than school. The two settled on a Margherita Pizza, their favorite, and two large Pepsi's with lots of ice.

"Gertie. Listen. I am so happy that you are home but I need to tell you something." She said as her eyes searched Gertie's face.

"What mom? Are you ok?" Gertie leaned into the table with her hands reaching out to grasp Celeste's hands. "What's wrong?"

"Oh baby nothing is *wrong*. Actually I am happier now than I have been in a very long time." The look in her eyes became real intense.

"Well then why are you looking so serious?" Gertie was confused by her sudden mood change.

"You know, when daddy and I split up I was in a dark place and I was lonely, which is why I took in Ryan and Michelle. I was hoping they could fill a void, especially at those times when you were gone with him. Having Michelle and Ryan there really helped me make it through the rough patch following the divorce."

"Awww mom I know."

"Well, what I want to tell you is that I am now in a *new* dating relationship."

"Mom, there is *nothing* wrong with you dating some-one else. Whew. I thought something was *wrong*." She said releasing her mom's hands. "You have been divorced for a while now and clearly daddy has no issues dating so what's the big deal?" Gertie asked taking a long sip of her drink. "So am I going to meet your new beau this trip?"

"You already know the *person* I am dating." She said smiling nervously as she patted the perspiration from her forehead.

"I do?"

"Yes… It's Michelle. I'm in a *relationship* with Michelle. I needed to tell you that before we get home." She said really quickly.

"What? Mom, No!" She blurted out just as the pizza arrived at the table. "Are you kidding me?"

"Is everything alright?" The waiter asked as he slowly placed the pizza on the table while looking back and forth between Gertie and Celeste.

"Yes, we are fine." Celeste responded with her eyes darting between the waiter and Gertie. "Can we please have some crushed red pepper and Parmesan Cheese?" She was glad that the waiter interrupted at that very moment. She needed time to gather her thoughts. As the waiter walked away she quickly turned her full attention back to Gertie who was crying with her head down on the table.

"Mom." Gertie whispered. "I'm confused. So are you telling me that you are *gay* now? I had no idea this is what you were going to tell me. That's ridiculous." She said throwing her napkin on the table and turning sideways to avoid eye contact with her mom.

"First of all, it's not *ridiculous* and this is *my* life." Celeste said hardening her facial expression. "You have a life. Your dad has a life…"

"But you were married and had a child." Gertie interrupted. "Who does that? Man, I wish I never came home. This is so unreal."

"Well, I'm glad you are home." Celeste said in a softer tone. "My sexual preference should not change anything between you and I. You are my child and I love you more than anything in this world. I just needed to tell you this in person *and* before we get to the house because Michelle is there. She loves you and you know that so I hope that you will be respectful about our relationship."

"I don't want her to love me. She's a dyke." Gertie exclaimed.

"She's not a *dyke* Gertie. That's very offensive. You need to learn how to respect people's differences. Trust and believe I will *never* tell *you* who to love. I'm in a good place in my life and you should want that for me." She explained as Gertie stayed turned away from her. "I often wondered why your dad and I never clicked on all cylinders and when God revealed *this* relationship to me it became clear that I was not living in my truth. You're grown now so you really need to grow up."

"I feel like someone just punched me in the stomach." She said pushing her plate away from her. "Can we just go to the house now? I'm tired."

"Ok. I'll have the waiter box up the pizza." Celeste had also lost her appetite.

Neither of them touched the pizza, and the ice was melting in their drinks by the time they finished their debate. They hurried back to the car forgetting the pizza on the table after having it boxed up to go.

The 45-minute ride to the house was quiet with the exception of the soft jazz playing in the car, and the sound of traffic all around them. Celeste's new lifestyle clearly explained her makeover. She was born again but not in a biblical sense Gertie thought.

Michelle was anxiously awaiting Gertie's arrival but she did not know that Celeste had broken the news of their relationship to Gertie before they got home. Gertie entered the house pulling her suitcase behind her. She pushed past Michelle and went directly to her room barely speaking. When she walked past Michelle's room, she quickly noted that it was extremely tidy. It did not look lived in at all so it was clear that Michelle had new sleeping quarters downstairs in the master bedroom. Celeste motioned for Michelle to remain silent as Gertie pushed past her. She followed Gertie to her room where she lay crying in her pillow. Celeste went to comfort her but Gertie pushed her away.

"I need to call my dad to let him know I made it safely." She said whimpering as she wiped her tears away with the heel of her hands.

"Ok. Go ahead. Call your dad. I'll give you some privacy." Celeste backed out of the room and gently closed the door behind her but stood outside in the hallway for a second to eavesdrop.

After listening for a few seconds she felt guilty eavesdropping so she returned to the downstairs den where Michelle was opening a bottle of her favorite drink, Yellow Tail Chardonnay. Michelle filled their glasses to the brim because she figured it was going to be one of those nights. Celeste was a lightweight when it came to alcohol so the wine quickly calmed her nerves as she shared the details of her conversation with Gertie. Michelle dealt with young hormonal girls on a regular basis in her role as high school basketball coach and teacher so Gertie's demeanor did not intimidate her, and in this circumstance she totally understood her attitude. The two drank wine and gathered snacks from the fridge when Celeste realized that she had left the damn pizza at the restaurant.

———————

Robert was at home preparing for a date with Clara and Savannah when his phone rang.

"I'm so glad you made it home safely baby cakes. Has your mom asked you about school yet?" Unbeknownst to Gertie he had already told Celeste about her poor grades but he wanted *her* to personally discuss it with her mom.

"No daddy, I have not told mom about my grades yet but I will." She was very solemn.

"What's wrong?" Robert noted that her mood was weird.

"Nothing. I'm just sleepy." She was not ready to talk about her mom's midlife crisis at that time.

"Ok then take your booty to bed and we will talk tomorrow." Robert said. He was in a good mood.

Gertie turned in for the night without going back to the den with her mom and Michelle. Winter break couldn't end fast enough she thought because things were not the same there at home and besides her friends were all over the place. Some of them were still away at college; others were working, and one friend was pregnant and shacking up with her boyfriend.

Gertie visited her maternal grandmother for a few days and after the initial shock of Celeste's transformation wore off she realized that her mom was happy with Michelle, which was much different than her mom ever was with her dad so she found herself softening her stance and she showed a more amenable spirit towards her mom *and* Michelle. When it was time to return to Cali, Celeste *and* Michelle took her to the airport but they stopped on the way and had pizza one final time that trip.

"Hey Mom, so, does daddy know about you and Michelle?" She asked during small talk at the table.

"No. That Negro doesn't tell me who *he* dates but you can tell him if you want, I don't care. By the way, we never talked about school. How were your grades this past semester?" Celeste asked lightheartedly already knowing from Robert what her grades were like.

"Not good mom." She was curt and to the point without looking up from her plate as she folded her large slice of pizza and prepared to stuff it in her mouth. "It was like I was in a daze the first semester but I will definitely do better next semester I promise you that." She said averting eye contact with her mom.

"Ok. I like how you owned that. Just remember this is *your* life and your dad and I want the best for you so please take this time in your life seriously and never settle." Celeste said in counselor mode.

"Mom. I'm going to graduate and I will make you and daddy proud." She said smiling at Celeste and Michelle.
The ladies finished their pizza and headed to the airport just in time to make the flight, which was oversold. It was a good thing Gertie was in First Class because her expensive seat was not up for grabs.

"Come on honey find your seat we are about to close the doors." The Flight Attendant said sternly as Gertie approached her seat. "Hurry now." The frazzled looking woman said as she tried to usher her into coach. She was nothing like the pretty flight attendant Ms. Foster who Gertie met on the previous flight.

"Excuse me." Gertie said as she stopped at Row 2. "Here's my seat right here." She said rolling her eyes at the disheveled woman.

"Can I please see your Boarding Pass?" She asked as Gertie went to open the overhead bin.
Gertie searched her backpack and pockets and could not find her Boarding Pass so the Flight Attendant had her sit temporarily in the Flight Attendant's seat to allow others to pass while she tried to verify her seat assignment.

"What's the problem?" Ms. Wanda asked as she hurried into the cabin and approached the Flight Attendant.

"The *problem* is that the passenger here says she is seated in First Class but she can't find her Boarding Pass." The woman explained looking harshly at Gertie.

"I can tell you for certain that she *is* in First Class. I book flights for her folks all the time. Let me look her up in the system and verify her seat. Give me a few minutes." Wanda said as she walked briskly back through the Jet Way.

Within minutes Ms. Wanda returned with a copy of the Boarding Pass, which indicated that Gertie was in fact seated in First Class. Row 2.

"Please forgive me young lady." The flight attendant insincerely offered. "I thought you were in Coach." She said dryly as Wanda stood by waiting for Gertie to take her seat.

"I know. But, I'm not. Excuse me please you are blocking my seat." *Rude bitch* Gertie thought as she slid down into her comfy seat as the frazzled Flight Attendant walked away towards the back of the plane closing overhead bins.

"You alright baby girl?" Wanda asked handing Gertie complimentary headphones and a blanket.

"Yes ma'am." Gertie responded smiling up at Wanda.

"I'm so glad I was working today. These motherfuckers get on my nerves thinking black folks can't afford shit." Wanda said under her breath. "Excuse my French honey but she pisses me off all the time. Anyway don't get me started. Tell your daddy I said *hi*. Have a safe flight." She said as she left the aircraft.

———◆———

After the boring two weeks at home with her mom and Michelle, Gertie looked forward to finishing winter break at her dad's house. On the ride from the airport she told her dad all about her trip and all about her mom's *revelation.*

"Girl, what are you talking about?" Robert asked as he applied the brakes hard enough to cause a whiplash. He abruptly pulled to the curb and put the car in park.

"You heard me right daddy. Mom is gay *and* Michelle is her girlfriend. I mean I know that J.R. is gay but I love him. I know my roommate is gay, and I can't stand her but I don't know how to feel about mom being gay. It's so crazy."

"Aww baby." Robert said reaching across the seat to hug Gertie. "I understand how you must be feeling and it sure explains a lot. Wow. Who woulda thunk it?" He was shocked to say the least.

They sat at curbside on Airport Blvd talking for about 20 minutes before they continued on their way home.

"Oh yeah and Ms. Wanda told me to tell you *hi.*" Gertie said.

CHAPTER 5

"ROOMIES, LOVERS AND FRIENDS"

GERTIE DIDN'T HAVE ANY PLANS for the remainder of winter break but she was happy to be chillin' at her dad's place versus her claustrophobic dorm room. When she wasn't with her dad she was with J.R., as she couldn't get in touch with Jaxon. J.R. was still living at home but hanging out most of the time in West Hollywood with some of his boy toys.

"Do you want to go with me to a parade?" J.R. was watching Gertie twirl around his room in one of his creations that he made for his midterm exam.

"I guess. What kind of parade?" She asked stopping mid twirl.

"It's the L.A. Pride Parade for the LGBTQ community."

"What the hell is L G B T Q?"

"Girl, it's a gay parade that's *all* you need to know. I'm queer honey and it's always a celebration!"

"Yes J.R. I know. And yes I will go with you. I'll celebrate my mother's new *gay* pride too. I guess."

"Girl shut up!" He squealed. "You mean to tell me yo mama done come to the other side?"

"Yup." She acknowledged nodding her head.

"Well then yes honey you *needs* to come and celebrate with me. I will let you know when it is."

"Ok. I'll be back in school I'm sure, but call me and if I am available I'll definitely go with you." Gertie wasn't a fan of parades but she agreed to go because J.R. asked and he was always fun to be around.

———◆———

Gertie lay in her room on the night before returning to campus reflecting back on her winter break. She believed that her introduction to J.R. as a young teen, and her recent introduction to Taylor kind of unknowingly prepared her for her mom's new lifestyle. She wondered what all of it meant. Was she too judgmental about Taylor and her teammates? What was the message she was supposed to get? Regardless of the message she still did not like Taylor and hated that they had to finish out the year as roommates.

Robert kissed Gertie goodbye at the door of her dorm room and promised to check in on her after he finished some work in his office. Taylor was laying face down on her unmade bed when Gertie entered the room. She gingerly laid her suitcase on the chair beside her bed and started to quietly unpack her belongings hoping Taylor wouldn't notice she was back. After a few minutes she noticed that Taylor had not moved. She was glad because she didn't want to engage in any frivolous small talk with her anyway.

After about 20 minutes Taylor still had not moved so Gertie walked towards her bed and stood close enough to see if Taylor was ignoring her or if something was wrong. As Gertie got closer Taylor lay still so she bent down slightly and listened to her breathing. She then called out to Taylor and she did not respond so she shook her. Taylor was still unresponsive. Gertie then called her name again loudly several times and still no response. She then turned Taylor over when she noted the blank stare in her eyes.

Gertie ran from the room and looked for the nearest Resident Assistant (RA).

"I think something is wrong with my room mate." Gertie said out of breath. "I can't wake her up." She said as the RA followed close behind her to the dorm room.

"Taylor! Taylor!" The RA yelled as she observed Taylor groggy. "I think she may have ingested something. Somebody call 9-1-1!" The RA yelled.

"Are you serious? Like an overdose? But she's an athlete and she doesn't drink or smoke." Gertie said as a crowd started to gather at the door.

"Well she's ingested *something*, so we need to get her to the hospital."

The RA stayed close by Taylor's side until Paramedics arrived. They transported her to County USC Medical Center where she was treated for an overdose of sleeping pills. When she came to she explained to the police that she hadn't slept in a few days due to family issues while on winter break so she mistakenly ingested too many sleeping pills. She was adamant she did not try to commit suicide so they did not refer her for a psychological evaluation due to no prior history. The women's basketball coach went to the hospital and drove Taylor back to the school. When she arrived back at the dorm Gertie was anxiously waiting for her.

"Taylor, are you ok?" Gertie asked as she jumped up from her bed.

"Yeah. I'm good." She said with her head down and her hands in her pockets. She was embarrassed.

"Girl you scared the shit out of me." Gertie put Taylor in a bear hug and momentarily lay her head on Taylor's chest.

"Thank you for getting me help." Taylor's voice was weak. She removed her hands from her pockets and hugged Gertie in return and then sank to the floor sobbing like a baby in Gertie's arms.

"Here, lie down. You need to get some rest." Gertie helped Taylor up onto her bed, removed her shoes, lay her down and covered her with a blanket. Gertie had an epiphany when Taylor broke down. People were hurting all around her; she was not the only one who had issues.

The next morning she awakened just as Taylor was returning from the community restroom. Taylor was dressed and ready for school. The girls felt a close connection to one another. They spoke to each other like long lost friends and got along famously as roommates and teammates from that point forward. Taylor was very protective of Gertie, and repeatedly cautioned Jaxon not to hurt her.

"So now ya'll besties?" Jaxon asked.

"She saved my life. If she didn't come to the room when she did I would not be here. After being around her these past few weeks I see that she really is a very sweet person. I guess we just got off on the wrong foot. I'm serious you better not hurt that girl. She really likes you."

"Ain't nobody *tryin'* to hurt homegirl."

"Are you guys an item or not?"

"I mean we cool but we not boyfriend and girlfriend." Jaxon clarified.

"Well you better tell *her* that. She thinks y'all are a couple."

"We cool. But when she not here I'm not gonna sit around and wait for her to come back. A man's gotta do what a man's gotta do." He boasted. "Anyway, I'm glad you feeling better big head."

———◆———

Jaxon was really hoping to compete in the 2000 Olympic summer games in Sydney, Australia. He had run track for most of his life and had trained and worked extremely hard during his high school years resulting in the full scholarship at USC. Track was his priority, *not* his relationships.

Gertie heard the rumors about Jaxon's sexual prowess and although she got butterflies in her stomach at the thought of having sex with him she was not about to be one of his conquests. She was quite smitten with him but she was not ready to give up her virginity to him or anyone else for that matter. She had heard about his screwing a pretty white cheerleader but that didn't change her stance just to solidify their relationship and keep the other girls at bay.

"No. I'm not ready yet Jaxon. We aren't even in an exclusive dating relationship according to you. Taylor told me what you said." Gertie was sick and tired of him pressuring her but she didn't want to end their *friendship*.

"You know I love you girl." He said slyly as he stood facing her rubbing her shoulders. "You need to suck my dick." He said pushing her down onto her bed and thrusting his pelvis towards her face.

"Hell no!" She yelled pushing him away from her as hard as she could. "I'm not sucking your nasty sweaty ass dick. That's just disrespectful." She said as she abruptly rose to her feet and rushed towards the door. "You can leave now." She said as she opened the door and motioned for him to leave her room.

Gertie slammed the door behind him and flung herself onto her bed where she lay crying for a little bit. She was done with him. Well at least for the time being.

Throughout the spring semester Gertie and Jaxon flirted with one another whenever they ran into each other on campus but that's as far as their relationship went. Occasionally she found him in her room hanging out with Taylor and at those times she politely excused herself and left to visit with friends until he was gone.

———◆———

The school year ended on a good note. Gertie had earned a position as 6th man on the team, coming off the bench much more often than other reserves; and her grade point average had risen to a strong 3.7. Robert and Celeste were happy about how well she bounced back.

When the school year ended Jaxon went home for the summer but maintained his training ritual. Gertie and Taylor and several of their teammates banded together and moved to a rental house close to campus, which greatly improved their camaraderie.

By Gertie's sophomore year she was fully acclimated to the California lifestyle but still looked forward to her short visits to New York for Christmas.

Celeste and Michelle were still in their respective careers, and their relationship was as strong as ever with an occasional jealous rant from Michelle whenever anyone gave Celeste too much attention. Michelle and Bea did not like each other. Bea thought Michelle took advantage of Celeste's loneliness, following her divorce. Bea went as far as accusing Michelle of *turning Celeste out*.

———◆———

By the end of Gertie's sophomore year she declared her major in *Political Science*; Taylor in *Sociology* and Jaxon in *Journalism/Mass Communications*. Jaxon and Gertie rekindled their superficial relationship and he vowed to be faithful if she would give him another chance. It was during *that* summer that she lost her virginity to him and not long afterwards the rumors of him screwing the blond cheerleader started again. Gertie was furious. She felt used but she couldn't resist his charm so she continued to have sex with him often, and everywhere; her house; his dorm; his car; and even under the biggest oak tree at Exposition Park near the school campus. They were both hot and horny. Gertie had started menstruating during her senior year in high school, however she had not been sexually active until her sophomore year in college with Jaxon so she had not thought about getting on a birth control regimen nor had she ensured that he wore a condom.

———•———

It was late in June 2000, when Jaxon was preparing for the Olympic Trials that were taking place that July in Sacramento. Gertie and her teammates were in a summer club ball league there at USC and during their time off they hosted basketball team hopefuls. She and Jaxon talked on the phone daily, sometimes several times a day when they were apart. They pledged their love for one another even though Gertie knew about his ongoing infidelity.

It was one warm summer night when Jaxon urged Taylor and Gertie to meet him and some friends at Tam's Night Club, a popular hangout near the campus. She and Taylor agreed to meet him. They looked forward to all that came along with the club atmosphere; watching their friends drink in excess and clown one another; and one night stands, which ended in the usual walk of shame on the morning after. Gertie made sure that she was looking hot in order to keep Jaxon's full attention throughout the night. Her hair was bouncing and behaving after getting the $25 Trojan Girl Weekend Special Press and Curl, at Simply Raw Hair Designers earlier in the day.

They had been at Tam's for a few hours when Jaxon, Taylor and Gertie decided to head back to campus. They made their way through the crowd and out onto Vermont Avenue walking towards their cars. Gertie was walking slightly ahead of Jaxon and Taylor attempting to cross Vermont when an older model Blue Buick sedan drove slowly past the crowd. The passenger yelled out the window a gang slogan then opened fire into the crowd. He fired several shots before the driver drove recklessly from the scene at a high rate of speed. The terror stricken crowd went wild running in every direction when they realized they were victims of a drive by shooting. Just as Gertie made it across the street she turned to see where Jaxon and Taylor were. They had all hit the deck. She yelled for them to get up as she scurried up and started to run away. Taylor caught up to Gertie in a frenzied state but when the girls turned to look for Jaxon they saw he was still lying on the ground trying to lift himself up off of the pavement.

"Hey!" Jaxon called out. "Help me! I can't get up!"

"Come on Jaxon! Get the fuck up man." Gertie yelled.

"Let's get out of here." She said stopping in her tracks.

"I can't feel my legs!" He yelled back to her from a push up position as the crowd of young folk ran all around him. When Gertie and Taylor reached Jaxon's location they realized that his legs were covered in blood. Gertie yelled for someone to call 9-1-1 as she knelt beside him trying to calm him down.

"Have I been shot?" Jaxon asked looking up at the sky with tears running down the side of his face from the corner of his eyes. "Please tell me I'm not shot? Oh my God please help me!" He screamed as he grimaced.

"Yes Jaxon, it looks like you *have* been shot." Gertie said frantically looking to see where the blood was coming from. "We are getting you some help." She was terrified. "I'm not going to leave you." She had never seen anything like this except in the movie *Boys In The Hood* when football star Ricky was killed in the alley near his house.

Paramedics arrived on scene quickly. Jaxon gave Gertie the keys to his car and she and Taylor followed the ambulance to the hospital in his car. Doctors immediately operated on both of Jaxon's legs. He was hit in one thigh and in the hamstring on the other leg. Gertie and Taylor stayed at the hospital until his family arrived. Robert rushed to the hospital to support Gertie and to check on the track star.

When Jaxon's mother, Deanna and his grandfather, Moses arrived Gertie and Taylor briefed them on what occurred. Moses was the only father figure in Jaxon's life. Deanna got pregnant her senior year in high school and never told anyone who Jaxon's father was. Moses was scared for Deanna to have the baby because his wife, Deanna's mother died at childbirth when she was born. Moses raised Deanna alone and vowed to help with Jaxon after convincing Deanna not to have an abortion. When the doctor approached the family to brief Jaxon's folks Gertie and Taylor listened in.

"It's difficult to say whether he will regain his world-class speed, but after physical therapy he should be back to running in a few months." Dr. Butler said. "He's in good spirits so that's a good thing."

"That boy strong." Moses said rather proudly squinting one eye. "He done run all his life so he ain't gonna let nothin' like this get him down. I don't know why nobody would wanna hurt him though." Moses said vigorously shaking his head. "He ain't no gang banger. Prolly somebody just jealous because he so popular."

"Well, I hope and pray that they catch *whoever* did this to your son." Dr. Butler said after listening to Moses rambling.

"Naw, he not my son ma'am. He my *grandson,* but thank you. People tells me all the time I look young enough to be his daddy." Moses said proudly.

"Hush Daddy." Deanna said as she smiled and wiped tears from her face. "Thank you doctor. Can we see him now?"

"Sure. But he needs his rest so don't stay too long." She warned. Her bedside manner was pleasant. She was motherly in her approach.

Robert stayed at the hospital for a while with Gertie and Taylor. He wasn't happy that Gertie was dating Jaxon but he sure didn't wish this tragedy on him or anyone else. When the police arrived at the hospital they interviewed the girls and asked if they knew if Jaxon had any gang ties. They assured the authorities Jaxon was not a gang member nor associate gang member. While briefing the cops Gertie's attention was drawn to Jaxon's family standing on the other side of the room talking to a black female LAPD Captain. The Captain was *tall and very attractive* Gertie thought to herself as she admired her meticulous uniform and the shiny bars on her collar. She and Taylor moseyed their way back near Deanna and Moses and listened in as the Captain assured the family they would catch the suspect(s) responsible for the heinous crime. Gertie then watched closely as the Captain walked a short distance away and greeted her dad with a hug. Robert and the Captain then chatted a bit before she sauntered away acknowledging everyone whom she passed with a slight nod of her head. Gertie knew her dad was dating and he was secretive so she thought for a moment that just maybe the Captain was one of her dad's women.

"Dad, how do you know the Captain?"

"Oh, she's friends with my buddy Chief Dandridge. You met Dandridge right?" Robert asked.

"Yes, of course dad. I see him all the time on campus."

"Captain Moore is very cool but she's married so don't get no ideas." Robert said playfully before changing the subject. "Now I told you about hanging out with that boy. He's from the 'hood, and I'm sure they were targeting *him* because out of all of those damn kids out there on that street why was *he* the only one shot? What does that tell you Gertie? He must be involved in some kinda shit so you need to stay away from his ass."

"Daddy, please stop! Yeah he's from the *'hood* but he is *not* a gang member. You met his mom and grandfather. They are good people *and* they want the best for him just like you and mom want for me so stop putting him down." She felt her dad was very insensitive at that moment and that was not like him. She expected that kind of scrutiny from her mother.

"Yeah I met them niggas and they are hood too, *and* yes I'm sure they want the best for him. I mean I hate the boy got shot but he is not for you Gertie. Not my baby. I'm just sayin'." Robert declared.

In spite of his serious injuries Jaxon was still in good spirits when he was discharged from the hospital a few days later. He endured three grueling months of physical therapy and as a result missed the trials for the 2000 Summer Games and that was devastating for him as his life long dream was to compete in the Olympics. Jaxon requested and received pain meds to help him cope with the physical pain and he needed them too for the mental anguish. When the doctors stopped prescribing the pain meds he found other ways to get his hands on opioids even after he didn't really need them anymore. Gertie noticed his mood swings but she dealt with them because she felt sorry for him and she still wanted to be with him so she didn't complain about his misuse of the pain meds.

By the start of their junior year Jaxon was well on the road to a full recovery and back to things as usual. He trained and prepared for the track season at USC while Gertie and Taylor travelled for basketball.

—◆—

Robert was still dating Clara, who consistently put pressure on him to get Savannah into USC that fall. Savannah had graduated Summa Cum Laude with her Associates Degree from Santa Monica City College, which was key to her easy acceptance into USC. Robert was apprehensive, but reckoned the campus at USC was big enough that she *and* Gertie would possibly not run in the same circles. It helped that Savannah did not live on campus. She had been working at the Fox Hills Mall for a couple of years and loved it so she thought it was better for her to commute, which was just fine with Robert.

During that winter break Gertie went home as usual. Celeste and Michelle were still going strong as a couple, however, Gertie learned that her mom's relationship with Bea was strained to the max and she didn't understand the full reason why so she went to visit Bea to find out for herself what was really going on.

"I just never liked that weird bitch. Not only is she an opportunist but also my gut tells me she is hiding something. I mean she's pretty much alienated your mom from most of our friends, especially from me." Bea said looking at Gertie over her glasses that were dangling on her perfectly shaped nose. "You want some wine doll face?"

"No Auntie I'm an athlete, remember? I'm not supposed to drink. So, have you told mom how you feel?" Gertie was concerned. She had known Bea all of her life and knew how close her mom and Bea were since college, long before Michelle came into the picture.

"Your mom does not agree with me that Michelle is manipulative. When she told me that she and Michelle were in a *dating relationship* I was fucking floored. I could not believe it. She swears that she is totally happy, and tells me that I should respect her decision, so rather than debate with her I just stopped going around when Michelle's home. I feel like I don't know your mom anymore." Bea said as she took a big gulp of her wine and licked her lips.

"Well, I don't understand this change in her lifestyle either but I can't blame Michelle for anything because she can't force mom to do anything she doesn't want to do. You guys will be ok. Give it some time ok?"

"Ok. I'll try." Bea said as she shook her head and poured herself another glass of wine. It was clear that she missed her best friend. She was clearly sulking.

"I'm heading back home tomorrow. I hope you will be able to make it out to my graduation next summer." Gertie said as she got up from the table and embraced Bea.

"I wouldn't miss it. I love you to the moon and back."

"I love you more. Later gator." Gertie said as she walked out the door waving miss America style.

———————

The second semester of Gertie's junior year she found herself questioning her feelings towards Jaxon. His wandering eye and cocky disposition was off putting. He had fully recovered from his leg injuries and was doing quite well in school academically. He was ghost most of the time unless he wanted to have sex with her. She was turning into his *bottom lady* and she didn't appreciate that so she started to push back whenever he was just on a sex mission. Sex was never spontaneous when they spent time together. Jaxon came around primarily when he was horny. Gertie gave in most often to his requests for sexual intercourse but she stood firm on not having oral sex with him because she knew he was screwing anything that looked like a girl. Taylor was the first to tell Gertie to *'leave that nigga alone'* when she saw Gertie upset by his antics.

———————

Savannah settled in nicely at USC and declared her major in Journalism. She made friends with many of the cheerleaders, and like most of them she pledged *AKA* with help from her daddy's wallet. It was expensive to pledge. Gertie on the other hand wanted to pledge *Delta* however, the pledging process was too time consuming for her as a student athlete so she planned to revisit pledging after college and maybe join a Graduate Chapter.

Gertie crossed paths many times with the cheerleaders however she didn't pay close attention to any of them in particular except for Barbie, the pretty blonde who was rumored to be sexing her man up. Savannah just kind of blended in with all the other pretty faces on the cheerleading squad with their tight little bodies and big boobs. Gertie's shapely but athletic build didn't lend itself to the girly kicks and gyrations the cheerleaders were known for. Savannah's big boobs, small waist and long wavy hair allowed her to fit right in with them. Gertie thought cheerleaders were not deserving of scholarships, as she didn't consider cheerleading to be a *real* sport.

———◆———

2001-During the summer of Gertie's junior year she secured a non-paid internship at the Sentinel Newspaper after meeting Mr. Blake, the owner of the paper at a community event held at her school earlier in the spring. She liked the connection the paper had with the various local political figures and mega churches in the area, and she loved the paper's connection to the black community in general in South L.A. She was about to graduate with her Degree in Political Science and she had no clue what she was going to do with it so she figured working at the Sentinel was a great start for her professional life. It was an interesting full summer for her. Starting with her being assigned to cover interesting stories for the paper.

On June 15, 2001, she covered her first story, the 55th NBA Championship. She was in the building at Staples Center when she witnessed the Lakers beat the Philadelphia 76ers 4 games to 1. She was ecstatic to see the players up close and personal.

That summer she also covered a story about Mexican Artist Frida Kahlo being the first Hispanic woman honored on a US Postage Stamp, and she covered Venus Williams beating Justine Henin in the 108th Wimbledon Women's Tennis Tournament. Those stories were exemplary of the type of girl power Gertie was proud to report on.

The summer was a blast but was coming to a close along with her Internship. She was preparing to head back to school but on August 25, 2001, she was tasked with covering her last story of the summer.

"Oh my God, Taylor. Did you hear about Aaliyah?"

"Nope. What happened? Is she pregnant or something?"

"Girl no. Haven't you seen the news? Aaliyah was killed in a plane crash along with several others in the Bahamas. They were returning from a video shoot."

"Oh no. That's so sad." Taylor said. "When you coming back to school? I miss your big head."

"This is my last week working so I'll see ya soon." Gertie said ending the call with tears in her eyes at the thought of her favorite singer, pretty Aaliyah dying so tragically.

———◆———

The start of Gertie's senior year had her feeling melancholy. She had experienced a lot during the time she was at USC and had established some friendships in college that she hoped would last forever. Robert was proud of how she rebounded after her dismal first year but she still wasn't where he thought she could have been in terms of her overall standing. She was maintaining a strong "B" average, which would not have gotten her into USC but it was good enough to keep her there so he was ok with that. Gertie decided to spend winter break that year at home in California instead of travelling to New York. After all, her mom would be coming to her graduation a few months later.

By the start of the spring semester Gertie and Jaxon were on good terms even though Taylor was still giving her the side eye for dealing with him. Taylor hated being so curt with her about Jaxon because she really cared about her and didn't want to hurt her feelings. She credited Gertie with saving her life during their freshman year so she vowed to always be there for her no matter the situation.

"You know Jaxon stopped messing with *Barbie* because *she's* engaged to one of the star football players." Gertie happily reported.

"Oh, that makes sense why he's back fucking with yo ass on the regular. Are you stupid or what?"

"That's fucked up Taylor."

"I'm just keeping it real with you. Now let's go. I'm hungry and you know how crowded it gets at Harold and Bells on Fridays." Taylor said zipping up her letterman's jacket.

Gertie had been craving seafood for a few days so Harold and Bells Creole Cuisine was just what the doctor ordered. After dinner, the girls went home and watched movies for a while before turning in. The next day Gertie got up bright and early to go work out before school but her stomach was a little queasy so she lay back down. She was restless and moments later she jumped up and ran to the bathroom. She threw up whatever was left in her system of the Po' Boy sandwich, coleslaw and fries that she ate the night before. Taylor heard her purging from a distance and asked if she was ok. Gertie told her she might have gotten a case of food poisoning from the seafood. After she threw up, she felt better and went on about her day. The next day she was sick to her stomach again and for a few more days after that until she finally decided to go to Urgent Care.

"Ms. Bellamy, when was your last period?" The nurse asked.

"Oh." She thought for a moment. "A few weeks ago. Actually I think I might be a little late." Her response to the question was tentative because she had actually lost track of her period because of her hectic school and travel schedule.

"Makes sense." The nurse said. "Young lady I do believe you are pregnant."

"Huh? There is *no way* I can be pregnant. I mean I *shouldn't* be pregnant." She tried to maintain her composure while she started to hyperventilate just a little bit.

"Obviously you are sexually active. Right? Are you on birth control? Using any protection?" The nurse fired off some routine questions. She was annoyed with Gertie's trifling denial. She wasn't stupid and she knew Gertie wasn't either. The nurse had seen one too many girls dummy down about their sexual activity and Gertie was no different.

"Well…sometimes…we use protection." Gertie responded slowly as she quickly recounted in her head all of her and Jaxon's sexual trysts *without* protection. It seemed fun at the time but the *shit just got real* she thought. She slowly got up thanked the nurse and abruptly left the clinic.

Gertie drove back to her apartment instead of going on to school. She went straight to her room where she buried her face in her pillow and cried for a good 10 minutes straight. *Fuck school* she thought as she lay there in the quiet house. Everyone else was gone. All she could think about was how disappointed her mom and dad were going to be when they found out, *if* they found out. She had a decision to make and it was not going to be an easy one. The hard part was deciding *what* to do next.

"Daddy." Gertie tried holding back her tears. "Are you going to be in your office for a minute? I need to talk to you."

"Yes, I'll be here a while. Are you ok? You sound like you've been crying. I can come to you."

"No. I'll come to you." Gertie knew that she would need privacy and her place was not amenable.

She grabbed her backpack and went straight to Robert's office. She held her head low as she maneuvered through the maze of students milling about on campus. When she walked into Robert's office she closed the door behind her and plopped down on the firm leather loveseat across from his desk and burst into tears.

"Girl *what* is going on?" Robert asked as he went to console her. He knew it wasn't her grades because he had been monitoring them closely and she was doing quite well. "Is it Jaxon? Did you all break up?"

"No daddy, we didn't break up. I'm pregnant." She said with her hands over her face.

"What in the hell are you talking about?" Robert pulled her hands away from shielding her face. "You are *pregnant*? How? I mean *why* Gertie? That's so irresponsible! How far along are you?" His compassion was quickly turning into fury.

"I didn't mean to daddy!"

"What the hell did you *mean* to do then? You are obviously out there having sex with no protection? I'm so disappointed in you. So what are you going to do now? I'm assuming *it's* Jaxon's baby, or am I wrong?" Robert stood in front of Gertie with his arms folded staring down at her waiting for a response to *all* of his questions.

"I'm so sorry daddy." She responded meekly. "The last thing I want to do is disappoint you or mom. I made a big mistake."

"You damn right you did." He said walking back to his desk. "Now what are you going to do? Where's Jaxon's ass? What is that nigga saying? What does *he* want you to do? You are about to graduate and you have gone and changed the trajectory of your future with this dumb ass *mistake* as you call it."

"I don't know what I'm going to do." Gertie gathered her belongings and headed for the door. "I'll talk to you later."

"Wait one damn minute. Have you told your mother?" Robert jumped up and rushed to the door to prevent her from leaving his office. "Sit yo ass down and get yourself together before you head back home." He said firmly handing her the phone. "Here. Call your mama."

"I'll call her later." She said rejecting the phone.

"No. You are calling her now and *we* are gonna have a family conversation today. Right now. This afternoon. Damn it." Robert was mad.

"Mom." Gertie's tone was tentative.

"Hey girlie what's up?" Celeste was distracted. She was busy in her office.

"I have something to tell you. Mom please don't get mad."

"What's wrong? Are you and your dad ok?"

"Yes mom, dad's fine but I…I'm pregnant." She blurted out.

"Awww shit! Are you fucking kidding me? What the hell is wrong with you?"

"I'm pregnant. I made a mistake."

"Who is the father?" Celeste asked.

"What do you mean *who's* the father? It's Jaxon mom. I don't sleep around."

"That ghetto ass trash. Why, Gertie? Why? I sure hope you are not going to keep *it*."

"You hope I'm not going to keep *it?*" Gertie instantly became angry. She didn't know what to expect from her mom but hoped she would be more supportive. "*It* is a *person* and Jaxon is not *ghetto trash* as you put it. You don't even know him *and* it's my decision if I keep *my baby* or not. Mom, remember you live in a glass house and should not be throwing stones. You're gay for God's sake!" She yelled into the phone.

Robert sat there with his arms folded seething while listening to Gertie's end of the conversation and seeing her balling her eyes out. He couldn't stand to see her that way. He grabbed the phone from her trembling hand.

"Celeste, what is your problem? If we are going to help this girl make the right decision we have to be more supportive and not judgmental. I get it. I snapped too when she told me but now that it has happened we need to pull it together. She is well aware of the consequences of her actions."

"Robert how could *you* let this happen?"

"How did *I* let it happen? She screwed that boy not me."

"Well I still say there is no way she should have this baby." Celeste barked.

"Obviously you didn't hear what I just said and you obviously didn't hear what Gertie said either. Whether she keeps the baby or not is *her* decision to make so you and I are going to let her and Jaxon's ass make *that* decision. I'll talk to you later." He tossed the phone back to Gertie.

"Mom, I'm sorry for all of this. I should have used protection."

"You damn right you should have. Here you are about to graduate and now this. You call me and let me know what you decide to do about this little situation. I need to get back to work."

"Ok later." Gertie squinted at the phone as she hung up. Gertie left her dad's office that day with a hug and a heavy heart. It was pretty clear from her conversation with her parents that she and she alone had some decisions to make. She went back to her place and lay down. Her roommates returned home one by one that afternoon as their classes let out. Taylor was the last to arrive home.

"Knock. Knock!" Taylor said bursting into Gertie's room. "Oh damn are you ok?" She asked when she noted Gertie's solemn mood.

"Why did you bother to knock if you weren't going to wait for me to answer? I don't feel well."

"I figured something was up when I didn't see you on campus today. You still sick from the food the other day?"

"Girl no...I'm fucking pregnant." She said as tears rolled down her cheeks.

"Are you serious? Is it Jaxon's?"

"Yes I'm serious and Jaxon is the *only* person I have ever had sex with! I can't believe *you* are asking me that shit too?"

"Shit. I didn't know. I'm just asking. Damn. I'm not being rude. Does he know?"

"Not yet."

"I'll talk to you when you are feeling better." She backed out of the room and let the door close softly behind her. She didn't like the way Gertie snapped at her.

———◆———

Gertie knew that she needed to tell Jaxon about her pregnancy especially now that Taylor knew. She hadn't seen him in a couple of days and that was unusual but she just figured he was doing his thing around campus so she let him be. They bickered often when they were together anyway, mostly about his cheating ways, so he steered clear of her on occasion so he didn't have to hear her mouth. Jaxon was walking across campus heading to his apartment when he heard Taylor calling his name.

"You hear me calling you."

"Damn girl. Yeah I hear you. What you want?" He responded laughing.

"You play too much. Have you talked to Gertie?" Taylor asked trying to catch her breath.

"No. Why?" I been in school all day. Where she at?"

"Boy just go see her please. She wasn't feeling well today." Taylor said trying to help expedite their meet up. Jaxon made a quick detour and followed Taylor back to her house not really giving much thought to what if anything was wrong. Once inside the house he chatted with her and her roommates for a little while in the living room. When Gertie heard his voice she jumped up from her bed, balled her bushy hair up on top of her head and ran towards the door to her room. She wasn't in the mood to join them in the living room.

"Hey Jaxon. Come here." She poked her head out of her bedroom door and motioned for him to come to her room.

"Hey girl." He excused himself from the other girls and walked towards Gertie's room. "I heard you was sick. What up with you?"

"Who told you I was *sick*?"

"Taylor told me you weren't feeling well. Why didn't *you* tell me? I ain't heard from you in a couple days and I didn't see you on campus today either." He wasn't really bothered by her absence because he had plenty of activities to occupy his time but he *was* genuinely concerned about her possibly being sick.

"I was taking care of some business that you and I need to talk about." She said closing the door behind him. She sat on the side of her bed with her head down avoiding eye contact with him for the most part.

"What business *we* got?" Jaxon asked standing next to her bed staring down at her.

"I'm pregnant Jaxon." She said without looking up.

"*Pregnant?* Who's the father?" He asked emotionless.

"Fuck you Jaxon!"

"I mean we don't even do it that much." He said backing away towards the door.

"Get the fuck out!" Gertie jumped up and pushed him into the door. She then pushed him out of the way, opened the door; and pushed him out of her room. Jaxon walked hurriedly past Taylor and the other girls and out of the house. After he ran out Taylor ran into Gertie's room.

"What in the hell just happened?"

"You know damn well what happened. You brought him here so I could tell him I was pregnant *and* he had the nerve to ask me the same dumb ass question you asked talkin' about '*who's the father*'? You both can go straight to hell for all I care." She was angry.

"I brought him here because I didn't want you to drag your feet telling him that you are pregnant."

"But you didn't know it was *his* baby remember so why would you go get *him*? I would have told him in my time but *no* you had to get involved. Well for the last time the baby *is* his and you can leave now." She said as she held the door open for Taylor to exit.

"Fuck it then." Taylor said as she walked out of the room. The cat was out of the bag. All parties knew Gertie was pregnant and no one was taking it well. Robert was disappointed that she had derailed her immediate future; Taylor thought she was dumb to stay messing around with Jaxon in the first place; Jaxon was dismissive as he was not willing to accept responsibility for the situation he helped to create, and Celeste was just not having any of it. Robert didn't tell Clara what was going on because he needed time to see what Gertie was going to do before he said anything to anyone.

——◆——

It was Gertie, Taylor and Jaxon's last semester in college and they were all trying to figure out which road to take in life. Jaxon's dream of competing in the Olympic games was dashed when he lost his competitive edge following his leg injuries so he did not know where he was headed after college but one thing he knew for sure was that he was not ready to start a family with Gertie or anyone else.

Taylor planned on becoming a Social Worker, which she thought would be a perfect use of her Degree. She was in the foster care system for most of her life and knew firsthand just how important it was to protect vulnerable children and support families in need of assistance.

Gertie wasn't sure of what she wanted to do with her Political Science degree. Her internship at the Sentinel Paper certainly put her in the right circles with local politicians but she didn't like what she saw with all of their posturing in the community, which was primarily self-serving. She thought that maybe she'd follow in her mom and dad's footsteps and garner the necessary credentials to teach or counsel. They all had decisions to make and one of Gertie's biggest decisions in life hung in the balance.

"Hey baby, I'm just calling to check on you and see how you are feeling." Celeste said hoping to hear that Gertie had taken care of her little situation.

"Hi Mom, I am feeling ok. I'm just trying to figure everything out." She was not in the mood to fight with her mom on the heels of arguing with Jaxon and Taylor.

"Well, how far along are you?"

"I'm about 3 months."

"Three months? Are you kidding me? You don't have much time if you are going to get rid of *it*."

"There you go with that *it* shit again. Mom, please let me work through this." She begged.

"So if you have *it* I guess you are not participating in your commencement exercises then right? Gertie you will be ruining your life if you have this baby. It's more than a notion to raise a child, especially by yourself."

"How do you know I will be by myself? In spite of Jaxon's philandering ways mom, I am hopeful that we can work things out because I never wanted to be nobody's baby mama."

"Looks like that's exactly what you are going to be if you keep this boy's baby. You are so close to graduating I can't believe you would throw your education away like this."

"What are you talking about? I'm finishing school and I will proudly walk across that stage with my big ass belly and all."

"Good luck with that. I tell you what. I refuse to attend your graduation under these circumstances. You will be parading your illegitimate child for the entire school to see. They are sure to gossip about *poor Gertie who got pregnant by the no good used to be track star.*"

"Ok. I'm done with this conversation. So, you are going to throw me away because I want to keep *my* baby? I can't with you." Gertie hung up the phone before Celeste could respond.

CHAPTER 6

"REVELATIONS"

———◆———

SEVERAL DAYS PASSED BEFORE GERTIE heard from her dad again. She was in a fog. She had made a terrible mistake by getting pregnant and neither of her parents nor Jaxon was happy about her situation. She swore to everyone that she *only* slept with Jaxon and she felt betrayed by all of those who suggested that she was sleeping around.

Robert assured her that he would support whatever decision she made and offered that Jaxon's response to the news of her pregnancy was how most young men would have responded so he really wasn't angry with him for that. Gertie felt empowered by her dad's supportive stance and told him that she was definitely keeping her child. When she told him about her mom refusing to attend her graduation he called Celeste.

"You know what?"

"What Robert?" Celeste answered. "What do you want?"

"You are a real piece of work. You have a lot of nerve..."

"I don't know why in the world you would encourage my child to have this baby!" She said angrily interrupting him. "She is going to ruin her life. She's *not* ready to raise a child."

"First of all, Gertie is about to be 22 years old so she's no *child*, and last I checked we are no longer married so you need to watch your tone with me you crazy bitch. I'm only talking to your ass because we need to have a united front when it comes to supporting *our* daughter."

"Well...I'm just sayin'." She said backing down a little bit. She was surprised by his harsh tone.

"I told Gertie that I'm prepared to help her. But trust me that Jaxon character is going to step up to the plate too and take care of *his* responsibility. If the nigga wants a paternity test I told Gertie I will pay for it."

"I don't care *who* the father is, I just want better for my daughter, like putting things in the right order. According to her, she and Jaxon aren't even in a monogamous relationship let alone planning to marry, so having a baby under these circumstances is a huge mistake."

"Well it's *her* mistake and she has to deal with the fall out from that. We just need to support her as best we can.

———————————

2002-A couple of months had gone by after Gertie broke the news to everyone about her pregnancy. Basketball season was over, which was perfect timing because she was not in any shape to play the high intensity sport. She had a great run. Taylor was voted *Player Of The Year* and was prepared to go overseas to play ball since she was not successful in joining the WNBA as she had hoped. Gertie and Taylor's relationship suffered for a little while after Gertie announced her pregnancy. However, Taylor appealed to Gertie that she was not being shady and explained that her question about whether Jaxon was the father or not was purely a rhetorical response and that she was simply shocked about the pregnancy.

After a long and sincere conversation Taylor and Gertie kissed and made up. Taylor told Gertie that she brought Jaxon to her room that day because she wanted him to face the music sooner rather than later and she apologized for not discussing her tactics with Gertie first.

———————

It was just weeks away from graduation day and Gertie was ecstatic about graduating Cum Laude considering her trifling start in college. Robert was extremely proud of her, and she was just as proud of herself in that she had not let her pregnancy derail her from graduating from college with such distinction.

Celeste called periodically to check on her, however, they never discussed whether Celeste was attending her graduation. Robert appealed to Celeste not to do something that she would regret later, and she agreed that she was speaking out of anger when she said she was not attending the graduation. She later told Robert that she planned on surprising Gertie and swore him to secrecy.

Jaxon avoided Gertie for weeks, during which time the rumors and speculation on campus about her baby's daddy grew exponentially. Taylor was finally able to impress upon him that he needed to meet with Gertie again in order to come to some type of resolve so they could move forward and get on with their lives after graduation. This time she told Gertie she was going to talk to Jaxon to avoid another falling out.

"Yo, I just don't think I'm the father. I don't know who else she been sleeping with." Jaxon was standing firm.

"We been good friends for a long time right?"

"*Fo sho.*" Jaxon uttered.

"Well then you need to listen to me bro. Gertie is *not* a liar and she does *not* sleep around I can promise you that. That girl loves you and I know you may not feel the same about her but if nothing else, ya'll need to at least get a paternity test. Have you even told your moms and Pops about what's going on? I know your Pops would make you do the right thing. You already know how he feels about taking care of your responsibilities. I remember him telling us that he talked your mama into *not* aborting your ass."

"Man why you gotta bring that up?"

"Because you seem to have forgotten where you came from."

"I mean I do love her but I ain't ready to settle down with no baby tho'. I ain't ready. Hell naw." He said under his breath.

"Oh shit. Really? You love Gertie? Wow. You need to tell *her* that dude. She has been so sad about this situation *and* she feels dejected by you. And if you aren't ready for a baby then you shoulda wrapped it up."

"*Dejected?* Oh you using real college words since you about to graduate huh? Ok then, I'm going to talk to my Pops then I'll go from there. I'll call her later."

"Ok big head. I'll talk to you later." Taylor couldn't believe she just might have gotten through to him.

———————◆———————

A few days after Taylor's meet with Jaxon, Chief Dandridge announced that a Press Conference was going to take place on campus just outside of the Town and Gown Ballroom, regarding Jaxon's shooting. Gertie was hesitant to attend the conference, but she was anxious to hear about the status of the investigation.

She was glowing and her belly was blossoming quite nicely. She was entering her third trimester and feeling well as she prepared for her impending graduation. She was nervous and excited at the same time about graduation but disappointed that her mom refused to attend. Taylor didn't know how to feel about

Gertie's pregnancy mainly because of Jaxon's *no good behind* as she referred to him. Nevertheless she vowed to be there for Gertie

On the afternoon of the Press Conference Taylor and Gertie left their classes early, and met up at a specified location close to the Ballroom so they could be together during the conference. Taylor spotted Gertie's wild mane a mile away. She had removed her braids since basketball season was over and her hair had grown a lot so it was quite full. Gertie, wearing her oversized letterman's jacket to shield her belly, was walking towards Taylor when they spotted each other. The crowd was growing fast and they wanted to be up close and personal so they walked as close to the front as they could get.

Robert was standing up front near the podium talking to his buddy Chief Dandridge, and Captain Moore was in close proximity to them, talking to Reporters. Gertie watched Moore like a hawk as she was in awe of the Captain ever since she met her at the hospital on the night Jaxon was shot. Gertie noticed Jaxon off in the distance walk up towards the Reporters and Captain Moore with Deanna and Moses close behind. She watched them from afar trying to secrete herself within the crowd so they didn't notice her.

Robert stepped aside so that Chief Dandridge could get the Press Conference underway. Jaxon, Deanna and Moses stood behind Captain Moore shoulder to shoulder with their arms locked as she stepped to the podium. Her uniform revealed every curve. She was a woman of a particular age but she looked amazingly youthful.

"It's with great pride that I announce today that we have captured the suspect responsible for shooting star athlete and Olympic hopeful Reginald Jaxon Atwater." Moore was so poised that Gertie hung on her every word and forgot that Jaxon was even standing behind her. "On the evening of the shooting it was speculated and rumored that Mr.

Atwater had gang ties but I am here to say with certainty and publicly that there is no evidence of him being a current gang member, nor any evidence indicating that he was ever a gang member or associate gang member. So, I want to put that assertion to rest as the possible motive for the shooting. This incident was however *gang related* in that it was considered a gang initiation for the perpetrator and Mr. Atwater just happened to be his random victim. I want to thank my Detectives for their incredible police work. I want to thank the community for your incredible partnership, and Chief Dandridge, thank you for your support and the assistance from the Department of Public Safety."

Just as the Press Conference ended Gertie turned to walk away when she heard someone calling her name. She and Taylor turned in unison when they saw Jaxon jogging in their direction as Captain Moore talked to Deanna and Moses in the distance. Gertie nervously pulled on the zipper of her jacket attempting to zip it up to conceal her bump from Jaxon but the zipper was stuck. They hadn't spoken in a few weeks in spite of Taylor's pleas for him to reach out to Gertie.

"What's up Mr. Atwater?" Gertie asked facetiously with her arms folded and Taylor standing next to her ogling Jaxon.

"Oh, so now I'm Mr. Atwater?" Jaxon chuckled trying not to focus on Gertie's baby bump.

"What do you want?" She asked abruptly readjusting her arms folded across her chest trying to keep the jacket closed.

"Taylor, can you excuse us please?" Jaxon looked shifty eyed in her direction.

"Sure. You good Gertie?" She asked as she slowly walked away backwards.

"Yes. I'm good Tay. I'll see you back at the house."

"I know I haven't been around but I have been trying to get myself together for graduation."

"Mmm Hmm." Was all Gertie could say at that point.

"I have been in a bad way because of my slow recovery, and then finding out that you were pregnant with my baby just put me in more of a funk." He said as he led Gertie to a cement bench where they sat side by side. "Anyway, I told my mom and Pops about the baby and they made me see that in spite of all that I was going through I was wrong for the way I responded to you, and they told me that I need to do the right thing by you." He said as he fidgeted with his fingers.

"So, it took *them* to tell you to do right by *me*? That's really sad. Well, I don't need your damn pity." Gertie saw a weakness in him at that moment that she did not like or respect.

"No girl! I'm just saying that they *confirmed* how I was already feeling. I guess I just said it wrong. Will you please accept my apology so we can move on?"

"Oh, I'm sorry but your apology sounded more like an excuse but if you are *apologizing* for acting like an ass-hole then yes I will accept your *apology* but where do we go from here?" She asked.

"I see your dad is here. Do you think we can all meet in his office to talk?"

"You mean all of us as in you, me, your mom and Pops and my dad?"

"Yeah. If that is ok?"

"Sure. But I don't want any surprises. What are we going to talk about?"

"My mom and Pops think that we all need to talk about *our* plans for the baby."

"Why can't *you* ever take the lead on *anything?* Seems like you are doing everything at your mom and Pop's prompting and that's so juvenile. It ain't cute."

"It was *my* idea to meet. You can ask them. I can't seem to do anything right according to you." She and the entire situation frustrated him.

"Ok well I'll see if my dad is available." She said as she and Jaxon got up and walked towards their respective parents. Robert was surprised at Jaxon's request as he was prepared to travel along this pregnancy journey with Gertie alone. Gertie motioned to Jaxon that the meet was a go then she walked with Robert the short distance to his office. The two talked briefly before Jaxon and his family caught up to them. That was the first time they had all been in each other's company after meeting at the hospital on the night Jaxon was shot. After exchanging pleasantries and superficial hugs Jaxon nervously started the conversation about why he asked to meet.

"Go ahead son. You got the floor." Moses said standing off to the side like a proud papa nodding and grinning as Jaxon began to speak.

"Well, uh I already apologized to Gertie for disrespecting her when she told me she was pregnant. I asked her who was the father because I didn't know what else to say at that moment. I know that she loves me, and I know she doesn't sleep around so I should have responded differently. I haven't been the best *boyfriend* and I know that I need to do the right thing and take care of the baby…our baby."

"Ok. I wasn't sure that we were *boyfriend and girlfriend* because you never openly acknowledged our relationship as such."

"I know. I know. But I do love you." He said in a low voice. "After talking to my family I realize that I have their full support so I feel the best thing to do is for us to raise *our* baby *together*."

"What do you mean *together*?" She asked rolling her eyes.

"I think we should get married. That's why I wanted us to meet with your dad." He said as he tried to grab Gertie's hand that was tightly tucked in her folded arms across her chest.

"Hold up. What are you doing Jaxon?" She asked pulling away from him as he attempted again to grab her hand. "We have *never* even talked about being in a serious relationship let alone getting married."

"I know, and we never talked about having a baby either so what. We did things out of order but I think with our families' support we can do this…we *should* do this for the sake of the baby if nothing else." He said as he peered around the room at his blushing parents.

Robert on the other hand was shocked and put off by Jaxon's bootleg proposal, which he believed was prompted by his family primarily because *they* wanted him to do right by Gertie.

"I appreciate you for stepping up and being a man about this but Gertie don't need no sympathy sham of a marriage." Robert said looking furtively between Jaxon and his folks. "Gertie has my full support, so she doesn't *have* to get married just for the *sake of the baby* as you put it."

"Daddy, Jaxon is right. I do love him and I believe him when he says he loves me too so yes I will marry you Jaxon." She said as she turned quickly from Robert to Jaxon.

"Mr. Bellamy, I promise you I will take good care of Gertie and the baby." Jaxon said peering over Gertie's shoulder as the two embraced. "I can see you are not happy about this."

"You damn right I'm not happy boy." Robert scoffed.

"Wait a minute Mr. Robert the *boy* has a name." Moses said as the huge grin disappeared from his face. "He done come to you like a man so you needs to show a little mo' respect. He is about to graduate from college just like yo baby and he's trying to do right by her so I understand your concerns but they done dipped they toes in the ocean so they needs to ride this wave that done come they way." Moses said as Deanna sat on the edge of her seat and cosigned his every word.

"I apologize. I don't mean to be rude." Robert said as he put some distance between him and Moses and returned to the other side of his desk. "I know you two are in fairy tale mode." Robert looked at Gertie and Jaxon still holding hands. "But I still think it's a good idea to move forward with the Paternity Test to avoid any issues later on down the road. Jaxon, I know you said you didn't mean to second-guess Gertie when she said the baby was yours but you need to be sure this baby *is* yours before you all move forward. It's just a simple blood test and I'll pay for it."

Robert wasn't sold on Jaxon because in his opinion he was still a little nigga from the 'hood and apt to change his stance once he was tired of playing house. Robert didn't trust him.

"I think that's a good idea too Mr. Robert." Deanna said nodding in agreement. "We don't need no Jerry Springer shit later on when y'all get mad at one another. This test needs to be done before ya'll move forward with this marriage plan."

"I agree. I will arrange for the test and for the results to be expedited."

The families embraced and engaged in small talk until they all went their separate ways. Jaxon walked Gertie home where they met back up with Taylor. They went into Gertie's room and briefed Taylor about the family meeting.

"Aww shit. Y'all niggas gettin' married for real? Get the fuck out of here! I can't believe this. Y'all fuckin' with me right?" Taylor hugged Jaxon from behind. "That's what I'm talking about. You doing the right thing bro."

"Girl calm down. We ain't married yet." He said as Gertie sat at the foot of her bed beaming like a Cheshire cat.

"Taylor can you leave now? I need to talk to my baby mama." Jaxon said playfully as he sauntered over to the bed to cuddle up next to Gertie.

"Yeah. Yeah. Yeah. Later asshole." She said as she left the room closing the door behind her.

It was two weeks until graduation and Gertie was scurrying around trying to make sure that she had everything she needed for the big day. She was growing daily and Jaxon was very attentive to her every need. She had not spoken with her mother about graduation anymore because the last time they spoke Celeste vowed not to attend.

It was the Friday before the Sunday commencement exercise when Jaxon showed up at Gertie's place bright and early. Taylor quietly let him in the front door while Gertie slept in her room. The two waited quietly in the living room for Robert to join them. Upon his arrival the three of them crept to Gertie's door. She was sleeping soundly but was startled by the knock on the door. She thought she was dreaming.

"Who is it?" Gertie sat straight up in bed wiping the slobber from her face.

"It's Taylor, Baby daddy and yo daddy. Can we come in?"

"Yeah." Gertie said groggily.

"Get up!" Taylor said opening the door.

"Oh hi Tay. Hi daddy. Hey Jaxon? What's going on?" She yawned big exposing all of her pretty white fillings.

"You heard Taylor. Get up. We getting married today." Jaxon said proudly. "We have an appointment for our blood tests at ten and then we gonna head downtown to City Hall to the Justice of the Peace."

"Whoa. Wait a minute." Gertie looked at her dad for confirmation while Taylor placed her slippers at her feet.

"Remember we talked about getting married before the baby comes, so I talked to our peeps and I say we get married now before we graduate so you can walk across that stage proudly as a married woman."

Jaxon was nervous. He was trying to live up to his Pop's expectations, and Robert was on board with his plan under the circumstances. Robert said very little when Jaxon met him to discuss his last minute wedding plan. He just went along for the ride.

"I will be there for moral support as I promised you guys. Gertie and I have already talked about her and the baby living with me at the house so Jaxon now that you all are getting married, I guess you will both be living with me until you all get on your feet. Clearly Gertie is in no position to get a job right now so with you all living with me you can take your time and look for work without the pressure of household expenses."

Jaxon welcomed the opportunity to live in Ladera versus Compton, where he grew up. He loved his parents to death but he wanted out of the '*hood* forever. Jaxon and Gertie only needed one witness for the wedding ceremony, however after he told his mother, grandfather and Robert about the impending nuptials they all wanted to be there, and of course Taylor invited herself.

"You guys need to leave so I can get dressed." Gertie ushered Jaxon and Taylor out of her room. "Wait daddy." She said as she grabbed a hold of Robert's sleeve stopping him in his tracks. "I guess I should call mom huh?"

"Nah, I'll call her while you get dressed. How do you feel? I mean don't feel like you have to do this just because Jaxon wants you to." He said with a smirk on his face.

"I'm good daddy. I mean I'm a little scared but hey I gotta put my big girl panties on like you always say right?"

"Ok well get your big girl panties on and you guys meet me at my office when you are ready to roll ok? I'm going to go call your mama."

Robert passed Taylor and Jaxon on his way out and also told *them* to meet him at his office when Gertie was ready.

Celeste was packing when the phone rang. She was running late and needed to hurry and get to the airport for her late evening flight.

"Hey Michelle is Celeste around?"

"Oh hi Robert." She responded dryly. She hated when he called. "Yes she's right here. Hold on." Without saying a word, she tossed the phone across the bed to Celeste and went back to packing her things. She was not looking forward to the trip but looked forward to seeing Gertie.

"Hey Rob. What's up?" Celeste was not expecting a call from him.

"I'll make it quick. We are on our way to the Justice of the Peace so Jaxon and Gertie can get married." He said in one fell swoop.

"Robert, I don't have time for this bullshit. I'm trying to pack and get to the airport." Michelle looked up in her direction when she noted the abrupt change in Celeste's tone.

"This is no *bullshit* heffa. Jaxon proposed to Gertie a couple of weeks ago. Gertie didn't tell you?"

"Hell no. She's still upset with me because I said I was not coming to the graduation. You didn't tell her did you?"

"No, I didn't spoil your little secret."

"First she gets knocked up and now she's having a shotgun wedding. I'm at a loss for words." Tears rolled down Celeste's cheeks as she stifled her cry. She didn't want Robert to know she was crying. "This is not how I planned for her life to be."

"It wasn't your shit to plan, and you know what they say, we make plans and God laughs. We are not in control of anything. Anyway, I have to get going because the kids should be here any minute."

"In spite of everything that's going on I'm still looking forward to my trip out there. I'll let you know when we arrive in L.A. and get settled into our hotel. We will be staying at the Renaissance LAX."

"That's cool but I'll just see you at the graduation." He said ending the call.

Robert was relieved that Celeste had come to her senses and agreed to attend Gertie's graduation. She had sworn him to secrecy about something yet again just so she could surprise Gertie. He was about tired of keeping her damn secrets as he had been living a double life for about 8 years partly because of her. Thankfully it was all about to be over. As soon as the graduation ceremonies were over Robert was going to end the charade.

———◆———

Gertie cried throughout the short wedding ceremony. She was such a water head. Jaxon kept looking at her raising his eyebrows as if to say *bitch for real*. He didn't understand that her emotions and hormones were out of control mostly due to her pregnancy. When it came time to sign the marriage license everyone was surprised when Gertie opted to keep her maiden name.

"What is the problem? You are married now so you have to take my last name." Jaxon said with a puzzled look on his face.

"There's no *problem*. I just want to keep my maiden name." She said as she dug her heels in.

"That's retarded Gertie and it's not right."

"Jaxon, a woman does not *have* to legally change her name to her husband's name. She is free to keep her own name, hyphenate her name or come up with a completely different name and I choose to keep mine because it's easier and if we ever divorce I want to maintain *my* identity rather than have a constant reminder of my connection to you."

"So, you already planning our divorce before the ink dries on the marriage license?"

"No, I just know that some marriages don't last, like my mother and father's marriage didn't last. I'm keeping my maiden name." She said firmly.

The family and court clerk stood by watching Gertie and Jaxon banter back and forth, as if they were watching a tennis match. Robert was surprised by his baby girl's firm stance about an issue he had never even thought about. What he also noticed in that brief exchange was just how much Jaxon and Gertie hadn't really talked and didn't really know one another.

"Ok. Ok." Robert said throwing his hands up. "It's obvious you all have some things to talk about but this is not the time or place. Gertie if you feel that strongly about this issue…"

"I do. I feel strongly about keeping my name." She said cutting Robert off.

"Well then sign your damn name whatever the hell that is and let's get out of here. You guys can revisit this topic later." Robert was getting fed up with what he considered a childish exchange.

"Yeah I agree with Mr. Robert." Moses said. "Let's get up outta here."

Once the ceremony was over the family headed off to El Cholo's Mexican Restaurant for good old drinks, and nachos with extra cheese. Gertie couldn't have a drink but she put a major dent in the chips and salsa like it was the last supper. Throughout the meal she kept looking down at her wedding ring sitting on her finger. She didn't know what she was feeling. Everything was moving so fast starting with her unexpected pregnancy. Robert, who was seated to her right, sensed her nervousness. He felt around under the table and grabbed her hand and squeezed it as confirmation that all was going to be ok. Gertie breathed a sigh of relief as she rested her head on her dad's shoulder.

After everyone was stuffed to capacity they waddled out of the restaurant one by one. Jaxon and the girls went to their respective homes where they spent the afternoon and evening packing so they could move out prior to graduation day. Gertie had already been taking things to her dad's home since she was already planning on moving there after school let out so she didn't have much left to pack.

———◆———

Clara had planned on attending Gertie's graduation so she arrived early at the school and met Robert in his office. Gertie knew Clara as one of Robert's ladies but that was all she knew about her. Robert had butterflies in his stomach at the thought of Savannah also graduating from the same school, however he was relieved when Savannah opted to participate in the Black Graduation Ceremony, which was a day after Gertie's ceremony.

"I think it's time for us to introduce the girls." Robert said pacing in front of his desk. "When Savannah's graduation ceremony is over tomorrow let's meet at my house and we will talk to them. I am so ready for this shit to be over for once and for all. They are grown and should be able to handle the news. I don't know why I let Celeste talk me into keeping this secret in the first place."

"They may be *old* enough but I don't think it's going to go over that well especially with Gertie because you stepped out on her mom and that's a hard pill for most girls to swallow." Clara said as she grabbed her purse from Robert's desk.

"Yeah I know. I know. Shit." Robert said shaking his head as he walked towards the door. "Does Savannah have all that she needs for her graduation tomorrow?"

"I talked to her last night and she said she did. She was asleep when I left the house this morning."

"Ok. Great. Well, I'll be close by if you need me. I'm so sorry Nanny couldn't make it out to see the girls graduate but at least Jocelyn is here. She rode in with me this morning and is out there saving seats for you and Celeste and her *partner.*"

"Whew, I'm not looking forward to meeting Ms. Celeste. I sure don't want any drama with her."

"She doesn't know *who* you are just yet and Jocelyn knows what's going on so you don't have to worry about her saying anything to point Celeste in your direction. Jocelyn can't stand her so I'm sure she will be sitting there laughing her ass off at the thought of what's going on."

Robert kissed Clara on the cheek and ushered her the rest of the way out of the door.

The crowd was growing fast outside the Doheny Library in the center of the campus where the proud graduates prepared to walk across the makeshift stage. Family members filed into their seats, and placed items on empty chairs to save them for latecomers. Robert sat amongst other staff and dignitaries close to where Jocelyn and Jaxon's family were seated. Clara sat in the row behind Jocelyn and the family to distance herself from Celeste. Robert had not seen Celeste since he went to New York for Gertie's high school graduation but he spotted her right away when he saw her and Michelle walk towards their seats. She looked better than he had ever seen her look. She looked 10 years younger and he loved her short hair cut. Celeste had no problem finding their seats when she saw Jocelyn waving wildly.

"Hey old lady how you doing?" Jocelyn greeted Celeste with a fake hug.

"Jocelyn, long time no see. I'm so glad you could make it out. Oh, this is my friend Michelle; Michelle, this is my sister in law, well *former* sister in law, Jocelyn." She said as the two women laughed about the clarification.

"You ain't married to my brother no more but I'm gonna always be your

sister-in-law as long as you Gertie's mama." Jocelyn said with her gold fronts glimmering in the sunlight. "Nice to meet you Michelle."

"Likewise." Michelle responded with a fake smile as she took her seat.

Celeste took her seat next to Michelle and noted that her attitude changed a bit. She wasn't as talkative as she was when they were alone.

"Are you good?" Celeste asked.

"Yes, I'm good." Michelle whispered back. "I just feel out of place in this atmosphere with you, and your ex-husband and *his* family, and I know Robert never really cared for me. So it just feels awkward." Michelle was pouting.

"Oh come on Michelle. Robert and I have been over for a very long time so you should not care what he thinks of you. I sure don't care. You're with me and he's got his life so don't be intimidated ok?" Michelle was always reticent around Bea *and* Robert and her complaints about them were starting to wear on Celeste's nerves.

Celeste spotted Robert seated next to the stage but was hesitant to acknowledge him because of Michelle's attitude. He waved when he and Celeste made eye contact but she nodded her head in return hoping Michelle didn't notice their interaction. She then looked around at the crowd and when she spotted Clara seated behind Jocelyn she nodded and smiled at her as well not knowing who she was. Clara nodded quickly in return. She was nervous.

Celeste saw Gertie standing amongst her peers, looking around feverishly. She could barely tell that she was pregnant under her pleated robe. When Gertie spotted Jocelyn the two waved and then she saw Celeste and Michelle sitting next to Jocelyn. They all turned in her direction and she jumped for joy and cupped her mouth with both hands. She was pleasantly surprised to see them all. Celeste and Michelle stood up and waved in return blowing kisses in her direction.

As the ceremony got underway Jaxon was amongst the first to be called to the stage as the graduates were called up in alphabetical order. Gertie graced the stage close behind him, as *her maiden* name was also early in the alphabet. The procession was long and boring as expected and as soon as it ended the entire row of family stood up and stretched their limbs while they waited for Gertie and Jaxon to join them. Clara stood up and walked the long way around to the front near where Robert was standing and talking with other staff members. Celeste and Michelle stayed put watching Gertie from a distance.

"You must be Gertie's mama." Moses said reaching out to shake Celeste's hand. "That girl look just like you."

"Yes. I'm Celeste." She said staring at Moses's hand reaching out from beneath his tight round belly that was peering through the opening in his suit coat. "And this is my friend Michelle."

"I guess we all family now." Deanna said proudly looking Celeste up and down like she was window-shopping. "It sure is nice to meet you. You are beautiful just like your daughter."

"Nice to meet you as well and thank you so much." Celeste said as Deanna leaned in for a hug as Moses loosened his grasp from Celeste's hand. *What sweet people.* Celeste thought to herself as she genuinely hugged Deanna.

"Mom! Mom!" Gertie called out as she skipped in Celeste's direction with Jaxon following close behind her.

"Hi baby!" Celeste walked to meet Gertie in the crowded aisle. "You look gorgeous natural hair and all! Oh yeah and Auntie Bea told me to tell you that she is sorry she couldn't make it to your graduation." Truth was that Bea did not want to attend because she couldn't stand to be around Michelle for that long. Rather than put Celeste in an awkward position she just told Celeste she couldn't make it.

"I thought you weren't coming." Gertie said as she hugged her mom tightly. "Michelle!" Gertie squealed as she broke away from her mom and grabbed Michelle's hand pulling her in for a hug. "This is Jaxon! Jaxon, this is my mom and Michelle."

"Hi Ma'am." Jaxon said as Celeste opened her arms for a hug.

"You sure *are* handsome." Celeste was pleasantly surprised by Jaxon's good looks.

"It's nice to meet you. I'll be right back Gertie." Jaxon said turning his attention to his parents.

Jaxon greeted Moses and Deanna while Gertie talked to her mom and Michelle. Robert and Clara started to walk towards the family when they heard a familiar voice.

"Mom! Dad!" Savannah yelled as she walked briskly towards him and Clara.

"Oh shit! Oh shit. Robert it's Savannah. What is she doing here?" Clara asked as she pulled Robert and quickly walked back in the opposite direction from where the family was gathered.

"I thought you said she was at home sleeping." He said with their backs turned towards the family.

"She *was* asleep and she never mentioned she was coming to today's graduation."

"Mom what are *you* doing here?" Savannah asked as she approached Robert and Clara.

"I'm here with your dad. What are *you* doing here today? You should be at home getting ready for your own graduation tomorrow. I thought you had a hair appointment this morning."

"I did but I changed it to this afternoon so I could come to see some of my friends who are graduating today." Savannah said looking around. "I'll be right back I see one of my friends." She said as she ran off.

"Savannah!" Robert yelled trying to stop her. "Savannah!"

"Hi Jaxon! Savannah said as she came face to face with Jaxon who was talking to his folks and holding hands with Gertie.

"Oh hey Savannah. What are you doing here girl?" He asked as everyone paused watching the dynamics between him and Savannah. It was real obvious that they knew each other well.

"Hi. I'm Gertie." She said looking back and forth between Jaxon and Savannah with a furrowed brow. "I'm Jaxon's *wife*."

"Jaxon's *wife*?" Savannah asked looking shocked at Jaxon.

"Jaxon, *who* is this girl?" Gertie asked stepping in between Savannah and Jaxon with her arms folded across her chest.

"I'm Savannah. That's who *this* girl is."

"Savannah, come here please." Robert demanded as he walked up and reached out to grab Savannah's arm once he and Clara finally caught up to her.

"Hold on Dad." Savannah said shaking loose of Robert's grasp. "Oh hey Auntie Jocelyn. What are *you* doing here? I don't graduate until tomorrow." Savannah said when she spotted Jocelyn close by.

"Hey baby girl." Jocelyn responded. Her heart went out to Robert. She had no idea this reveal would unfold in this way. She couldn't wait to tell Nanny about this shit.

"Come here Savannah!" Clara demanded as she yanked on Savannah's arm trying to pull her away from the family. Savannah jerked away from her grasp and stepped back towards Gertie and Jaxon. She struggled to put everything into perspective with Jaxon suddenly being married.

"*Dad*?" Gertie echoed. "Who is your *dad*?" Gertie pushed through Jaxon and Savannah and rushed towards Robert. "He's *my* dad." She said as she held out her arms to shield Robert from Savannah who turned sharply towards them and stared Gertie up and down.

"Hold on girls!" Robert yelled as he grabbed Gertie by her shoulders and gently moved her to the side. He was all discombobulated as he looked around and into the faces of Clara, Jocelyn, Celeste, Michelle, Deanna and Moses standing off to the side staring at him. The scene was chaotic.

Robert was lost in thought and forgot he was in the middle of the school campus. Luckily there was so much going on around him with people talking and taking pictures that all of their antics went unnoticed by others.

"What is going on here Robert?" Celeste asked looking around furtively hoping no one noticed *their* family drama. "Is *she* who I think she is?" Celeste locked eyes with Clara who was standing alongside Robert. "Oh. I know exactly who *she* is."

"Who do you think *she* is mom?" Gertie asked looking at her mom and dad for answers. "I'm so confused. What is going on?"

Jocelyn tugged at Deanna and Moses simultaneously and asked them to please excuse Robert and his family so they could have some privacy. Jaxon stayed glued to Gertie's side with his head hung low. He did not want to be there but knew he had better not leave.

"No problem. I don't know what the hell is going on but I guess we will leave y'all be." Moses responded. "Jaxon. Come here son."

"It was nice meeting y'all." Deanna said to Jocelyn, Celeste and Michelle as she and Moses slowly walked away. They waited off to the side for Jaxon to come to them.

"Son, what in the hell is going on?" Moses asked as the three sat in an empty row of seats across the aisle from where Robert and his family were engrossed in deep conversation and finger pointing.

"Pops I don't know? I mean I know that girl Savannah from here at school but I don't know what else is going on with her and Gertie and the rest of the family. They all seem to know each other but I don't know how."

"Ok well we going to go on home and you call us later when you find out what is going on with these niggas." Moses said.

"Ok. I will." Jaxon backed away from Moses and Deanna and jogged back to Gertie.

When Jaxon got back to her, Robert and Celeste were still in a heated debate.

"Yeah, Celeste, go ahead and tell Gertie who *she* is since you know so goddam much?" He said looking between Celeste and Savannah who were standing close to Clara.

"Mom! Dad!" Savannah said pleading for them to listen to her. "Who are these people?" She asked.

"No! Robert, *you* need to tell *everyone* what is going on. You and *Clara* created this mess so you can have the floor." She said folding her arms as Michelle sat back down.

Clara remained silent but looked at Robert with her lips pursed. She did not want to fight with Celeste in front of the diminishing crowd but she was getting mad at all the inferences being thrown her way.

"Yeah you are damn right I created this mess so I will handle it." Robert agreed as he grabbed each girl by an arm. "Come with me." He said to Gertie and Savannah as he pulled them away from the group. "Don't say shit else just come with me to my office."

"Come on Michelle, we don't need to stay here for this bullshit." Celeste said as she grabbed her purse from the chair.

"Celeste, you shut the fuck up because your entire life has been a lie so don't get me started on you." Robert yelled as he continued to walk away with the girls in tow.

"Fuck you Robert. Gertie call me when you get home." Celeste yelled as she walked away with Michelle.

"Hold on Celeste. Let me talk to you for a minute?" Robert said in an exasperated tone as he stopped in his tracks and released his grasp on the girls. "You girls stay right here and don't say a word to each other. I'll be right back."

"What?" Celeste asked as she turned abruptly in his direction. "I'll meet you at the car Michelle." Celeste said as she walked gingerly to meet Robert. She didn't know what to make of his sudden request.

"Let me tell you something." He said in a low tone through his clenched teeth as he walked to within inches of Celeste. "I have put up with your *bullshit* for a long time so how dare you act like this is all beneath you when you are partly responsible for this façade that you and I carried on for all of these years. I should have been a man and stood up to your wicked ass a long time ago but no I tried to please you and tried to salvage our little fucked up marriage. You put me through holy hell and now I know why. You fucking carpet muncher." Robert rattled off.

"Are you done?" Celeste asked nonchalantly with her arms folded across her chest as Robert's hot breath blanketed her face.

"No! I'm not done. Let me finish! Now, that you are finally living in your truth I thought that maybe, just maybe you would be a better person moving forward in your *new* life but I see that will never happen because you are still just as evil as you wanna be. But I'll tell you something else; you will never, ever have another opportunity to disrespect me again after today. You can go straight to hell!" He said backing away from her. "Now I'm done!" He tugged at his shirt and popped his neck.

"Like I said, fuck you Robert." Celeste pointed her finger at him and tried to poke him in the forehead. He swatted her hand away just as she turned to walk away at a double time pace. She couldn't wait to return home.

"Let's go girls." Robert said as he turned and reached for the girls' arms again and pulled them along towards his office. They had stayed put just as he directed and watched the exchange between him and Celeste.

Jocelyn, Jaxon and Clara also witnessed the exchange with Robert and Celeste but kept their distance because they could see Robert was breathing fire.

"Ok, so where in the heck *we* gonna go?" Jocelyn asked looking at Clara and Jaxon.

"I guess we can go sit outside of Robert's office and wait for him to finish talking to the girls. I'm sure they will all need some moral support when they are done." Clara said with a worried look on her face. She felt bad for Robert and this mess she helped to create.

"Can somebody *please* tell *me* what's going on?" Jaxon asked. He was still very confused.

"I'm going to leave that conversation for you and your wife, new nephew." Jocelyn said shaking her head as the three slowly walked in the direction of Robert's office. "Welcome to the family."

When Jocelyn, Clara and Jaxon arrived at Robert's office, Clara listened at the closed door. She could hear Robert doing most of the talking but could not hear what he was saying or discern how the girls were responding. The girls were sitting on opposite sides of the room facing each other trying not to make eye contact with one another.

"I don't know how else to say this so I will get right to the point. You guys *are* sisters." Robert was searching for the right words.

"How can that be?" Gertie asked.

"Yeah how can that be?" Asked Savannah.

"I fucked up that's how. Clara and I were high school sweethearts but we split up when we went away to different colleges. We later married different people. When her husband passed away she went home to Mississippi to sell their home and I was in town for the holidays that year, and we *hooked up*." Robert explained.

"What do you mean you all *hooked up*? Savannah asked angrily. "You make it sound like my mom was a prostitute or something."

"Savannah shut the fuck up and let me finish!"

"Yeah shut up. Ain't nobody calling your mama no ho." Gertie offered.

"Girls! Both of you please let me explain, please." Robert pleaded. "I had an extramarital affair with your mother Savannah while I was still married to Gertie's mom. Your mom got pregnant with you but she didn't tell me about you until you were 10 years old. She was trying to protect my marriage and although I appreciated her for doing that it was probably not the right thing to do. Anyway, when I found out about you I told my wife and she and I decided to keep you a secret from our friends and her family, *and* you Gertie. However, I accepted full responsibility for you financially and have been in your life ever since as a loving father. When my marriage dissolved a few years later Clara and I rekindled our relationship and Celeste moved on with her life but I still wasn't ready for you girls to meet because I thought you all were too young to really understand. So there, whether y'all like it or not you are sisters, I love you both and I hope you will forgive me for my transgression. I also hope that you can learn to accept and love each other too one day." Robert breathed a big sigh of relief.

"Wow…well, I don't know about accepting her as my sister because clearly she came here today to see Jaxon, and I need to know what that is all about before we can move forward." Gertie said staring at Savannah.

"Jaxon and I are *friends*." Savannah responded with a smirk on her face.

"Have you all slept together?" Gertie asked while bracing herself for the answer.

"You need to ask your *husband*." Savannah got up and ran out of Robert's office slamming the door behind her. As soon as the door closed she ran smack into her mom, Jocelyn and Jaxon sitting outside the door.

"Savannah!" Clara yelled as she ran past them tripping over Jocelyn's feet.

Robert followed Savannah leaving Gertie sitting in the office with her head resting in the palm of her hands. She was numb. It was too much information to digest and the baby was extra active because of all of the excitement.

Savannah stopped running when she looked back and saw her mom following close behind.

"Mom, I can't believe you slept with a married man. I guess the apple doesn't fall far from the tree huh?" Savannah asked squaring off with Clara.

"You don't get to talk to me that way. I am still your mother. Yes I made a huge mistake but you will still respect me!" Clara quipped. "What do you mean *the apple doesn't fall far from the tree?*"

"You know exactly what I mean mother." Savannah said sarcastically.

"Did you sleep with Jaxon?" Clara knew Savannah was sexually active since high school so she wasn't surprised if she had slept with him.

"Yup. We did it a few times. But I didn't know that he was married."

"I know, but now you do so that can't happen again. Do you hear me?" Clara asked holding Savannah by her shoulders. "Do You Hear Me?"

"Whoa, so now you got morals all of a sudden...?" Savannah said. She barely got the words out when Clara slapped her so hard her large hoop earrings went flying in opposite directions.

"Let me tell you something little girl." Clara said as she gathered a hand full of Savannah's tube top in her closed fist. "You keep trying me. I am not fucking with you. You leave Jaxon alone and I mean it." She said angrily as she released her grasp on Savannah's top and then turned and walked back towards Robert's office leaving her crying and searching for her earrings.

Robert, Gertie, Jaxon and Jocelyn were all still in front of Robert's office when Clara returned.

"How's Savannah?" Robert asked as he walked towards Clara.

"She's ok I guess. I'll talk to her again when I get home." Clara was exasperated. "I think I'm going to go on home. I'll call you later. Are you ok Gertie?" Clara went to grab Gertie's hand and she pulled away. "Ok." Clara said as she looked up at Robert and mouthed, "I'll call you later." She then blew a kiss at Jocelyn who returned the gesture as Clara walked away.

"Whew, I need a drink." Robert said lightheartedly looking at Jocelyn, Gertie and Jaxon as they all walked towards the parking lot.

"You ain't said nothing but a word brother let's go. All this damn arguing done gave me a headache." Jocelyn chuckled for a second until she looked up and saw the dreadful look on Gertie's face.

"I'm tired. I just want to go home and lay down." Gertie said looking at Jaxon.

Savannah had not given Gertie a straight answer but her gut told her that Jaxon had slept with Savannah. She couldn't bring herself to ask him about it because she did not really want to know, and didn't want to give him an opportunity to lie about it.

"Ok baby you and Jaxon go on home and I'm going to take Jocelyn to get something to eat. You guys get something to take home to eat and you get some rest ok?"

The ride home with Jaxon was quiet. Gertie looked out of the passenger window the entire way home. She had butterflies in her stomach thinking about his ongoing cheating ways and unfortunately unbeknownst to him he had slept with her very own sister. She was sick to her stomach and it was long past the morning sickness phase of her pregnancy so she knew it was due to the exhaustive afternoon's activities. When Jaxon pulled into the driveway at the house he ran around to the passenger side and opened her door. She exited the car without saying a word and marched right into the house, and went straight to the bedroom and slammed the door. Jaxon followed her and opened the door. She was laying curled up on the bed in a fetal position.

"Are you ok? I know you ain't mad at me because of what your sister said are you? I ain't screw that girl. I mean we hung out a few times but we didn't do anything."

"Jaxon, save it. You screw anything that moves."

"Well believe what you want." He was dismissive because he was lying.

"Oh I will. I wish I never got pregnant by you. I'm so embarrassed and that bitch will be a constant reminder of your infidelity because I *know* you screwed her while we were dating. You just need to slow your roll and stop fucking *everybody*."

"I'm going to get something to eat." Jaxon rolled his eyes without responding to her rant. "You want me to bring you something back? You need to eat."

"I'm not hungry." Gertie responded with her eyes closed trying to erase the scene from earlier.

"Ima bring you something back anyway because you need to eat. I'll be *right* back." He was genuinely concerned about her so he was bringing her some food back whether she wanted it or not.

"That's fine. I'm sure I will be hungry later." Gertie relented as she struggled to get comfy.

As soon as Jaxon left she picked up her phone to call her mom and saw she had a few missed calls and a voicemail already from her. Celeste apologized for not staying to support her but she thought it was best she leave to keep the peace with Robert. She reminded Gertie that she was leaving early on the next morning.

———◆———

Jaxon pulled into the crowded little parking lot at Woody's Barbeque and parked. He sat there for a few seconds then pulled out his new cell phone.

"Hey Ma, where is Pops?" He finally had a chance to call them.

"Boy, what the hell happened out there today? I mean they had more drama than a little bit. Is Gertie ok? Who is the other girl?" Deanna was firing off questions.

"Hey Boy." Moses said picking up another phone extension in the house. "Tell me and your mama what's going on."

"Well it looks like Mr. Bellamy had an affair years ago with Ms. Clara and she got pregnant with Savannah. Then

Savannah and Gertie came here to go to college and they just found out about each other today. Man it's bananas!"

"Oh wow...I can't believe he put Gertie's poor mama through all that." Deanna felt bad for Celeste.

"Her mama don't care because she gay anyway."

"Hold up a minute so that white girl was her man?" Moses asked.

"Daddy, she ain't a man. Be nice." Deanna was trying to be politically correct.

"Anyway, I gotta get this food and get back to the house before Gertie thinks I'm out doing something wrong. I'll call you guys tomorrow."

"Alright son. Be good and kiss Gertie for us. Poor girl." Deanna said about her new daughter in law.

Gertie was busy getting things ready for the baby's arrival and Robert and Clara made sure that she had everything she needed for the nursery. Jaxon was diligent in his job search immediately after graduation but was not having any luck. He had no clue what he wanted to do with his Journalism Degree. After futile efforts to find work, Robert promised him that he would talk to Chief Dandridge about a job with USC's Department of Public Safety if he wanted him to. He had never thought about a career in law enforcement and definitely didn't want to be a security guard at his alma mater. Gertie on the other hand had been exploring the idea of becoming a police officer ever since she laid eyes on Captain Moore.

"Jaxon, you don't have to do it if you don't want to. My dad is just trying to help. You are not having any luck getting a job on your own." She said trying to appeal to his better judgment.

"I know, but where I grew up niggas hated cops and I was one of them niggas. So how am I gonna *be* one?"

"Oh so this is about your ghetto ass friends and how you look to them? You need to grow up. You have a baby on the way."

"I mean I appreciate your dad for wanting to help but I don't know." He said shaking his head.

"What do you mean *you don't know*? We have been out of school now for a few weeks and you have to do *something* pretty soon. We are about to have this baby and the last of your scholarship money is pretty much gone so what are we going to do when that's completely gone? I will not have my dad taking care of no grown ass man." She said becoming annoyed with his immaturity.

"I will take it as a *last resort* but I ain't stayin' there long." He conceded.

"Whatever. You just need a damn job."

———◆———

A couple of months after graduating from college Jaxon was offered and accepted a job with the Department of Public Safety thanks to Robert and Dandridge. Contrary to his expectations it turned out to be a pretty cool gig. He felt empowered wearing the uniform, and he loved the camaraderie he had developed with the officers who worked at the nearby LAPD's Southwest Division. The bonus was that he was still on the college campus with all of the pretty young girls, some of whom remembered him and others he didn't know who simply just loved a man in uniform.

Chief Dandridge was an excellent role model and he ran a tight ship so Jaxon was not free to roam as much as he thought he would be able to. Oftentimes he stopped by Robert's office to low key complain or just to shoot the shit about a lot of nothing.

"I heard you were doing a great job." Robert said like a proud papa. "Dandridge is really pleased with your performance."

"Man you clockin' me? I mean I know you helped me get the job but I'm a grown ass man and Chief should not be reporting back to you. That's not cool." Jaxon chuckled nervously. He tried to make light of it but he was serious.

"He didn't *report* back to me man I asked him how you were doing. But I get it. You a man so I apologize if you think I'm checking up on you. That shit won't happen again." Robert dropped his pen on his desk. He was put off by Jaxon's comment. "Hold on, it's Gertie calling me." Robert said looking at the caller ID on his office phone. "Hey Gertie are you ok?"

"Yes daddy I'm good but I think my water just broke. I tried calling Jaxon but he's not answering his cell phone." She said somewhat out of breath.

"Jaxon is right here in my office and the reception is bad around here. I'll be right there. Here's Jaxon." Robert said as he handed the phone to Jaxon and simultaneously grabbed his jacket from the back of his chair.

"What's going on? You good?" Jaxon asked.

"I think my water just broke. I went to the bathroom and peed for a long time." She said excitedly.

"I'm going to go and let my boss know I gotta leave and I'll be right there ok?"

"Ok. I'll wait here until one of you guys get here."

"I'll go get Gertie and you can meet us at the hospital ok?" Robert told Jaxon loud enough for Gertie to hear on her end.

"Did you hear your dad?"

"Oh wait. Clara is off today." Robert offered. "It's Columbus Day. I'll have her take you to the hospital and we can just meet you guys there."

"Ok! Hurry up." She sounded nervous.

"Ok we will be there soon!" Jaxon was excited.

Robert called Clara who agreed to take Gertie to the hospital. While en route to DPS headquarters Jaxon called Moses and Deanna. They happily agreed to meet at the hospital.

"What horspital she at son?" Moses asked holding the phone for Deanna to also hear the conversation. He never could pronounce hospital correctly.

"She's gonna be at Cedars Sinai. Are ya'll coming?"

"Hell yeah we comin'!" Deanna said.

"Ok. I'll see you guys there."

On October 14, 2002, Gertie gave birth to a baby boy, Joel "Marcus" Atwater.

CHAPTER 7

"I'm Out of Shape-You Can't Shoot"

———◆———

"Don't hold his head like that Jaxon." Gertie scolded.

"You need to calm down. I'm not going to hurt him. He's my son too."

"I'm sorry we dragged you two out with the baby being so young and all but we really want you to share in our special day." Clara said looking back at Gertie and Jaxon in the back seat of the roomy Ford Expedition that Robert rented for a comfortable ride to Las Vegas.

"Is Savannah coming?" Gertie asked hesitantly.

"Yes. She's going to fly in so we will pick her up from the airport early tomorrow."

ROBERT AND CLARA HAD RECENTLY celebrated their 50th birthdays and were ready to spend the rest of their lives together so they planned a New Years Eve wedding in Las Vegas. Gertie wasn't too thrilled about taking the baby out so soon but she couldn't miss her dad's wedding. It was bitter sweet. She wasn't looking forward to seeing Savannah but knew she also had a right to be there at *her* parents' wedding.

The ceremony was quaint in the Little White Chapel on the strip. Clara wore a form fitting off white satin two-piece suit with a pillbox hat and matching Podeswa shoes. She looked amazing. Not a day over 35.

2003-The Vegas excursion was a weekend turnaround trip as they all had to get back to work except for Gertie who was still *bonding.* Robert had spent the weeks leading up to the wedding preparing Clara's townhouse for Gertie and Jaxon to move in there upon their return from Vegas as Clara was moving in with him. Savannah was renting a plush apartment in Studio City with one of her sorority sisters so she wasn't planning on moving back into the townhouse where she grew up.

While in Vegas Gertie ran across one of Jaxon's old prescription bottles discarded in the small bathroom trash can.

"Jaxon are you still taking these pain pills?"

"Why are you snooping through my stuff?" He responded with an attitude.

"I wasn't *snooping.* The bottle was in plain sight in the damn bathroom trash."

"I'm taking the pain meds because my legs still hurt from time to time. Don't worry my doctor says he's not going to prescribe me anymore pills because he doesn't want me to become addicted." He realized she was really concerned so he softened his tone.

"The extra strength Tylenol should work just fine. You really don't need the prescription drugs."

"Well I guess I won't have any choice but to take the Tylenol since my doctor is trippin'." He conceded. Gertie was satisfied knowing the doctor had things under control.

Gertie was getting antsy at home with the baby while everyone else worked. Jaxon had a decent salary at DPS and overtime was plentiful with all of the sports events and other special events held at the school and nearby Coliseum and Sports Arena. They were able to live ok off of his salary but Gertie found herself having to get money from her dad from time to time to help and she didn't like using him like that but she had no choice because Jaxon didn't manage well and she was at his mercy since she didn't work.

After five months of bonding she was tired of cooking and cleaning in between the baby's naps so she started looking for work.

"Guess what?"

"What?"

"Remember when I was an intern at the Sentinel? Well I been looking for a job and they offered me a full time position."

"I don't remember you being an Intern there but ok. So what are you gonna be doing?" Jaxon asked.

"I'll be a writer for the paper. I think I'm going to take it. There is a daycare right across the street from the office so that will be perfect for Marcus." She was excited about going back to work.

"Sounds good." He was halfway listening to her.
Gertie called Mr. Blake and accepted the job. She couldn't wait to get started.

"How do I look?" She asked looking at herself in the full-length mirror admiring how well her body bounced back after the baby. It had been 5 months and her long walks pushing the stroller around the Fox Hills Mall had paid off.

"You know you fine girl. Them old niggas over there at the paper better not be pushing up on you." He said thrusting his pelvis into Gertie's backside. He also admired her image in the mirror while looking over her shoulder.

"Boy you are too funny. You barely *push up* on me anymore and I'm your wife." She said pushing him off of her with her behind. "I gotta go. Enjoy your day off with your son."

Gertie had not seen Taylor since their graduation but they talked on the phone often. Taylor wasn't successful in her bid to play basketball overseas so she settled on working at Gold's Gym as a Personal Trainer until she could find a job with real benefits. She had applied for a Social Worker position with the County but had not heard anything from them in months.

Taylor and Jaxon's relationship waned significantly after college. He was tired of her complaining about his cheating ways. He also didn't like that she consistently warned Gertie that he was not good for her and wasn't going to change. She loved him like a brother but she loved her friendship with Gertie even more.

"I haven't heard from you in a cool minute." Taylor said.

"I know. I am working now." Gertie said in a low tone.

"Why are you whispering? I can hardly hear you. Where are you working at?"

"At the Sentinel Newspaper. I'm at work right now and guess what?" Gertie asked not waiting for an answer. "Guess what my first assignment is?"

"Girl what? I'm not in the mood for your guessing games. The last time you told me about your assignment at the paper was when Aaliyah died so just tell me. I have a client coming in a few minutes."

"Ok. Tay. I am going to be interviewing the only four African American Female Lieutenant's on LAPD *and* Captain Moore. Remember her?"

"Yeah. I remember her."

"I'm super excited. This police stuff is so exciting to me. Anyway I know you gotta go and so do I so I'll talk to you later and tell you all about the interview ok?"

"Ok. I can't wait to hear all about it. Later." Taylor smiled a she closed her phone and slipped it back into her pants pocket shaking her head at Gertie's excitement.

Gertie told Jaxon about her impending assignment and he was less than enthused. He was happy at DPS but had never thought about joining the LAPD.

"That's cool but I don't know why you are all excited. It's just an interview. Ain't that what you supposed to do when you work for a newspaper?" He was rocking the baby to sleep while Gertie cleaned the kitchen. "I mean I used to not like cops at all but since I been around them a lot lately they cool as fuck." He said.

"They are regular people just like you and I Jaxon. So now you wanna be the real Po Po?" She asked hoping he said yes.

"I don't know about all of that. I wanna be able to carry a gun and shit and not just be no Top Flight Security on a college campus especially in South L.A. I need some protection." He proclaimed.

"I think we should do it Jaxon." Gertie said excitedly as she dried her hands and tossed the dish towel on the counter. "They have great pay and benefits." She said walking towards him with a huge grin on her face.

"I don't know. I'll think about it." He said as he got up to go put the baby to bed.

When the day came for the interview. The four Lieutenants showed up on time and ready for the inquiry. Gertie greeted them as a group and introduced herself. She did a cursory assessment of each woman as they engaged in small talk while waiting for Captain Moore to show up.

Lieutenant Mason was short and stocky wearing a twisted wig and black rimmed glasses; Lieutenant Norton was a tall woman a little thick in the mid section with a pretty face and light freckles on her smooth butterscotch skin. She had a lighthearted personality. Lieutenant Torrance was a petite woman with a short haircut to die for. She wore her uniform well and carried herself with authority and lastly Lieutenant Newby was tall and fit. She was a star basketball player when she was in college at San Jose State and she was the head basketball coach for the LAPD's women's team.

"Ok she's here. Captain Moore is in the building." Gertie announced. "We will get started as soon as she is done talking to Mr. Blake." She told the others.

"Ms. Bellamy, have you ever thought of law enforcement as a career?" Lieutenant Torrance asked.

"I had not really thought about it until I met Captain Moore, who inspired me to write this story on the five of you." Gertie was surprised by the question. "I'm sure that after this interview I will be convinced one way or the other."

"I'm sorry I'm late." Moore said as she sauntered into the room. She looked cute in her suit and the other women all verbalized just how cute they thought she was too as they greeted one another before Gertie started the interview.

The women genuinely seemed to like each other. They acted more like sorority sisters than law enforcement colleagues. There was a familiarity amongst them that said loud and clear *we are sisters* over and above all else and Gertie loved their camaraderie.

"So ladies, I appreciate the opportunity to interview you all." She was in reporter mode. "I want to know a little bit about you and why you chose this career with the LAPD. Captain Moore I will start with you if you don't mind."

"I came from a single parent home raised by my mother. I grew up in Michigan and came here to California when I was 14; I have two teen aged sons and an ex-husband from hell." Moore said as the women all laughed in unison.

"Girl you ain't ever lied." Lieutenant Norton added. "That man put you through holy hell."

"Anyway my husband was also on the job but retired and is now the Chief of Police in Riverside, Ca. I chose law enforcement because I needed a job after I graduated from college and LAPD was hiring so I went for it. I had a rough time on probation like most women did at that time but I stayed the course and promoted up through the ranks." She proudly proclaimed.

Lieutenants Norton, Torrance, Newby and Mason followed suit with their individual testimonies. One common theme was that these women were all strong dedicated women who loved their jobs in spite of their hard times. The five were all so different. They looked different; they spoke of vastly different experiences; and they all had different energy. Gertie thought that the Captain was the most inspiring.

"I want to thank you all again for allowing me this incredible interview in helping me gain insight into your leadership roles on the LAPD." Gertie gushed.

"So when are you signing up?" Lieutenant Torrance asked as the others all nodded in agreement.

"You said you played basketball for USC right? Well you know you can play for the Department. I'm sure that Lieutenant Newby would love to have you on her team." Lt. Torrance said.

"Ok. That's good to know." Gertie quickly pondered the thought of having that opportunity. "You ladies are such an inspiration to me. I'm going to seriously consider joining the Department for real. Again, thanks so much, and as soon as I have finished the article I will make sure that you each get a copy of the paper."

The women laughed and talked for a few minutes as they prepared to leave. Mr. Blake stopped Captain Moore before she walked out.

"Patrice, you know who this is?" Mr. Blake asked pointing to Gertie.

"No. I don't think so." Moore said studying Gertie's face.

"You know my buddy Robert? The Dean at USC?"

"Yeah. Yeah. Yeah!" Captain Moore responded excitedly. "Yes I do remember he said he had a daughter at USC."

"Actually she is married to Jaxon Atwater the young man who was shot near campus a couple of years ago." He said looking between Gertie and Captain Moore.

"Yup. That's me." Gertie said as she raised her hand sheepishly and waved with just her fingertips. "We never formally met but I remember you from the hospital and the Press Conference and I have admired you ever since."

"Oh. It's so nice to actually meet you. Your daddy told me you recently graduated so it's nice to put a face with a name. I hope your hubby is doing well. Good luck to the both of you." Captain Moore said opening up her arms to embrace Gertie. "Tell your daddy I said hello and I'll stop in to see him real soon."

"Thank you so much ma'am. I will definitely tell him." Gertie could not wait to get home and tell Jaxon all about her interview. She picked up the baby from day care and on her way home called her dad.

"Captain Moore told me to tell you *hello* and that she'll stop by and see you next time she's on campus. She's so cool dad." Gertie said reflecting on her time spent with the women.

"Yeah. She likes to stop by and shoot the shit. That woman can talk her ass off." He said as he chuckled. "I'm glad your interview went well."

"I'm really thinking about applying for a job with LAPD."

"Really? Dispatcher?" Robert asked.

"Heck no. I think I want to be a cop. There are so many possibilities on the force. One of the Lieutenants I interviewed is in charge of Recruitment and another is the Women's Basketball Coach. Can you imagine being paid to play basketball? Man, that would be the bomb."

"Girl. Calm down. What does Jaxon say about all of this? You have a baby now remember. I don't know if it's a good idea. That job is very dangerous." Robert said confused by her new job interest.

"Daddy ain't anything any more dangerous than going to college in South Central Los Angeles At least as a cop I will be able to carry a gun and protect myself, *and* my baby. Jaxon is thinking about doing it too instead of being unarmed campus security. Most of the women I interviewed today have children. Matter of fact did you know that Captain Moore has two teenaged sons? I'm really giving it some serious thought." She said with conviction.

"Right. Right." Robert said. He was listening intently and taking in all that she shared. "Baby girl it sounds like your mind is pretty much made up. I just want you and Jaxon to be happy in your careers."

"I'll keep you posted." She said.

"Ok then." Robert replied.

"Talk to you later."

When Gertie got home she talked to Jaxon at length and they agreed they would start the LAPD hiring process. She felt the need to also tell her mother about her decision to join the force.

"Why would you want to do that? That job is so beneath you." Celeste remarked surprised by the news.

"What? What are you talking about? It's a respectable job and there are many cops from great families and most of them have college degrees. So what are you talking about?" She was really surprised by her mother's stance.

"Most cops are *bottom feeders*. They really have no status in society in general. They are trained just like mechanics and others who are low on the totem pole."

"Wow. I can't believe what I am hearing. Mom you are a trip. How about you being afraid for my safety? How about *I support whatever you want daughter*? Oh no, you have to put down a very noble profession; people who actually put other people's lives before their own." Gertie was livid.

"I'm sorry. I'm sorry. I didn't mean to hurt your feelings. But that's how I feel. I know I'm generalizing but I just never thought in a million years that you would graduate from a top notch university and then go to work as a *cop*."

"You don't get it. You should hear yourself. You of all people should not be judging anybody. Anyway, I gotta go." Gertie hung up the phone without saying good-bye. That was becoming a habit with them. "Whew that woman is a trip." Gertie said to Jaxon when she hung up the phone. Gertie became increasingly angry as she relayed the conversation with her mom to Jaxon and then to her dad. She and her mom's relationship had never fully recovered since their falling out over her pregnancy; followed by Celeste's initial refusal to attend the graduation, and then her rude remarks about the police profession was the icing on the cake.

"Daddy I can't deal with her. I'm serious. I don't know how you put up with her for all of those years. She was furious about me wanting to join the police department and called cops *bottom feeders*. She's so rude."

"I know. But that's your mom and you have to find a way to deal with her but on *your* terms. She *is* a real piece of work."

"Well enough about her. It's official. Jaxon and I are applying to join the LAPD. I'm so excited!"

"Oh really? *Both* of you gonna do it? Well let me know what I can do to help. I mean I know you will probably need help with the baby so Clara and I will do whatever we can." He said.

———◆———

Gertie and Jaxon remained on their jobs while they processed with the City. They simultaneously breezed through the written test; oral interview; and physical abilities test. However, when they got to the medical examination Jaxon was notified that his process was deferred, as he needed further evaluation and clearance due to his previous leg injuries.

"I knew this shit was going to happen." He said reading the notice intently.

"Let me see that." Gertie said taking the letter from him. "All you have to do is be reevaluated and I'm sure you will be cleared to move forward." She felt positive.

"I thought I made it through the physical with no problem because they didn't say anything when I was there so I don't get it." He was very disappointed and looked defeated. "I'm going to call and see what I need to do in order to appeal."

"Ok and I'll call Lieutenant Torrance and get some
advice from her since she's in charge of Recruitment."
Gertie did in fact call Lieutenant Torrance and was assured
that she would have someone look into Jaxon's situation and get
back to *him* as soon as possible. Within days of her call, Jaxon's
assigned mentor called and notified him that he was resched-
uled for a physical examination.

A few days later he showed up at the appointed time and
within a couple of weeks he was cleared to move forward in
the process. Meanwhile Gertie was in the background phase
of the process and looked forward to getting an Academy start
date.

She was nervous about entering the academy because she
was warned about the physical training, which was the biggest
stumbling block for most women trying to make it on the force.
Her mentor told her about the Candidate Assistance Program
(CAPS), which allowed her to work out several times a week to
get into tip-top shape before going into Academy. She told her
dad and Clara about the program that took place during the
evening hours and they agreed to babysit while Jaxon worked.
When Gertie told Jaxon about the classes he was lukewarm about
the opportunity.

"You go right ahead. I don't need those classes." He said
proudly.

"Jaxon, you can't go anyway because of your evening
work schedule but you still need to run on your own so
you will be in shape when you get a start date." She said.

"Girl I'm a world class athlete so I'll be good." He said
dismissing her concern.

"You haven't run in a cool minute dude." Gertie
believed Jaxon was delusional about his physical abilities
at that point. "But ok. Do you *boo boo*." She said rolling her
eyes at him.

Gertie and Jaxon passed their background investigations with flying colors and received their Academy start dates in the mail. They were scheduled to start the class in mid December 2003.

"Oh shit! We're in the *same* class. Oh man. Hopefully one of our parents can take Marcus to day care because our start time will be too early for us to take him."

"I'm sure my Pops can help but they live so far we would have to leave Marcus there overnight during the week." Jaxon offered.

"Uh, that's not happening. I need to see my baby every day so I'll see if *my* dad is serious about him and Clara helping. They live much closer than your folks."

"Ok, well you ask them."

When Gertie expressed her childcare concerns to Robert he agreed to help. Clara was still off on disability due to her recent carpal tunnel hand surgery so she welcomed the opportunity to bond with Marcus. Gertie and Jaxon left Marcus at Robert's house during the week so they would not have to get him up so early in the mornings and in the evenings they went to Robert's and hung out there until Marcus's bedtime so they spent time with him every day. On Fridays they picked him up and took him home for the weekend.

———◆———

The holidays were fast approaching as Gertie and Jaxon prepared for their first week in the Academy. They were excited and scared at the same time. Gertie neatly braided her hair in two French braids connected at the nape of her neck and Jaxon shaved his head bald for easy upkeep. They were eager to get the next 6 months over with.

"I have put his milk and juice in the fridge and his snacks are in the Pantry. Everything else, his diapers, wipes and

Desitin ointment are all in his diaper bag." Gertie said as she and Jaxon prepared to leave Marcus with them that first night.

"Come here I need to show you something." Clara said motioning for Gertie and Jaxon to follow her.

"Oh wow. Thank you so much!" Gertie exclaimed entering the room Clara had prepared for Marcus. It was fully furnished, tastefully decorated, and stocked with diapers, clothes and toys.

"Robert and I figured since he's going to be with us part time he may as well have his own room. So I will put all of his things away and you can just leave them here so you don't have to pack anything for him anymore. I will restock as needed." Clara said with Marcus on her hip.

———◆———

The first week of the Academy was stressful but pretty much uneventful until that first Friday. Gertie and Jaxon planned to meet at the car at the end of each day. The Physical Fitness Qualification Test was administered after lunch that afternoon. The recruits were warned ahead of time not to eat too heavy and to definitely stay away from the cafeteria's famous grill cheese sandwich and clam chowder as they were sure to cause bubble guts, which could impact their ability to effectively perform their sit ups and grueling *Burpees.*

On that Friday Jaxon finished first and was leaning against the car with his arms folded across his chest when Gertie walked up to the car.

"Man this is some bullshit for real." He said with his head hanging low.

"What happened?" Gertie asked handing Jaxon her duffle bag to load in the trunk. "What's wrong?"

"They saying I didn't pass my Physical Fitness Qualification Test so I'm disqualified *again*." He said shaking his head with an angry brow as he closed the door behind Gertie and jogged around to the driver's side.

"How did you *not* pass?" Gertie was perplexed by the news.

"Apparently my *run* was too slow." He said driving away from the curb.

"Get out of here! Jaxon. That is exactly why I told you that you had to run in your spare time but *no* you a *world class athlete*, as you put it, so you didn't need to run everyday." She said mocking Jaxon's mantra. "You have already quit your job, now what are you going to do?"

"Calm down girl. Check this out." He said excitedly. "They said..."

"*They* who Jaxon?" Gertie interrupted.

"The Sergeant I met with during my exit interview said I can go into this Academy Training Program and the City will continue to pay me my recruit salary. I will work at the Academy in the Captain's office for a few hours a day and the rest of the day I will work out and run, and then I will go into the next available Academy class in a month or two. So *that's* what I'm going to do." Jaxon said proudly.

"Wow, ok. That's very cool." Gertie responded breathing a sigh of relief. "So *now* I hope you will take your physical fitness routine seriously." She chided.

"Yeah. Whatever." He said rolling his eyes.

Jaxon and Gertie went to her dad's house that evening and told Robert and Clara all about their first week.

"Man I can't believe you didn't pass the Physical Fitness Test." Robert said to Jaxon while looking at Gertie with his eyebrows raised.

"Man, they are trippin'." He said shaking his head. "Just because I didn't complete the run in under 15 minutes."

"Well at least he still has a job." Gertie added.

"How? Where?" Robert asked.

"He's going into a paid program at the Academy to prepare him for the *next* class." Gertie explained to her dad. "He's going to be just fine. Whew I'm tired. It's been a long week."

———◆———

Gertie was afraid to relax too much on those first few weekends while in the Academy because she knew she would have to withstand the rigors of physical training come Monday mornings and she never knew what to expect during those training exercises. Jaxon on the other hand was not under the same pressure during that time period because as part of the Academy Training Program he was scheduled to spend the first half of his workday in the Captain's office photocopying and preparing training binders for the active recruits, and he completed each day with a required workout regimen.

On occasion, when Jaxon and Gertie arrived at Robert's house in the evenings Savannah would be there visiting. She loved Marcus but she didn't dare show her affection when they were around. There was always tension whenever they were all there together. Savannah and Gertie were jealous of each other for different reasons. Gertie felt like an outsider now that Robert was married to Savannah's mom and Savannah was jealous that Gertie had snagged fine ass Jaxon and had a baby by him.

Gertie was off to a good start in the Academy and Jaxon was rebounding from his rude awakening. He was no longer a *world-class athlete* and that realization was hard for him to fathom. His unexpected detour served him well though. The next

Academy class was slated to start two months later, and Jaxon was cleared to join that class in mid February 2004.

"No more clerical work for me. That shit is for the birds. I'm ready to join the big boys." He said breaking the news to Gertie about his impending new start date.

"That's cool. I hope you are really ready this time because it's not easy." She said. "I hate running and I get nervous shooting with the instructors yelling in my damn ear."

"You should be used to it by now. You can't let them get to you. It's all a game and you know that. I'm used to coaches yelling at me over the years so these drill instructors can't be any worse than them." He said nonchalantly.

"Yeah right, like your ass *used* to run fast too, but you failed the Physical Fitness Qualification Test so don't be cocky. You had better be prepared."

———◆———

Jaxon was getting used to the idea of becoming a *real* Police Officer. He felt totally comfortable in the Academy environment after working there for two months prior to entering the actual training for the second time. Gertie tried to prepare him for what lay ahead, as she had already been where he was going. The only area she could not prepare him for was shooting. He was 3 months in and Gertie was in month 5 and looking forward to her badge ceremony and impending graduation.

"Damn it." She said nervously fastening her seatbelt. "I can not afford to flunk out of this damn Academy." She proclaimed with tears in her eyes.

"How are you going to flunk out? You only have a month to go." Jaxon said wondering what she was talking about.

"I can't fucking shoot! I failed Combat Qualification today and have to go for remediation tomorrow and then

attempt to qualify again. If I double fail I will be termi-
nated and have to start the entire fucking process all over
again." She said bursting into tears.

"First me, now you. I was out of shape and now yo ass
can't shoot!" He said laughing. "We can't seem to get this
shit right." He was making light of their situations but
really felt bad for Gertie.

"This is not funny Jaxon!" Gertie blurted out as she
punched him in his arm. "Our situations are totally different. You were being lazy but I have been working my
butt off. Besides, there are only a few of us women left so
they *want* me to flunk out!" She said as her head swiveled
in Jaxon's direction.

"Don't get mad at me shit." He said rubbing his arm.
"You know good and damn well *they* ain't going to let you
double fail because *they* say *they* need black females badly.
You know they got a hiring quota."

———◆———

Gertie's remediation was low stress. It was just she and the instructor on the shooting range with no spectators or other shooters
to add to her nervousness. She listened intently as Officer Clark
provided her with specific directions from the booth. It felt like
she was in the Wizard of Oz at that moment as she only heard his
voice but could not see him.

"Are you loaded and ready for live fire?" Clark asked over
the loud speaker from the sky booth.

"Yes sir." She nervously gestured with a hand wave.
Clark was extremely patient and there were no instructors yelling in her ear. He was impressed with how well she handled her
weapon for starters.

"Ok you will have 25 seconds for this first round of fire ok?" Clark advised. "Two to the body; two to the head on each target; speed reload and repeat that sequence." He said slow and deliberate making sure that she understood his every command. "The first phase of fire will be from 21 feet from a holstered position. When the targets face you will fire 12 rounds in 25 seconds. Now, take your time and make good shots. Twenty-five seconds is a long time. You will fire two to the right body; two to the left body and a head shot on each target; then perform an out of battery speed reload, repeat the sequence then conduct an in-battery reload and holster a loaded weapon. Twelve rounds; when the targets face. *Attention!*"

Gertie had heard these same commands for weeks and she never had an issue qualifying before. It was *do or die* this time and she was determined to pass. Jaxon waited anxiously for her at the car as it was at the end of the day and his class was let out early. Gertie nailed every shot in the 9 and 10 rings on each target.

"Ok. Bellamy, go ahead and inspect your targets then pick up your brass and put it in the green bucket. I'll meet you outside in a few minutes." Clark said as he shut down the equipment in the tower.

"Yes sir."

Gertie ran to inspect the black silhouette targets stapled to the stiff brown cardboard. She quickly knelt down and did as instructed and picked up all the brass in sight; hers and everybody else's that was left behind by other shooters from earlier in the day. Just as she finished, Clark appeared in the tunnel behind the row of targets and she watched as he forcefully removed her targets from the pivoting cradles. She nervously dumped the shells she had collected into a green receptacle, and at a double time pace walked out from the Range and into the adjacent parking lot.

She waited there for a few minutes when Clark walked up behind her.

"Here ya go kiddo. Keep this for your records." Clark said handing her the shooting receipt. "I will let Captain know that you passed. You're actually a pretty good shot. You just have to find a way to calm your nerves when you qualify or I will be seeing you a lot on your second and possibly third attempts after you are out in the field. Congratulations and good luck out there."

"Thanks sir, but I still have a month to go."

"Oh, I know, but you don't have to qualify again until *after* you graduate so *I* won't see you again until then. Do you know where you are going yet?"

"Yes sir, I'm going to North Hollywood." She responded proudly now that she passed her requalification. She felt confident.

"Keep your head up and be safe." Clark said as he smiled and walked away. He looked like a Chinese Clark Kent with his chiseled features and big horn rimmed glasses. Gertie thought he was very handsome.

"Thank you so much sir." She said as she breathed a huge sigh of relief and walked away.

She was beaming from the inside out and could barely contain the huge grin that grew across her face as she skipped down hill and through the Academy gates to the street where she jogged the half a mile to her car. She could not wait to tell Jaxon that she had passed her qualification.

"I still got a job! I did it! I passed!" She squealed as she sprinted towards the car waving her qualification receipt in the air.

"Good. So now you can calm the fuck down." Jaxon said.

The last month in the academy was a whirlwind. Gertie passed her self-defense test with flying colors, which boosted her confidence ten fold. Jaxon watched from the sidelines as she pranced around the Academy with her classmates. She looked forward to graduating and hoped that her mother would come out but she was doubtful.

"Hey Michelle. How are you? Is my mom around?" Gertie was short and to the point.

"Hi Gertie. How's everything with you? How's everyone?" Michelle asked earnestly happy to hear her voice.

"Everything is great. I'm about to graduate from the Police Academy."

"*Police Academy?*" Michelle asked. "I didn't know that you were in the Police Academy."

"Wait, mom didn't tell you?" Gertie was very surprised. "Are you serious Michelle? Mom *never* told you that Jaxon and I are in the Police Academy?"

"Uh...no, but I'm sure she probably just forgot." Michelle was surprised but realized she had stepped on it.

"She didn't forget Michelle. Mom made some very disparaging remarks about the status of police officers in society when I told her Jaxon and I were going into the Academy so she didn't forget. She just didn't tell *you.*" She said angrily. "I gotta go. Don't even bother to tell her I called."

———◆———

Gertie was sitting on the chaise lounge as Jaxon entered the living room with his boots dangling from his hands. She was crying.

"What is wrong with you?" Jaxon asked with a scowl on his face. "What happened?"

"Nothing *happened.*"

"You ain't crying for nothing girl. What's wrong?" Jaxon asked laying the boots and Kiwi shoe paste on top of the newspaper spread out on the dining room table.

"I just spoke with Michelle."

"Is your mom ok?" He asked as he hurriedly walked towards Gertie.

"Yeah that bitch is ok." She said with a stiff upper lip. "Can you believe she never even told Michelle that I was in the Police Academy?"

"Get out of here. You're kidding me right?"

"Nope. I wish I was." Gertie sat up straight with her legs straddling the chaise.

"Why wouldn't she tell her?" Jaxon was confused.

"Because she's an uppity bitch who thinks she is better than *everybody*."

"But what does that have to do with her not telling Michelle you are going to be a cop?"

"Jaxon, she thinks that cops are *bottom feeders*."

"What the hell is that?" He asked. He was having problems connecting the dots.

"Never mind Jaxon. I don't want to talk about it." She didn't feel like rehashing her conversation with her mom while trying to explain shit to Jaxon. "Bottom line, she doesn't want me to be a cop."

"Oh. So she mad that's why she didn't tell Michelle?"

"Yeah. Pretty much. I called her to see if she was coming to my graduation and Michelle answered the phone. When I told her I was about to graduate from the Academy she was shocked, as mom never told her." Gertie said shaking her head.

"Oh shit. That's pretty foul."

———◆———

The sun shone bright on graduation day as Gertie and her classmates scurried around with lint brushes in hand inspecting each other's gig lines. Her uniform was a little big, as she had lost weight since her fitting just a few short weeks before. She tucked and tucked until her shirt was nice and taught inside of her trousers. She looked like a little girl playing dress up with the oversized hat dangling on her head. She walked out of the women's locker room and peered over into the field as family and friends and LAPD Command Staff and City leaders filed onto the field. She was hoping that her mother would surprise her like she did at her college graduation but she didn't see any-one from her family except for Jaxon who along with his class-mates were setting up chairs under the VIP canopies. Jaxon looked up just in time to catch her watching him. A tinge of jealousy overcame his attitude as he quickly looked away while lining up the fold up chairs. He was just *the help* at that moment.

"Hey Jaxon." Robert called out as he walked towards the VIP seating area. "I guess I found the right spot."

"You're sitting here next to Captain Moore and Chief Dandridge."

"Yeah. I'm Moore's guest."

"Where is everyone in the *Fam Bam* sitting?" Jaxon asked.

"They are in the front row. Over there." He said point-ing in their direction.

"Oh. I see them." He said when he spotted his mother waving and grinning at him.

"This is going to be you in a couple of months boy." Robert said poking Jaxon in his firm pecs. "Whew you are solid. They are gonna love you in the field."

"Yeah, I guess, if I ever make it out there. Man, I'm sup-posed to be graduating today with Gertie. I wish I hadn't failed the physical abilities test."

"Look here, everything happens for a reason and it wasn't for you to stay in that class. The way that you and

Gertie fight ya'll both would have been kicked out of the Academy by now if you stayed in the same class. You will be out in no time at all." Robert proclaimed.

"You right about that." Jaxon said as he chuckled. "I'm going to go say hi to my mom and Pops and Ms. Clara." Jaxon went over to where the family was seated and hugged everyone and picked up and kissed Marcus. He was as cute as he could be with his thick curly hair and chin dimple. After exchanging pleasantries Jaxon went back to work and then joined his classmates in a corner of the field after the VIP set up was complete. He was anxious to see Gertie in her full Class-A uniform.

Jaxon watched Gertie and her classmates line up on the track ready to march onto the grass part of the field. She couldn't stop smiling as she nervously tried to stabilize her hat on her head. She spotted her dad sitting with the dignitaries; and then looked around the crowd until she spotted Clara, who was holding Marcus. She then spotted Jaxon who was way across the field. The gang was all there except for Celeste. She felt a tinge of sadness then shook it off quickly as she listened intently to the Drill Instructor's reminders about the impending gun inspection commands. Gertie's thick hair was freshly pressed and pulled back into a low shiny bun instead of the two French braids she had worn for months.

The graduation was ceremonial as usual ending with a thunderous applause and police hats flung in the air by the graduates. Following the ceremony Jaxon found Gertie and the family in the crowd. He said his quick goodbyes and double-timed it off the field and back to the bungalows where his last class of the day was being held.

Robert treated the family to lunch at Harold and Bells before heading home. After lunch Gertie took Marcus home with her. She was looking forward to her class party later that evening in the bar area of El Cholo's. She couldn't wait to dress up and wear her hair down. Most of all she was looking forward to her favorite nachos and Strawberry Margaritas.

"I'll stay home with Marcus and you go on and enjoy yourself." Jaxon said when he arrived home later that afternoon.

"Are you sure? I don't really want to go alone."

"Yes. I'm sure. I really don't think it's a good idea for me to go since I'm still in the Academy."

"Yeah, you might be right." She agreed. "I promise, I won't be out long. I'll be on the graveyard shift and I start work tomorrow night, which is actually for Sunday. I will need to get back home at a decent hour and get my stuff together and then get some rest before I have to go in tomorrow night."

"Stay out as long as you want. It's cool." He responded nonchalantly.

Gertie noted a hint of an attitude in his voice. He grabbed Marcus from her lap and sat on the floor playing with him low key ignoring her. Gertie didn't say anything because she didn't want to start an argument. She thought for a second maybe she was being too sensitive.

"Hey did your dad and Clara go home after ya'll ate?" Jaxon asked without looking up at her.

"I think so, why?" She was puzzled by the question.

"Just asking. Me and Marcus might go hang out with them until you get back."

"Ok. That's cool." She was happy that he wanted to go hang out with her dad. "I'm sure they would like that. Just call first to make sure they are going to be home."

"For sure." Jaxon said as he followed Gertie into the bedroom. "What are you wearing tonight?"

"Some jeans, heels and a tank top. I'm not getting dressed up. It's a restaurant so it's not a real party location."

"You wearing your hair down?"

"Jaxon! Damn. What is this? An interrogation?" She asked. She was tired of his questions, which she felt were fueled by jealousy.

"Well you are going out partying *without* me so I think I have a right to ask."

"No. Your ass is just insecure." She said.

"Whatever. I just don't want them punks in your class hitting on my wife." He said walking up behind her loosely wrapping his arms around her neck.

"Nope. Don't even think about getting started I gotta go. Hold that thought though. I'll be back soon." She said as she wiggled out of his embrace and combed through her loose curls, which were hanging down way past her shoulders. "Ok, I'm out of here." She said as she bent down to kiss Marcus's forehead and then pecked Jaxon on the lips before walking out of the door.

Jaxon wasted no time calling Robert. He was definitely jealous that Gertie was a full-fledged police officer and he was still in training. He hated that she was celebrating and he was not.

"Hi Ms. Clara this is Jaxon."

"Hi baby. Is everything alright?" She was surprised by his call.

"Yes ma'am. Everything is cool. Gertie just went to her class graduation party."

"Oh, that's right. You didn't want to go?"

"Naw. We didn't think I should go since I'm still in the Academy you know?"

"That makes sense." Clara agreed.

"I wanted to know if I can bring Marcus over there while I go visit my Pops. I'll be back to get him in a couple hours."

"You don't think Moses wants to see Marcus too?" She asked. She was surprised by his impromptu babysitting request.

"Well, my Pops is not feeling well so I didn't want to take Marcus over there in case he's resting."

"Oh ok I understand. Marcus is welcome over here anytime and we are in for the night so bring him on over." She was happy Marcus was coming over because she had really gotten attached to him.

Robert was nodding off in his recliner in the den when Jaxon called and spoke to Clara so he didn't know what was going on. At about 8:15 Jaxon showed up at the door with Marcus.

"Who's at the door?" Robert asked looking at Clara as she walked towards the door. "Are you expecting somebody?"

"Yes. That should be Jaxon dropping my baby off. I'm sorry I forgot to tell you."

"Hey man." Robert said as Jaxon entered the house holding Marcus's tiny hand.

"Hi baby!" Clara exclaimed as Marcus bolted towards her and away from Jaxon.

"Oh it's like that huh?" He chuckled at Marcus's excitement to see Clara.

"Hey where's Gertie?" Robert looked around and behind Jaxon.

"She went to her class party."

"Why aren't you with her?" He asked.

"I didn't wanna go since I'm still in the Academy."

"Oh that's a good idea."

"I should be back to get Marcus in a couple of hours." He said walking back towards the door.

"Take your time. Marcus is in good hands. We will see you when you get back." Clara responded cheerfully as she closed the door behind him.

———————•———————

Gertie's classmates almost didn't recognize her with her hair down, and in her civilian attire. For the first time they saw her real beauty. She was tall and slender with an athletic build, and long thick hair. She had a great time getting to know her classmates on a different level that evening. After a couple of hours she decided it was time to go so she gathered her things and headed for her car. Her classmate Karisma Jackson the only other black female in her class was close behind her.

"Oooh girl I need to get home before my baby's daddy brings my daughter home. He's such an asshole." Karisma said as she and Gertie waited on line to pay for the Valet.

"Yeah I need to get home too because I have to work tomorrow night." Gertie said excitedly. "My baby's daddy is at home *with* my baby but his ass ain't answering the damn phone."

"Ok girl drive safe and I'll call you next week and we can compare notes about our first week in the field." Karisma said as she entered her car searching her purse for tip money. "I'm assigned to Wilshire Division where my dad used to be the Captain. He says I will love it there."

"Ok. Well I hope the same is true for me at North Hollywood." Gertie said as the Valet drove her car up right behind Karisma's car.

Gertie called the house to tell Jaxon she was on her way home but there was still no answer. She made her way home in the thick Saturday night city traffic and when she drove into the garage she noticed that his car was not there. She thought maybe he parked on the street. She went into the house and noted it was very quiet and all the lights were off except for the under the cabinets lights in the kitchen.

"Jaxon!" Gertie yelled into the darkness. "Jaxon!" She yelled once again. She then called her dad's house because she remembered that he said he was going to hang with Robert and Clara for a bit.

"Hi daddy. I'm sorry. Were you asleep?"

"Hey baby girl. Naw I'm just sitting up here trying to get your child to go to sleep." Robert chuckled in a low voice. "Clara is knocked out over there on the couch and I'm watching some bullshit Lifetime movie she had on. What's up?"

"Is Jaxon there?"

"Oh no baby he was here earlier but he called a while ago and said he was gonna be staying the night at his mama's house because his grandfather isn't feeling well."

"Oh, ok. I wonder why he didn't call me and tell me he left Marcus there with you. I'm so sorry daddy." Gertie said trying not to sound angry. "I'll be right over to get him."

"Now why would you do that? He's fine right here. Call Jaxon and check on his granddad and you stay at home and get some sleep. You have a big day tomorrow. Are you excited?" Robert asked.

"Yeah. I'm excited daddy. But I'm scared. I heard them streets ain't no joke."

"Girl, you going to North Hollywood. It ain't like you are going to South Central L.A." Robert said as he laughed

"Whatever. They got crazies in the Valley too. I'm coming to get my baby." She said. "I'll see you in a few."

"Ok then. He probably wants to go with you anyway because this little boy ain't trying to go to sleep no time soon." Robert said conceding.

Gertie went right back to her car and drove to her dad's to get Marcus. It had been a long day. She was tired, and nervous about Jaxon's whereabouts. The knock at the door startled Robert who had dozed off with Marcus squirming in his lap.

"Hey." Robert said as he opened the door with Marcus at his side.

"What time is it? Where's my baby?" Clara asked as Gertie walked into the room. "Oh hey Gertie. What are you doing here?"

"I went home and my family was missing."

"Oh yeah, Jaxon is staying the night with his folks. Didn't he call you?"

"No, and that really pisses me off." She said angrily.

"Maybe he didn't want to bother you at your party." Robert said defending Jaxon.

"Daddy, please. He should have at least called or texted to tell me what was going on." She was visibly upset and a little embarrassed. She picked up Marcus and looked around the room for his shoes. "Thank you guys for keeping him. That was *not* part of the plan for this evening but I'll take that up with Jaxon." Gertie nervously dressed Marcus for the nighttime weather.

By midnight she still had not heard from Jaxon and she didn't know whether to be mad or concerned. Marcus was fast asleep in his room and she lay in her bed staring up at the ceiling. She was growing angrier by the minute and decided to try calling him once again.

"Hi Moses." Gertie said tentatively. "I'm so sorry to bother you this late but can I please speak to Jaxon? He isn't answering his cell phone."

"Hey baby. I wasn't sleep. I'm just sitting here watching late night TV. Is everything ok?"

"Yes everything is ok I just need to talk to Jaxon."

"Baby, Jaxon ain't here and I have not heard from him since we left your graduation today."

"Oh really? Well...I went to my class graduation party earlier tonight and he was supposed to stay home with Marcus. Then he told *me* he was going to go hang out at my Dad's but instead he left Marcus with my dad and told *him* he was going to go check on *you* because *you* were not feeling well." Gertie's voice started to tremble. She felt like a 5 year old tattling.

"Look baby I don't know what is going on or why he would say I'm not feeling well. I ain't heard from him but when I do he is going to get an ear full from me." Moses was confused but had a feeling that Jaxon was up to no good.

"Ok thank you so much Moses. Goodnight."

"I'm so sorry baby." Moses said as he slowly placed the phone on the receiver.

Gertie flung her phone across the bed and sat straight up in the bed. She was fuming. She tried feverishly to reach Jaxon on his cell but it kept going straight to voicemail. She didn't understand what was going on with him but pretty much surmised that he was out screwing around. Her mind was all over the place wondering where he was and with whom. She had finally fallen off into a deep sleep when Jaxon's keys hitting the dresser awakened her.

"Where in the hell have you been?" She asked jumping up from the bed.

"I was out with my boys." He responded bending down to hug her.

"Oh hell no!" She said pushing him away. "You're drunk and you stink!" She was furious and couldn't believe he was so reckless by driving under the influence. "Are you fucking kidding me? You could lose your job and then what Jaxon? Huh? Then what? You are so irresponsible.

I thought you were going to check on your granddad but come to find out he wasn't even ill like you said."

"Oh, so you checkin' up on me?" He asked barely understandable.

"I was looking for my *husband* who just happens to be a damn liar. So I was not *checking up* on you asshole." She yelled watching him strip down to his underwear.

He face planted across the bed and within minutes fell off to sleep with Gertie standing over him. He was sloppy drunk and she was angry and in tears. She needed to get some sleep because she had to report for duty later that night and she needed her mind right for her first night in the field. Gertie left Jaxon sprawled out across the bed and headed off to Marcus's room. She lifted him out of the crib and cuddled with him on the twin bed in his room. She wanted no parts of Jaxon.

Gertie got up bright and early after only sleeping for a couple of hours. She needed to sleep but was nervous about her first night on patrol. She did some light cleaning and got her gear ready for work before lying back down. Jaxon still had two months to go in the Academy and Gertie was on morning watch so it was going to be tough trying to sync their schedules with Clara to ensure that Marcus was dropped off and picked up.

"Jaxon, how are we going to do this? You have to be at work too early to drop Marcus off and I get off too late to get home before you have to leave." She said as he shuffled into the kitchen rubbing his forehead. He clearly had a hang over.

"I'm sorry about last night. I ran into my homie on my way to my mom's house and we went to his house and I had a little too much to drink." Jaxon offered looking in the fridge.

"Jaxon. Please stop with the lies. Your grandfather didn't even know you were coming over there *and* he wasn't sick like you told my dad. You were probably with some bitch, which is why you left Marcus with my dad in the first place. I'm not stupid."

"Girl you are trippin'. You can go out but I can't?" Jaxon poured himself a tall glass of orange juice.

"Oh, so you're mad because I went out to my class party? That's fucking retarded. We agreed on me going alone and for good reason. I totally understand if you wanted to go out but you didn't have to lie about where you went. I'm not putting up with your bullshit antics like when we were in college. That isn't happening. So, why is it that your granddad didn't know you were coming over?"

"That's because I talked to my *mom* and *she* told me he wasn't feeling well."

"Yeah but you never made it there. So what's up with that?" Gertie stood at the table preparing her utility belt making sure her equipment was in the right order.

"I told you I ran into my homie. Damn." He would not make eye contact with her. "You always think I'm with some bitch. I'm not fucking around." He said convincingly as he wrapped his arms around her from behind. Gertie softened her stance as she slowly turned around in his arms until she was facing him. She wanted to believe him but she was skeptical. He kissed her forehead reassuringly. He really loved her but she had some serious trust issues with him and he had integrity issues.

"Daddy, is Clara there? I need to talk to you both." Gertie said after placing her war bag by the door.

"She's right here. We are just having a little breakfast. Did Jaxon make it home?"

"Yes. He's here. We were talking about our schedules and realize we do need help with getting Marcus to child care in the mornings."

"Ok. Clara and I will stop by in a little bit and we can discuss it then. I wanna see you before you go to work tonight." Robert said.

"Ok. Come by soon before I lay back down."

"Of course baby doll. We will come by as soon as we finish eating."

"Ok. See you in a little bit."

Gertie played with Marcus while she lay on the couch waiting for Robert and Clara's visit. Jaxon sat close by at her feet as they watched TV. She had dozed off on the couch when the doorbell rang. Only about an hour had passed but she was still tired from being up so late trying to track Jaxon down. In just a few short hours she would have to report for duty.

"I got it." Jaxon said as Gertie sat up on the couch.

"Hey boy. I see you made it home huh?" Robert gave Jaxon a half hug on his way in the door. Jaxon then hugged Clara who was following close behind.

"Yeah." He responded as Robert quickly passed.

"Hey daddy."

"You getting nervous about tonight?" He asked bending down to hug Gertie.

"Actually, I'm excited. Jaxon has to be at work before I get off so we definitely need your help. I hate to ask but I don't want to start off expressing a hardship at work based on child care issues, at least not until I get off of probation."

"No problem. We will continue to help take Marcus to daycare and/or pick him up on the days that you work, until you all can do it yourselves." Clara said looking at Robert for reassurance.

Gertie felt a great sense of relief and promised not to abuse their kindness as she peered over at Jaxon hoping he held the same sentiment. They chatted for a bit before heading home for the evening. Jaxon walked them out and then took Marcus out to the park. After everyone left Gertie went to get a few hours of sleep in her cozy bedroom.

CHAPTER 8

"STREET LIFE"

Summer 2004-"15A49. Hairston and Bellamy!" The Watch Commander barked peering over his round clear rim glasses.

"Here!" Hairston responded nonchalantly.

"Here, sir!" Gertie exclaimed loudly.

THE WATCH COMMANDER CONTINUED ON with calling roll before sending the troops out into the cold of night. Gertie's first partner, Wilton Hairston, a 30 something year old male white with thinning sandy blond hair was a 9-year veteran and had a reputation for being a good family man. She was Hairston's first female partner ever and unlike some of his male peers he welcomed her with open arms from day one.

"Where are you from kid?" Hairston was pumping gas while Gertie nervously loaded the shotgun.

"I'm from *here* sir. Los Angeles. Well, I went to college here but I was born and raised in Upstate New York." She nervously responded with her eyes stayed on the shotgun. She couldn't afford to make any mistakes at this stage in the game.

"Oh yeah? Where'd ya go to college?" He asked as he loaded his war bag into the trunk.

"USC sir." She said without making eye contact as she entered the passenger side of the vehicle and started to prepare her Daily Field Activities Report.

Gertie and Hairston engaged in small talk as he drove out of the station parking lot. He discussed his expectations and expressed the need for her to know her whereabouts at all times.

"Your head should always be on a swivel. Whenever I turn you make note of the street I just turned onto. You got that?"

"Yes sir."

"*15A49, 15A49, Officer Involved Traffic Collision at Ventura and Laurel Canyon. Respond Code 2!*" The police dispatcher said in her hurried tone.

"Roger!" Gertie said taking her cue from Hairston to respond to the Dispatcher.

As they neared the traffic collision scene she noted fire engines and ambulances crowding the streets with their flashing emergency lights a blaze. They exited their vehicle in a hurry just in time to see the driver officer being extracted from the mangled wreckage of the black and white police vehicle. The police unit had been in pursuit; lost control and collided with a power pole. The driver was a rookie who had only been out in the field for one month and it was his first time driving. He was a bloody mess with severe cuts to his face from the impact with the windshield, as well as from his coke bottle glasses, from which glass particles were imbedded in his face.

"He obviously wasn't wearing a seatbelt. Let that be a lesson young lady." Hairston warned as they maintained a perimeter around the wreckage.

"Wow. I hope he will be alright." Gertie watched the paramedics strap the young officer to a gurney preparing him for transportation to the hospital.

"He'll be in a lot of pain but I think he will make it." Hairston said. "Thank God his partner was not seriously injured.

"Yeah that's good."

Gertie was more shaken than the partner officer and saddened by the officer's injuries due to the traffic collision, but she was in awe of the Detectives who responded to the scene especially the female Detective who was in charge.

"So, why do the Detectives respond to traffic collisions?" Gertie asked.

"They are our traffic Detectives and they respond to *all* collisions involving death, severe injuries, criminal activity and any possibility of city liability. I'm glad you got to see this tonight rookie. Remember this, there are more officers killed in traffic collisions annually than from shootings."

"Yes sir." She responded as she had done all night in response to all of his teachable moments.

"Ok let's head in so you can finish your reports." He said yawning and squinting at the rising sun.

"Yes sir." Gertie responded for one final time during that shift.

Gertie felt overwhelmed on her first night even though it was spent mostly at the traffic collision scene. Even still she was very excited and proud to be a Los Angeles Police Officer. She couldn't wait to get home and get some sleep and then come back and do it all over again the next night. She wanted so badly to see Marcus but he was already at daycare when she got off. She thought about calling Jaxon on her way home but he was in class so she would have to wait to talk to him when he got home. She was hoping that maybe they could spend a few hours together before she headed back to work. She decided to call Clara instead to check in and see how things went getting Marcus off to daycare that morning. They chatted about her first night in the field and she confirmed with Clara that Jaxon was picking Marcus up on his way from the Academy that day.

Gertie had no problem falling off to sleep that morning because she was mentally drained from the previous night's events at work. She had invested in black out drapes for their bedroom so she could block out the ungodly sun during the day. She was asleep for a few hours when the house phone ringing awakened her.

"Hello." Gertie was groggy.

"Hi!" Said the chipper voice on the other end. "Mrs. Atwater?"

"Huh?" She muttered. She was so sleepy.

"Is this Mrs. Atwater?" The woman asked. "I'm calling to see who is picking up Marcus today?"

"Oh yes. Yes this is she." Gertie sat up in the bed trying to gather her senses. "What time is it?"

"Ma'am it's 6:15 and our daycare closed at 6." The woman said. "I will be here for a little while longer so Marcus is fine but I will have to leave soon."

"Oh no. I'm so sorry!" Gertie exclaimed fully coming to her senses. "I'll be right there. I'm so so sorry. I understand there is a late fee and I will pay it when I get there."

"Don't worry about it. It's the first time and these things do happen. I'll see you when you get here!" The woman was very understanding.

Gertie dialed Jaxon's number feverishly to see where in the hell he was. She was furious wondering why he had not picked up Marcus when he got off.

"Stay home girl I'm on my way now to get him. I stopped by my mom's and I didn't realize it was so late. I knew you were asleep so I figured I would just stay out until it was time to get him. I lost track of time."

"Ok Jaxon. I know my baby is probably hungry by now. You could have gotten him early and taken him *with you* to see your mom." Gertie was wide-awake at that point so she got up and fixed a light dinner.

When Jaxon walked in with Marcus, her fury turned into pure joy when she laid eyes on her cute baby boy. He was growing so fast and she loved witnessing his growth spurts. He would be turning 2 soon and she was noticing early signs of the terrible two's. Her eyes darted a quick dirty look at Jaxon as she grabbed Marcus from his arms. She still had a couple of hours before she had to report for duty.

"What you cooking?"

"Spaghetti." She replied dryly. She was very annoyed with him most of the time and that day was no different.

"Mmm that sounds good." He said as she mixed the ground turkey in with the organic pasta sauce.

"Marcus *loves* my spaghetti and there will be enough leftover for a couple of days. I'm not off until the weekend." She responded.

"I'm surprised they letting you off on a weekend." Jaxon said. "I heard probationers don't get good days off."

"Well, at my division we get the same days off as our FTO's so we get the same good days off they get." They finished dinner, after which time Gertie laid back down for a little bit before heading off to work.

———————

After Gertie was in the field for a couple of months Jaxon graduated on schedule and was assigned to 77th Street Division in South L.A. He was excited about working in that part of town because he was told that it would best prepare him for his dream job of working Metro. He eventually wanted to be a member of the elite SWAT team.

The family was happy and proud watching Jaxon stand tall at his graduation. Moses and Deanna remembered having that same proud feeling when he graduated from USC.

"We will meet you guys at Dulan's." Robert said to Moses at the end of the ceremony as they made their way through the crowd and walked down the hill from the Academy towards their cars.

"Ok. See y'all over there." Moses responded happily with Deanna walking closely behind him.

"I'm going to the car and wait for Jaxon. He's changing. We will be right there." Gertie said holding Marcus's hand as everyone walked in different directions towards their respective vehicles.

Gertie was tired because she had worked the night before but she was happy to be on the first of a couple of days off that night. She was about to start her third month in the field but not looking forward to changing training officers because she was warned about some of them who were not as tolerant of female officers as Hairston was. Gertie experienced the typical bullshit that most rookies were subjected to especially female officers, being talked down to or ignored all together but it was nothing she couldn't handle.

Dulan's Soul Food Restaurant was crowded as usual. It was Friday afternoon and soul food was a popular food option for black people on Fridays. The levity was welcoming when Gertie and Jaxon entered the warm and friendly restaurant. Moses and Deanna had grabbed one of the bigger tables for all of them and had pulled up a high chair for Marcus.

"Here, sit my boy right here." Moses said pointing to the high chair. "I haven't seen him in a while."

"Well you should have Jaxon bring him to see you sometimes. Actually he was supposed to come see you a while ago. Right Jaxon?" Gertie was being facetious.

"And I told you what happened." He said looking sternly at Gertie. "I told you I was with my boy and I got sidetracked and never made it to my folks house like I planned."

"Whatever." Gertie remarked looking around the table at everyone staring at them during their brief exchange. "Daddy and Clara I can't thank you guys enough for being there for us and helping out so much with Marcus. I didn't realize it would be so hard to be a cop with a small child."

"Don't worry about Marcus. You just focus on work."
Robert said touching Gertie's hand. "Clara and I are here
for guys. I'm so proud of you both."

"That's what's up." Jaxon said reaching for the menu.

"I wish we could help more." Deanna sincerely offered.
"But my hours at work are all over the place and we live
so far from you guys so neither daddy nor I can help. But
if ya'll need us in an emergency situation we will do what
we can to help ok?" She said as Moses shook his head in
agreement.

"I totally understand and we really appreciate you all too.
Marcus is a lucky little boy." Gertie said as she took a long sip
of her Iced Tea wishing it were a Long Island Ice Tea.

2005-Gertie and Jaxon compared stories about their training
officers and the stark differences between the Valley Division,
where she worked and the South L.A. Division where he roamed.
By the start of the New Year Clara was notified that her Wells
Fargo branch was being taken over by Chase Bank, which com-
promised her maintaining her high level position. After expressing her displeasure about the takeover Robert suggested that she
just retire. She gladly agreed and retired before the conversion
of her branch into Chase Bank was fully complete. She was grateful for the opportunity to retire earlier than expected and Gertie
was happy that she agreed to care for Marcus full time until he
was old enough to attend school. Clara's decision to retire was a
win win situation for everyone.

Jaxon continued his pattern of being irresponsible and staying out way beyond his work hours. He and Gertie were at odds
for weeks about his disappearing acts and his unwillingness to
help with Marcus. He was quick to leave Marcus with Clara and

Robert even when he was available to care for him. They didn't mind helping out but they too were becoming annoyed with his trifling ways. The more Gertie complained to Jaxon the more strained their relationship became.

On one of Jaxon's late nights out Gertie was in need of a good friend to talk to so she reached out to Karisma whom she had not spoken with in a few weeks.

"What are you up to?" Gertie was glad that Karisma answered the phone.

"I'm off today and getting ready to take Morgan to her dance class. What are you doing?"

"Just here at home. I'm off too." Gertie said solemnly.

"What's wrong?" Karisma motioned for Morgan to go get in the car. She then grabbed her purse and set the alarm before heading out with the phone pinned between her ear and shoulder.

"I'm so tired of Jaxon's bullshit. I don't know if I can do this."

"You don't know if you can do *what?*"

"Marcus is *his* child too and he needs to help me but he's not. It's not fair to my dad and Clara when he shirks his responsibility. I'm just tired and don't need this added stress. Plus I have a training officer from hell right now and he had the nerve to give me an unsatisfactory rating talking about my tactics were bad on a call we responded to. I can't take it. I think I'm going to resign and convert to a civilian job within the Department until I can find something else I really want to do with my life."

"And why would you do that after you worked so hard to get to where you are? I'm not going to let you do that. Have you talked to your dad?" Karisma found herself getting angry about Gertie's situation. "Where's Jaxon's ass?"

"He *claims* he's over there with his mama but shit I don't really know. He lies so damn much."

"I'm going to drop Morgan off at Debbie Allen's Dance Academy and I'm coming over since it's not that far from you. You got any wine?"

"Yes I do but I'm sippin' on this Long Island Ice Tea." Gertie perked up when Karisma said she was coming over. "I'll see you when you get here chica." She said as she jumped up and tidied up real quick. She had been in a funk. She needed to vacuum and clean the few dishes that were in the sink from the night before. Just as she hung up the phone rang.

"Don't tell me you changed your mind and you aren't coming over." Gertie said turning off the vacuum.

"What are you talking about?" Taylor asked.

"Oh Tay!!! What's up? Where have you been?" Gertie asked without giving Taylor a chance to respond.

"Damn girl. Who were you expectin'? I just talked to yo big head husband. He told me you were off today and that you were at home."

"Umph. Yeah I'm here. Did he call you or did you call him?"

"What difference does it make? What are you up to?" Taylor asked.

"I just wanted to know because I haven't heard from you in a while so I just figured he called you to vent because he knows I am sick of his ass. Anyway it doesn't matter I'm just happy to hear from you. I'm waiting on my friend Karisma to come over so I thought you were her calling me back. You coming over?"

"Well since you having company already I guess I *will* stop by." Taylor said.

"Ok cool. I'll see you in a little bit. Hey…hey stop and get yourself something to eat because you are a greedy bitch and I don't have anything here for you to eat. Matter of fact, you can bring me some Louisiana Fried Chicken and some Dirty Rice. I haven't had that greasy shit in a while. See you when you get here. Bye!" Gertie said hanging up before Taylor could say *no*."

Gertie was excited that two of her very best friends were coming over. She had been so consumed with work and Jaxon's antics that she hadn't found time to relax. Karisma arrived first.

"I'm coming girl! Gertie yelled as she hurried towards the door with Marcus right on her heels.

"Hey!" Karisma exclaimed as Gertie swung open the door. "Aww he's so cute!" Karisma picked up Marcus and kissed his cheeks.

"Come on in. I have a glass of wine waiting for you?" Gertie said after the two women embraced.

"I can't drink too much because I have to pick up Morgan in a couple of hours. Girl what is going on with you and Jaxon?" She asked right away as she kicked her shoes off and curled up on the love seat.

"Whew…where do I start? He barely picks up my baby on time when it's his turn and he stays out to all times of the night. Thank God for my dad and Clara. They have really been there for me." Gertie mustered a smug grin.

"What about *his* mama? She can't help?" Karisma asked with attitude.

"She would love to but unfortunately her work schedule won't allow it and besides they live way the hell over there in Lynwood. It's just too far."

"Oh…I see." Karisma responded.

"My friend from college, and Jaxon's best friend is on *her* way over here so we can't talk about him when she gets here unless she brings him up ok?" Gertie warned.

"*She?*" Karisma questioned.

"Naw bitch it ain't like that. They grew up together *and* she's gay."

"Oh. Gotcha. Ok then." Karisma chuckled.

"Knock. Knock." Taylor said as she poked her head in while opening the front door. Gertie had failed to lock it after Karisma entered. "Gertie! It's me." Taylor yelled before entering all the way.

"Hey Tay. Come on in."

Gertie introduced the two women. Karisma and Taylor hit it off right away. They talked for a couple of hours while chowing down on fried chicken washed down by *Moscoto* and *Lambrusco*. Karisma and Taylor talked about their respective relationships after Gertie reiterated her ongoing problems with Jaxon.

"Gertie. You know I love Jaxon like a brother but you have been putting up with his shit for a long time now. You deserve better. I'm just saying."

"Yeah I know. You have always said that but leaving him is easier said than done especially now that we have Marcus. So how is it going at Gold's Gym? How's the personal training coming along?" Gertie asked changing the subject.

"Man I'm trying to get out of there but they are still not hiring at the County."

"What job are you applying for with the County?" Karisma asked.

"My Degree is in Sociology and I want to be a Social Worker. I was in the system for years so I kind of want to give back but the County hasn't been hiring Social Workers for a while now.

"Oh that's too bad." Karisma offered.

"You know where you need to be?" Gertie asked. "You need to come on the job. I'm surprised your buddy Jaxon hasn't tried to recruit you."

"Well actually he has."

"And? What's up?" Gertie asked.

"Girl. Yes. You need to do that." Karisma said shaking her head in agreement.

"You say you want to give back. What better way is there than by being a cop?" Gertie added.

"Yeah you will have plenty of opportunity to give back as a cop." Karisma said shaking her head.

"I don't know." Taylor said.

"The Department does not care that you are *gay* I'm serious Tay you need to really consider it. It's a great career. We have great benefits *and* a pension."

"I agree. I mean there are some assholes on the Department like in any other profession but it's a really good job. I'm having a good time working Wilshire Division." Karisma said downing her last gulp of wine.

"Look at ya'll, real life LAPD poster girls. Jaxon told me the same things so I'll look into it because I'm tired of training delusional fat bitches. They think they fooling me when they come to the gym talkin' about all the stuff they doing at home in between our sessions when they really just eating they asses off. Talking 'bout *my metabolism done slowed down.* "I tell them '*No Bitch. You just eating all the wrong shit*'!" Taylor said breaking into hearty laughter.

The women laughed out loud for a few minutes as they finished off the Fried Chicken and Dirty Rice. Karisma hugged the ladies and excused herself so that she could go get Morgan. Taylor kicked off her shoes and curled up on the chaise as Gertie went to put Marcus to bed.

"So, is Jaxon still over his mom's?" Taylor asked as Gertie walked away towards Marcus's room.

"Yup right where his ass needs to be. He don't do shit around here so I told him I don't need him here."

"Ya'll need to get it together and try to work this shit out." She said as Gertie walked back into the room. "Especially since ya'll have a baby and you guys are now on the job together."

"Well *he* needs to get it together or I'm going to take my baby and run. He has a good job so I'll at least get child support." Gertie boasted.

"He's not going anywhere. Find us a movie to watch." Taylor felt good being there with her favorite girlfriend. Before the movie could get started good Taylor nodded off. When she was good and sleep, Gertie covered her with a blanket and then went to bed. She didn't hear from Jaxon until the next morning after she and Taylor finished breakfast.

"Hey." Gertie said when the Caller ID indicated it was Jaxon calling.

"What are you doing?"

"Getting my stuff ready for work."

"I'm *at* work. I'll be home right after I get off if that's ok."

"I guess..."

"I talked to Taylor and as usual she talked some sense into my head. You and Marcus deserve better." Jaxon sounded sincere.

"Yeah she just left. She came over last night and we had a long talk before she passed out. Karisma was here too and I think we talked Taylor into joining the Department."

"I tried to recruit her a while ago but I guess she listened to you ladies." He was happy that Gertie changed the subject.

"I'm about to take Marcus to my dad's house so I can get some sleep. I'll see you when you get home."

Jaxon and Gertie literally kissed and made up when he got home that evening. He vowed to do better and was good on his word for a little while before his disappearing acts started again. His favorite new outing was on Pay Day Wednesdays when he hung out at the Academy Lounge where he drank and partied with fellow officers and Police Dispatchers. Many of the Dispatchers were starving for attention especially from the men in blue; even the married men. Jaxon *loved* the attention he received from them. The more he drank the more flirtatious he became. He made it a point to schedule his days off on Wednesdays so he was available for the special gatherings, and when he couldn't get those Wednesdays off he still managed to make his way to the Academy for quick visits before continuing Patrol at his Division on those nights.

Gertie had heard about the Pay Day Wednesdays and some of her male coworkers tried to get her to partake in the biweekly festivities. She wasn't interested in hanging out with the guys especially in that atmosphere; after all, she was a married woman and needed to spend her spare time at home. She had no idea that Jaxon was a regular participant in those activities.

———◆———

Gertie ended her 18-month probationary period at North Hollywood and was beyond happy about her transfer into Northeast Division. She didn't know anything about the Echo Park area of Los Angeles but she looked forward to learning her way around. She also looked forward to having more independence and was exploring opportunities to promote to the next level.

Gertie stayed in touch with her mom even though their relationship was strained more than ever since she joined the

Department. After a while they got back to talking more on a regular basis and got caught up on each other's lives. Michelle and Celeste were still going strong and Bea was still Celeste's bestie but she only came around when Michelle wasn't home.

"Hey Mom how is everything there in the Big Apple? I am finally off probation and just transferred to another Division."

"Wow that was fast. I know you won't believe this but I am very proud of you. In spite of my bad attitude you still did the damn thang and now you are one of LAPD's finest."

"Thanks mom. I really appreciate that coming from you."

"How's Jaxon? Is he doing better since his dismal start?"

"Jaxon has done pretty well since he went *back* into the Academy but he's still an asshole."

"What is his problem?"

"He just needs to grow up that's all."

"Is he messing around?" Celeste asked.

"I don't know. Probably. He's supposed to be at work when he's out late but I never know with him."

"Well you better *know*. Don't let him play you. You need to pay attention and let him know you ain't no fool."

"Mom, trust me he knows I'm no fool. I just don't have any proof of his messing around and I ain't about to start looking for shit because I'm sure I'll find something if I do. What's done in the dark will surely come to light so I'll just wait."

"Ok baby, enough about Jaxon's ass. How are your dad and *Miss Clara?*"

"You mean *Mrs. Bellamy?*" Gertie teased. "Actually they are doing very well. Clara just retired from the bank and she keeps Marcus full time for me on the days I work. She's really a sweetheart so you need to get over your issue with her. You don't like men any damn way so why are you trippin'?"

"Oh no you didn't. So you taking up for *her*? I'm your mama." Celeste said laughing. "That's very cool. I wish I were closer so I could spend more time with you and Marcus. Maybe he can come spend some time with me next summer."

"I would love that mother. That sounds like a plan. We will work out the details later."

"How's Grandma Rose? She's getting up there in age. What is she, about 95? 96? I haven't talked to her in quite a while. Please tell her I asked about her when you talk to her."

"I sure will. I really need to call her." Gertie said. "Ok mom I'll talk to you soon. I love you."

"I love you too." Celeste smiled as she hung up the phone.

———————

Gertie made it a point to call Grandma Rose often. She really was getting up there in age and had slowed down a lot but she was still a mess and in her right mind. Thank God Jocelyn was still there in Biloxi otherwise Robert was seriously thinking about moving her to California. Gertie was on her way home one afternoon in late August when she received a call from her dad.

"Hey baby girl have you been watching the news?"

"No. What's going on?" She heard the worry in her dad's voice.

"A hurricane has hit the Mississippi Gulf Coast. The Mayor is saying it is like a tsunami and I can't get a hold of Jocelyn or Nanny." Robert was slightly panicking.

"Calm down daddy." Gertie had never heard her dad panic before. "I'm sure they are both just fine."

"But I can't get through to anyone. The news is reporting that about 90% of the buildings along the Coast and in the neighboring Gulfport have been destroyed and most of the churches have either been destroyed or severely damaged, including St. Michael's Catholic Church where Nanny usually goes to Mass." Robert was shaking his head in disbelief. He felt so helpless.

"Daddy, we will just have to keep trying until we get through to someone. Ok? I'll see you in a little bit. I'm on my way over there right now. Try not to worry?"

Robert was nervous and losing hope when CNN reported that the hurricane-force winds had persisted for about 17 hours. Finally Jocelyn was finally able to make contact with Robert. Thank God she was safe at a Red Cross center with her boys.

"Don't cry sis. I'm sure Nanny is okay." Robert said trying to comfort her long distance. "You have to let the authorities do their job. I'm worried too."

"They sayin' that a lot of peoples is dead brother. Lord I hope Nanny's ok. I talked to her right before I went to work yesterday and I was gonna stop by on my lunch break when I saw that the storm was getting pretty bad." Jocelyn broke down and cried uncontrollably. "I shoulda just took her home with me last night when the news said we was on storm watch. Oh Lord."

"Listen, don't start blaming yourself. Just start praying that she is ok." Robert said.

"Ok. I gotta go now so somebody else can use the phone. I'll call back when I can." Jocelyn said as she hung up the phone.

The day after the hurricane touched down Robert, Clara, Gertie, Jaxon and Savannah held vigil at his house waiting for word about Nanny's whereabouts.

Two days after the hurricane touched down the news confirmed 53 fatalities in Biloxi but there was still no information on Nanny's whereabouts. Robert appealed to his friend Chief Dandridge to *please reach out* to law enforcement in Biloxi to try and locate her.

"Ok bro. I just got off of the phone and of the 53 confirmed fatalities, one has been identified as a 53 year old male; one an identified 22 year old woman, and there's a 90-95 year old Jane Doe."

"Oh no!" Robert shrieked.

"It's a slow identifying process under the circumstances. I *came* here instead of calling you because it appears that they may have tentatively identified the Jane Doe as a Ms. Rose Malveaux, that's your Nanny right?

"Oh my God...No!" Gertie said as they all gasped in unison.

"Yeah, someone recognized her by her gold fronts but they need a family member to positively identify her." Dandridge said rubbing Robert's shoulder.

"Ok bro. Thanks for your help. Let me call the Red Cross and try to get a hold of Jocelyn." Robert said through his tears.

"I got it man. Let me call the authorities and have *them* find your sister." Dandridge offered. "You just sit tight." Dandridge called several numbers until he finally got through to the Red Cross where Jocelyn was last known to be.

"Ma'am, hold on. Here's your brother." Dandridge said handing his cell phone to Robert.

"Jocelyn! I think they found Nanny." He said screaming into the phone while the family formed a circle surrounding him holding hands.

"Oh thank you Jesus!" Jocelyn exclaimed.

"No. Jocelyn! I'm so sorry. I should be there with you..."

"What? Why? What are you sorry about boy? Where is Nanny? I'll go to her."

"She's dead Jocelyn and they need you to go to the Morgue and identify her body."

"So how you know she dead if ain't nobody identified her body yet?"

"The cops have *tentatively* identified her by her front teeth but they need a family member to *positively* identify her. So please go and then call me back."

"Oh my lord." Jocelyn commented stifling her cry with her boys, Ricky and Stevie by her side.

After Robert hung up the phone he, Clara and the girls cried and hugged it out in his kitchen while Jaxon kept Marcus busy in the den. Marcus was too young to understand what was going on and Jaxon was devoid of emotion because he had never met Nanny in person. Even still he felt bad for the family. He couldn't imagine losing Moses or Deanna.

Robert immediately booked a flight to Biloxi as soon as the airport reopened. Jocelyn's home was gutted by the storm surge, however the structure was still solid enough to allow for repair. Jocelyn and her boys remained at the Red Cross location for a few days until they were provided temporary housing. She didn't know how she wanted to move forward long term so she waited for Robert to get there so he could help her figure everything out.

Robert's first order of business when he got to Mississippi was to make arrangements to have Nanny cremated without any consideration of a Memorial Service under the circumstances, and secondly to deal with disposing of her property, which was pretty much destroyed. Everyone and everything in Biloxi was in such disarray he decided to take Nanny's ashes back to California with him.

"I wanna go too." Jocelyn said pouting.

"Go where?" Robert was caught off guard by her comment.

"To California with you."

"Are you serious?"

"I sure am. I can't stay here brother." She said nervously. "I don't wanna be here without Nanny. The lady at FEMA told me that the Government is planning on givin' some homeowners the option to sell they properties, and my house is repairable so I'm hoping it's in the area they talking about buying." She said wiping her tears from her puffy eyes. She hadn't slept in days.

"Well, I will stay here for as long as you need me to so I can help you make some decisions, and if you *really* want to move to California we will make it work sis. They got plenty of Walmarts in California for you to transfer to, and we can get Stevie and Ricky into a good school out there." Robert was actually relieved that she was willing to move. "I won't worry about you if you are with me in California so I like that plan." He said hugging Jocelyn tight.

The next couple of weeks were dismal in Biloxi with the death and destruction as a constant reminder of the tragedy that many families there faced. Robert got Jocelyn and the boys a room at the hotel where he was staying while he was there so they could be close while getting Nanny's business in order. They were happy to hang out at the hotel because their temporary housing left a lot to be desired. Before Robert left he was able to help get Jocelyn settled into better temporary housing and he encouraged her to seek a job transfer to California as soon as possible.

———◆———

Savannah and Gertie had not seen much of each other following their unusual introduction at their college graduation. They had only communicated when they happened to run into each other at their dad's home. They remained very distant up until Nanny's death.

While Robert was gone Gertie and Savannah stayed with Clara on most days when they weren't working. They were like three peas in a pod while waiting for Robert to return home. They all loved Nanny as each of them had their own special relationship with her. During the time Robert was gone Jaxon stopped by the house after work on occasion and spent time with the ladies, and played with Marcus for a bit before going on home for the night. His presence made Savannah feel most awkward but she knew she *needed* to move on from their previous dalliance.

"Looks like you are making quite a name for yourself over there at Channel 5 News." Gertie said striking up a conversation with Savannah after Jaxon went home one evening. She was trying to break the ice. "How do you like being a Reporter? It looks cool."

"Yeah. It's *very* cool." Savannah said. "I can't wait to get out of the field and move into one of those Anchor chairs though. I guess I just have to wait my turn." She said as she chuckled nervously. "So how's cop life? Mom told me Jaxon had some kind of issues early on. How's *he* doing now?"

"He's fine." Gertie responded curtly. "You know you and Jaxon's past is still a sore subject with me. I mean I know you guys didn't know back then that you and I were related but it still stings a little knowing you guys fucked around." Gertie said trying really hard not to get mad.

"I realize that my past relationship with Jaxon is a sore spot with you. I get it. It was an unfortunate liaison considering that we are sisters but it's impossible to unwind the clock so hopefully we can just move forward." She remarked staring Gertie right in the eye. "*Trust me* I would have never knowingly disrespected your relationship or marriage or anyone else's marriage for that matter. I hope you will get to a place where you can trust me."

"You are right. I'm more upset with Jaxon because he is a serial cheater and it's just sad that he bagged my sister even though he didn't know it. That's why niggas need to keep their junk in the trunk *especially* when their asses are in committed relationships." She said laughing. "Anyway, I too am hoping that we can move past this drama."
Both girls turned when they saw Clara walk into the room talking on the phone.

"You know death has a funny way of bringing people closer together." Robert said.

"Yeah I guess. Nanny's death has kinda been a blessing in disguise because I have never seen our girls talk so much to each other, and civilly." She said looking off in the distance at Gertie and Savannah who were laughing and talking like two long lost friends.

"Jocelyn wants to move to California but I told her she can't live with us because them boys are just too damn bad. I mean I love my sister but she can't live with me. I will help her from a distance. As long as she is close and I can lay eyes on her from time to time I'm good." He said shaking his head.

"Robert you are so crazy. You better leave them kids alone. They just need a father figure and I nominate you Robert Bellamy to fill that void." Clara laughed out loud causing the girls to turn again and look in her direction.

"Shit. I'm serious." Robert said still laughing.

"I'm ok with whatever you want to do. We are family and I'm glad we are in a position to help Jocelyn."

"That's what I love about you. You are so giving but I'm giving her all of the insurance money from Nanny's estate so she should be good for a while. I'll call you when I land tomorrow." Robert was tired.

After Clara got off the phone she briefed the girls about Jocelyn relocating. That was one of the evenings that Jaxon stopped by the house on his way home from work. The ladies all noticed that he was acting *weird*.

"Have you been drinking?" Gertie asked in front of Clara and Savannah.

"Hell naw girl." He snapped. "I'm just tired."

"Oh ok. I'm sorry but you are acting a little weird. Are you still taking those pain meds?" Gertie whispered as she pulled Jaxon away from where Clara and Savannah were sitting.

"Yeah. I need them." Her line of questioning annoyed him.

"I thought the doctor would not give you any more pain pills so you must have gotten more from somewhere else. *Please* stop taking them." Gertie pleaded.

"She has a valid point Jaxon." Clara said overhearing their conversation.

"Why are ya'll trippin'? I only take the pills when my legs hurt. I'm not addicted." He swiftly grabbed his keys from the table and left in a huff without making contact with Marcus as intended.

———◆———

Robert returned home on a mission. He had helped get Jocelyn set up in her new place in Biloxi and now he needed to find suitable housing for her in California. He shared with Chief Dandridge that he was searching for a place when Dandridge told him that he owned rental property north of the San Fernando Valley.

"It's a 4 bedroom home in West Palmdale. It's a little far from where you live in Ladera but you should make a drive out there and take a look at the property." Dandridge suggested. "I'm going to rent it out for $1550 per month but I can be flexible for you my brother."

"That sounds real good bro." Robert said as he and Dandridge chatted over drinks at their favorite watering hole Little John's. "That's very affordable *and* the house looks really nice from the pics you showed me."

"I'm glad you approve my brother. I grew up in that house and my mama, who was also a single parent like your sister, took great care of the property. Mama's getting up there in age so I moved her in with me about a year ago and I'm still getting the house ready to rent out. I have been taking my time. They are really building up out there in Palmdale and adding some great restaurants and stores so I think she will like it out there."

"You don't have to sell me on the house man. My sister is coming from a country ass area in Mississippi so I think she will be ok living in Palmdale."

"Ok. Well if you are sure you want it..."

"Yes man. I'm sure I want it." Robert said interrupting Dandridge.

"Then I can have it ready in a few weeks. I will go ahead and have it painted *and* have the new carpet installed." He said happy to help his friend, and relieved that he didn't have to look for renters.

"Man, thank you so much. I feel so bad that Nanny went out like this, and that Jocelyn has to uproot her family due to the devastation caused by this damn hurricane." Robert said tearing up.

"Yeah. Mother Nature is something else." Dandridge said reaching over to give Robert dap. "But don't worry about it man I got you."

Jocelyn was happy to find out that there were several job openings at Walmarts throughout Southern California. She couldn't wait to share the news with Robert.

———◆———

It had been a few weeks since Gertie and Karisma talked Taylor into applying for the LAPD.

"Hey Gertie. What's up?" Taylor asked.

"What's up with you? You sound like something is wrong. I can call you back."

"No. I'm sorry. I'm just in my head I guess. Backgrounds disqualified me from continuing on in the LAPD process, talking about I might have *suicidal tendencies* from that time I went to the hospital when we was in college. They saying I need to be further assessed by the Department Psychologist before they can let me continue on in the process."

"Oh shit. Are you serious?" Gertie had forgotten all about Taylor's sleeping pill episode. "I wonder who told them about that incident because I sure didn't." Gertie assured Taylor.

"*I* told them…"

"What?" Gertie interrupted. "Why did you tell them about that?"

"Because *you* told me that omitting information was the same as lying. One of the questions on the Psych Eval asked if I had ever done anything resulting in police response and I answered *yes*. When the analyst asked me about it during my interview, I told her about *that* incident. Man I fucked up huh?"

"No." Gertie said abruptly. "You did the right thing. I'll call and talk to Lieutenant Torrance and get some advice from her. Don't worry ok? I was just calling to check in on you. I did not expect this was going on. Why didn't you call me?"

"I was embarrassed. So do you think the Lieutenant will talk to *you* about *me?*"

"I don't know, but she told me if I ever needed *anything* to call her. Well damn it I need some information for my BFF so I'm calling her. I'll hit you up after I talk to her."

"Ok. That's what's up. I feel better already. Thank you." Taylor was happy that Gertie had called after all.

"No problem. On another note have you talked to Jaxon lately?"

"Yeah. He called the other day all hyper and shit. Talking about he's training with some guys from Metro because he wants to eventually get into SWAT." Taylor laughed.

"Oh really? Mmm." *That's probably why he's been taking more pain medication.* Gertie thought to herself. "Ok well I'll talk at ya later." Gertie wondered why Jaxon had not mentioned his Metro workouts to her.

"Wait. Are ya'll ok?" Taylor asked surprised by Gertie's question.

"Yeah. Yeah we are ok. I just wondered if you had heard from him that's all."

"Alright then. Talk at ya later." Taylor said ending the call.

During Gertie's early months at Northeast she mostly worked the front desk or the Report Car. When she worked the front desk she made routine notifications to Detectives, or directed citizens to the Detective section. She took every opportunity to hang out in the squad room especially when she was working the Report Car. She would secrete herself in a corner at an empty desk and complete her reports without all of the interruptions by officers in the Report Writing Room. She loved the camaraderie in the Detective section and hoped that one day she could join their ranks.

Gertie worked diligently on refining her skills in Patrol. She was the first responder at several crime scenes; some of which were high profile, where she was oftentimes tasked with notifying Detectives about the various incidents. She was barely off of probation so she figured it would be a very long time before she would have an opportunity to actually work in a Detective assignment but she still took time to foster some relationships and learn the lay of the land.

On most occasions when she ended up in Detectives she asked for advice, and for direction in completing her investigations. It was on one of those days while back in Detectives that the Kit Room Officer, Bobby Boon, gently tapped her on the shoulder.

"Oh hey Boon." Gertie was startled by the contact. "What's crackin'?"

"Girl, Communications been trying to contact you. You don't show out to the station." He said with a toothpick extending from the side of his juicy lips.

"Oh shit!" She exclaimed under her breath as she scrambled for her radio. "*11U1 show me out to the station.*" Gertie said quietly into the radio.

"Roger 11U1." The dispatcher responded loudly. Gertie's radio was loud. "11U1 please see the watch commander."

"Roger ma'am." She said turning the volume down so she didn't disturb the detectives.

Gertie jumped up and darted out towards the watch commander's office leaving her reports scattered all over a squad table.

"Yes sir." Gertie said when she reached the watch commander. She was out of breath.

"What you got going on kid? Communications Division has been broadcasting you as Code 1 for a while now. You obviously forgot to show yourself out to the station."

"I sure did. I'm so sorry sir I have been in Detectives for a little while completing my reports. But I'm Code 6 now."

"Well go back there and check in with Detective Martin in Homicide. He needs a female arrestee searched."

"Yes sir!" She said as she hurriedly walked away relieved that that was all he wanted with her.

Detective Phillip Joseph Martin or PJ, was the Detective 3, Homicide Coordinator in charge of the team of homicide Detectives there at Northeast. He ran a tight ship and was lovingly referred to by his Detectives as *Big Poppa* even though he was not really a big man. He was a tall bald caramel colored specimen and very much easy on the eyes. He was a no-nonsense, but caring boss and he was an amazing investigator with a wide variety of Detective experience but Homicide was his specialty. When Gertie approached the Homicide Unit she observed Detectives around a squad table separating and sorting through all types of personal property or evidence so she was tentative in her approach.

"I'm looking for Detective Martin." She said tapping Detective Loren Baldwin lightly on the shoulder.

"Yeah." Baldwin said turning sharply to look at her. "What do you need?"

"Uh…" Gertie stammered. "The watch commander sent me back here to see Detective Martin."

"PJ!" Loren yelled across the squad room turning away from Gertie.

She looked around and spotted a well dressed male black Detective stroll towards them holding a female arrestee by her bicep pulling her along.

"Sir, the watch commander sent me back here to see you." She said standing tall as PJ approached.

"*Sir?* Don't call me that shit. My name is PJ."

"Oh. Ok. PJ sir. I mean PJ." Gertie said as she giggled.

"Ok *Bellamy*." PJ said slowly, looking at her shiny name-plate. "I need you to search my arrestee. Have you done this before?"

"Yes sir a few times. This is a felony search right?" She asked.

"Yes. Ok then girl. I mean *Officer Bellamy*. Handle your business." PJ chuckled.

PJ and Gertie walked a short distance to the nearest women's restroom in the front lobby of the station.

"Go on in and clear the restroom." He ordered still hold-ing on to the arrestee.

Gertie walked in and peered underneath each stall and pushed open each door and visually *cleared* each stall. She then returned to the hallway and took the arrestee from PJ's grasp and stepped back inside the empty restroom while he stood guard just outside the door.

Gertie put on some rubber gloves and gave the arrestee step by step instructions. The arrestee handed her clothes to Gertie one piece at a time as directed. Gertie checked each clothing item carefully before dropping them onto the floor. Once the arrestee was completely naked Gertie continued on with her commands. "*Stick out your tongue; lift it up; run your fingers through your hair; turn around, bend over, reach around and spread open your vagina.* Gertie then bent over and peered inside the arrestee's crevices, which is when she noted the clear baggie partially secreted inside the woman's vagina. Gertie directed her to remove the baggie and hand it to her. Gertie was grossed out. She thought the strip search was very humiliating for arrestees and she hated the process for herself even more but it had to be done and now she totally understood why. *This bitch has drugs on her* Gertie thought.

"Here you go Detective PJ." Gertie said as she handed the arrestee over to him with one hand and the small cellophane baggy containing a white powdery substance with the other hand.

"Well damn?" PJ said shaking his head and holding the baggy up in his gloved hand away from his face. "You know what this is right?"

"No. Not exactly but it looks like Cocaine." Gertie responded.

"Yup that's what it looks like but we have to test it to be sure. It could be Crystal Meth. We'll see." PJ said after securing the arrestee in a nearby holding tank.

PJ was happy to finally see another black female police officer at Northeast. There had not been one there in Patrol for several years. Gertie was thrilled that she had personally met a real Detective up close and personal and he seemed cool but she was intimidated by his bravado. He invited her to watch him perform the preliminary test on the drugs, which in fact tested positive for Cocaine. She was in awe watching as the Q-Tip changed colors signifying a positive reading for the narcotic. PJ released Gertie, booked his arrestee and had Loren book the narco.

Gertie returned to her reports still spread out across the squad table just as she left them. Ever so often she looked up and saw PJ walking around the squad room barking out orders and laughing and talking with his sidekick Loren and others in the office. She didn't know if she liked him just yet because he was very curt and he cursed like a sailor, but she was impressed by his status if nothing else.

———•———

Things at home with Jaxon were shaky at best. He was still evasive about his whereabouts from time to time but he readily admitted to his extracurricular activities when Gertie asked him.

"Yeah I have been going to Pay Day Wednesdays after working out with the Metro guys." He said.

"So why didn't you just tell *me* that? I had to hear from Taylor that you are working out with the SWAT guys and hanging out at Pay Day Wednesdays. I've heard about the groupies who also hang out up there. I don't want any drama because I know how you are."

"What you mean you know how *I* am? I ain't doin' shit with nobody. I'm just hangin' out with the fellas."

"Ok. Well if we are going to coexist on this Department we have to be open and honest about what we are doing." She said lightly punching him in the shoulder.

"Aww girl you ain't got nothin' to worry about." He said blocking his midsection from her playful jabs.

———•———

It had been a couple of months since the horrific hurricane touched down in Mississippi leaving devastation in its wake and uprooting Jocelyn and her boys. Robert still could not believe his Nanny was gone. Every time he checked in with Jocelyn they ended their call in tears.

"So the government *is* buying my house brother because they are planning a low income condominium community in that area." Jocelyn reported to Robert. "I'm so glad we are coming out there because I can be close to you *and* get a fresh start."

"Well thanks to my friend, I have a rental house for you. It's really nice too. So what's happening with your job transfer?"

"Looks like they got two Super Walmarts with Manager positions available in a place called *West Palmdale*."

"Oh wow, that's exactly where my friend's rental property is located."

"Ok. Well now that you got me a house out there I'll tell my boss I will take one of them jobs in Palmdale."

"That is a clear sign that Palmdale is *the* best housing option for you and the boys. God is good."

"Yes indeed he is. All the time." Jocelyn said. "I guess I'll get these gold fronts taken off since I'm coming to California. I don't wanna embarrass you."

"Yeah that's a great idea because that's some country shit right there sis. They don't do that here in Cali. That's some dirty south hood shit." Robert said.

"Ha ha ha! You have always been so bougie brother." Jocelyn said as she laughed hysterically.

"I'm just glad you and the boys are coming out." Robert said.

———◆———

Taylor was finally cleared to start the November class. She was so ready to leave Gold's Gym and get a real paycheck *and* real benefits. She had prayed for a job with good medical benefits.

"Lieutenant Torrance assured me that you would get in. Your revaluation revealed no tangible evidence of mental illness or suicidal tendencies so the Department approved your Appeal and is moving you forward in the process." Gertie said. "I'm so glad that I reached out to her and that she kept her word to help."

"That's what I'm talking about. Girl I *need* this job. I'm so tired of this raggedy ass personal trainer shit. Half the people I see whine more than they work out. I can't stand it so thank you Gertie."

"Are you up for this challenge?"

"What challenge?" Taylor asked.

"For this Academy crap? It's not bad but the Academy is designed for you to fail. I know you are tough but you can't let them get to you. I'm so excited for you. Finally the Three Amigos are going to be back together again. Woo hoo!" Gertie exclaimed.

"Three Amigos?"

"Duh! You, me and Jaxon!"

"Oh. Yeah! Duh." Taylor laughed.

———————

Gertie thrived in the field and developed a great relationship with Detectives PJ and Loren but it was her outstanding report writing skills and detailed preliminary investigations, as reported by her Training Officers and Detectives, that got the attention of higher ups.

"Bellamy! Come here when you get done." PJ yelled when he saw her in the squad room one day talking to Detective Marisol Ramirez, the Detective 3 in charge of the Sexual Assault Table. It was late in the afternoon so the squad room was pretty deserted.

"Yes sir." She yelled back before returning her attention to Detective Ramirez.

"I'm going to talk to the Lieutenant and see if I can get you back here on loan to help us with this serial sexual assault case we are investigating." Marisol said in her thick Spanish accent.

"Oh ok. That would be great. Thank you ma'am." Gertie was surprised by the offer with her being so new to the Division.

"Don't get too excited." Marisol scolded. "I'm only asking for *you* because I need a female investigator because I believe the women at the strip club would be more comfortable talking to a woman and you conducted a couple of the preliminary investigations on my cases and they were very thorough with great follow up possibilities. One of my Detectives is off on Bonding Leave so you are the best bang for my buck."

"Oh ok. Thanks ma'am."

"After our Deployment Meeting the Watch Commander will let you know if you are coming back here or not." She said without looking up from signing a stack of reports.

"Yes ma'am." Gertie made an about face when Marisol was done then she scurried over to PJ's desk.

"Sir you needed to see me?"

"Yes. What did *she* want with you?" PJ asked.

"To tell me I might be coming back here to work for her on some investigations."

"Umph." PJ uttered. "Watch out for her. She can be messy."

Gertie didn't know the dynamics between all of the Detectives but she was sure she didn't want to get mixed up in their squabbles. She was thrilled about the opportunity to work with Detectives and looked forward to working for a woman because she certainly appreciated *girl power.*

The Watch Commander wasn't happy about losing Gertie from Patrol and expressed his displeasure in the deployment meeting but ultimately Marisol won because solving the serial sexual assault case was more important than anything going on in the Division at that time according to the Bureau Chief. Later in the morning following the very heated meeting the Watch Commander notified Gertie that she was in fact going on loan to Detectives indefinitely, and that she should report to Marisol right away.

"You will be on a 5/40 schedule, which means Monday-Friday 8:30AM-5PM, weekends off. You got that Mija?" Marisol directed when Gertie went to see her.

"Yes ma'am. Got it." She responded.

"Report back here first thing Monday morning."

"Should I wear my Class A or Class C Uniform?"

"*Neither.* You need to wear *business* attire. No uniform. You hear me? Oh yeah, and none of them CFM's you young chicas like to wear." She said looking Gertie up and down noting her amazing figure.

"Oh ok ma'am… I will make sure that I am dressed appropriately."

Gertie literally ran into PJ as she walked into the break room right after leaving Marisol. He had coffee in one hand and a Butterfinger candy bar in the other. She stopped just in time to avoid a collision with him.

"Damn it! You almost made me spill my shit." PJ barked sitting his cup down on a nearby table and straightening his tie. "What's up with you young lady? I mean *Bellamy.* I understand that you are definitely coming back to Detectives on loan." He said taking a big bite from his crunchy Butterfinger leaving orange crumbles all up in his meticulous mustache.

"Yes sir. I just met with Detective Ramirez about my new assignment."

"Yeah the Watch Commander did *not* want to let you go, and our Lieutenant reluctantly agreed to let you come back talking about you are *too new* to the Division and there are others more deserving of the break from Patrol but she agreed to let you come back after Marisol convinced her. You know the Lieutenant and Marisol are good friends and classmates. I can't stand Marisol's ass. She is unhappy and doesn't like *anybody* so you better watch your back." PJ warned as Loren stood off to the side shaking his head in agreement. PJ was very intolerant of Marisol as she was always creating unnecessary tension throughout the entire squad room with *everyone,* sworn and civilian.

"Don't get me wrong you should take her up on the opportunity to work Detectives but just know she is *not* to be trusted." Loren added.

"Oh wow. Ok. Thanks for the heads up guys. So, I need to ask y'all something."

"What do you need?" PJ asked picking up his coffee.

"What are CFM's?"

"Ha ha ha!" PJ broke out into laughter. "*Whaaat?* Who said anything about CFM's?"

"Detective Ramirez told me to wear business attire but no CFM's." Gertie was puzzled by his laughter.

"CFM stands for *Come Fuck Me* referring to very high heel women's pumps!" He responded still laughing hysterically.

"Why would she think I would wear *those* and what *you* know about CFM's?" Gertie asked.

"Girl, don't play with me. My baby wears the hell out of some CFM's when we playin' around at home." PJ said taking a sip of his coffee as Loren walked out of the break room.

Gertie and PJ laughed for a few more minutes as they engaged in small talk when they spotted Lieutenant Bettye Lane, a tall dark skinned woman with big hips, walk past the door, back up and poke her head into the break room. She was very well dressed in a skirt suit with a crisp white shirt and low heel pumps. She wore a short pixie wig, which framed her perfectly round face nicely. She was fairly attractive but thought she was cuter than she was.

"PJ, can you please stop by my office when you are done?" Lane asked looking Gertie up and down and then back at PJ with a fake grin on her face.

"Sure L.T. I'll be right there." PJ said coldly as he slowly balled up his candy wrapper and tossed it in a nearby trash can. He wiped the crumbs from his mustache before heading out.

"Whew. She seems mean." Gertie whispered to PJ after Lane walked away.

"Did you see how she looked at you but didn't really acknowledge you? Actually her bark is bigger than her bite. But she is still a hot ass mess too." He said shaking his head.

"Really? Ok." Gertie left the break room looking in each direction hoping not to run into the Lieutenant again.

"Be good." PJ said as he followed her into the hall. "I will see you bright and early on Monday...*Detective!* Hey. Hey. Hey." PJ yelled.

"Yes?" Gertie stopped abruptly and turned to see what he wanted.

"Don't be late!"

Gertie waved with a huge grin on her face. *He's a cool dude.* She thought as she hurried to the locker room. PJ walked past Lane's door and on to his desk where he prepared to go end of watch then he remembered that she wanted to see him so he grabbed his things and headed back to her office.

"Hey L.T. What's up?" He asked nonchalantly pushing her door all the way open.

"Oh hey PJ." She said as she watered the small plants behind her desk. "Have a seat."

"Nah. I'm good." He was ready to go home.

"I just wanted to pull your coat tail..."

"Pull my coat tail? About what?" He asked interrupting her.

"Well, I have been hearing *people* talking about you and Officer Bellamy."

"Me and Officer Bellamy? Why?" He was instantly annoyed.

"PJ, it's not that serious..." Lane started.

"Well then why are you *pulling my coat tail* if it *ain't that serious*? What asshole is talking shit and why don't they come to me with this crap?" He asked shaking his head. "I can't fucking talk to anybody without these motherfuckers around here starting shit. Are you kidding me? First of all, my wife is on this damn job and I have nothing but respect for her *and* that young woman." He said laying his things on a nearby chair.

"I'm just telling you *people* are talking. Apparently Bellamy's always back at your desk so I just thought I would let you know what they are saying." Lane went from watering her plants to feather dusting her credenza without making eye contact with PJ.

"Please do me a favor L.T."

"What?" Lane asked turning to look at PJ.

"Please leave my *coat tail* alone because I am not doing anything wrong. This is a bright young woman who happens to be an attractive black female, *and* she just happens to talk to me, a black motherfuckin' Detective." He was flustered. "Nobody ever says anything about the little bottle blond Community Relations Officer who is always all up Loren's ass huh? I guess *that's* ok because she's a perky little kiss ass. So you can miss me with all that bullshit. If you want to take a complaint, then go for it otherwise I got murders to solve."

"Calm down PJ. I'm just telling you what I'm hearing because she will be working back in Detectives soon and I need to make sure nothing is going on. I don't want any sexual harassment type issues." She said not commenting on his profane rant.

"But you *know* me and you know my wife, and I don't fuck around so instead of you promoting this type of bullshit you need to just shut it down. I know where it's coming from." He said pacing back and forth in front of Lane's desk. "I believe Marisol is starting *this* shit. Isn't she?"

"I didn't say that..." Lane offered.

"You don't have to! You *and* Marisol are just jealous of this hot young thang." He said shaking his hips, and his finger in Lane's face and laughing as she backed her face away from his finger. "I definitely ain't got time for none of Marisol's bullshit and I can't believe *you* jumped right on her band wagon but I hear you loud and clear L.T. Can I please be excused now?" He asked as he picked up his things from the chair.

"I didn't mean to piss you off. You know I totally respect you and appreciate your leadership."

"Well then you of all people should not be entertaining these types of rumors. You had a damn fit when your domestic violence incident took on a life of its own *and* when people here were talking shit about you getting your ass beat by that weed head husband of yours. Instead of allowing the rumors to persist I shut that shit down and protected you and your reputation as much as I could." PJ reminded her. "So you need to shut Marisol down when she starts spewing this nonsense. I ain't got time for this. Now I gotta go for real unless you paying me overtime."

PJ saw through bullshit like no other so Lane had no choice but to back down when he went off on her about his *perceived* inappropriate relationship with Gertie. He wasn't having it. Lane didn't expect him to peep her hole card so quickly but he was exactly right in his assessment. Marisol had gone to Lane right after the Deployment Meeting and expressed concern about Gertie being a little *too friendly* with PJ and Loren. He knew without a doubt that she was behind this drama and he was right.

———————

Gertie couldn't wait to tell her dad about her new job opportunity. She figured Jaxon would be envious of her amazing new assignment but she still needed to tell him also.

"That's amazing!" Clara exclaimed when Gertie told her the news. Robert was sitting close by.

"I'm going to stop by Ross and TJ Maxx on my way home before I pick up Marcus ok? I have to get some low heel shoes and panty hose for my required *business attire*."

"Ok take your time. We will be here." Clara said. "I'm so excited for you. Your dad says congratulations and he will see you when you get here."

"Ok! See you guys in a little bit. I'm going to call Jaxon now."

———————

"Hey. Are you on your way to work?" Gertie asked excitedly.

"Yeah. I *just* finished my workout." He responded nonchalantly.

"Guess what?"

"What?"

"I'm going to Detectives next month." Gertie exclaimed.

"For what?"

"I'm going to be temporarily working the Sexual Assault Table." She shrieked, barely able to contain herself.

"Ok but why are *you* going there?"

"To *work*…Jaxon. They requested that I go on loan to help with a serial rape case because one of their Detectives is off on Bonding Leave." She was annoyed by his hint of an attitude. "Just like you are all hyped about going to Metro I'm just as excited about working Detectives and you know that. I thought you would be happy for me getting this opportunity so soon. Anyway I can see that you are not so I'll talk to you later." She said preparing to hang up the phone.

"Why are you trippin'?" Jaxon asked hurriedly before she could hang up. "What do you want me to say? I *am* happy for you. I'm just rushing to get to work on time. I always seem to lose track of time when I work out that's all." He said trying to smooth things over. He really found it hard to mask his competitive spirit. Working Metro was a *lofty goal* for him at that point but her goal was coming to fruition.

———◆———

Monday could not come fast enough. Gertie got up bright and early and got dressed in her favorite dress and new low heel pumps with her hair slicked back and pulled into a low neat shiny bun. She felt officious. She kissed Marcus and Jaxon good-bye and happily drove into work.

"Damn Bellamy you clean up good girl!" Loren said admiring her business look when she walked into the squad room. "Hey boss, look at Bellamy."

"Where you get that damn church dress from?" PJ asked staring at her white Peter Pan collar. "Is that your idea of *business attire?*"

"What's wrong with what I'm wearing?" She asked looking down at her dress suddenly feeling embarrassed by her appearance. She *thought* her long flair dress with the lace collar and her short strand of white pearls was appropriate *business attire* until she looked around the room and noted that the female Detectives were wearing pant or skirt suits with button down blouses or sweaters.

"Nothing's *wrong* with what you have on. Actually you look really nice. It just looks like you on your way to church." PJ remarked patting her on her shoulder as he and Loren passed her on their way out of the office.

"Thanks." Gertie said under her breath as she slightly moved rebuffing his tap on the shoulder.

"You mad?" PJ asked stopping in his tracks when he noted her body language.

"Nah...I'm cool." She said with her head down.

"Well you look mad!" He remarked jokingly as he and Loren and other Detectives in the room laughed at his taunting. Even Marisol took pleasure in the banter. Gertie sat there fuming as she twirled a pen in between her fingers and stared off into space. *The nerve of this asshole to poke fun at me in front of all these guys* she thought as she watched out of the corner of her eye PJ and Loren walk out of the squad room. She got up as soon as they cleared the doorway, and went to the women's locker room where she sat by her locker for a few minutes trying to gather her thoughts. She was angry and it was only the first day. After a few minutes of solitude she regained her composure, took a deep breath and went back into the squad room ready to work.

"Are you ok?" Marisol asked displaying some compassion.

"I'm fine ma'am. I'm just happy to be here." She professed, mustering a fake half smile. *Maybe I shouldn't buy into what PJ is saying about her* Gertie thought. "Thanks for this opportunity ma'am." She said looking Marisol in the eye.

"You are very welcome Mija. Hey don't let these guys get to you. They really don't want *us* here but they better get used to us because we are here to stay baby. These guys can be such assholes." Marisol said as she retrieved a huge binder from the edge of her desk. "I'm going to give you all of these Crime Reports; Follow Up Reports and Chronological Logs to review to bring you up to speed on our sex assault cases from the strip club and when you are done with that I'll give you further direction."

"Is it just you and I working this case?" Gertie asked noting the empty desks all around her.

"Oh no. I don't carry cases. I am the *Coordinator* so I *supervise* and *manage* the Detectives on the table. You will be working with Detective Ruby Jones. She's on her long vacation." Marisol said handing Gertie a huge blue binder. Gertie felt a warm welcome from Marisol. She seemed nice enough but she was still going to watch her back like PJ and Loren warned. She was mad at PJ at that moment for clowning her but she believed he was just poking fun and not really being malicious. At least she hoped he wasn't.

Gertie and Jaxon's schedules finally allowed for them to take Marcus to school and pick him up without imposing on Clara too much. Jaxon dropped Marcus off on his way to work and Gertie picked him up on her way home, which provided Clara with a much break from her full time babysitting duties at least for a little while.

CHAPTER 9

"Double Duty"

———◆———

Jaxon's probationary period at 77th Division was almost over and he was ready to move on to a new division as he was fed up with how probationers were treated at 77th. He didn't like it when his old crotchety training officers, who had been in the south end for way too long, expected him to acquiesce to the beat downs they dealt to the underprivileged; and how they expected him to be ok with the poor customer service they provided on a regular basis to the law-abiding black residents in South L.A. He hated being referred to as a *sell out* by his people whenever he responded to calls for service where black folks were acting up and he was forced to take action. He was very much conflicted except when it was time to kick butt and take names, which is what he did with the asshole gang members and other punks who wreaked havoc in the neighborhood.

Finally the time had come. Jaxon transferred into Southwest Division after passing probation in one of the busiest and most dangerous areas of the City. He felt pretty invincible after surviving 77th Division and thought that he was prepared physically and mentally to work Metro but he was told by his work out buddies that it wasn't going to be that easy for him to get in the elite division.

———◆———

From day one Southwest had a different vibe than 77th. Instead of working the field on a regular basis Jaxon was oftentimes assigned to the front desk and on occasion assigned to work with probationary officers in the field when their assigned Training Officers were on days off.

The front desk at Southwest was extremely busy but not always due to citizens in need of help or assistance. Jaxon marveled at the cute police groupies who came into the station looking for officers to hang out with. They brought in food and pastries for officers to enjoy all the while trying to strike up personal relationships. Officers were notorious for turning those on duty contacts into off duty relationships, which were frowned upon by the Department. Those contacts usually weren't an issue until those dating situations went south and/or became toxic resulting in the women expressing their scorn by filing complaints against the officers for some type of mistreatment real or perceived.

The groupies knew the disciplinary system better than most officers they messed around with especially the young dumb cops who thought they knew everything. Most often when these complaints came in, the Department sanctioned the officers for *CUBO (Conduct Unbecoming An Officer)* primarily because they would have met the women while in the performance of their duties. All other alleged violations committed were dealt with *in addition* to the *CUBO*. The heavy make-up, tussled hair, real and fake, and the tight jeans and cleavage blinded Jaxon, just as it did his peer officers. In spite of those risky relationships some officers just couldn't resist all that temptation and many paid dearly for their indiscretions.

———◆———

South L.A. didn't offer a lot of safe and desirable dining options for officers in the field, so they frequented the local City contracted hospitals where the nursing staff welcomed them with open arms. The break room refrigerators were always chock full of bottled water, juices, prepackaged dry ass sandwiches and a variety of chips to fill the officers bellies while in a safe environment. There were always rooms full of officers resting their weary eyes while waiting for arrestees to be medically treated, or officers who simply stopped by for a much-needed respite from the field. Some officers routinely hid out at the hospitals and spent quality time with the nursing staff, especially on night watch.

When Jaxon was introduced to the hospital break room it became abundantly clear to him that many of the nurses there were actually officers' wives or mistresses. He thought that was way cool because he felt that same type of connection with the pretty sexy Police Dispatchers who cozied up next to him and other officers on Pay Day Wednesdays at the Academy.

———◆———

Jaxon's inconsiderate ways and irresponsible actions at home were a consistent source of frustration for Gertie. He acted like it was a chore to drop Marcus off or pick him up; housework was beneath him, his spending was out of control and he stayed out in the streets until the wee hours of the morning especially on his days off.

"I really think we need to go our separate ways." Gertie said one morning after a night of Jaxon's unjustified late night activities.

"I told you I'm trying to get into Metro so I *have* to get my workouts in and sometimes I have to go *after* work if I can't make it to the gym beforehand." Jaxon reasoned.

"I get that but you have a *family* and you need to spend some time with *us* and you need to *help me.* I feel like I'm raising Marcus with my parents and that's not fair to them. We don't go anywhere or do anything together and you don't do shit around here. Like the faucet in the spare bathroom has been broken for weeks and you keep saying you are going to fix it. I can't keep on like this." She was really fed up.

"Ok so what you want me to do?" He asked with his workout bag in one hand and his keys in the other. "I have been working a lot and I still help with Marcus when I can, *and* I don't remember you telling me the faucet was broken."

"Help *when you can*? Are you kidding me? And as far as the faucet you don't listen to anything I say and you are never here for me to remind you of anything."

"Ok I'll look at it tomorrow and I promise I will fix it or I'll call someone to have it fixed. I'm outta of here. I gotta go work out." He said bending down to kiss Marcus's forehead. He then leaned in to kiss Gertie but she turned away. "Oh so it's like that huh?" He asked leaning back staring at her. "I'll see you later then." He said walking out of the door.

Gertie was suspicious of Jaxon's late night activities and his lack-adaisical attitude was getting on her nerves. She knew that he had an insatiable appetite for sex and they weren't intimate that much so her gut told her he was definitely messing around. She didn't want to admit it but she was checked out too however, she wasn't going to be the one to end the marriage until she was able to figure out *how* she was going to make it by herself finan-cially. She followed Jaxon out into the garage with Marcus in her arms. She felt so lost. He watched as she slowly disappeared behind the garage door as it closed. He was going to one of his happy places.

———◆———

"Hey Jaxon. I haven't seen you in a few weeks." Alexa said when she spotted him sitting at the Academy Lounge bar drinking a beer. He was relaxed.

"Oh hey girl, yeah I've been on night watch so it's been hard for me to come here unless I'm on a day off like I am today." He said as he pecked Alexa on her soft cheek. "You are so damn sexy." He whispered pulling her closer in between his legs, looking at her from head to toe pausing ever so slightly at her big breasts.

"Boy!" She said as she chuckled slightly pushing his shoulder away from her as he pulled her closer to him. "You need to stop!" She exclaimed. She continued to giggle incessantly while slowly relaxing in between his legs. She felt comfortable there.

Alexa was a single mother of a 9 year-old boy. She didn't know who her son's father was and she had stopped her search long ago. She was a cute brown skinned, weave wearing hood chick with deep dimples on both cheeks and big pretty white teeth. She wanted a better life than her humble beginnings offered as a former welfare recipient, so she followed in her mother's footsteps after a little prodding and joined the LAPD family as a Police Dispatcher.

Alexa had great benefits as a Dispatcher, which allowed her to get those pretty white veneers on her front teeth to cover the huge gap she grew up with. Jaxon had flirted with her from the first day he started going to Pay Day Wednesdays. Although she wasn't nearly as pretty or as classy as Gertie, he thought she was *very* sexy and he imagined himself having kinky sex with her. She dressed provocatively all the time even when she was in her Flight Attendant style uniform. Her crisp white blouses always puckered in between the buttons, and her pants were always so damn tight they offered a pronounced camel toe from every angle. She left *nothing* to the imagination.

Alexa's non-uniform attire primarily consisted of low cut tops and tight low-rise jeans, which revealed the top of her thong whenever she slightly bent over. Her breasts and butt, both of which were ample, unlike Gertie's svelte persona, mesmerized Jaxon. She was determined to find herself a man and she didn't care if he was married. She often told her girlfriends that if the man didn't care about *his* marriage why should she? That was *his* problem not hers as she saw it.

"What you about to get into?" Alexa asked when she saw Jaxon check his watch more than once.

"I don't know. What about you?" He responded slyly looking her up and down occasionally licking his top lip.

"Well I'm waiting on my girls so we can have some drinks. Them bitches better hurry up." She said slowly scanning the room. "They should be here any minute... Oh speaking of the devil. There they are!" She said. When she spotted them walking towards the glass double doors from the Rock Garden. She quickly wiggled out from between Jaxon's legs.

Jaxon knew Alexa's dispatcher friends too but some of them were married, and some of them had made their rounds with dating various cops. This would be Jaxon's first rodeo with one of these fast-talking broadcasting vixens.

"Call me when you leave here and maybe I can stop by." Jaxon whispered to Alexa on his way out as she got settled in at the bar surrounded by her friends.

"Ok. Bye." She said nervously hoping her girls weren't paying them any attention.

"I'm gonna get out of here." He said loud enough for everyone to hear. "Don't forget to call me." He whispered to Alexa as he walked past her.

———◆———

Jaxon had not seen much of Moses and Deanna since he transferred to Southwest but he talked to them often on the phone. He told them about his ongoing issues with Gertie and used his *issues* with her as the primary reason he did not bring Marcus to see them. Truth was that he wasn't really trying that hard and when Gertie asked him to take Marcus to see his folks he always had an excuse as to why he *couldn't. Moses is sick; Mom's gotta work.* Blah. Blah. Blah. Excuses. Excuses. Gertie was tired of asking him and too ornery to take Marcus herself.

"I'm gonna go see my moms." Jaxon said when he called to check Gertie's temperature after leaving Pay Day Wednesday. "I might spend the night since I have to work so early tomorrow."

"Why do you *have* to go in early tomorrow Jaxon?" Gertie asked.

"I'm going out with Detectives in the morning to serve search warrants at a couple of gang locations in Lower Baldwin Hills."

"Oh ok. That's cool." Gertie said nonchalantly. "I'll see you when I see you then. I guess."

"I'll fix the faucet when I get home tomorrow. Ok?"

"You said you were gonna look at it *today* when you got off but that's not going to happen now that you have decided to go visit your folks." She said chuckling to herself and shaking her head. "Don't worry about it. Clara never cancelled the Home Warranty here at the condo so I will make a claim and have it fixed."

"Oh ok that's what's up." He said. He was relieved that he didn't have to fix it after all.

"Ok. I'll see you later." Gertie said sternly. She knew her marriage was over but still longed for his attention and most importantly his touch, which she hadn't felt in months.

"Don't trip. I'll get Marcus from daycare tomorrow and we will be home when you get off. Maybe we can go out for a bite to eat." Jaxon bargained.

"Yeah. Yeah. Yeah." Gertie said looking off into space with Marcus at her feet peering up at her. "Later." She said ending the call.

———◆———

Alexa couldn't wait to leave her girlfriends and call Jaxon to see what was up with him. She thought he was *fine* as did every other woman he came in contact with. There was definitely a mutual attraction and she hoped that her call to him would lead to a late night booty call.

"Hey what's up?" Jaxon asked walking into another room leaving Moses and Deanna watching TV in the tiny cluttered den.

"You told me to call you so here I am." Alexa said as she pulled her 1999 Datsun into her cracked driveway. She lived behind her mother's home in a two-bedroom guesthouse. It was actually pretty nicely done on the inside. It was like a bachelorette pad because most often her son stayed in the main house with her mom and her stepfather. "What you trying to get into?" She asked.

"What you want me to get into? You want some company?"

"You coming over?" Alexa asked.

"I can. If you want me to." Jaxon said getting excited at the possibilities that lay ahead of him. "Where you live girl?"

"I'm at 62nd and Gramercy Place. I'll text you my address. Are you coming for real? Don't play with me Jaxon."

"I ain't playing. Send me your address and I promise I won't stay long." He said.

"Pull all the way to the back house and park behind my car." Alexa advised.

"Ok I'll see you soon. I'll call when I'm outside so you can open the door."

Jaxon excused himself and told Moses and Deanna that he was heading home and that he would bring Marcus to see them real soon.

"Ok baby. It was so good to see you. I just hope that you and Gertie can get it together for Marcus's sake. Gertie is a good girl and ya'll really need to work through your issues." Deanna was concerned.

"Yeah son. You need to go on home and ya'll needs to talk through your issues. Life is too short and y'all got a good future ahead of you. You need to keep yo dick in yo pants and work it out wit yo wife."

"Daddy!" Deanna squealed. "What his dick gotta do with anything?"

"I wasn't born yesterday and I knows that when a man ain't happy at home instead of working shit out they goes out and complicates shit by fuckin' around and I hope you ain't doing that son." Moses warned.

"Pops." Jaxon said as he chuckled out loud. "I'm good. Gertie and I are going to work things out. I'm going home now. I'll call you guys tomorrow." He said as he bent down to kiss his old man on the forehead.

"I'll walk you out." Deanna said as she followed him to the door looking back at Moses shaking her head. He was a mess but *he was right*. She thought.

The two embraced at the door. Jaxon then jogged to his car parked at the curb as Deanna stood in the doorway watching him drive off. He called Alexa when he pulled into her driveway.

"Open the door. I'm outside." He said as he reached into the back seat for his duffle bag. By the time he turned back around he looked up and saw Alexa standing in the dark doorway of her house.

"Come on in." She whispered waving for him to hurry and come inside. "What's in the bag?" She asked as he passed her in the doorway. She wasn't expecting him to stay the night.

"My gun. Girl you know you live in the 'hood and I'm not about to leave my shit in the car. Besides, your baby daddy might show up and I might have to shoot a nigga."

"Oh you got jokes." She said as she closed the door behind him. "I ain't seen my baby daddy since my baby was a baby and he's 9. Anyway have a seat. You want something to drink?"

"Nah. I'm good. I had a few beers already and I'm trying to watch my intake while I'm training for Metro." Jaxon explained.

"Oh I feel you." She said as she bent down to light a candle on the coffee table in front of where he was sitting.

"Where is your son?" He asked looking around.

"He's up in the front house with my mama." She said.

"Ok. So basically you have your very own woman cave then huh?" Jaxon asked poking his head into the doors of the various rooms. "It's really nice in here. It's very deceiving from the outside."

"Why? Because it's in the '*hood*?" Alexa asked pushing Jaxon onto the couch.

She straddled him and put her arms around his neck as he sank further into the couch. She was bursting out of her white wife beater with side boob oozing out of both sides and her butt cheeks were bubbling out of her booty shorts. They wasted no time engaging in what would be the first of many trysts. They licked and sucked on one another for a couple of hours. She knew he was married to a cop but she didn't know his wife and didn't care to ever meet her. After all, his wife had what she wanted, him. In spite of their non-committed relationship they were like moths to a flame whenever they were together. Their visits were as often as their schedules allowed and their rendezvous' were always at Alexa's house.

Within a few short months Jaxon's nose was wide open. Pay Day Wednesdays were spent at Alexa's house instead of at the Academy. He didn't want to flaunt their relationship in that open environment for all to see especially since Gertie was on the job. After a several months of their routine Alexa started to ask more and more questions about the status of his marriage. She seemed obsessed with Gertie and always asked about her whenever she was around her sworn coworkers. Alexa wanted to know if they knew Gertie; what kind of person she was; *and* she was interested in knowing if they knew what Gertie and Jaxon's marriage was like. She was disenchanted whenever she heard good things about Gertie. People described how pretty she was and how she and Jaxon were the *cutest couple ever.*

"I already told you I'm trying to find the right time to leave her." Jaxon said with Alexa lying on his chest.

"Oh, so you want your cake and eat it too." She said rolling off of his chest and onto her side with her long wavy hair weave falling over her breasts. "I didn't sign up to be nobody's side chick *forever.* I want security for me *and* my son just like your wife has. I don't want to live behind my mama forever. I want my own place *and* I need a new car. So basically I want the same shit your baby's mama has." She said angrily as she sat straight up in bed drawing the sheet to cover her breasts.

"You know what? I'm not doing this with you." Jaxon got up and abruptly stepped into his underwear that lay on the floor next to the bed.

"You not doing *what?*" She asked snapping her head in his direction.

"I'm not going to have you putting pressure on me when you knew what *this* was when we got together. You knew I was married when we decided to *hook up* so why are you tripping now? I thought we were cool." He added getting dressed in a hurry.

"*Hook up?* Oh, that's all this is to you, a *hook up?*" Alexa asked as she jumped up from the bed draped in the top sheet. "I can *hook up* with a bunch of niggas out there but I been fucking around with your monkey ass. So why don't you go home to your perfect little wifey and leave me the hell alone!" She said following close behind Jaxon poking him in the back as he slowly walked towards the door. When he stopped to get his keys from the hall table she grabbed his duffle bag from the floor and threw it out of the front door.

"Hey! What the hell! When you calm down and come to your senses you call me." He said arrogantly as she lightly pushed him through the doorway. "I'm out." He said as he picked up his bag and turned and looked at her standing in the doorway wrapped in the bed sheet.

"Bye bitch ass nigga!" She screamed and then slammed the door.

———◆———

*2006-*Gertie was working out well on the Sex Table and was learning a lot. The serial sex assault case primarily involved Strippers working at a couple of Gentlemen's Clubs in the division. She had reviewed Crime Reports and Chronological Logs and had gleaned critical leads from them, which she pointed out to Marisol.

"Ma'am, I was reviewing this Chrono entry and I see where Robbery Homicide Division (RHD) notified the

Investigating Officer of DNA results that came in a few weeks back but there is no mention of the results ever being picked up or reviewed." She advised standing over Marisol pointing to the document as Marisol took the report from her and read the entry for herself.

"Good job Mija." Marisol said after reading the entry and those that followed. "You are right. It doesn't look like there was any *follow up* to that entry. I need you to call RHD and set up a time to go there and pick up the report." She directed. She was impressed with Gertie's attention to detail but disappointed in her seasoned investigator whose case it was.

"Right away ma'am. Do you mind if I go to the graduation at the Academy while I'm out?" Gertie asked expecting Marisol to decline her request. "My friend from college, who I recruited is graduating today and I told her I would try to make it if I could."

"Of course Mija. Just make sure that you put yourself Code 6 so that Communications is not looking for you." She said looking Gertie up and down.

"Thank you so much ma'am. I promise I will go Code 6 and I won't be there long." She said as she backed away towards her desk.

"By the way, you look really nice. I *love* your suit. Very tasteful." Marisol said like a proud mama sending her child off to school on the first day.

"Oh thanks! I went shopping in my step mom's closet. She has great taste." Gertie said as she put her jacket on and walked towards the Kit Room to check out a squad car and radio.

Taylor looked amazing in her uniform with her neatly done corn-rows tucked beneath her hat. She was tall and lanky and looked confident as she prepared to march onto the field with her class-mates. Her 6 months in the academy were uneventful. She was in shape, and an outstanding shooter so she did not encounter the issues Jaxon or Gertie faced with their physical fitness and shooting debacles. Taylor was embarking on a great career and was looking forward to her new journey as a Los Angeles Police Officer alongside her best friends. Her foster dad took time out of his busy schedule to attend her graduation. After all, she routinely stopped by Lynwood High School whenever she could to support him in his coaching and mentoring endeavors. She hadn't heard from her foster mother since the divorce.

Taylor spotted Gertie in the crowd and waved her arms to get her attention. Gertie responded likewise when she saw Taylor's skinny arms waving in the air.

"Man I am so glad to be out this bitch." Taylor said as she and Gertie embraced.

"Yo, I want some!" Jaxon ran up behind the two women and embraced them both. "Group hug! Damn man you made it *and* you coming to Southwest with me. That's what I'm talking about." He said as they dispersed from their group hug. "Hey babe." Jaxon said turning towards Gertie. He leaned in for a personal hug and a quick peck on the lips to Gertie's surprise.

"Hey Jaxon." She responded as she slightly pulled away trying not to be too obvious. "I didn't think you were going to make it since you have to work tonight." She said with a side eye. "But I'm glad you did." She faked being pleasant.

"Man, I don't know if I want to be at the same division with you Jaxon. You gonna be clownin' me and shit and I gotta take it because I'm on probation." Taylor said as the three of them laughed.

"Girl, I'm going to watch out for you." He said like the big boy on campus. "Southwest is no joke. Are you ready?"

"I guess." Taylor quipped. "Shit if you can do it anybody can!"

"The three amigos are back together again! That's what I'm talking about." Jaxon exclaimed.

Taylor had not been around to witness *all* the changes that had occurred in Gertie and Jaxon's relationship but she picked up on the shade Gertie threw Jaxon that day.

"I have to go." Gertie said. "I need to go to RHD to pick up some DNA evidence." She boasted.

"What's RHD?" Taylor asked fanning with her hat. It was unseasonably hot for May.

"Yeah Ms. big shot, what's RHD?" Jaxon asked jumping on the bandwagon.

"Shut the fuck up Jaxon." Gertie said. "It's *Robbery Homicide Division* and I'm just a gopher so don't get it twisted I'm no *big shot*. I'm just telling you guys what I'm doing."

"I feel you sis. Thanks for the explanation." Taylor said cutting her eyes at Jaxon.

"I wasn't being funny. I'm really proud of you. At least you are working Detectives and that's huge so don't be so sensitive pretty girl." Jaxon added.

"Ok." Gertie said softening her tone. She hugged Jaxon and Taylor and left them standing on the field.

"What's up with you and Gertie?" Taylor asked Jaxon as Gertie walked away. "I haven't talked to you guys much but I know yo ass and I'm sure you have done something to piss her off."

"She be trippin' man." Jaxon said shaking his head looking to make sure Gertie was still walking away. "She be nagging me too much about *everything*. You remember how she was in college. She still doing that same shit so we be arguing and then I leave for a few days and go stay with my peeps to get away from her ass."

"Mmm hmm." Taylor said with a smirk on her face.

"What? You don't believe me? See you always take her side. Damn."

"I'm sure you haven't changed. You should have stayed a bachelor. Anyway, I better not hear no shit about you fuckin' around at Southwest. I'm going to be watching you Jaxon."

"Oh lord. Now I wish you weren't coming to Southwest. I thought you put in to go to Wilshire." He said rolling his eyes.

"Yeah I did but I'm the lowest shit on the totem pole so they sent me where they thought they needed me." She said. "But I'm cool with going to Southwest."

"Alright. I gotta go get a work out in before I head off to work." Jaxon said as he hugged her one last time.

"I'll see you at work in a few days. I'm off for the rest of the weekend and by the way I'm on day watch."

"Ok. Let me know if you need anything. Remember to wear a long sleeve shirt; have all of your shit and have your gear shined or you gonna catch hell." Jaxon warned.

"Damn nigga ok!" Taylor said jogging away backwards from him and into the crowd still mingling on the field.

———◆———

Jaxon hadn't seen Alexa in a few weeks and he was missing her body like crazy. After several weeks of his calls going straight to voicemail he was happy to see her one evening at Pay Day Wednesday. She ignored him when she first spotted him at the bar until she saw him joking around with a few of her coworkers. She then decided to join the group to see what the levity was all about. She was hoping that he was not pushing up on anyone else.

"What ya'll talkin' about over here?" She asked playfully.

"Hey you." Jaxon said trying not to look at her for too long. "We are just laughing about stupid shit. Hey why ya'll leavin'?" Jaxon asked the group as they all excused themselves one by one leaving him and Alexa alone. Alexa then took a seat at the bar in between Jaxon and Grayson, Jaxon's Metro mentor who started playing with Alexa's fake locks.

"Dude, will you please stop?" Alexa pulled away from Grayson.

"You weren't saying that last night." Grayson laughed out loud as he walked away hurriedly towards a group of his friends sitting at a nearby table.

"You wish." Alexa retorted as she grabbed her purse from the bar. "I gotta go." Alexa had a one-night stand with Grayson before she met Jaxon. She was bitter when she realized he wasn't interested in dating her so she hated when he showed up at Pay Day Wednesdays. She hoped he and Jaxon had not compared notes.

"You going to be home tomorrow?" Jaxon asked.

"You still married?" She responded as he walked closely behind her towards the exit.

"Oh here we go again. Yes, I'm still married and you know that. But I have something for you." He said following her into the parking lot.

"What time tomorrow? I have to go to a Parent Teacher Conference at my son's school after work but I should be home by 6:30 or 7. What's up?" She asked dryly.

"You'll see. I will stop by about 7:30." Jaxon said standing in the doorway of her driver's side door. "I think you will like what I have for you."

"Oh ok." She said as he backed away from the car allowing her to close the door.

Jaxon went home that night as happy as a lark because he had reconnected with Alexa. When he arrived at home Gertie was bathing Marcus.

"I got that." Jaxon said as he helped her to her feet and knelt down in her place beside the tub to finish bathing Marcus.

"To what do I owe this honor?" Gertie asked looking down at him. She noted he was happier than he had been in the past few weeks but she just chalked it up to endorphins kicking in from his recent workout.

"I'm going in a little early tomorrow." He warned.

"Why? What's going on? How early?"

"Don't worry I'll drop Marcus off at your dad's before I go in." He said. "I'm gonna get my work out in and go in to finish up some reports I didn't finish the other day." He revealed.

"What are you talking about? You can't hold on to reports for days like that." Gertie was stunned to find out he was not following the rules with such little time on the job. "Did you at least get report numbers so the reports show in the system?"

"Calm down. We do it all the time at Southwest because it's so busy there and they trying to cut down on the overtime so we have been allowed to hold on to reports until our next working day." Jaxon explained.

"Yeah but Jaxon you have been off for a few days now so clearly it's been longer than *the next day*." She shook her head in disgust. "That's so trifling." She said under her breath.

"You think you know everything just because you a big time fake ass Detective." He said as he wrapped Marcus in a towel and carried him to his bedroom to finish drying him off.

"You know what?" Gertie remarked standing in the doorway of Marcus's room. "I am sick of your smart ass comments about my job. They sought *me* out for this *fake ass* Detective assignment. I didn't go looking for it so I would appreciate it if you would keep your negative comments to yourself. I'm so sick of you!" She yelled looking at him putting on Marcus's pajama pants.

"Not now Gertie!" He said pulling Marcus close to button his shirt. "He don't need to hear this." He scolded as he tucked Marcus in bed and walked towards her partially blocking the doorway.

"Boy, please!" She exclaimed as he pushed her out of the door way and into the hallway. He closed Marcus's door behind him then proceeded down the hallway. "I'm keeping it real with my son! Kids are not stupid Jaxon. I'm not about to walk around here like some little perfect family and pretend that everything is hunky dory when clearly it's not!" She was angry.

"He's a kid!" Jaxon yelled as he tried to go around her in the narrow hallway.

"I know he's a kid." She said lowering her voice trying to calm herself down. "I'm going to bed." He said as Gertie allowed him to pass her. She returned to Marcus's room to make sure he was ok. She knelt beside the bed and said a quick prayer into the Power Rangers comforter then kissed her baby boy goodnight.

Gertie climbed up in the bed next to Jaxon who had just lain down after a very quick shower. She reached over to gently touch his shoulder when he pulled away with his back still towards her. She was trying not to go to bed angry as her dad had always suggested but when he rebuffed her contact she got angry all over again and said *fuck it.*

"You obviously have someone else." She said realizing he was no longer interested in being intimate with her. They hadn't had sex in months, and they argued more often than they didn't.

"Go to sleep." Jaxon said. "I told you I have to get up early."

CHAPTER 10

"OUT OF CONTROL"

———◆———

JAXON GOT UP BRIGHT AND early just as he planned. Gertie had already gone and taken Marcus to school. Marcus was in Pre-K at a school close to the house so it was convenient for Clara to pick him up when necessary.

Jaxon was happy he didn't have to get Marcus off to school that day so he took his time getting dressed and left the house a little earlier than usual. Instead of going straight to work he went directly to the Credit Union at the Academy.

"Hey Jaxon!" Audrey said as soon as he walked in. She was the Manager at the Academy Branch and she loved when her favorite clients came in and Jaxon and Gertie were two of her favorites.

"Oh hey Audrey. How you doing girl?" He asked when he saw her in the distance.

"I'm good. How's my girl?"

"She's good. I'll tell her you asked about her." He replied. He was being fake.

"Ok. Please do. I haven't seen her in a while." Audrey said noticing that Jaxon was waiting in line for a Loan Officer. "Sign in and someone will be right with you ok?" She offered as she turned to walk back to her office.

"Ok thanks." Jaxon said as he took a seat and waited nervously for the next available Loan Officer.

"How can I help you?" The jovial loan officer asked. Miranda was Audrey's most efficient Loan Officer, and dear friend.

"I want to apply for a car loan." He said in a low tone.

"Will there be a co-borrower on the loan?" Miranda asked getting her computer set up to look up Jaxon's account.

"Uh...no. I'll be the only one on the loan. I haven't picked out a car yet but I want to know how much I can get preapproved for. I want to finance the *whole* amount. It won't be an expensive car. Is that possible?" Jaxon asked.

"Of course. Based on your credit rating we can get you approved for $35-$40,000 by yourself. How's that sound?"

"Cool. Thank you." He was relieved that he could qualify for the loan without Gertie.

Jaxon completed all of the necessary paperwork; left the credit union after getting his loan approved and went right to work. He went to the locker room and retrieved his Posse Box containing the incomplete crime reports. There were *several* reports that needed to be completed. He still had a couple of hours before roll call started but he went ahead and got dressed early and *then* went into the messy Report Writing Room to complete the reports. He finished just in time to submit the reports for approval to the on duty Watch Commander before it was time for PM Watch roll call.

"Atwater, what are you doing here so early?" The Watch Commander asked accepting the reports from him. Lieutenant Thomas was a lazy old bastard who hated reviewing crime reports especially close to his end of watch.

"My Watch Commander let me hold on to these reports the other night to avoid overtime." Jaxon advised.

"You're only supposed to hold reports if you are working the next day. These reports are three days old." Thomas said as he angrily flipped through the reports looking at the dates. "Did you wait until today to get the report numbers too?" He asked.

"No sir. I got the report numbers before I went home the other day."

"Well that's good. At least you did that right. Next time don't hold so many reports, and definitely not for so many days." Thomas said as he shoved the reports in Jaxon's direction after signing them. He barely reviewed them. He didn't give a shit if they were correct. He was ready to go home.

"Yes sir." Jaxon said as he accepted the reports back. "Thank you sir." He said *mean muggin'* the L.T. as he turned and briskly walked away towards the Records Unit.

Jaxon dropped the reports off in Records and went in search of something to snack on before roll call. He sat at a small table in the corner of the big break room and called his Moms and Pops to check in with them and then he called Gertie.

"Hey." Jaxon said lighthearted as soon as Gertie answered the phone. "I just saw your girl."

"Who?" Gertie asked somewhat happy to hear from Jaxon.

"Taylor. She was at the gas pumps getting ready to go end of watch when I got here. She looked goofy as fuck!" Jaxon laughed.

"Ha ha ha! You're stupid Jaxon. "She looks goofy? For real?"

"Yeah because she's so fuckin' skinny. She needs to gain some weight to deal with these niggas out here in these streets." He added.

"I'm sure she will after she gets settled in the field. They ran like crazy in the Academy so she lost a lot of weight and she wasn't that big to begin with. Leave her alone." Gertie defended Taylor.

"Alright. I won't clown her to her face. Anyway I'm about to go to roll call. I'll see you tonight when I get home. Kiss my boy for me. Love you." Jaxon said before hanging up the phone.

"Ok. Be safe out there." Gertie said looking at the phone surprised by the stranger on the other end. *He's in a good mood* she thought as she hung up the phone.

Jaxon looked at his watch and realized he still had a few minutes before roll call so he made one more call.

"Hello there sexy."

"Hi Jaxon. How are you?" Alexa asked trying to contain herself. She was happy that he called but she tried not to sound too excited. "Are you still coming over tonight?" She asked quietly while monitoring radio calls at her work cubicle. She had just finished broadcasting a pursuit. She had a great voice for radio.

"Yes. I'm going to ask for an early out so I can stop by. Remember I have something for you."

"Ok I'll see you in a little bit then." Alexa said hanging up the phone. She had Jaxon right where she wanted him. She knew he couldn't resist all of her chocolate weave wearing sexiness for too long.

"Later." Jaxon said. He hung up and headed to roll call.

Jaxon approached his favorite Sergeant while waiting for roll call to start. He requested to be allowed to work the Report Car because he needed an *early out* to handle a *family emergency*. Sergeant Lewis was happy to oblige.

"So what time you trying to leave?" Sergeant Lewis asked.

"I need to leave by 7 sir."

"Ok. Just finish whatever reports you have *before* you go end of watch." Sergeant Lewis directed. "Lieutenant Thomas told me you turned in a bunch of late reports that you held onto for a few days. Dude, that can't happen again. Oh yeah, *and* you also need to return the narco evidence you checked out a couple of weeks ago for one of your Court cases. It came up on the Property Dispo Sheet as *Outstanding* for more than 30 days. Boy you are slippin'. Check in with me before you leave so I can make sure you did everything and I can sign you out."

"Yes sir and I forgot I still had the evidence envelope in my locker. I'll return it as soon as I come in tomorrow."

"No. You do that shit tonight before you leave or your little *family emergency* is gonna have to wait to be resolved." Lewis said as Jaxon went to walk away.

Jaxon couldn't get out of the station fast enough that evening. After checking out with Sergeant Lewis he drove right to Alexa's place. Her car was parked in the back yard near her front door as usual. He parked on the street and slithered down the long dark driveway back to her house. She came to the door wearing a sexy teddy and a robe slightly open.

"Girl put some clothes on." Jaxon quipped as he entered the house and closed the door behind him.

"Ugh that's rude." She said closing her robe and backing away from him.

"I'm taking you somewhere. Go put your clothes on. You need to hurry." Jaxon said with a shit-eating grin on his face. "Just throw something on real quick." He took a seat on the couch while she hurried towards her bedroom.

"Where are you taking me?" She yelled from the room as she squeezed into the tightest jeans she could find.

"Just get dressed."

"Ok. I'm almost ready." She said as she struggled to pull her sweater down over her boobs. "For real though, where are we going?" She asked. "I don't like surprises."

"Oh you will like *this* surprise." He assured her.

Jaxon led Alexa to his black BMW 5 Series with dark tinted windows. He opened the door for her and once she was inside the car he closed the door and ran around to the driver's side; got in and took off like a racecar driver.

"Whoa! Why you driving so fast?" Alexa asked.

"You'll see. Just sit back and relax. We will be where we are going in a few minutes."

The ride was short to Inner City Honda on Manchester. When he pulled into the parking lot a swarm of salesmen approached his shiny BMW just as he parked. He got out and talked to one of the salesman for a few minutes while Alexa remained in the car. She sneakily opened the glove box while eyeballing Jaxon and then quickly looked at his Vehicle Registration where she noted his Fox Hills address. She then looked back at the child's booster seat and shook her head. She was mad at herself for resuming their relationship but she was snapped out of her stupor when he tapped on her window.

"Get out. I need you to come with me and pick out a car." He said opening her car door.

"Stop playing Jaxon. Are you serious?" She tried hard to contain her excitement.

"I'm serious girl get out."

"Why are you doing this?" She asked as she stopped in her tracks before getting all the way out of the car. "I don't want no drama with you or your wife because I'm sure she doesn't know about this. Right?"

"*I* want to do this for *you*." Jaxon said standing over her. "Don't you worry about my wife. I'm just trying to find the best time to leave her. I mean I already asked her for a divorce. In the meantime I want to show *you* how much I *care about you*." Jaxon offered dangling that 4 wheel carrot in her face.

"Ok well if you are serious about moving forward with your divorce then I accept your gift. Lord knows I need a new car." She said as he pulled her the rest of the way out of his car.

It didn't take long for Alexa to pick out a brand spanking new, sparkling white, Honda Accord with black leather interior. After the deal was done Jaxon followed her back to her house and on the way there he called home.

"Hey sleepy head." Jaxon said.

"Hey you." Gertie responded. "What's up? What time is it?" She was awakened by his call.

"Uh…I'm going to be a little bit overtime but…but I'll be home early enough to take Marcus to school ok?"

"Ok. What did you guys get into tonight that has you working overtime *again*?" Gertie asked sitting up in bed. She had a funny feeling in the pit of her stomach but she didn't know what to make of it at that moment.

"Southwest is crazy!" He said excitedly. "We got a late arrest. Anyway I gotta go." He said as he pulled up in front of Alexa's house. "I'll see you in a few hours. I won't wake you up when I get home."

"Ok. I'll see you later. Be careful." Gertie said as she ended the call.

———◆———

Marisol mentored Gertie and took up for her whenever others in the office objected to her working in Detectives with such little time on the job. She was impressed with Gertie's work ethic and let her feelings be known.

"So, how is Bellamy *really* working out?" Lieutenant Lane asked during the monthly Deployment Meeting.

"Actually ma'am she is doing quite well." Marisol proudly reported. "She's a very smart young lady."

"When will Moselle return from Bonding Leave?" Lane asked.

"She was supposed to return next month but I just received an updated doctor's note putting her off for another 2 months, which puts me in a real bind because I have *another* Detective on his Long Vacation during that same time period. I really can't afford to lose Bellamy right now." Marisol complained.

"If I let you keep her another month we are going to have to give her bonus pay for working out of class for too long per her MOU so we might need to rotate her out and get another officer in to take her place." Lane advised.

"Oh no. I'd really hate to lose *her*. We have made some headway with the case that you are on my ass to solve. I hate to admit this but it's Bellamy who discovered the critical lead in Moselle's Chrono." Marisol added. "Also, shouldn't we be able to advertise for Moselle's Detective Trainee position since she'll be off for more than 6 months with this latest extension? I mean her baby will be damn near grown by the time she returns to work!" Marisol said as they all laughed.

"I think you're right." Lane agreed. "I'll have my Adjutant check with Position Control to see if we can advertise Moselle's Trainee spot since she will be gone for so long. I'm happy to hear that Bellamy is earning her keep." Lane said without looking up from her meeting notes.

"Yeah and for the record..." PJ started as he looked slowly around the room. "For the *asshole* who pulled the Lieutenant's *coat tail*, I'm not fuckin' Officer Bellamy.

"PJ…!" L.T. Lane scoffed as she looked up abruptly from her notes.

"Well you said *people* were talking. So, let's get this shit out on the table right now." He said landing his gaze on Marisol. "Somebody got something to say to me let's talk about it now." He said falling back in his chair with his arms folded.

"All I said was that Bellamy *seemed* a little *familiar* with you PJ and you know how this new generation is always screaming sexual harassment. That's the *only* reason I said anything." Marisol offered. "I brought it to the Lieutenant's attention to avoid any issues down the road."

"I *knew* you were behind this bullshit Marisol. I knew it! You really need to mind your own damn business, woman. I swear."

"Whatever PJ." Marisol said as she pursed her lips and started doodling on a piece of paper.

"*Whatever* my black ass. You just keep my name out of your mouth." He said. He was fed up with her *sneaky* ways over the years they had worked together.

"Ok guys come on. I'm sorry I said anything to you PJ. I should have just paid attention and only said something if *I* saw something myself." Lane was mad that PJ brought it up in front of the snitch.

"So, is that it? Are we done?" PJ asked gathering his things to get ready to leave.

"Almost PJ." Lane said. "Wait a minute…you know Lt. Pineda is going off to have surgery so I'm going to need you to provide oversight for the Gang Unit while he is off ok? Can you handle that for me?" Lane asked.

"Who's going off?" PJ was half listening because he was still miffed.

"*Gil.* Gil Pineda."

"Oh. Oh. Oh. Gil. Ok sure L.T. Whatever you need." He said regaining his composure. He never stayed angry for too long. "I'll go talk to Gil and have him bring me up to speed on his guys and what's going on in the unit that I need to know about."

"Cool beans." Lane said smiling at PJ. "Ok, *now* we are done. Marisol I will let you know if I'm able to advertise for Moselle's Trainee position and if so you can give Bellamy a heads up so she can get prepared for the Oral Interview since you like her so much. Before you do though, check and make sure that she is *eligible* to even apply for the position. She has such little time on."

"Ok. Will do L.T." Marisol agreed.

———◆———

Jaxon ended his call with Gertie and walked down the long dark driveway to Alexa's house. The hood on her new car was still warm to the touch. She had left the door unlocked for him to go in. The house was dark but he could see the dim light on in Alexa's bedroom. He heard the water running in the shower as he approached the bedroom door. When she saw his shadow she wiped the fog from the glass shower door and watched him standing in the doorway leaning against the doorjamb admiring her silhouette.

"Get in." She said poking her head out of the shower door. "C'mon." She said waving him in her direction.

"You ain't gotta tell me twice." Jaxon said as he quickly undressed leaving his clothes strewn about the bathroom floor.

"Thank you for my car." She squealed wrapping her arms around Jaxon's neck. "I love it."

"You're welcome sexy lady." He took the loofa from her hand and turned her around and started to wash her smooth back. When he reached the small of her back he dropped the loofa and slowly turned her back towards him. Jaxon pressed his slick body against hers away from the waterfall where they made out in the fog for a few minutes.

"Let's get out." He whispered with a tinge of guilt at the thought of Gertie turning over in their bed at home alone. He quickly shook off his thoughts of her at the sight of Alexa's naked body glistening under the dim light when she walked ahead of him and out of the bathroom.

"So what is the catch to me having this car?" She asked drying off. "You know you can't *buy* me." She warned.

"I'm not trying to *buy* you. You said you need a car so I want you to have a new car as a way of showing you how much I *care* about you." He said as he dried off while sitting on the side of the queen size bed that pretty much filled the small room. "Come here." He said as he baited her around the bed and into his open arms.

Jaxon and Alexa had sex for hours and in the heat of passion Alexa muttered *I love you.* He heard her but didn't respond to her utterance. He kept his rhythm until he was done then he rolled off of her and onto his back as she stayed lying on her back. She was low key fuming because she couldn't believe he had just bought her a car but he could not bring himself to say *I love you* back to her. She lay there quietly as he turned onto his side with his back towards her. After a few minutes he fell off to sleep. A little while later Alexa finally went to sleep too and just as she did she felt Jaxon sit straight up in bed.

"Oh shit! What time is it?" He asked picking up his cell phone from the bedside table and squinting at the screen.

"It's 3:45." He had three missed calls from Gertie. "Fuck

me! I gotta go. Shit. Shit. Shit." He said as he rushed around getting dressed in the dimly lit bedroom. "I never meant to stay here this long."

"Oh. I thought you were spending the night." Alexa said wiping the sleep from her eyes.

"Hell naw. You know I wasn't spending the night. Don't trip Alexa." Jaxon said. He was annoyed.

"Ain't nobody trippin'. I just *thought* you were staying since it didn't seem like you were in a hurry to leave." She said trying not to piss him off since he had *just* bought her the car. She really tried to contain her jealousy too. "So when am I going to see you again?"

"I don't know. I'll call you later." He said as he rushed out of the room.

Jaxon was happy to be back in Alexa's good graces but he was growing tired of her demands for him to leave Gertie; and she complained about him not openly expressing his *love* for her, so his visits became less frequent after that night of bliss in the shower. He soon realized that he needed to find *another* way to feed his sexual appetite because Alexa was getting stingy with the poo nanny.

Due to Alexa's change in shift from Day Watch to Night Watch, she and Jaxon switched up their routine and had their on again off again meet ups in the early afternoons before they each went in to work. Jaxon welcomed that change because he thought it was sure to rejuvenate their relationship.

———◆———

Gertie thought Jaxon's ego was out of control and her biggest pet peeve was that his alleged *overtime* hours did not correspond with an increased amount on his bi-weekly paychecks. She and Jaxon argued about that and everything else to the point that she gave in and started to look for evidence of his *fucking around*. She even used Taylor on occasion to spy on him at work. Taylor's reports were primarily that she saw him working hard in the field. Taylor was not aware of his relationship with Alexa or anyone else.

———◆———

Gertie was officially assigned as a Detective Trainee after she aced the interview with PJ and Loren's help. She was proud to go to work everyday sporting her new wardrobe thanks to Clara. She fell right into the fold in Detectives and was getting used to the jargon, and the protocol they employed during their daily routines. She loved how Detectives bantered back and forth with each other and came together on Search Warrants and other field activities, and unusual occurrences. For the most part they were a tight knit crew. PJ explained to Gertie that she needed to buckle down and pass the *damn Detective Exam* or she would lose her Trainee Position and have to return to Patrol.

"I can do that. I think. What do you think PJ?" Gertie asked.

"Shit. If your ass can't pass the test after four damn years in Detectives you deserve to go back to Patrol." He said. "I'll tell you what. When you need to know something or there is something you don't quite understand you need to come to me or Loren in private." PJ told Gertie. "If the Detectives back here know you don't know shit they will undermine you at every turn and try to make you look bad." He said. "Because you know they don't want you back here with your little time on the job."

"Oh damn. Ok. Gotcha." Gertie responded surprised by PJ's candor.

Gertie did exactly what PJ said and sought his advice relative to her follow up investigations. There was no way that she was going to ask Marisol for frivolous advice and chance being ridiculed in front of everyone as Gertie had seen happen with other more tenured Detectives. All in all the Detective Squad Room was still a great place to be.

Home was another story. When she wasn't at work she spent a lot of her spare time at her dad's house with him and Clara and Marcus and on occasion she commiserated with her girl Karisma over the phone or at Little John's during happy hour libations. Gertie was even developing a more solid relationship with Savannah who was a fan favorite on the Channel 5 News, which made Gertie proud.

"I don't know daddy." Gertie said shaking her head while talking to Robert and Clara at her dad's house one day after church. "I don't think me and Jaxon are going to make it."

"Only *you* know what's going on in *your* marriage so only *you* can call it when it's time." Robert said gently placing his overflowing coffee cup on the table before sitting back down with Clara and Gertie. "What's that nigga up to *now*?" Robert asked as Clara chuckled under her breath.

"Damn daddy, do I complain that much?" Gertie asked glancing over at Clara sipping her coffee and reading the paper.

"Girl, you don't have to complain. I'm living this shit right with you so I *see* what's going on. He's either late picking up Marcus, if at all; he doesn't come around us as much as he used to; he works all hours of the night and day, and when you all are together you argue about dumb shit. Did I miss anything?" Robert asked looking at Gertie over his glasses. "I'm sick of his ass too but I will not be a third party in *your* marriage. Just know I got you and I support whatever *you* decide to do."

"Thanks daddy." Gertie said as she got up and kissed the top of his smooth bald head. He had started to shave his full head of hair rather than dye the gray. "I love you so much Daddy."

"I love you too baby girl but you still ain't told me what that nigga is up to lately." Robert said as they broke out into hearty laughter.

"You read me so well. It's just more of the same except that I notice he's losing weight and he's jittery at times. I think he's overindulging in his pain meds again that he's *not* getting from his doctor."

"He's still working out a lot trying to make it to Metro right?" Robert verified. "That's probably why he's losing weight but the meds could be causing him to be jittery. Good thing you are paying attention."

"A while I brought up that he was acting weird and he got all bent out of shape so I don't say anything anymore. I just watch him."

"Oh. I see. Ok well hopefully he is not addicted to pain meds." Robert said studying the worried look on Gertie's face. "So how's your new job in Detectives baby?" He asked changing the subject.

"Oh daddy it's great! I think I have found my niche." She said.

"*Everything* is your niche." Robert laughed. "You said that about the job at the Sentinel too."

"No. I *liked* my job at the Sentinel but you are thinking about how much I *loved* interviewing the black female Lieutenants and Captain Moore. Anyway law enforcement rose to the top of my list of careers after that interview. My heart was not set on working at a black owned newspaper forever. Oh yeah and Ms. Clara, thanks for the suits. They are perfect!"

"I'm so glad you could use them. I feel better giving them to you versus giving them to the Goodwill." Clara said joyfully still focused on her newspaper.

———◆———

Jaxon was successful in his bid for Field Training Officer at Southwest and he was proud to report his promotion to the family, especially to Gertie. Even though they didn't get along she was genuinely happy for him.

In spite of his weight loss he still looked sharp in his uniform, and he had great field experience having worked at two busy divisions in high crime areas. Jaxon's supervisors at Southwest usually sought him out to work specialized details targeting identified gang members and other career criminals wanted by Detectives. His male peers loved his confidence and admired how he worked. He was known for his hardcore tactics.

"Jaxon!" The watch commander yelled from the front of roll call.

"Here Sir!" He responded loud and boisterous just like the Marines in the room.

"Evans!" The watch commander continued.

"Here Sir!" The pudgy rookie responded from the front row. He was a handsome fella with big brown eyes.

"You guys are going to be assigned a Specialized Detail tonight so I need you to go back and see the Robbery Coordinator after roll call." The Watch Commander advised.

Jaxon and his brand new rookie partner headed out in the field after meeting with the Robbery Detectives. They were assigned to conduct surveillance in the area of 43rd and Crenshaw looking for a Robbery suspect responsible for robbing fast food restaurants up and down the Crenshaw corridor.

It was the middle of their shift when Jaxon pulled into the parking lot of the McDonald's on the northeast corner of 43rd and Crenshaw where he drove through and picked up a bite to eat in the car. He returned to the parking lot where he backed into a parking stall facing Crenshaw. The windows were down as he and his partner sat there listening to the police radio. A few minutes later a woman appeared from the darkness and approached the passenger side of the vehicle startling Evans."

"Hey y'all. Who ya'll lookin' for ova here?" The woman asked.

"Whoa!" Remarked Evans. As he turned sharply in her direction shining his flashlight in her used to be pretty face. She was obviously a street prostitute. She was clean but had clearly been out in them streets for a while looking just like Felicia from the movie Friday.

"Hey man. You ain't gotta blind me wit that light and shit. Come on now." She pleaded as she bent down and peered past Evans and into the car looking over at Jaxon, who was looking back in her direction with his hand on his gun.

"Oh. You gonna shoot me?" The woman asked as she started to laugh hysterically. "Hey don't I know you?" She asked with her laugh stopping abruptly. "Didn't you go to Audubon Jr. High School?" She asked looking more intently at Jaxon.

"Hey yeah...I think I remember you." Jaxon said pondering. "Cynda. Right?" He asked squinting ar her face.

"Hell yeah! It's me! I *knew* that was you."

"What are you doing out here in these streets girl?" He asked as he moved his hand from his gun and placed it back on the steering wheel while leaning forward and talking to Cynda. Evans sat quietly with is upper body pressed back against the seat so Jaxon and Cynda could talk freely around him.

"Oh, you know..." Cynda responded.

"No, I don't *know* but I have a pretty good idea." Jaxon replied as he chuckled.

The two continued to talk as Cynda stood outside the door. The radio was quiet and the traffic in the area was light. The guys finished their meals and tossed the trash bags on the rear floorboard.

"You know I always wanted to fuck a cop." Cynda said out of the blue leaning her head further into the car window as Evans slightly pushed her shoulders back away from the car.

"Oh yeah?" Jaxon asked as he thought for a moment picking his teeth with a toothpick. "Get in the back seat. Yeah get in." He instructed as Evans looked sharply in his direction.

"For real?" Cynda asked surprised by Jaxon's response.

"Yes girl for real..." He said.

"Wait man. Are you serious?" Evans asked under his breath.

"Man just sit over there and chill. I'm in charge of *this* car." Jaxon quietly told Evans while he reached around and opened the door from the inside and watched as Cynda climbed into the back seat. They were in a supervisor's vehicle so there was no cage separating the front and rear seats. "Now lean forward and put your hands behind your back and pretend like you are hand-cuffed." Jaxon said after Cynda closed the door. Jaxon slowly drove out of the parking lot and into a nearby alley behind McDonald's.

Jaxon drove all the way into the dead end alley past the closed businesses rear doors, turned the car around facing out, and put the car in park.

"You stay here." Jaxon told Cynda as he and Evans got out of the car.

"Ok, but where *you* goin'?" She asked trying desperately to open the back door, which she couldn't do from inside.

"Just stay there." Jaxon directed. "I'm not going far."

"Look man, I need you to go wait down there at the mouth of the alley," Jaxon said to Evans pointing towards the entrance of the alley. "Down there by 43rd, and don't let nobody in here. Period. Ok?" He said quietly.

"Sir, are you for real?" Evans asked with his eyebrows raised. He thought he was being punk'd or about to participate in some crazy hazing ritual.

"Yes man. *For real.*" Jaxon said. "Just do what I say. I won't be long. Nobody should be looking for us but still listen to the radio." Jaxon said as he reached down, deactivated his flashing lights and killed his headlights then opened the driver's door.

Jaxon removed his uniform shirt and gun belt and carefully laid them on the front seat. He then went to the back driver's side door and opened it and while standing in the doorway pulled his pants down around his knees. He stood facing the car with his bare ass facing the closed buildings in the dark alley.

"Come here." He said motioning for Cynda to slide over towards the door where he was standing with his erect penis dangling between his legs. "Suck my dick." Jaxon said and Cynda gladly obliged. She went right to work. She wasn't shy.

After a few minutes of Jaxon lightly guiding Cynda's pie hole onto his erect penis he looked furtively around the area before pushing her down onto her back across the back seat.

"Scoot up and pull your pants down." He directed. She happily pulled her sweatpants down and watched as he rolled a condom onto his erect penis. She anxiously waited then he thrust his penis inside of her.

Jaxon and Cynda had sex for a few minutes until headlights aiming towards the police car spooked him. He pulled out quickly and peered up through the foggy front windshield where he saw Evans's silhouette directing a car away from the alley with his flashlight.

"Get up." Jaxon ordered as he quickly backed his rear end out of the back seat of the car. He rushed to his feet and quickly pulled his pants up. "Hurry up girl! Pull your pants up and sit up." He said as he closed the door and ran back around to the front driver's door.

"Ok. Damn." Cynda said. She was mad that the *sexcapade* ended so abruptly. "You taste good."

"Shut up girl. Come on." Jaxon hurried and dressed fully and then got back into the driver's seat. He turned on his emergency lights and drove to the mouth of the alley with Cynda leaning forward in the back seat.

"Hey man. You good?" Jaxon asked Evans while looking around nervously.

"I guess." Evans said without making eye contact when he entered the car.

"Hey...you cute too. You wanna see my pussy?" Cynda asked leaning forward with her elbows perched up on the back of the seat in between Jaxon and Evans. "I wanna suck your dick too."

"That's not going to happen. Now sit back." Evans scolded as he raised his elbow towards her head and nudged her further back in the seat.

Jaxon drove back to the McDonald's parking lot and told Cynda to *get out*. He then drove off as soon as she got out of the car.

"Hey man you know what goes on in the car stays in the car, right?" Jaxon warned Evans.

"Yes sir." Evans responded with his eyes stayed straight ahead. He was disgusted by what he had just witnessed and did not know what to make of the experience. The night felt weird from that point forward.

———◆———

Taylor finally had a weekend off so she called Gertie and suggested they meet up so they could catch up and talk shop. Taylor was in a good place. She was a strong probationer and the guys loved her. It didn't hurt that she was a USC Trojan Alum and tall and athletic. She was not a *typical chick* as noted by most of her male partners. She would tie up with the best of the street hoodlums and not ever wince when faced with physical altercations in the field.

"Let's meet at El Cholo's. I need some of them Nachos in my life." Taylor said. "Is Karisma off?" Taylor really liked Karisma.

"Ok El Cholo's sounds good. Let me call Karisma and see what she's doing." Gertie said. "I'll tell her to meet us there. I can't wait to see you Tay!" Gertie squealed. She needed her friends now more than ever.

Gertie dropped Marcus off at her dad's and called Karisma to verify she was on her way to the restaurant. Karisma was a Detective Trainee at South Bureau Homicide so she had the weekends off too. Everyone expected Karisma to promote fast since her daddy was a Captain on the Department.

"Hey girl!" Gertie exclaimed when Karisma walked into the restaurant.

"Hey girlfriend. I'm so happy you called. I was so fucking bored at home alone. Morgan is with the donor this weekend."

"You need to stop calling that man that."

"Well, shit we been separated for 3 years and he has yet to pay me one dime of child support. The nigga has a good job and is always posting shit on Facebook about his dinner dates and sending flowers to his sorry ass girlfriend. Fuck him! He's just a sperm donor."

"I can't believe you didn't have a date lined up for tonight."

"I didn't feel like being bothered with that sorry ass Roman tonight."

"You are crazy as hell!" Gertie broke into laughter. They were still waiting for Taylor.

"Let's order a drink." Gertie said.

"I want a Strawberry Margarita. What you drinking?" Karisma asked. "First round is on me."

"I want a Cadillac Margarita with a shot of top shelf Tequila on the side." Gertie said.

"Shit! Bitch, where you trying to go? This is a milc race. Slow your roll." Karisma warned as she walked away towards the bar.

"I know. But I got issues." Gertie said just as Taylor walked into the restaurant looking around.

"Perfect timing!" Karisma said when she saw Taylor walk in. "'Bout time your ass got here. What *you* drinking?" Karisma embraced Taylor. "Gertie is over there talking to some strangers." Karisma said pointing to Gertie in the waiting area. "First round is on me. What ya want?"

"Get me a Vodka and Cranberry." Taylor said as the Maître D approached Karisma to advise that their table was ready.

"Gertie!" Karisma yelled in the noisy restaurant. "Our table is ready."

"Here I come. Oh hey Tay! I didn't see you walk in." Gertie took her drink from Karisma and they all followed the Hostess to their booth.

Gertie almost didn't recognize Taylor. She looked so much like a man she forgot for a moment that she was actually a woman. Gertie climbed into one side of the booth and Karisma and Taylor sat across from her.

"So what's going on ya'll?" Taylor asked after they got settled into the booth.

"For starters I think I'm headed for divorce." Gertie announced. "I don't know Jaxon anymore. I know that's your bestie Tay but he is a piece of work." She said shaking her head.

"Nope. I don't want to hear it. I told you way back in college to leave that nigga alone. But *no* you just had to have his ass. I love him but he ain't no good and I always told you that." She reminded Gertie.

"I thought once I had Marcus he would change."

"That's what women *always* think. They have a child and then things will miraculously change." Karisma said interrupting Gertie.

"But he's getting worse. Have you seen him lately?"

"Yeah. I see him from time to time in passing." She said shrugging her shoulders. "I know one thing, the probationers are scared to work with him."

"Really? Why?" Gertie asked.

"They say he always be harassing the prostitutes and they feel sorry for *the prostitutes,* which is really sad when the cops feel sorry for the prostitutes." Taylor said.

"You didn't tell me Jaxon is a freak Gertie." Karisma said laughing. "Oh shit what's wrong?" She asked when she saw that Gertie wasn't laughing. "I'm so sorry. I was just playing."

"I know. I'm just so tired of his bullshit." She said with tears running down her face. Taylor reached out to grab her hand to console her as she continued. "He hardly helps with Marcus and I think he's fucking around because he's *allegedly* working overtime almost every night." Gertie said as she quickly dried her tears. "Have *you* seen him lately Karisma? He's lost a ton of weight. I also think he's addicted to his prescription meds."

"Oh yeah because of his past leg injury huh?"

"Yeah, but I can't really feel sorry for him." Gertie quickly recovered from her mini break down. "I'm tired of crying over this punk bitch." She proclaimed as she quickly looked in the waitresses' direction. "Ma'am can I get another Margarita and a shot of top shelf Tequila on the side?"

"Sure. Are you guys ready to order?" The waitress asked as she pointed to the menus and identified the *Specials*. The women all placed their orders before the waitress went off to get Gertie's drink. They ate, drank and talked for about two hours.

"Y'all know what?" Taylor asked as the evening was winding down and they were all pretty relaxed and full.

"What girlfriend?" Gertie asked searching the basket for some tortilla chip scraps.

"I think I want to have sex reassignment surgery." Taylor said quickly followed by a big gulp of her Vodka/ Cranberry elixir.

"Are you serious?" Gertie asked looking up at Taylor.

"I sure am." Taylor looked Gertie right in the eye.

"I mean if you *are* serious I'm here to offer my support but *please* do your research. I don't want you walking around here half woman/half man. I want you to be whole mentally and physically. I definitely want you to live in your truth whether woman or man." Gertie said.

Gertie left the restaurant thinking that maybe, just maybe her problems were not so bad after all. Her heart went out to Taylor but at least *she* was trying to live in her truth.

Jaxon was adamant that he did not want to change shifts from Night Watch to Day Watch when Sergeant Lewis notified him that he was due to be bumped. So he bypassed the Lieutenant Watch Commander and went right to the Captain. He begged the Captain to allow him to stay on Night Watch. He had a *routine* while on Night Watch that he was not ready to change. His productivity stats were great so the Captain obliged and told the Lieutenant to allow him to stay on night watch for another 3 months as long as it didn't interfere with deployment numbers and didn't disrupt the bump process for someone else.

Jaxon thrived on night watch. He frequented the motels in the area and whenever he saw prostitutes roaming he detained them and ran them for warrants. He knew the hotel owners in the area and most of them allowed officers to use rooms to interview suspects, or for command post operations whenever there was an Unusual Occurrence in the area. To keep those relationships in tact officers provided extra patrol at those hotbeds for illegal activity and the hotel owners welcomed the partnership.

"Here, run her for warrants." Jaxon said to his brand new probationer.

"Yes sir." Officer Monroe said as he took the whore's California Identification from Jaxon.

"Stand here and put your hands on the hood of the car." Jaxon told the prostitute they stopped for Jaywalking.

"Man, please don't take me to jail." She pleaded as she cried aloud. "My baby is at home with my mama and I need to go pick her up before it gets too late." She said through her crocodile tears.

"You weren't thinking about your baby when you were out here selling your ass for crack now were you?" Jaxon asked standing behind the whore as she leaned over the car. "I just stopped you for Jaywalking. Is there something else I need to know?"

"Sir." Monroe said as he walked towards Jaxon. "She has a Failure to Appear Warrant for a previous 647 B PC violation."

"Ok. Cuff her ass." Jaxon directed as he stepped back. "Don't put her in the car yet though. Just watch her and I'll be right back. I gotta go to the office." Jaxon said as he jogged the short distance to the office.

"Officer, is there a problem?" The hotel owner asked in his thick Indian-American accent as he looked out the window at the flashing lights. "She's a regular around here. I have had to run her off a few times but she keeps coming back."

"I just need to talk to her about some crimes in the area so can I please get the keys to an available room. I won't be long." Jaxon assured the owner.

"Sure officer. Actually, the room right in front of your squad car is available. I'll open it for you." He said as he searched a cabinet for the right key.

"Ok. Thanks man. I'll be waiting for you over there." Jaxon walked briskly back towards his police car.

The hotel owner hurriedly walked in Jaxon's direction with a big ring of keys dangling from his hand. He opened the door and then walked back to the office.

Officer Monroe was a brand spankin' new rookie officer with no idea of what real police work was all about. He was just happy to be out in the field and eager to learn from his new Training

Officer. Monroe didn't know what to make of the hotel scene or Jaxon's leadership at that point.

"Yo, Monroe did you put us Code 6 here?" Jaxon asked as he walked into the room pulling the whore by the arm.

"Yes sir I did." The rookie said nervously standing outside of the passenger door with his police radio in his hand visually scanning the area.

"Good job. You stay by the car and I'll leave this door open a little bit so you can hear what's going on in case one of us needs help ok?"

"Yes sir." Monroe answered as he leaned against the rear of the car for the best vantage point.

"Stop all that damn crying!" Jaxon said in a low no nonsense tone to the handcuffed whore as he guided her further into the hotel room. "You wanna go home right?"

"Yes. Please. I promise I will take care of my warrants." The whore said as Jaxon removed the cuffs and shoved them into his back pocket. He then pushed her down onto the bed.

"You suck my dick and I'll let you go." He said with his crotch just inches from the whore's face as she sat on the edge of the bed with her hands down by her side clutching the bed covers.

"I don't want to suck your dick you fucking dirty cop!" She said still crying and turning her head from side to side trying to avoid staring into his crotch as he straddled her legs.

"Well then your ass is going to jail." He said as he quickly backed up and grabbed her by the arm trying to pull her up from the bed. She dug her heels into the dirty carpet and tried to yank her arm away from him.

"Come on. Let's go!" He said as he tried again to pull her up to her feet.

"Ok! Ok! I'll do it." The whore yelled. "But, you are gonna let me go right?" She asked as she wiped the tears from her face.

"You cooperate and I'll see what I can do." Jaxon said as he backed away and removed his gun belt.

Jaxon laid his belt on the bed behind where the whore was seated; unbuttoned and unzipped his pants and dropped them to just above his knees. He pulled out his erect penis, reached behind her neck with one hand and grabbed his penis with the other and forced it in her mouth holding her neck steady for 1-2 minutes while she orally copulated him.

"Get up." He said after the deed was done. He put his gear back on and watched as the whore wiped her mouth vigorously with her dirty sleeve. She was disgusted.

Jaxon walked over to the door and peeked out when he saw his partner still leaning against the back of the running squad car with his radio in hand. The streets around the hotel were busy so the ambient noise in the area was pretty loud. A couple of minutes later Jaxon and the whore walked out of the room.

"Hey partner, she just sucked my dick." He said proudly. "Your turn."

"No!" The whore screamed. "Please don't make me do it again." She said crying hysterically.

"No. I...I...I don't want to sir." Monroe said turning his nose up at the whore.

"Ok. Remove the cuffs." Jaxon said to Monroe as the whore looked at him in amazement. "If I see your black ass around here again I'm going to take your stanky ass to jail. You hear me?"

"Yes sir!" She said as she scurried off into the darkness.

Jaxon and Monroe reentered their squad car and slowly drove away as they watched the whore disappear into the night with her scuffed run over platform shoes.

Jaxon continued that routine for weeks. He stopped whores and ran them and if they had warrants he demanded sexual favors in return for them avoiding arrest. He even got bold enough to meet up with repeat customers like Cynda when he was off duty. He was out of control, which is why probationers avoided him like the plague whenever they could. None of them ever reported Jaxon's incredulous activity to a supervisor.

———◆———

One afternoon when Jaxon was off work he decided to go see his Pops while Deanna was at work. Gertie was picking Marcus up that day as usual. After visiting for a little while he asked Moses if he could use his car to run to the store.

"Yeah son. You know you can always use my car. But what's wrong with *yo* car?" He asked.

"Nothing. I just want to drive the Cadillac. I haven't driven it in a while." He had learned to drive using the Cadi.

"Ok son. Well do me a favor and get me some gas while you out." Moses requested. He was happy that Jaxon was spending some time with him that evening.

"I'll be right back Pops." He grabbed the car keys from the hall table and headed out.

Jaxon made his way into 77th division his old stomping grounds where he drove up and down Figueroa Street for about 20 minutes before he spotted a scattering of prostitutes on the stroll. He slowed down and turned off Figueroa onto 47th street where he slowly pulled to the curb and stopped. He rolled his passenger window down and motioned for one of the girls to come to his car. The only white girl in the mix walked to the car and engaged him in small talk as they each tried to make sure that the other was *not* the police.

Jaxon knew the whore looked too raggedy to be anybody's cop, and the whore knew the vice cops didn't normally drive big ass, old ass Cadi's, so they both let down their guards and agreed on a cheap blow job. The whore got into the car and Jaxon drove away slowly with her in the front passenger seat. He turned into a nearby alley where he parked with just his parking lights on. The whore went right to work orally copulating Jaxon and when she finished she immediately asked for payment.

"Get out the fuckin' car!" Jaxon reached across her and opened the passenger door and tried to push her out of the car.

"You give me my fuckin' money asshole!" She demanded as she stumbled out of the car holding tightly onto the inside door handle to keep from falling to the gravel.

"Bitch! I'm not playin' with you...get out! I'm not paying you shit." He said as he reached inside his t-shirt collar and pulled out his badge that was hanging on a chain. When the whore saw the badge she let go of the door handle and slowly backed away from the car anticipating the arrival of police cars. She just knew she had been stung. Jaxon exited the car, ran around to the passenger side and quickly closed the door as the whore backed away into the dark alley cursing at him.

Jaxon pulled a 2" revolver from his back pocket and as the whore turned to run away he fired one shot in her direction. He then nervously ran back around to the driver's side and sped away with his headlights still off. The whore ran back to Figueroa where she hysterically recounted the incident to her friends who were still on the stroll. She then flagged down a passing black and white police car and reported the incident to officers who found the whore's story unbelievable but they still took an Assault With A Deadly Weapon crime report. Jaxon returned Moses's car with a full tank of gas and stayed and visited for a while before heading home.

———◆———

Gertie had heard the rumors that Jaxon was hanging out with a Dispatcher but she didn't know who the *skank* was. She was not about to go looking for confirmation because she knew she'd find something if she did. She figured what was done in the dark would surely come to light at some point. She longed for her mom now more than ever but she was so far away. She hadn't talked to Bea in a while either so she thought she would check in with them.

"Hi Auntie. How are you?" Gertie was happy to hear Bea's voice.

"Hey baby doll. Are you ok?"

"Yes. I'm really good." Gertie said trying to sound happy. "Did Mom tell you I'm working Detectives now?"

"No babe. You know we don't talk as much anymore." Bea said.

"I hate that you all are still not talking."

"It's just not the same since she's been with Michelle. I do not like that woman and she's not fond of me either." Bea chuckled making light of the situation for Gertie's sake. "Well, she's not fond of *anyone* close to your mom for that matter. Something is not right with her Gertie. I'm telling you. I just can't put my finger on it." Bea proclaimed. "She's too possessive."

"You have always said that. But I hope you are wrong. That's not cool that after all of these years you and mom have let Michelle come between you all's friendship. That makes me sad. I wish I were closer. I miss you guys terribly." Gertie was feeling melancholy.

"I miss you too hun. So, how are your dad and Ms. Clara, and Jaxon and that cute baby of yours?" Bea asked changing the subject.

"Everybody is great." Gertie exclaimed. "How's Papa Larry?"

"Larry has been a little under the weather since the stock market crashed but other than that he's good."

"Ok. I just wanted to hear your voice. I'm happy that you are well. Hopefully I will see you soon. I love you. I'm gonna call mom now."

"I love you the most. Be careful. Bye bye for now." Bea said slowly hanging up the phone.

———◆———

"Hey mom. How are you?"

"Hey honey. I'm good. I'm sorry I haven't called that much but Grandma Gigi has been sick so I have been spending a lot of time with her."

"Is she staying with you?" Gertie asked.

"No she's still being stubborn about moving in with me so I hired a caretaker to be with her at her house."

"Mom, please be careful with that. Those people be stealing and mistreating old folks."

"The person I hired was vetted by an Agency *and* Michelle and I have been making sure that one of us stops by mom's house every day.

"Ok that's good. How *are* you and Michelle?" Gertie asked.

"We're good. She's still teaching and coaching."

"What's up with you and Bea? I called her to check in and she said she hasn't seen much of you because she and Michelle are not fond of one another."

"Well I wasn't fond of Larry either when they first got together but I didn't distance myself from her. I can't believe she had the gall to discuss our relationship with you behind my back."

"Mom. Don't get defensive. I have seen how Michelle gets when we are all around. She retreats and gets weirdly quiet but when it's just you me and her she's a totally different person." Gertie reminded her mom.

"I guess but Bea is *exceptionally* annoyed by her and I don't want to have to choose between my mate and my best friend. The problem is, when Bea has an intuition about someone she's usually right and I think that's what has me bothered the most. Anyway, I don't see any reason to *not* trust Michelle or question her intentions. She's been a great friend and confidant thus far."

"Ok mom, you don't have to convince me. I know Michelle remember. I love all of you guys and I just wish you and Auntie Bea could rekindle your friendship. I feel better knowing she's there for you."

"You know what babe? Some friendships are meant to last a season and others a lifetime and maybe our season has passed. I hate to admit it but that may be just what's happening here. Anyway how are my baby and Jaxon?"

"Marcus is great. He's growing so fast mom. You really need to come visit soon but if not I can bring him to you next summer." Gertie offered.

"I would love to keep him for the summer. I'm sure Michelle would too. She loves kids."

"Ok well we will talk about that more later. Jaxon is still getting on my nerves. He's very immature and irresponsible. I can barely stand him right now."

"What's new? I know that's your husband but he can't get right according to you. His people are sweet but they are ghetto so what do you expect?" Celeste said in her uppity tone.

"Ok. There you go." Gertie said not surprised by her mother's commentary. "I thought with your alternative lifestyle and all the judgment associated with that you had somewhat changed but I guess not. I just wanted to check on you and I see you are good so I'll talk to you later." Gertie hung up the phone without waiting for a response. *Some things never change* she thought.

CHAPTER 11

"ABOVE THE LAW"

———◆———

JAXON WAS FEELING POWERFUL IN his role as a Field Training Officer and supervisors believed he was working hard at training probationers. But actually he was working harder managing his extracurricular activities with Alexa and the street whores. After weeks of his escapades, his dabbling in prostitution activity turned into pure addiction.

What he didn't realize was that word was getting out amongst the hookers in Southwest Area that there was a *cop who is raping prostitutes.* One of the whores he detained was angry that she was arrested *after* she relented and had sex with him, so she contacted the Law Offices of Johnny Cochran and filed a lawsuit accusing Jaxon of *Rape.* The whores who jumped on the bandwagon all remembered it was Officer Atwater who had stopped them. When the Department was notified of the lawsuit an administrative complaint was also initiated against Jaxon. He never thought for a moment that those *broke down ho's* as he referred to them would ever complain; let alone file a lawsuit.

———◆———

Gertie thanked God everyday for her 9 to 5, Monday-Friday job, and how it came at just the right time, since she was effectively a single parent. Robert and Clara were fully aware of Gertie and

Jaxon's fractured relationship so they continued to help with Marcus mainly to relieve Gertie's stress. Even Savannah came around more and more and she and Gertie became quite close in spite of their rocky past. They actually laughed at the fact that both of them slept with Jaxon's *sorry ass* in college as the two recalled when Gertie told her their marriage was pretty much over.

"Girl, I see he still hasn't tamed that little dick of his." Savannah said as the two laughed hysterically.

"You're right about that. You want some more wine?"

"Yes please. So, tell me about this bitch he's supposed to be fucking with now." Savannah asked. After she got over the initial shock of Jaxon and Gertie being married she lost all interest in him. She no longer found him to be attractive.

"I'm pretty sure she is a Police Dispatcher. Well, at least that's what I kind of confirmed." Gertie said.

"Really? So you know who she is?" Savannah asked.

"Oh I know exactly who she is *now*. I wasn't sure until a couple of weeks ago when Jaxon and I went to a promotional party together. Anyway the heffa made it a point to introduce herself to me. She walked her little ass over to where we were standing and spoke to Jaxon, and then turned and introduced herself to me. She extended her crusty little hand and smiled all big with her fake ass teeth. I don't think she expected me to be there *with* him.

"Oh wow." Savannah laughed at Gertie's description. "Did you shake her crusty ass hand?"

"Yes regretfully because I didn't realize at the time who she was. Anyway later on that evening I saw her and Jaxon huddled up in a corner engaged in a heated discussion, so I put two and two together and I figured she must be the one he's fucking. There was absolutely no reason for her to be upset with him unless they were *involved* in some personal way." She said reflecting back on that night.

"I'm so sorry." Savannah genuinely felt bad for Gertie listening to her recount the story.

"I don't deserve this shit. I didn't force him to marry me. It was *his* idea to get married but I was careless by getting pregnant by him so I agreed to the marriage. I'm so done with him. Every time I think I'm strong enough to move on, I get emotional and stay. I need to muster up the strength to leave. I really do."

"Then if he makes you feel this bad you really need to kick him to the curb for real." Savannah was disgusted by Jaxon's ongoing antics. She didn't like him at all.

"But I can't afford to maintain this household by myself. And I refuse to accept any more handouts from my dad and Clara. They do enough for me and Marcus as it is." Gertie said.

"You know what? I'll move in with you if you need me to. My roommate moved in with her boyfriend and I'm on a month-to-month lease right now so you just say the word and I'm here. I'm getting tired of apartment living anyway and I don't like living alone."

"Ok. That would help me a lot." Gertie perked up. "I would be ok financially by myself if I hadn't *just* bought that damn car and I increased my deferred comp withdrawals."

"Don't worry about anything. *If* you guys don't work things out I will move in and we can help each other. I'm sure mom and dad would love that too. Savannah declared. "Now, can we *please* watch the damn movie? I'm tired of talking about Jaxon."

"You got it." Gertie picked up her wine glass and curled up on the couch with Marcus in her lap.

———◆———

Captain Weintraub from Internal Affairs showed up bright and early to meet with Captain Dawson at Southwest Station. He said it was imperative that they discuss Jaxon's administrative investigation in person.

"I'm sure my investigators have briefed you on the case right?" Weintraub asked taking a big gulp of his coffee.

"No. Actually they have not. I have been off the past few days."

"Well you should be hearing from Detective Terri Martin or Sergeant Roger Barrett soon and they will provide you with ongoing briefings from here on out. First thing is Atwater needs to be removed from the field immediately. The case is classified as "Highly Confidential" due to the seriousness of the allegations and we can't afford for any case information to be revealed prematurely. I also have a surveillance squad assigned to follow him around during off hours to ensure that he does not engage in any criminal activity while we are conducting our investigation. Please make sure that he doesn't have access to *any* City vehicles while he's on duty. It's too risky for him to be in the field and we sure can't afford for our surveillance team to also follow him around at work and at home." Weintraub explained.

"Ok. I will make sure of that." Dawson said. "I believe we've had some issues recently with this officer returning evidence late to Property Division following his court appearances *and* he's been written up for holding on to crime reports for way too long." Dawson said reflecting on recent complaints he received from supervisors about Jaxon. "Looks like we might have a bad apple here huh?"

"Well, we don't know yet the extent to which he's bad, and we sure don't want to pass judgment before the investigation is complete." Weintraub cautioned. "But clearly this young man might have some serious issues.

"I will meet with him today when he gets in and advise him of the nature of the investigation, and I'll make sure that he is closely monitored by supervision until you all are ready for me to relieve him from duty." Dawson said.

"Ok. Great." Weintraub said as he got up to leave.

As soon as Weintraub left, Dawson summonsed all of the on-duty supervisors to his office and advised them of the nature of the *Highly Confidential* investigation, and impressed upon them the need to closely monitor Jaxon. When he reported for duty that evening, Dawson told him about the investigation and warned him that he was not to leave the station for any reason, and lastly that he was being moved to the day watch shift on his next working day.

Jaxon was startled by the news of the lawsuit and the corresponding personnel complaint investigation. He asserted his innocence claiming that the *prostitutes were just trying to get back* at him for arresting them. Dawson assured him that he would be treated fairly throughout the process.

After hearing the news the first person Jaxon called was Gertie.

"Man they are buggin' over here." He said.

"*Who's* buggin'?" Gertie asked. "What are you talking about?" She wasn't used to him calling her so early in his shift.

"The Captain is saying that some prostitutes are complaining that I did *something* to them, but they won't tell me exactly what these whores are saying I supposedly did. Talkin' about I'll know when Internal Affairs interviews me." He said trying to convince himself that he hadn't done anything wrong. "And they moving me to Day Watch so they can *watch me*." He said shaking his head.

"Well, you are just going to have to let the investigation run its course and if you haven't done *anything wrong* I'm sure you will be just fine." *Maybe the investigation was enough to scare him straight and make him act right.* Gertie thought to herself.

"Ok. I'll see you later." Jaxon realized that Gertie wasn't buying his sympathy routine.

"I guess you won't be working that much overtime at the desk huh?"

"I see you got jokes. I gotta go." He said. He was mad that she was making light of his situation.

Gertie was happy Jaxon was benched *and* on Day Watch because that made it harder for him to find an excuse to hang out at all times of the night. The first few days he was at the desk he helped a little more at home by picking up Marcus from school, but on his days off surveillance crews reported that he was hanging out with Alexa or visiting with his mom and Pops. Being confined to the desk was definitely stifling him and kept him from feeding his craving as often.

Gertie was uncomfortable with what was going on with Jaxon so she told him she didn't want him picking up Marcus because he was still very fidgety and she expressed her concerns and repeatedly urged him to see his doctor. He blamed his weight loss and disheveled appearance on stress caused by the complaint at work. Gertie had no clue that he was under surveillance. She worried about him in general based on what she knew was going on but her concern was short lived.

Gertie notified Marisol that their rape suspect was identified by DNA evidence as 44 year-old Terrence Collins.

"You did a great job interviewing the ladies at the club yesterday." Marisol said. "I heard several of them positively identified our suspect in the photo line up."

"Yes ma'am they sure did." Gertie said proudly. "I'm about to go to the DA's Office right now to get an Arrest Warrant for Mr. Collins."

"Very good Mija."

On her way to the DA's office Gertie stopped by the Academy Café for a salad and some of their famous clam chowder and homemade croutons. After eating, she walked down the hill to the Credit Union to get some cash.

"Hey Gertie!" Audrey yelled from behind the counter. "Long time no see."

"I know. I've been busy girl. You know I'm working Detectives over here at Northeast."

"Oh no I didn't know. That's very cool. Now that you are in the Division, don't be a stranger." Audrey said as she walked from behind the counter and hugged Gertie. "So, how are you liking your new car?" She asked casually.

"Girl I've had my car for over a year now and I financed with BMW Financial because they had a better rate than you guys at the time. You must be thinking of someone else." Gertie said as Audrey shrugged her shoulders with a puzzled look on her face.

"Oh. I know Jaxon came in here a couple of months ago and got a car loan so I thought you guys got a new car. Maybe I *am* confusing you guys with someone else." She said innocently. Audrey's recall about Jaxon recently purchasing a new car was unsettling. She could have sworn he recently got a car loan.

"Ok well let me get in line so I can get some money and I'll talk to you later." Gertie said as she turned her attention to the teller. "How can I help you today ma'am?"

"I need to make a withdrawal but can you also tell me what the interest rate is on the new car loan my husband recently got?" Gertie asked.

"Sure. Let me see. You know he actually got a really good rate." The teller boasted. It's only 1.9 % and that's way lower than what Honda Financial was offering at that time and of course you know we offer the free GAP Insurance so it's good you all went with us."

"Oh yeah. *Honda* was way higher and I remember that insurance perk." Gertie responded softly. "Thank you so much." She said finishing up her cash withdrawal transaction.

Gertie couldn't believe that Jaxon had actually bought a car without her knowledge. She didn't understand it and couldn't wait to ask him about it. She went on to the DA's office and secured an Arrest Warrant for her rape suspect before going end of watch that afternoon.

———◆———

Jaxon was asleep on the couch when she and Marcus arrived home. She went quietly and bathed Marcus and put him in his room with his Happy Meal to watch cartoons. Jaxon was sound asleep and didn't flinch when she returned to the living room so she nudged him.

"Hey." Gertie said poking Jaxon hard in the side of his temple. "Wake up."

"Hey watch it." He cautioned. "I'm tired." He said as he slowly sat up rubbing the area where she poked him. "Where's Marcus?'

"He's in his room. So you really that tired from working the front desk? Really?" Gertie was being facetious.

"Yeah nigga from working the front desk." Jaxon did not understand where her aggression was coming from.

"You know I went into the Credit Union today and I saw Audrey and she asked me how I liked my new car. Did you buy a new car Jaxon?"

"No. I ain't bought no car." He responded as he sat up erect on the couch.

"Oh, so Audrey is lying about *our* new car?"

"What Audrey got to do with this?"

"She asked me how I liked *my new car* asshole. That's what and I had no idea what she was talking about so I had the teller check our account and I found out *we* just bought a brand new cute little Honda. So what in the hell is going on?"

"*Nothin'* is going on." He said.

"I really can't do this."

"You can't do *what*?" He asked looking up at Gertie with a scowl on his face still acting confused.

"I don't know you." She said fuming about his bold face lies. "I want to know right now who you bought a fucking car for Jaxon!" She screamed at the top of her lungs.

"Damn girl! Ok! I was trying to help out a friend who needs a car. That's all." He realized that he could not wiggle his way out of the lie since Gertie already had the receipts.

"Oh so now you the fucking Salvation Army? What *friend* Jaxon? Please don't tell me you are talking about one of your *bitches*. It's probably the one I met at the party huh? Is it her? I'm going to need you to get the fucking car back. Now!"

"I can't do that." He said with his head hanging low.

"Then you need to get the fuck out of here because I won't put up with this kind of bullshit. You are so fucking disrespectful. What a sorry example of a man you are. You're pitiful."

"Where am I supposed to go? This is my house too." He got up from the couch and commenced to sloppily folding his blanket.

"I don't care where the hell you go but you can't stay here." Gertie snatched the blanket from him and balled it up and threw it on the couch. "Why don't you go stay with the bitch you bought the car for? I'm sure she would love that."

"Oh. It's like that? Ok I'm out of here." He relented and quickly walked towards the bedroom. "I don't need you or your stuck up ass family." He mumbled with Gertie following close behind him to the bedroom.

"There's the Jaxon I know." Gertie said. "You smug, cocky bastard!" She shouted.

Jaxon packed most of his personal items and loaded them up in his car. He then called Deanna and told her that Gertie had kicked him out so he was on his way to her house.

"Come on baby." Deanna said consoling her man-child.

"Daddy, Jaxon said Gertie done put him out so he's on his way here." Deanna said to Moses while Jaxon was still on the phone. He was half asleep in his recliner.

"Oh lord." Moses said slowly sitting up straight and squinting in Deanna's direction. "What the hell is wrong with them kids? What Jaxon do to that girl now?" He knew full well Jaxon was the main one with issues.

"I don't know but he's crying." Deanna said sensing that her son was in a bad way, she just didn't know how bad or exactly why.

Martin and Barrett contacted many of the prostitutes in the Southwest Area, and interviewed them at Cochran's Law Office. Many of them jumped on the bandwagon and joined the lawsuit against the City. Cynda was not one of them.

"Yeah, I had sex a few times with Officer Atwater." Cynda recalled proudly. "The first time we did it in the police car in the alley behind McDonald's."

"At 43rd and Crenshaw right?" Martin asked.

"Yeah. How you know?" Cynda asked.

"I *am* the investigator on this case. That's how I know." Martin said as they all laughed. "Do you remember what Atwater's partner looked like on the day you met him at McDonald's?"

"Yeah, kinda. He was a tall black dude, and a little pudgy with big brown eyes. I don't remember his name though."

"So, are you certain that the officer you had sex with in the black and white was Officer Atwater?" Martin asked.

"Yeah. I *know* him. We went to junior high school together but everybody called him Jax or Jaxon and not *Atwater.*"

"Ok, very good. So did he ever *force* you to have sex with him?" Martin asked.

"Nah. I went up to his police car the first time I seen him and we talked for a little bit while him and his part-ner was eating. Then I told him I always wanted to *fuck a cop.* Excuse my language." Cynda said snickering. "Then we went into the alley and did *it.* After that night we went to different motels around here but I think he was off work because he was just wearing jeans and a t-shirt *and* driving his own car."

"Did he ever pay you for your *services?*" Martin asked.

"Nope. He brought me cocaine instead of paying me." Cynda said. "He knows I'm an addict. Shit erybody know that." She said bobbing her head up and down. "Can I go now? My daughter gonna wonder where I am." Cynda couldn't sit still for long.

"Yes. Sure. I have nothing further. What about you partner?"

"No. I think you covered pretty much everything." Barrett added.

"Cynda. Do you have anything else you want to tell us?"

"Y'all know it was my friend who said that Jaxon forced her to have sex with him or he was gonna arrest her for warrants."

"Oh yeah?" Martin asked as her head turned sharply in Barrett's direction. "What is *her* name?" Martin asked. She was intrigued by this new information.

"Her name is Sunshine. Well that's her street name. I don't know her real name but I can show you where she hang out at." Cynda offered. "But y'all gotta give me a ride home after that if I show you."

"Ok...That's no problem. We will give you a ride home after you show us where *Sunshine* hangs out ok?" Martin bargained.

"Ok. Let's roll." Barrett said packing up the last bit of his things.

Investigators located Sunshine right where Cynda led them. Sunshine confirmed that Jaxon forced her to have sex with him in exchange for not arresting her for warrants, and then she told investigators about her friend who was shot at by an off duty LAPD officer *after she sucked the cop's dick*. Martin and Barrett thought they had struck gold after meeting up with Cynda and Sunshine. They came upon more and more information at every turn. After meeting with Sunshine investigators went to Southwest station to update Captain Dawson on their preliminary findings.

"Sir it looks like there *are* several women accusing Atwater of sexual assault."

"Oh wow. Ok." Dawson said shaking his head. "I understand that you all have interviewed quite a few of my officers over the past few days to determine who Atwater's partners were on the nights some of the alleged acts occurred." Dawson said still shaking his head in disbelief.

"As a matter of fact we have identified two partner officers who witnessed some inappropriate activity and we have added them to the complaint for acquiescing."

"Ok. I'll need their names so we can bench them as well." Dawson confirmed.

"Yes sir. They are Byron Evans and Richard Monroe. We just interviewed them earlier today. Evans was working with Atwater on the night he had *consensual* sex in the black and white and Monroe was Atwater's partner when he allegedly raped one of the prostitutes at the motel in exchange for not being arrested.

"And neither one of these punks had enough integrity or common sense for that matter to report this egregious activity to a supervisor?" Dawson asked.

"They sure didn't." Barrett said shaking his head. "They each independently confirmed what occurred and each expressed that they were *afraid* to report what they witnessed."

"Fucking cowards. They don't deserve to be Los Angeles Police Officers." Dawson scolded as he loosened his necktie.

"Oh yeah *and* we even connected Atwater to an ADW that occurred in 77th Division where he was assigned before he came to Southwest." Martin reported. "One of the whores...I mean *prostitutes* down there on the stroll in 77th said she was solicited by an off duty officer to perform oral sex in his car and after she did the deed he allegedly refused to pay her; kicked her out of his car and then he shot at her as she ran away. The report shows the man was driving an older model gray Cadillac with red interior and the suspect basically matches Atwater's description."

"Wow. The plot thickens." Dawson commented.

"Yes. It sure does. We need to conduct a few more interviews so can you please hold off on relieving him from duty until we give you the word?" Martin asked.

"Sure thing." Dawson said. "As long as he is under surveillance we are good. Please keep me posted. I'll wait until you all give me the word."

Gertie was feeling so much better after she kicked Jaxon out of the house. Their relationship had deteriorated to the point that she could barely stand to be around him. He tried calling her when he was working but she let all of his calls go straight to voicemail. Savannah kept her word and moved in with Gertie not long after he moved out and the sisters got along famously. They were both busy and oftentimes when they were at home together they shared stories about their respective jobs. It was always fun catching up.

Gertie was at work one day a couple of weeks after Jaxon moved out when she received a message to call Sergeant Barrett from Internal Affairs Division.

"Hello. May I speak to Sergeant Barrett?"

"This is Sergeant Barrett. May I help you?"

"I'm Officer Bellamy and I received a message to call you."

"Oh yes. Thanks for calling me back so quickly. I need to interview you as a witness on a case I'm investigating."

"Ok Sir."

"You can have a League Representative or someone you trust present during the interview." Barrett advised.

"Ok. Can I have my dad with me in the interview?" Gertie was clueless about the Department's disciplinary process and protocol.

"Uh no." Barrett said laughing. "It has to be someone on the Department like a Union Rep from the Protective League."

"Oh ok." She said laughing out loud. "Well you said someone I *trust*. Can I at least know what it is that I'm supposed to have witnessed?" Gertie asked. She had heard horror stories about Internal Affairs so she was scared to meet with them.

"We will tell you when we meet with you." He said.

"Ok sir I can come on my next day off." Gertie offered.

"Uh. That's a negative. We will interview you on duty and this is an urgent matter. You just need to notify your supervisor and get a Rep." Barrett advised.

"Ok sir. Do I come to you or will you come here to my station?" Gertie asked.

"We will need you to meet us at Parker Center Room 608. Does today at 2 work for you?"

"Yes sir. I think so. I'll let my supervisor know and hopefully I can get a Rep and I'll see you at 2." She said as she slowly hung up the phone.

Marisol was at her desk approving reports when she overheard some of Gertie's end of the conversation.

"Ma'am, I just got a call from Internal Affairs and they said they need to interview me as a witness on a case."

"Ok. When do they want to interview you?" Marisol asked.

"Today at 2 PM."

"Oh that's short notice. Those assholes are so wrong for that." Marisol said. "Make sure you get a Rep because witnesses sometimes find themselves as accused." Marisol advised.

"Yeah, he told me it's an urgent matter and advised me to bring a Rep to the interview."

"Ok good well call the League and have a Rep meet you at your interview and call the DA's office and follow up on our warrant while you are out. We need to get this damn rapist behind bars." Marisol said handing Gertie a piece of paper with numbers to the League and the DA's office on it.

Gertie grabbed her jacket and headed to her interview after calling the League and ensuring that a Rep was going to join her. She arrived at Parker Center by 1:30 and waited in the downstairs lobby until her Rep arrived. She was nervous because she didn't know what to expect. Her Rep, an older male white veteran Detective walked up to her and introduced himself. They exchanged pleasantries and then headed for the elevator.

"Just tell the truth as you know it." Detective Williams warned. "Don't add anything unless they ask you specific follow up questions. Basically *just* answer the questions. Got it?"

"Yes Sir. Got it." Gertie proclaimed staring up into her Rep's thick mustache.

Gertie and Williams waited outside the interview room for a few minutes, when a female Detective emerged from the room and approached them. Gertie was caught off guard by her beauty and style.

"Hi. I'm Detective Martin." She said with her raspy voice, reaching out to shake Williams's hand. "And you must be Officer Bellamy?"

"Yes ma'am." Gertie tentatively extended her hand.

"Come on in." Martin said joyfully shaking Gertie's hand. "We are ready." She said leading them into the interview room. "This is Sergeant Barrett." Barrett an extremely tall male black Sergeant stood to shake Gertie and Williams's hands before inviting them to sit across the table from him and Martin.

"Do you know *why* you are here?" Martin asked getting right down to business.

"No." Gertie looked at the mounds of binders on the squad table in the small interview room. "I was only told that I am being interviewed as a *witness*."

"Ok. That is correct. *Right now* you are just a witness." Martin confirmed.

"Right *now*?" Gertie asked. "What do you mean *right now*?"

"Remember what I told you Bellamy." Williams warned as Gertie shook her head.

"Who is Jaxon Atwater to you?"

"My soon to be ex husband." *Bingo.* Gertie thought. It was clear then that the interview had to do with Jaxon's drama.

"Oh really? Soon to be ex?" Martin asked sitting back in her chair.

"Well, I haven't filed for divorce yet but I kicked him out of my house." Gertie was gearing up to tell her life story. "He's been gone now for a few weeks now."

"Just answer the question Bellamy." Williams whispered trying to subtly reel her back in before she started talking too much.

"You *are* just a witness and I am hoping that we can just get some clarification from you about some things going on with Officer Atwater." Martin scoured over her notes. "Did he tell you about this complaint?"

"Yes ma'am. I mean he said he was assigned to the desk because of some prostitutes complaining about him arresting them for warrants. That's all he told me."

"What do you know about his drug use?" Martin asked.

"I know at one point he was taking a lot of pain kill-ers. He was shot when we were in college and ever since then he's been overindulging in his pain meds that were prescribed for him. We argued about that a lot because I didn't want him to become addicted. But he didn't lis-ten to me." Gertie said as Williams nudged her under the table. She rolled her eyes at him in return.

"Good for you." Barrett said. "So, you don't know of any *other* drug use?" Barrett sensed that she really *did not* have a clue as to what all was going on with her *soon to be ex husband.*

"No sir, that's all I know about any drug use." Her voice was slightly quivering. She knew that they knew a lot more than they were willing to share. She was confused.

"Bellamy, what kinds of cars do you and Atwater drive?" Martin asked.

"We both drive BMW's." Gertie said looking puzzled. "He drives a 5 Series Sedan and I drive an X5 SUV."

"Did either of you ever own or drive a Gray Cadillac with red interior?" Martin asked looking down at the ADW Crime Report.

"No, *but* Moses, Jaxon's grandfather drives a Gray Cadillac." Gertie responded. There was no rhyme or rea-son for some of the questions being asked. Well, at least she couldn't follow. "Is Moses involved in this case too?" She asked.

"Not that we know of." Martin responded noncha-lantly. She could tell Gertie was blindsided by the inves-tigation. "In due time everything will be clear to you." Martin commiserated with Gertie. She liked her. "That's all that *I* have." She said turning to Barrett.

"I don't have any further." Barrett said looking at Gertie. "I am ordering you not to discuss this investigation

with anyone except for your Commanding Officer. Any
violation of this order could result in charges against you
for insubordination. Do you understand?"

"Yes sir." Gertie said looking back and forth between
Martin, Williams and Barrett.
They all rose in unison and shook hands before Gertie and her
Rep headed out. Williams walked close behind Gertie patting her
on the back as they walked to the elevator. When they reached
the ground floor Gertie thanked him.

"You did good." Williams said shaking his head. "It looks like
your ex might be facing some serious allegations though."

"Yeah. I guess."

"You keep your head up young lady." Williams said.

"They were asking me so much that I couldn't get a
good sense of the totality of what's going on. I'm sure I'll
find out soon enough." She said mustering a smile.

"The good thing is it doesn't look like they suspect you
of anything or they would have read you your rights. So, you
should be good. If you have any questions please don't hesi-
tate to call me." He said handing Gertie his business card.

"Ok. Thanks so much for everything." She said as they
parted ways. Gertie then headed to the DA's office to follow up on her Arrest warrant. She decided to *go* there
versus calling since she was so close.
Gertie could not wait to get off work that evening so she could
call Karisma. She knew she would get in trouble if the powers to
be found out she violated the gag order but she had to talk to
somebody about this shit.

"Hey girl. What are you doing?" Gertie asked chomping at
the bit to blurt out what was going on.

"On my way to Court because of a damn ticket I wrote
two years ago when I was still in the field." Karisma said
nonchalantly. "What's up?"

"Are you sitting down?" Gertie asked.

"Oh lord. What's going on?"

"Remember when Taylor told us that the probationers at Southwest were scared to work with Jaxon because some prostitutes were making complaints about him?"

"Yeah."

"Why did I just get interviewed by Internal Affairs?" Gertie asked rhetorically.

"I don't know. Why?" Karisma asked as she carefully pulled into a compact parking stall under the Municipal Court building.

"I was ordered not to discuss the investigation but they didn't tell *me* shit. I told *them* everything so I don't really know anything about the investigation to tell. Anyway... anyway, I'm only telling *you* this but if you tell anyone I swear..."

"Girl how long have you known me and how much crazy personal shit have I shared with you? I ain't saying nothin' to nobody." Karisma promised.

"I know. I know."

"So just tell me." Karisma urged. "I'm already running late for Court."

"Ok. So look, I think this nigga Jaxon *is* really fucking with prostitutes *and* I think he's on drugs." Gertie blurted out.

"Get the fuck outta here!" Karisma exclaimed. She was stunned.

"Yes! *Now* everything makes total sense; the weight loss; the jumpy disposition and hanging out at all times of the day and night. I don't know what all happened with these ho's but I think he is in some serious trouble." Gertie proclaimed.

"Damn...I wish I had time to hear all about this right now but I gotta go. I will call you when I'm out of Court.

I can't wait to hear this shit." Karisma said grabbing her briefcase from the passenger seat.

"Ok. Don't forget to call me." She said driving through El Pollo Loco for some dry ass chicken breasts. "I'll talk at ya later." Gertie said.

Martin and Barrett called and advised Dawson that they would be back bright and early on the next morning to interview Jaxon as they had pretty much interviewed all of the key people germain to the allegations and discussed the case with the filing DA. Dawson said he would see them then. Surveillance teams picked up Jaxon when he left work that afternoon and they stayed on him until he turned in for the night at his grand-dad's home where they saw the back of the grey Cadillac in the open garage at the rear of the house.

———◆———

Martin and Barrett showed up at Southwest station early the next morning just as they said they would. They had the ammo they needed against Jaxon but needed to conduct search warrants to solidify their case against him so they contacted the various Internal Affairs team members and set their multi location search warrant plan in motion. They went directly to Captain Dawson's office where he was awaiting their arrival.

"Jaxon's at the front desk right now." Dawson advised. "I'll call him in and take his weapon before we head upstairs to search his locker."

"Has the locker room been cleared?" Martin asked.

"Yes. Are you all ready?"

"Yes. Let's do this." Martin said as she notified all team members via Radio to get ready to make entry into their respective locations. One of Martin and Barrett's search teams was ready to serve search warrants on Moses's car and home, and another was set to search Jaxon's vehicle while she and Barrett remained inside Southwest to search his locker.

"Sgt. Lewis, get Atwater and bring him to my office." Dawson said poking his head out of his door into the outer office.

"Jaxon Atwater!" Lewis yelled from the Watch Commander's office to the front desk.

"Yes sir." Jaxon said as he walked the short distance to the Watch Commander's office.

"Hat and books." He said. Jaxon knew that meant for him to gather all of his personal items from his workspace, and bring everything with him.

"Sir what's going on?" He asked. He wasn't used to Lewis's stern tone. Lewis was normally a jovial character and always in a good mood.

"Bring your stuff man and come with me to the Captain's Office." He said motioning for Jaxon to walk ahead of him.

Jaxon entered the Captain's Office where he came face to face with Martin, Barrett and Dawson. He was caught off guard by their presence.

"Officer Atwater. I'm Detective Martin and this is my partner Sergeant Barrett. We are here to interview you on your personnel complaint so I'm going to allow you time to call the League and get a Rep. The nature of the allegations are *Rape Under Color of Authority* and *Conduct Unbecoming an Officer.* You have an hour to get someone to respond here to the station." Martin said as she motioned for him to sit in the chair closest to the phone in Dawson's office.

"Whoa. I didn't rape nobody!" He blurted out. He was animated and his uniform appearance was subpar.

"Get your Rep Atwater then we will talk." Barrett said looking sternly at him. "But before you do that I'm going to need you to remove your gun belt and sit it on the Captain's desk."

"Why are you taking my gun man?" Jaxon asked sheepishly. "Man, this ain't right."

"Atwater, I see you are agitated." Dawson said in a comforting tone. "But I need you to calm down. I have to ensure everyone's safety." He said knowing that he was relieving Jaxon from duty as soon as the search and interview was done.

As soon as Jaxon's Rep responded, Martin and Barrett went right in questioning him about the various allegations. Throughout the interview Jaxon maintained his innocence. When asked about his drug use he vehemently denied any illicit drug use but was still ordered to submit to a drug test. While waiting for the results from the pee test Martin verified that the search teams were all ready to go.

"Officer Atwater we have search warrants, for your locker, your home and your car."

"Wait!" Jaxon exclaimed. "Why are you guys searching my house? Man that's foul! I didn't do nothin'. These ho's are lying on me." He said quickly rising to his feet.

"Sit down son." Dawson said forcefully guiding Jaxon back down to a seated position by pressing down on his shoulders.

"We are done with this portion of the interview." Martin advised. "Now we need you to accompany us to your locker while we search."

"Yes ma'am." Jaxon responded with his head hanging low.

"Come on. Let's go." Barrett said motioning for Jaxon to get up from his seat. "Martin, can you notify the other teams now?" He asked looking back at Martin who was walking close behind.

"Already done partner." Martin said as she smiled and saluted Barrett. They were always on the same page. They worked well together.

By the time Martin and Barrett reached Jaxon's locker, Martin had received confirmation that the other team members had made entry into Moses's house, and had eyes on his car parked in the driveway behind the house; and Jaxon's car, which was in the covered parking structure right behind Southwest station.

———— •◆• ————

Moses was home alone when officers arrived. He was startled by the loud knock at the door. He jumped to his feet; slid into his house shoes and shuffled to the front door.

"Who in the hell is knocking on my goddamn door like the fuckin' police?" Moses asked in his booming voice as he peered through the blinds and out onto the front porch. It was *the fuckin' police* he thought to himself when he saw officers with their guns drawn at his front door. His anger then turned to fear. "What's going on?" He backed away from the door when he saw the guns drawn. "Is my boy ok?"

"Sir, we have a warrant to search your home *and* your car." The Detective advised.

"What in the hell are you talking about man? Are you sure you have the right house?" Moses asked overwhelmed by the officers' presence outside his door.

"Yes sir. I believe we do." The Detective said as he looked quickly at the warrant. Is this Jaxon Atwater's residence?" The Detective asked coldly as he handed Moses a copy of the warrant.

"Yes, he's staying here *right now* but why are you searching *my* house and *my* car? Where's Jaxon? Why you not searching *his* house?"

"Mr..."

"*Atwater!*" Moses yelled cutting the Detective off. "What the hell is going on?" Moses quickly unfolded the Warrant and glanced at it.

"Sir, is there anyone else in the home right now?" The Detective asked as he slowly followed the uniformed officers into the residence.

"Naw. I'm here by myself. My daughter's at work, thank you Jesus otherwise she would lose her damn mind with ya'll bursting in here like this." Moses exclaimed as he sat down on the couch where Detectives directed him. "Sir, what may I ask are y'all looking for?" Moses asked softening his tone. He was out of breath. "I don't do no wrong shit so you ain't gonna find nothin' up in here." Moses couldn't believe what was going on. "I need to call my grandson." He uttered as officers stood by and others searched.

"Sir. Your *grandson* is at Southwest station and *he's* the reason why we are here. I promise you we won't be long. Just so you know, we are taking before and after photos to ensure that we are respectful of your property. I really wish we could tell you more but we can't. You have a copy of the warrant for your review and you'll have to ask your grandson what's going on." The Detective said trying to calm Moses down.

Moses sat there as the Detectives searched throughout his house. The house phone kept ringing but he was not allowed to answer it, which frustrated him even more.

"Why in the hell are ya'll searchin' my car though?" Moses asked when he saw through the open blinds, Detectives at the back of his house rummaging through his Cadillac. "I don't know what ya'll lookin' for but you muthafukas betta not cut my goddamn seats I know that." Moses said almost in tears. He had never experienced anything like this in his life. He was a God-fearing man and law-abiding citizen.

Meanwhile, Jaxon's locker search yielded a lot of treasures. Martin and Barrett were downright embarrassed for him as they rifled through his belongings. In between the mounds of dirty t-shirts and socks were crumpled crime reports; a 2-inch revolver with an obliterated serial number; and multiple evidence envelopes that still had drugs in them.

"Atwater. What is going on with these crime reports and evidence envelopes?" Dawson asked looking over Barrett's shoulder as he searched. Martin could not believe her eyes. "Is there some reason why you have all of these reports and this evidence in your locker?" Dawson asked shaking his head. "Now it makes sense why we were getting all the Property Dispo notices and we couldn't locate the evidence."

"Captain." Martin said as she pulled Dawson aside. "I'm going to need you to just watch the search but don't interrogate Atwater in this setting or we might be in violation of his rights. Trust me sir we will ask all of the questions you need asked to get to the truth of the matter."

"Yeah you're right. I just can't believe what I'm seeing. Sorry Detective."

"Ma'am." The drug-testing officer was trying to get Martin's attention away from Dawson. "Can I talk to you for a moment?" He asked as he motioned for her to follow him.

"Sure. What's up?" Martin asked as she followed behind the officer to another part of the locker room.

"I have Atwater's drug test results." The officer said with his eyebrows raised.

"Oh yeah?" Martin remarked. "I'm listening."

"He tested *positive* for Amphetamines and Cocaine." The officer said.

"Oh damn. Really? Wow." Martin said. She couldn't get to Barrett fast enough to share the news.

"Hey partner." Martin said interrupting Barrett's search.

"Yeah." Barrett replied as he walked towards her and the drug-testing officer.

"We are going to have to re-interview Atwater's ass again." Martin said. "We need to discuss our findings from the various search locations and these damn drug test results."

"There is something seriously wrong with this dude." Barrett said locking eyes with Martin. "You good?" He asked seeing the sad look on her face.

"Yes. I'm just disgusted with this young officer. I feel bad for his family especially his child and that pretty young woman who married this fool." Martin said shaking her head with tears welling up in her eyes. "This is just sad on so many levels."

———◆———

Gertie was on her way back to her division when she received a call from Lt. Lane. She was surprised to hear directly from the Lieutenant.

"Where are you?" Lane asked.

"I'm on my way back to the station ma'am. I had an interview with Internal Affairs and I *just* left the DA's office. Am I in trouble or something?" Gertie asked. She was still a little unnerved by the IA interview.

"No. You're not in trouble. I just need you to go home." Lane directed.

"Ma'am is there something wrong at my house?"

"Internal Affairs is standing by to serve a search warrant at your house and they don't want to breach the door so they want you to meet them there and let them in. I'm enroute as well."

"Oh my God!" Gertie exclaimed. "Should I get my Rep or Attorney? I haven't done anything so I don't know why they are searching *my* house." Gertie said. She was shaking and then got mad because she knew exactly what was going on. "Does this have anything to do with my *soon to be ex-husband?*"

"I don't know. I guess we will find out when we get there. I have already told Marisol that you are going to be with me so you don't need to call her. I'll approve your overtime."

"Ok ma'am. I'll come get my car from the station and then head home."

Gertie drove as fast as she could to get to her house before they booted her door. She was in tears and scared. She couldn't imagine what Internal Affairs would be looking for at her house. She hated Jaxon so much for all that he was putting her through. She needed to call her dad to tell him what was going on. She didn't care if she got in trouble for not abiding by the Department's *Gag Order.*

"Daddy!"

"What's up girl? What's going on?" Robert said in a low voice. "I'm about to step into a meeting."

"They are about to serve a search warrant on my house! I can't believe this!" She was incensed. "That fucker Jaxon is under investigation for some shit he did with some prostitutes and now they are searching *my* house."

"*They* who?" Robert asked.

"Internal Affairs!" Gertie yelled.

"Ok just calm down. It's going to be ok. I'll get out of this meeting and come right over." Robert said.

"Ok daddy. Thank you." She said breathing a sigh of relief. She felt better knowing that her dad would be there to support her.

Deanna arrived at home just as the Detectives were wrapping up their search at her house so they allowed her to go right in.

"Daddy what the hell is going on? Are you ok? Where's Jaxon?" She asked out of breath. She had literally run into the house.

"Girl, I don't know *what* is going on. I guess I'm ok and I don't know where the hell Jaxon is. He left for work this morning and that's the last time I seen him." Moses said exasperated.

"Ms. Cartwright from down the street said the police was here but I couldn't get through to you to find out what was going on. I have been calling the house for a while and you weren't answering. That's why I just came on home." She said sitting next to Moses on the couch.

"I heard the phone ringing but they wouldn't let me answer the damn thang until they was finished searching." Moses said as he handed Deanna a copy of the warrant.

"What is *this*?" She asked unfolding the warrant.

"That's what they give me. Talking about they had to search my car and my house because of something Jaxon done did." Moses said. He looked defeated.

"Ok sir, ma'am, we are done. Do you want to look around to make sure everything looks fine?" The Lieutenant assigned to that location asked as the team dispersed and headed to their vehicles parked every which way in front of Moses's home.

"You damn right I wanna check to make sure y'all ain't wrecked my home or car." He said as he jumped to his feet and shuffled his way throughout the house poking his head in and out of doors and then he went outside to inspect his car. Deanna followed close behind him looking over his shoulder.

———◆———

Detectives stood by waiting for Gertie to respond to her residence. When she finally arrived she nervously opened her front door and allowed them in. Lt. Lane arrived a few minutes later while Detectives were briefly explaining to Gertie why they were there.

"Sir, I told Detectives this morning that Jaxon, I mean *Atwater* moved out of our home weeks ago so I don't know what you expect to find here? None of his things are here." She didn't hold back even though she knew Lt. Lane was all ears. "This is just so ridiculous." She said under her breath as she reluctantly took a seat at her dining room table with her arms folded.

"Listen. I know you are upset but just let them do their job and get out of your hair." Lt. Lane said as she joined Gertie at the kitchen table. "You have a copy of the warrant and in due time all will be revealed. Investigators have assured me that you *are* still only a witness so try to relax."

"Then why are they searching *my* house like I'm some criminal?" She asked as she observed an officer escort her dad into the dining room.

"Hey baby." Robert said reaching out to hug Gertie.

"Daddy. I'm so glad you are here." She jumped to her feet and hugged him tight. "I don't know what Jaxon has done but I'm so pissed at him right now I don't know what to do."

"I know. But you have to let the investigators do their job and then we can figure this shit out when they leave."

"Hi. I'm Bettye Lane, Gertie's Lieutenant." Lane said as she stood to her feet and reached out to shake Robert's hand.

"I'm so sorry Lieutenant." Gertie said as she pulled away from her dad's embrace. "I didn't mean to be rude."

"No. You're good. I understand your manners might be a little challenged under the circumstances." Lane chuckled. She was earnestly trying to lighten the mood.

"Nice to meet you Lieutenant. Wow, so you are in charge of all of the Detectives over there at your Precinct?" Robert asked looking Lane up and down in admiration.

"*Division* daddy." Gertie said correcting him.

"I see where Gertie gets her inspiration from." Robert said ignoring Gertie's correction.

"Looks like they are wrapping up." Lane said leaning in close to whisper in Gertie's ear. "*And* you were right they didn't find anything."

"Ok ma'am." The officer said to Gertie. "We are done. Do you want to come and check to make sure everything looks ok?"

"Yes. I do." She was annoyed at the thought of Jaxon causing this drama.

Gertie took a quick look around and reported to the Internal Affairs Detectives that everything looked fine. Lane was fast on her heels as she looked about the house while Robert remained seated at the dining room table. Lt. Lane signed off on the inspection.

Martin and Barrett walked back to the locker where Dawson was babysitting Jaxon. They were pretty much done and had a ton of evidence to assess and book. Martin checked in with the team members at each of the other locations and directed all of them to meet her and Barrett at Southwest Division to discuss their respective search results.

After the debriefing it was discovered that there was nothing of evidentiary value found at Gertie's home nor Moses's home, however Moses's car matched the description of the car driven by the *suspect* in the ADW shooting incident, and Atwater definitely matched the description of the suspect in that instance.

Martin and Barrett took Jaxon into a private interview room and asked him a series of follow up questions about his drug use, the ADW and the crime reports and drug evidence found in his locker. In spite of being warned about providing false and misleading statements he lied repeatedly to them about his drug use, and played dumb about the crime reports and drug evidence he failed to return to Property Division. He just sat there with a smug look on his face. *The lights were on but clearly no one was home.* Martin thought.

After 2 hours of their good guy bad guy tactics Jaxon broke down and finally admitted to having a drug problem. He told investigators he had siphoned cocaine from the bulk evidence he checked out of Property Division for Court, and lastly he admitted to committing the ADW against the white hooker on Figueroa. He cried so hard that Martin found herself comforting him. She genuinely felt bad for him as a person. He was a lost soul.

"Captain, we are prepared to book Atwater for *Rape Under Color of Authority* and *Assault With A Deadly Weapon* as well as the theft of narcotics." Martin advised Dawson. "He has begged us to allow him to go to rehab but I told him based on the totality of the circumstances he will be going to jail due to the seriousness of the crimes that he has alleg-edly committed. Hopefully somewhere along the way just maybe he can get some help with his addiction. But today he's being booked for his criminal activity."

"How did we fail this young man?" Dawson asked. "I mean obviously supervisors weren't paying attention to anything going on with him." He looked directly at Sergeant Lewis who was standing close by avoiding eye contact. "This officer looks a mess. He's not the same young man I met during Orientation when he came here months ago *and* I understand he was a stellar athlete in college." Dawson acknowledged.

"We will notify the Chief's Office and Media Relations about the arrest." Martin advised. "I just need you to sign the Booking Approval and we will be out of your hair." Martin was glum. *Another black man lost to the system* she thought.

"Ok. I'll relieve him from duty before you all transport him." Dawson said.

"I will call and have them clear the jail." Barrett offered.

———•———

News travelled fast after the notifications up the chain of com-mand were made. Southwest Area was abuzz. The news permeated every section and unit in the Division as well as every entity within the entire Police Department. Taylor was working on that morn-ing and heard the rumblings in the station but was scared to call Gertie. Within a couple of hours Jaxon was in a holding tank at the County Jail in downtown Los Angeles while Gertie and Moses compared notes about Search Warrants served at their respective properties. Gertie shared what she knew about the nature of the allegations against him with her dad, Moses and Deanna.

"Oh my lord. I had no idea." Deanna said as she spoke with Gertie on the phone. Moses was sitting near by just as Robert was sitting close to Gertie on her end when she told all that she knew. "Are we able to talk to Jaxon? I need to talk to my son. I'm sure he's scared."

"You won't be able to talk to him until he calls you." Gertie told Deanna. "He will probably be *K10 status* to keep him from other inmates for safety reasons since he's a cop so he should be ok, well as good as he can be under the circumstances. Deanna and Moses I have to call you back. I have a call coming in." Gertie said as she abruptly ended her call with them.

"Hey Gertie." Savannah said speaking low and fast. "I just heard about Jaxon. I am being sent out to cover his arraignment tomorrow. I can't believe this. Did you know *anything*? You never said anything to me."

"Nope. I only knew that he was under investigation for some alleged inappropriate actions with some prostitutes he arrested that's all. Then IA contacted me today and ordered me in for an interview as a witness then the motherfuckers served a search warrant at our house; Jaxon's mom's house; his granddads car, and Jaxon's locker. I was devastated when I realized today that the allegations were possibly true when they arrested Jaxon."

"Yeah they are saying he is being arraigned for Rape and Assault With A Deadly Weapon." Savannah reported. "I can't believe they searched our house though." She shook her head in disbelief. "Anyway I have to go. I'll keep you posted about what I hear on this end. Look at the news at 6PM ok? There's going to be a Press Conference."

Jaxon was finally able to call and talk to his folks about what was going on. They consoled him as best they could and promised to get him an Attorney.

Robert, Clara and Savannah rallied around Gertie and Marcus. Taylor and Karisma agreed to help Gertie get through this rough patch as well. They were all in disbelief. Gertie's main concern was how she was going to approach the situation with her son when he got older.

———◆———

Gertie was embarrassed to return to work following Jaxon's arrest. She was sure that everyone knew what happened, however luckily for her many people didn't make the connection between them since their last names were different.

Gertie was surprised that neither Marisol nor PJ mentioned the fiasco. They acted normal but it was awkward when she encountered Lt. Lane because clearly she knew about the Search Warrant and investigation. To Gertie's surprise Lane acted very nice to her in passing.

"Bellamy, can I see you for a minute in my office?" Lane asked while walking aimlessly through the squad room talking to different people.

"Sure ma'am." Gertie glanced up at Marisol to see her reaction to Lane's impromptu request and Marisol didn't seem concerned about the meet.

"Come on in." Lane said as Gertie gently tapped on the open door to Lane's office a few minutes later.

"I just want to chat a little bit. Close the door."

"Ok." Gertie said gently closing the door.

"I want to make sure that you are ok." She motioned for Gertie to sit in one of the comfy oversized leather chairs across from her. "What you just went through was huge and I want you to know that I'm here if you ever want or need to talk." "Thank you so much ma'am. It's been really hard but I have tried to be strong. I'm so hurt and embarrassed." *She seems sincere.* Gertie thought.

"I totally understand but you haven't done *anything wrong* and that was made very clear by the outcome of the investigation." Lane handed Gertie a tissue.

"I have kept it all bottled up inside because I haven't wanted to talk about it. I didn't want to even talk to my dad, and he's my biggest supporter. I definitely can't talk to my mom because she never supported my relationship with Jaxon in the first place." Gertie said wiping tears from her cheeks.

"Well, it's probably best that you don't discuss it around here because people will definitely try to use it against *you*. Honey I have been subjected to rumor mongering my entire career and it's no fun to be the object of rumors. I just want to make sure that you are ok. On another note, according to Marisol you are doing a great job so I am really happy that you got the Trainee Position. Keep up the good work and please let me know if you need anything."

"Thank you so much ma'am. I appreciate your concern and your kind words." Gertie stood to her feet and quickly peered at herself in a mirror on the back of Lane's door. She wiped her eyes again and fluffed her hair before opening the door.

"You're welcome." Lane said following close behind Gertie patting her on the shoulder as they walked out of her office.

Gertie felt good about her exchange with Lane. She was encouraged by the pep talk and was empowered to stand up for herself if she was ever approached and/or shaded about Jaxon's situation.

———◆———

After a plea deal Jaxon was sentenced to 6 years in State Prison in Northern California. Gertie told her family that she would *never* visit him in prison, which meant she was not ever taking Marcus to see him either. Her decision didn't sit well with Deanna and Moses.

Soon after Jaxon's sentencing, he was fired from LAPD and Alexa's car loan went into instant default status when Gertie closed her and Jaxon's joint Credit Union account ceasing the automatic car payments. Alexa knew Jaxon was arrested but she kept driving the car he bought for her until the Credit Union finally repossessed it a few months later. She was upset and tried to get them to put the car in her name but her credit was not strong enough so they denied her request for a loan. She thanked her lucky stars that she still had her old piece of shit Datsun so she arranged for them to pick up the Honda after she exchanged the new tires from the new car with the bald tires from her old piece of shit.

Gertie was quick to finalize her divorce from Jaxon. It was bitter sweet but the prison sentence gave her the closure she needed to end the saga with him.

"Hey baby girl don't worry about anything. We got you and Marcus." Robert said.

"I can't believe I didn't know about some of the things he was doing." She thought about all the signs she had seen with Jaxon especially over the previous year.

"You had no way of knowing all that he was up to. Don't beat yourself up. Have you talked to your mama?"

"No. I really don't want to hear her mouth." Gertie said shaking her head vigorously.

"I'm so glad that Savannah is here with me. That helps a lot." She said.

"Yeah I'm glad too. You know we can refinance the condo to make it more affordable for you to be able to live there alone. You and Savannah may not want to live together forever."

"Ok that sounds like a plan. I'm so glad the place is still in Clara's name because otherwise I would have to sell it as part of the divorce settlement. Thanks for everything daddy."

Savannah and Gertie had grown to be very close but they agreed that they needed their privacy so Clara refinanced the condo as suggested and put it in Gertie's name and pulled out some equity for Savannah to buy her a place of her own. The girls were set in their respective spaces and happy to be moving forward.

———◆———

Gertie was adjusting to single life pretty well. She and Karisma hung out more often after her divorce. They were both single and on the hunt to find new loves. Karisma had been single for a few years and Gertie for all intent and purposes was too, however following the divorce she was free to *officially* date other men. Gertie could never bring herself to cheat on Jaxon even though he was always unfaithful to her.

Gertie was very attractive and friendly, so she was never devoid of male suitors or dating prospects. Her perspective on relationships was tarnished a bit because she was burned so terribly by her first love so she was hard to penetrate literally and figuratively by the men who tried to date her.

Karisma had no inhibitions about dating and was not shy to make the first move when she saw a suitable specimen she was interested in. She was more than comfortable with having a one-night stand versus cultivating a healthy relationship. She and Gertie oftentimes disagreed about her entertaining her new male *friends with benefits* at her house. Gertie didn't like that Karisma allowed her men to meet Morgan, her self appointed

God Daughter, so early in her relationships. She didn't trust the strange men around Morgan. Even though the ladies disagreed about Karisma's parenting choices they were still the very best of friends; they truly loved each other and had each other's backs.

------●------

"Hey I haven't talked to you since Jaxon was arrested so I'm just checking on you." Taylor was shaken by Jaxon's conviction for such violent crimes.

"I'm still in disbelief, but I've been good." Gertie said.

"I heard the rumors about the prostitutes accusing him of all kinds of shit, but never in a million years did I think that he was doing anything like that. He is handsome *and* he has a family who loves him. What's up with that?" Taylor asked.

"He's a *sociopath* Taylor. There's no other way to explain it." Gertie said after listening to Taylor describe Jaxon.

"Yeah, I guess. So you and Marcus are good right?"

"Yes, Tay we're good. This was not the best way to end my relationship with Jaxon but I'm glad it's behind me and I can move on."

"But you can't really move on. You have a child by this man so how's that going to work?" Taylor asked. "I mean you have to take his son to see him."

"That ain't happening. I don't want my son inside no damn prison. That's not an environment for any young child especially not mine.

"So you mean he won't see his son for 6 years?" Taylor was surprised by Gertie's stance.

"Nope. He made his bed. He shoulda thought about the consequences when he so recklessly engaged them nasty ass whores." Gertie was getting angry with Taylor for being all up in her business in that way. "I can't believe you are in favor of *my child* being subjected to that environment. *I* don't want to see him in prison so why would I take my child to visit him? I will let Marcus decide when he is older if he wants a relationship with his father. As far as I'm concerned Jaxon forfeited his parental rights when he was convicted for his violent criminal activity and drug use."

"I feel you. I didn't think of it that way." Taylor conceded.

"Of course you didn't because you are not a parent."

"Ok. Ok. Understood. Anyway on another note me and Cassie are back together." Taylor happily reported.

"Really? But you guys didn't get along that well when ya'll dated in college. I always loved Cassie because she was our first teammate to welcome me on the team with open arms." Gertie recalled.

"I know. Our relationship *was* pretty volatile in college." Taylor chuckled. "But we are older and wiser."

"Girl you ain't that much older. But if you guys are good with it then I'm happy for you. We have to get together soon and we need to talk about playing on the women's basketball team. You know Sergeant Alese right?" Gertie asked.

"I know *who* she is but I never said anything to her and she's never said anything to me."

"She must not know that you played ball in college. You are so damn skinny now so you don't look like a baller any more. You look like an Ethiopian runner." Gertie laughed.

"Well if *you* play, I will too." Taylor told Gertie. "Let me know. Let's do dinner soon; you, me, Cassie and Karisma."

"That sounds good. I'll plan it. I'll talk to you later." Gertie said hanging up the phone.

CHAPTER 12

"MOVING ON"

GERTIE WAS READY TO MOVE on with her love life and her cool vibe invited suitors on and off the job. She was a little hesitant to date another officer because being married to one turned out to be the biggest nightmare of her life.

Robert suggested that she get stronger in her faith to help her come to some sort of resolve with her situation with Jaxon, and he suggested that she specifically seek spiritual guidance relative to her raising Marcus without his father in his life. Gertie was ready and willing to actively incorporate Jesus into her life. She had been lazy about attending church when her dad, Ms. Pearl and J.R. all tried over the years to get her to go with them.

Although they both still lived in close proximity to one another Gertie and J.R. hadn't seen much of each other after they both went to college. All she could think about when J.R. invited her to church was seeing him pleasuring the youth choir director when they attended the church Lock-In as teens.

"Daddy you are starting to sound like J.R. and Ms. Pearl but I guess you are right. I definitely need more Jesus in my life." Gertie opined when she thought about what had been going on in her life.

"Did J.R. tell you that Ms. Pearl had a stroke?" Robert asked.

"No. I haven't talked to him in a while so I need to call him. I'm really surprised he didn't tell me about Ms. Pearl."

"Now don't you get mad when I call you on Saturday night and remind you about church on Sunday morning." Robert warned.

"I won't daddy. I promise. I'll call J.R. later. I need to get back to work. My break is over. Thanks for calling. I love you old man." She hung up the phone and returned to work.

When Gertie walked back into the squad room she saw PJ giving some young gang officers their marching orders for the day.

Gertie didn't recognize any of the officers but there was one who was staring at her a little too long. She thought he was handsome but he was not her type. He was a little shorter and more buffed than she liked so she turned her nose up and tried not to make eye contact with him.

———◆———

It had been a few weeks since Gertie picked up her serial Rape suspect's Arrest Warrant from the DA's office.

"Bellamy, I was reading your Chrono and I see where your *due diligence* efforts are mostly computer runs and not much field activity. I need you to grab somebody and go out in the field ok Mija?" Marisol said in an encouraging tone.

"Yes ma'am." Gertie didn't realize what the totality of *due diligence* encompassed so she made a mental note to ask PJ about it outside of Marisol's presence.

"Here look at this report. It looks like we may have another rape victim; it's a new girl who just started dancing at the club a few weeks ago. I need you to go show her the photo line up so we can see if her case is related to our series." Marisol advised. "Mija, on another note how are you doing? I know what happened with your husband and I want you to know I'm glad he didn't take you down with him with the drug use and theft allegations and all."

"Thanks ma'am. I'm fine. Just trying to move on." Gertie wasn't surprised that she knew the details of Jaxon's case because most of them were released in the media. "I'm just sorry my judgment was so faulty when picking a mate. Thanks for checking on me."

"Sure thing. Well, I'm going to take off. You'll be here until 5 right?" Marisol confirmed.

"Yes ma'am. I'm the late person this week. Enjoy your weekend ma'am."

It was too late to conduct field follow-ups on that Friday afternoon and Marisol was leaving so Gertie thought it was the perfect time to pick PJ's brain before going home.

"You know you have a secret admirer." PJ said as soon as Gertie walked towards his desk.

"Oh lord. I am *not* trying to hook up with another officer. Not after what I went through with my wayward ex-husband." Gertie said staring down at PJ.

"Yeah. I feel you. So what's going on?" PJ didn't press the issue at that time.

"Oh you know…"

"No I don't know that's why I'm asking you. Anyway, I heard you are kicking butt over there on the Sex Table."

"Oh wow. Thanks for *that* feedback. Actually, Marisol is a nice lady." She said.

"Fuck her!" PJ quipped looking up at Gertie and laughing.

"No but for real I'm learning a lot from her and she and Lt. Lane have been very supportive of me. But I do have a question."

"About what?"

"What is *due dil-i-gence.*"

"Oh, so your new *mentors* didn't explain *that* to you? You obviously ain't learning that damn much." PJ was being sarcastic.

"Never mind." Gertie said as she turned to walk away. "You're a mess PJ." She said shaking her head.

"Come here girl!" He said waving her back to him. "Bellamy! Come here damn it."

"Nope. Nevermind." She said stopping in her tracks.

"Can I *please* speak with you for a moment Officer Bellamy?" PJ asked in his best fake proper voice.

"Ok." Gertie uttered as she slowly made an about face and slowly walked back to his desk.

"Sit down." He said pointing to the chair next to his desk. "Sit yo ass down. Now what you wanna know about *due diligence?*"

"What is *it?*" Gertie asked as she sat down.

"In a nutshell it's where you have to make frequent, timely and thorough follow up investigations when you are attempting to serve Arrest Warrants." PJ rattled off. "You can't just sit behind a desk and do a bunch of computer checks and pray for some new shit to just miraculously pop up. You have to also take your ass out in the field and knock on some doors and shake some bushes and try to find these dirt bags you are looking for. You get it?"

"Oh. Ok. Yeah. I get it. It sounds so officious when you say conduct *due diligence* but it's actually a very simple concept. Cool beans." Gertie said smiling at how simple it seemed.

"It's an investigative *protocol* that as a Detective, you need to fully understand and utilize." PJ said in a teachable moment with Gertie. He loved teachable moments. He was regarded as an excellent trainer.

"Thank you. I'm going to get out of here now. You have a good weekend Detective PJ." Gertie said walking back to her desk.

———◆———

It was Friday and Gertie was ready to get her mingle on so she called Karisma for them to meet up at El Cholo's for happy hour.

She felt so liberated. Karisma didn't answer the phone so Gertie texted her. Karisma texted back that she was in an interview but she agreed to the meet up later in the evening.

Gertie headed to the restaurant straight from work and while waiting for Karisma, she called J.R.

"Hey bitch. How you dooooin'?" He asked in his best Wendy Williams impersonation.

"You are a mess J.R. I'm doing well *bitch*. Thank you very much." Gertie was so happy to hear J.R.'s cheerful voice. She loved his spirit. "I'm so sorry to hear about Ms. Pearl."

"Oh thank you girl. She just had a *mild* stroke. Thank you Jesus. She still in erybody's business especially mines so she is just fine." J.R. said using his finest slang.

"That's good to know that she's good. You know I love me some Ms. Pearl. Anyway my daddy is telling me I need to go to church..."

"Yes Lordt!" J.R. said cutting her off. "Yes you needs Jesus hunty!" He teased.

"Are you still going to First Baptist?"

"Uh yes Lordt!" J.R. exclaimed loudly. "You wanna go with me this Sunday?" He was *so damn animated*. Gertie thought.

"Hey why not? Living as a heathen ain't getting me no where. You heard about Jaxon right?"

"Oh yes girl. Now look. I coulda sucked his little dick and we coulda kept it all in the family instead of him runnin' around fuckin' with all them nasty whores."

"Ok J.R. you are just nasty."

"Girl I'm just kidding. But really how have you been since his ass went to prison?"

"I'm actually in a really good place mentally. Just happy we hadn't been intimate for a while or I would be scared to death wondering if he brought something home to me. I dodged a bullet for real. What have *you* been up to? Where you working now?" Gertie asked.

"I have been awesome and amazing!" J.R. squealed. "I'm working for Mossimo designing jeans and jackets for his denim line at Target. Girl we puttin' them Kardashians to shame with they sorry ass clothing line at Sears. Ha!" He said with flair.

"Oh damn! You are way too funny. You need to meet me and my friend Karisma for happy hour today so you can entertain us."

"Oh I can't hunty. I gots myself a date." He proudly reported. "Maybe next time. But, I will see you bright and early at church on Sunday right honey chile? Remember they got the children's ministry across the street at the Allen House."

"Boy bye. I think I'll keep my child with *me* because you was sucking dick at the church when we were kids and that ain't happening with my baby." Gertie said laughing.

"Girl. Stop it! They have a wonderful ministry for the babies *and* great supervision so stop playin' heffa. Take the boy across the damn street so *we* can enjoy church."

"Ok then." Gertie said still laughing. "I'll think about it. Anyway I'll see your crazy butt on Sunday."

Robert was so happy that Gertie was agreeable to going to church. When Sunday rolled around he didn't even have to call to remind her. He and Clara waited for her and Marcus to arrive at their house so they could all ride together due to the limited parking at and around the church. Besides, they were going to breakfast afterwards so riding together was perfect. J.R. was already seated next to Ms. Pearl on the front row when Gertie walked into the church.

"Hey boo." She mouthed when she walked in and spotted J.R. "Come sit with me."

"Ok." J.R. responded turning to Ms. Pearl telling her he was going to go sit with Gertie.

"Scoot over." J.R. said as he pushed Gertie further into the pew with his full hips. "Oh yes! The Brookin's Choir is singing today! They my favorite." He was too excited.

"Boy calm down. You are in church." Gertie scolded.

"I know and I'm about to get my *praise* on too." J.R. sat up straight and happily watched the choir march in.

"Heyyyyy is that *Ra-shon* up there?" Gertie asked squinting and pointing towards the choir members as they took their places behind the Altar.

"Girl yassss! That's his fine ass. I mean *behind*. Look at me up here cussin' in church. My bad." J.R. said checking himself.

"Oh lord. Are you crushing on him J.R.?" Gertie asked.

"Nope. Been there done that." He said keeping a straight face.

"What do you mean? You been there done *what?*" Gertie asked turning her head sharply in J.R.'s direction.

"I *tried it* girl. Well not *tried it* like that but I hit on him before when we were younger and he shut it all the way down." J.R. whispered as the choir was ending their first song. "He choked the shit out of me! Lord forgive me for cussin' again. Anyway he made it very clear that he was straight as an arrow." J.R. folded his hands in his lap and crossed his legs at the ankle like an old church lady.

Growing up, Rashon lived with his mother down the street from Robert in Ladera and Gertie met him when she visited her dad during her first summer in California. She had a huge crush on him throughout her teenage years but he paid her no attention.

Gertie hadn't seen him in a few years but wanted to speak to him and possibly catch up. She hoped he would remember her. When Rashon marched out of the sanctuary after 8 O'Clock church service ended he was standing tall and was as *handsome as he wanted to be* Gertie thought. She told her dad she was going to go say *hi* to Rashon so he and Clara agreed to go across the street to get Marcus from the children's ministry.

"I'll meet you at the car daddy." She said walking in the direction she last saw Rashon headed.

"Ok take your time I'm going to meet with Pastor before we get Marcus. I'll see you at the car in a little bit."

"Hi Rashon!" Gertie said catching up to Rashon with J.R. stepping on the back of her sling backs.

"Oops I'm sorry. I lost my balance." He said cupping his hand over his mouth when she looked coldly back in his direction. "Oh hey Rashon." J.R. said in his sweetest voice waving only with his fingertips.

"Oh hey man. How you doing?" Rashon asked in his deepest baritone voice trying not to look at J.R. for too long. He didn't want to send his flirty behind any wrong signals he thought to himself.

"Do you remember me?" Gertie asked taking back the conversation.

"Of course I remember you. Wow. You have grown into a beautiful young woman." He said looking Gertie up and down with an innocent respectful smile on his face.

"Oh I guess." Gertie said as she snickered a little. She was blushing big time. "You guys sounded amazing up there." Gertie commented.

"Oooh y'all sure did." J.R. chimed in.

"I think Ms. Pearl is looking for you." Gertie said turning around and squinting at J.R.

"Yeah you right. I better get going. I'll call you later." He said winking at Gertie as he pranced away.

"Later." Gertie said waving goodbye to him with a fake grin on her face. "So, how long have you been singing in the choir?" She asked returning her attention to Rashon as she looked down quickly at his hands. She noticed he was not wearing a wedding ring. *That's good* she thought.

"I have been singing in the choir off and on since I was a teenager."

"Nice. Well, I really just wanted to say hello." She said nervously. "I gotta go because my dad is waiting for me."

"Ok. So are you a member here at First Baptist?" Rashon asked continuing the conversation. "I haven't seen you here before."

"No. Not yet." Gertie had a sly grin on her face.

"I take that to mean you are considering joining?"

"I'll see. Yeah. I'll see."

"Anyway, it is really nice to see you again. Are you going to be at your dad's later?" Rashon asked.

"Yeah. Sure, I *can* be." She said clearly flirting with the man.

"Ok, well actually I moved back home with my mom so maybe we can get together this afternoon and catch up. I have to sing at ten and twelve and then I'll be home."

"Ok. That sounds good." Gertie said walking slowly backwards away from him.

She had butterflies in her stomach at the thought of meeting up with him and hopefully getting to know him as an adult. She only had memories of him as a teenager, when he paid her absolutely no attention. There was a four-year age difference and Rashon had the same girlfriend all through high school when Gertie was crushing on him so he was definitely unavailable then. There was a red flag however when he mentioned to Gertie that he was *back* living with his mother. Gertie wondered what that was all about. She was sure to find out at some point and preferred sooner rather than later.

Rashon was true to his word and went to Robert's house to visit with Gertie not long after he returned home from church. They talked for a couple of hours about their lives and about their past relationships. Gertie was most interested in knowing what happened with him and his high school sweetheart, and Rashon wanted to know all about her baby's daddy. They had an honest exchange, which clarified why he was back living with his mother. He shared that his *high school sweetheart,* whom he later married, got pregnant by another man, which was the reason why they divorced; and Gertie shared that her ex; a former cop was in prison.

"Oh my God Rashon, it's been so good catching up with you. I hope you won't be a stranger." Gertie said walking him to the door.

"Trust me I won't be." Rashon said hugging her goodbye.

As soon as Gertie closed the door she curled up on the couch in the den and called Karisma. Robert and Clara were out back having coffee and dessert on the patio watching Marcus play in the yard.

"Karisma. Girl. I went to church today and I think I might have met my next husband. Well I didn't *just* meet him. We met when we were teens. He lives down the street from my dad but I saw him this morning at church and afterwards he came over to the house and we talked about some of *everything.*"

"Hold up. Slow the fuck down. Can you please take a breath? So you went to church? That's new."

"I know. Remember I told you my daddy suggested I get closer with the Lord?" She reminded Karisma.

"Oh yeah. I remember that."

"Well I followed his advice and I'm so glad I did." Gertie was truly ecstatic. "His name is *Rashon*."

"Oooh I like the name. Very ethnic and sexy I might add." Karisma remarked.

"He is tall *and* handsome with milk chocolate brown skin. He's about 6'2" and about 198 lbs with a body chiseled from head to toe. Girl he is fine!"

"Damn. Did you pull out a measuring tape and measure the nigga or what?" Karisma asked as the two laughed. "So let me get this straight you were at church acting like you was at a club? Thought you went to find *Jesus*."

"Hell naw I didn't measure his ass. But I did size him up though. I'm just sharing with my best friend so don't hate." Gertie remarked.

"Ok. So, what size shoe *does* he wear? I know you didn't miss that in your assessment."

"Sure didn't. He looks to be about a 12 wide." Gertie said as she continued to laugh. "Anyway I just wanted to share my Sunday shenanigans with you. I'm about to head home now. I have to work in the morning."

"Ok. Me too. Keep me posted on your developments with sexy chocolate." Karisma said.

"I sure will."

———◆———

Gertie and Rashon dated for about a year when his mother, Mrs. Edwards, sold her house in Ladera and she and Rashon moved in with his grandmother in the Mid City area of Los Angeles. His grandmother had Alzheimer's and needed assistance. Mrs. Edwards did not want to put her in a home so she and Rashon moved in to help take care of her full time. Unfortunately only 3 weeks after they relocated, his grandmother died in her sleep.

Rashon was a devout Christian and Gertie had become a faithful servant after they started dating. She thought he was a great influence on her and felt they were compatible in so many ways. They fell in love and were ecstatic that everything was going so well. About 3 months after moving to his grandmother's home Rashon landed a job as a Stockbroker with a prestigious brokerage firm in Downtown L.A a job he had waited on for months.

Rashon loved the fact that Gertie was a police officer. He thought it was a noble profession and it was sexy for a woman to be a cop. He willingly shined Gertie's work boots on a weekly basis and even helped her study for the Detective Exam, which she needed to pass in order to keep her position as a Detective Trainee.

Rashon and Gertie both had great careers and were moving full steam ahead in their lives together. It had been a long time since she was truly happy and Rashon made her happy. Rashon was also very attentive to Marcus and even offered to go with Gertie to take him to see Jaxon in prison. He thought that was the *Christian* thing to do but she refused and begged him not to ever bring it up again. She stood firm about not taking her child to the prison and he respected her decision. Rashon didn't have any children but he understood where she was coming from as a parent of a black male child.

Life was good and Rashon and Gertie thought about taking their relationship to the next level by moving in together because loved being together 24/7. She was cautious however, and reminded Rashon that she had a child and needed to set a good example for him *and* she offered that shacking up was not *Christian like*. Obviously Rashon had *lost his Christian focus* Gertie thought. She and Rashon decided against moving in together but they were tighter than ever.

Rashon's office was pretty close to Northeast station so whenever he was out and about he would drop off lunch for Gertie, which is how everyone in Northeast Detectives came to know him as her *boyfriend*. There were several times when his car was in the shop and Gertie allowed him to use hers. He would take her to work and pick her up so it was obvious to everyone that they were in a *committed* relationship.

After about 4 months at his new job Rashon began to have problems. He was under an unusual amount of pressure as a new stockbroker and was stressing out primarily about securing the Series 7 certification that he needed in order to *keep* his job. After he finally secured his license Gertie breathed a sigh of relief but for Rashon the stressors of his job seemed to quadruple instead of diminish.

Rashon worked extremely long hours and had to acquire and maintain a certain amount of accounts in order to be successful. Gertie started to notice a dramatic change in his disposition. He had never really drunk alcohol other than a little wine every now and then, but he started drinking brown liquor heavily and started eating infrequently.

Gertie had the same knots in her stomach she had when she and Jaxon started having issues so she called her dad for advice.

"Baby girl, you gotta follow your heart. Don't jump to conclusions with this man because Jaxon's ass was no good." Robert reasoned. "Rashon seems like a good man *and* he's a Christian. It doesn't mean he's perfect, but I believe his heart is in the right place and he deserves a chance."

"I agree daddy. I'm not giving up on him I'm just scared because I'm watching his decline." She was really concerned. "I'm so glad we didn't move in together. That would have been all bad especially for Marcus."

"Oh yeah. Good girl. I'm so happy you are putting your son first."

"Well I learned from the best." She said smiling. "Ok daddy please pray for Rashon. I want the best for him. For us."

"You are always in my prayers sweetness. Let me know if there is anything I can do to help the brother." Robert said hearing the concern in Gertie's voice. "Goodnight my love."

"Goodnight daddy."

———◆———

The workload was building on the sex table. Moselle had finally returned to work but she caused such a scene with Marisol for allowing Gertie to work her cases that Lt. Lane had no choice but to move her crazy ass to another table. Lane was nice enough to allow Moselle to pick *which* table she wanted to work and she picked the Juvenile Table. She made it clear to anyone who listened that Gertie was responsible for her being moved. She complained that she was written up because Gertie was *brown nosing* and found the DNA lead that *allegedly* went overlooked by her. Gertie didn't pay Moselle any mind. She ignored her and her petty antics, as did everyone else.

———◆———

Gertie was so stressed out about her *new* relationship that after months of studying she failed her first attempt at the Detective's Exam. She wasn't retaining anything in her cloudy brain. She did not want PJ to find out right away that she didn't pass the test but she knew eventually he would when she didn't show up on the promotional list.

One afternoon PJ was working late with the gang unit and Marisol and Gertie were working late sorting through reports looking for more leads to try to locate their rape suspect. Marisol went out for a smoke break, which gave PJ the perfect opportunity to strike up a conversation with Gertie.

"So what the fuck happened with the test?" He asked trying not to talk too loud.

"What happened with what?" Gertie asked. She heard him but didn't want to talk about it.

"Look. You heard me. Don't play dumb heffa." PJ said. "I told you all the shit you needed to know about working Detectives *and* I made sure that you knew about all the good seminars to go to and you still fuckin' flunked the damn test. Where they do that at?" PJ asked shaking his head.

"I know. PJ." Gertie said throwing her hands in the air and turning to look at him as he walked towards her. "I appreciate all of your help but I have had a hard time this past year and now my *new* boyfriend is acting all weird and shit. I just have too many distractions I guess."

"I know that life sometimes gets in the way girlfriend but you need to get your priorities in order. I'm just sayin'. The last thing you want is to have to take your black ass back to Patrol. Them streets ain't nothin' nice." PJ said sitting in a chair next to Gertie with his feet up on the desk.

"Yeah. You right." She said looking at him. "Now I really have to get it together because I only have two more years or one more test, whichever comes first right?" Gertie asked. "My *black ass* ain't going back to Patrol. Believe that homie." Gertie said trying to lighten the mood.

"That's my girl." PJ said offering solace. "Don't beat yourself up. You will do it next time."

"I better." Gertie said as Marisol walked back to her desk.

"You better what?" Marisol asked looking at Gertie.

"Damn woman. Mind your business! Me and Bellamy were having a private conversation." PJ said swiveling around planting his feet on the floor. "Oh that's right. I'm not supposed to be talking to you Officer Bellamy."

"Oh shut up asshole." Marisol said looking at PJ. "Are you all talking about her *not* passing the Detective's Exam?"

"Yeah. Since you all up in the kool-aid and must know. Yes that's what we were talking about. She been working for your ass and obviously you ain't do shit to help her pass the test." PJ said.

"Nobody helped *me* pass no test Mijo." Marisol said throwing a piece of balled up paper at PJ.

"Ain't that a bitch *Mija*?" PJ said teasing Marisol. "Some kinda fucked up leader you are."

PJ and Marisol bantered back and forth for a few more minutes until he decided he had enough. He said goodbye to everyone and went end of watch.

"Mija, I know you have been going through a lot lately so I totally understand why you didn't pass the test. Don't beat yourself up." Marisol said.

"PJ said the same thing." Gertie said surprised that Marisol was so empathetic.

"Fuck PJ." Marisol said as the two laughed hysterically. "As soon as you are done we can get out of here." Marisol started to pack her things to leave.

"Ok. Whew. I needed that laugh. Goodnight ma'am."

Gertie expressed her concerns to Rashon about his weird behavior. She was really trying not to nag. He appreciated her genuine care and concern but it wasn't enough to ward off his demons. One Friday night Rashon and Gertie were chilling at her house and Marcus was with Robert and Clara for the weekend so Robert could take him to his T-ball games. Gertie let Rashon use her car to go to the store since his car was parked all the way down the street. He was gone for so long, that she fell off to asleep. When he finally came back to the house, he wreaked of alcohol. She didn't say anything to him, but she was mad as hell. The next morning she noticed that her car was not in the garage. She woke him up and asked where he parked her car.

"Excuse me? What in the hell do you mean you don't remember?" She was standing over him. He was laying face up in the bed. "Where are my car keys?" She asked angrily.

Gertie hurried outside in search of her car and saw it parked on the street in front of her condo complex with the front end smashed in. She panicked and ran back inside.

"Rashon what happened to my fucking car?" Gertie yelled.

"I told you I don't remember." He said as he sat up on the side of the bed with his head cradled in the palms of his hands. By the look on his face Gertie really believed that he had no memory of crashing her car.

Gertie was a nervous wreck because she thought that at any moment a cop was going to knock on her door and tell her that her car was involved in a *hit and run*. After hours of waiting she was thankful that no one ever showed up so she called and reported to the insurance company that her car was hit while parked on the street in front of her house. It was at that moment that she realized something was really *wrong* with Rashon. She just didn't know what.

Rashon's stress reached a dangerous level on another night. Gertie thought he was having a heart attack so she took him to Daniel Freeman Hospital emergency. It turned out he just had an *anxiety attack*. She had her own stressors at work in Detectives, but nothing like what Rashon was experiencing with his job.

A few days after Rashon's anxiety attack, they bedded down at around 9 pm after she put Marcus to bed. They were both exhausted. They weren't living together but he spent a lot of nights at her house. At around 3 am Gertie woke up and realized that Rashon wasn't in the bed. She had to get up for work in a few hours so she didn't *need that bullshit* she thought. She got up and walked into the living room and saw Rashon kneeling on the floor, butt ass naked in front of her coffee table. The lights were off in the room, but the flames from two burning candles illuminated the table. Next to the burning candles was one of Gertie's black dinner plates and on the plate were two round slices of banana; representing two eyes, and four vanilla wafer cookies in a half moon shape; resembling a smile. She walked back to the bedroom and stood in the doorway looking into the living room in total disbelief, almost in shock actually. She quickly checked on Marcus and he was still fast asleep so she made sure his door was closed.

"Rashon *what* are you doing?" Gertie whispered as she quietly walked back into the living room.

"God has revealed some wonderful things to me." He jumped up and walked towards Gertie and then grabbed her gingerly by her arms. "Come. Come pray with me, sit down and pray with me." He requested gently pulling her over to the coffee table. "This is my alter and I'm praying for wisdom and financial success." He said looking like a crazy fool. Gertie didn't recognize *that* man.

She didn't understand what was going on, but she knew it wasn't good. Rashon then started chanting and praying over the plate of bananas and vanilla wafers.

"What the fuck is going on here Rashon?" Gertie asked softly trying not to awaken Marcus but trying to bring Rashon back to reality. "You need to sleep." She suggested.

"Please pray with me babe." He begged pulling on her arm trying to pull her down to the table.

Gertie looked at him sideways but she gave in and knelt down beside him and silently prayed long and hard that God would bring him back to his senses while *he* cited his very *different* prayer aloud.

After about an hour or so, Rashon satisfied that Gertie had prayed with him returned to bed and fell off to sleep. She took that opportunity to call his mother. She told Mrs. Edwards about Rashon's anxiety attack days before, and about this recent manic episode earlier that night. Mrs. Edwards asked if Gertie could bring him home and she said she would try.

Gertie could not go back to sleep so she just lay there on top of the covers staring up at the ceiling fan until the sunrays pierced the blinds in her room. She was so tired from dealing with Rashon that she called in sick that morning. Although she was dead tired she went ahead and took Marcus to school so she could be free to deal with Rashon without Marcus being there. When she returned home Rashon was still asleep. *Thank God.* She thought. After watching him sleep for a little bit she woke him up and convinced him to let her drive him home so he could pray with his *mom* and share with *her* the wisdom that *he* received from God. Rashon happily agreed to go home.

Gertie breathed a sigh of relief after getting him in the car. She was hoping to go back home and get some much needed sleep but once they arrived at Rashon's house, he became very hyped and paced from one room to the next telling his mom about his *epiphany*. Mrs. Edwards was able to calm him down and convinced him to take a nice hot bath. Gertie rushed into the bathroom to run the water while Mrs. Edwards kept him occupied. Gertie was hopeful that the warm salt water would calm him down and help soothe his body and mind. While he was bathing, she returned to the den to talk to his mom.

"He's really scaring me." Gertie couldn't believe what was happening.

"I am so sorry about all of this." Mrs. Edwards said.

"I really think he might be on drugs or he is having a nervous breakdown." Gertie offered.

"No! I don't believe for a moment that he is on drugs and I can't believe my baby is having a nervous breakdown either. At least I hope not." She said. "That's just so hard to fathom. He is such a strong man, vibrant, intelligent and warm." She said reminiscing about better times she had with her son before he started to stress out.

"Yeah, but he is not the same person *right now*." Gertie said.

When Gertie went to check on Rashon he was sitting in the tub with a thick layer of white cream smeared all over his hair, face, arms and chest; it was everywhere! It was his mom's night cream that he had spread all over his body.

"Rashon. What are you doing?" Gertie asked calmly trying not to excite him.

"I'm cleansing my soul baby." He said looking like Casper The Friendly Ghost. "You need to get in the tub with me to cleanse *your* soul." He said laying back closing his eyes.

Gertie ran and got Mrs. Edwards so she could witness his bizarre behavior first hand. Exhausted from the previous night and put off by his strange behavior, Gertie told his mother that she needed to go home and get some sleep. She left Rashon in his mother's care; went and got Marcus from school and then went home and passed out.

Gertie didn't tell her dad or Karisma about what was going on because she was too embarrassed. She thought she had moved on from Jaxon's craziness and into a solid loving relationship when she was really just treading water with this relationship.

———◆———

Gertie hadn't talked to her mom since Jaxon was sentenced so she finally broke down and called her.

"Hey mom. I'm just checking to see how you are doing."

"Hey baby I'm good. How is everything with you? You sound tired." Celeste sensed Gertie's low energy. "How have you and Marcus been since Jaxon went away?"

"Marcus and I are doing well. Dad and Clara are a tremendous help." Gertie pointed out.

"That's good." Celeste said rolling her eyes. "I wish I could be closer so *I* could help."

"I know mom. How's Michelle?"

"Michelle is great. So are you dating yet?"

"Kind of. I mean it's nothing serious."

"Tell me about him." Celeste said. She was super friendly. Gertie thought maybe she had been drinking. Alcohol always made her nicer.

"For starters he's tall dark and handsome but we aren't serious mom." Gertie didn't dare tell her mom the truth about Rashon even though Celeste appeared to be in a great mood. She figured she and Rashon were not going to make it so *what was the point in sharing* she thought?

"Ok. Well at least you are getting back out there. That's a good thing." Celeste offered.

"Yup sure is." Gertie said holding back tears.

———◆———

Gertie was happy to go back to work to try to get her mind off of Rashon but after a couple of days she decided to call Mrs. Edwards to check on him.

"He finally got some rest." She sounded worn out. "He's sleeping right now. I stayed home from work these past couple of days to take care of him. How are you?"

"I'm good. I'm at work but just thought I would check to see how you are holding up."

"I'm doing ok under the circumstances. Thanks so much for thinking of me."

———————

Things were heating up with the strip club case after the newest rape incident occurred. The Bureau Chief was riding Lt. Lane about solving the case and Lane passed that stress on to Marisol who passed that stress down to her investigators.

"You know shit rolls down hill." Marisol quipped in her pep talk with her investigators. "We need to get more creative with our efforts and locate and arrest this suspect. He's out there somewhere and I need you all to find him before he strikes again."

"Ma'am these strippers are so elusive because they have warrants and other shady stuff going on." Gertie said. "I heard that some of them are even low key prostituting so they do not trust the police. It's like pulling teeth to get them to talk to us."

"I get all of that which is why I say we have to be *creative*." Marisol replied. "I'm going to talk to Lt. Lane to see if we can get a couple of undercover officers to conduct surveillance at the two Gentlemen's clubs. We've already distributed the Wanted Poster all over the city so officers know what this guy looks like, and Bellamy went to roll call to make sure the troops have all updated crime information." Marisol told her crew. "I'm a little frustrated with the Command Staff, who don't understand all of the issues we face with solving these damn cases." Marisol acknowledged to her team. "They are so unrealistic in their goal setting and overall expectations. I'm trying not to pass my frustration down to you all. Let's see if we can make some headway with surveillance but in the mean time get out there and find this bastard."

Gertie was happy it was Friday but she was not looking forward to the weekend since her relationship was literally falling apart. She was thinking about putting things on hold with Rashon but she felt bad about abandoning him in his time of need. *That's not love* she thought.

Gertie was on her way to get Marcus that afternoon when she received a call from Mrs. Edwards.

"Hi baby. I hate to bother you but I have taken so much time off work dealing with Rashon I want to know if you can come over to be with him this weekend because I *have* to go to work or I'm going to lose my job. He *is* still acting a little weird and he hasn't gone into his office all week."

"Ok." Gertie said in an exasperated tone. "I'll come over in the morning and stay while you are at work. But I will need to get back home as early as possible so I can spend some time with *my* son." Gertie was tired of baby-sitting Rashon. They weren't married so *for better or worse* was not a consideration in their relationship at that point.

"Thank you so much. You are so good at calming him down. I really appreciate you. Actually he listens to you more than he does me." Mrs. Edwards opined.

"I try but you may have to seek *professional* help for him. Things at work are really heating up for me so I need to stay focused *and* I need to make sure *my son* is taken care of too." She said firmly reminding Mrs. Edwards that she had a *young* child who needed her undivided attention. Gertie called her dad and briefly explained to him what was going on. He agreed to take Marcus to T-Ball practice the next morning so she could go and help with Rashon.

On the next morning Mrs. Edwards went off to work as soon as Gertie arrived. It was obvious to Gertie that she had not gotten much sleep because she looked really tired. Rashon was still asleep so Gertie decided to fix him some breakfast but she needed to use the bathroom first.

She was in the bathroom with the door closed when she heard Rashon walking in the hallway right outside the door. Then she heard a loud banging and loud thud outside of the door. She jumped up from the toilet, pulled up her sweat pants and rushed to the door to investigate. To her surprise the door would not open. Gertie tried again and it still wouldn't open. She then banged on the door and called out to Rashon, but nothing. He had somehow barricaded her inside the bathroom.

Gertie could hear Rashon mumbling to himself on the other side of the door, but she couldn't make out what he was saying. She tried desperately to open the door but it appeared to be jammed. Then she heard him whisper to her through the door. '*You are the devil, you must be destroyed!*'

"Rashon! What in the fuck are you doing?" Gertie's heart sank. Her first thought was *Damn I left my gun in my car!* "Rashon! Please let me out! Let me out! Open this damn door!" She demanded pulling on the door handle as he continued to mumble on the other side of the door.

For ten minutes she banged on the door and nothing. The door wouldn't budge. Then she smelled gas coming through the crack in the door and it was strong. At that point she realized that she was trapped and Rashon had most likely turned on the gas, clearly trying to kill her, *the devil*! Gertie kicked, and kicked and finally kicked a big hole in the bathroom door. Once she was able to wiggle out through the hole in the door, she was scared to move about the house because she didn't know where Rashon was. Her instinct was to call her dad but she didn't want to involve him in this crazy mess, at least not yet.

Gertie quickly realized that the gas smell was coming from the kitchen, so she slowly moved in that direction while looking for Rashon every step of the way. He was not in the house but she noticed the front door was wide open. She quickly ran to the kitchen stepping on a few half-lit matches strewn about the floor near the stove. It looked like he had tried to ignite the burners on the gas stove but he failed however, all the burners were left in the on position with no flames, which was the source of the strong gas smell. Gertie immediately turned off the stove and went in search of Rashon.

When she approached the front door she saw blood on the floor, and the word *DEVIL* written in blood *on* the door. She was scared that Rashon might be armed with a knife and might have cut himself. She grabbed her car keys, got in her car, and grabbed her 2-inch revolver from her glove box and placed it in her pants picket. She drove to the nearest payphone because she did not remember where she laid her cell phone down, and she didn't have time to go back in the house to look for it. She needed to find Rashon. While in the midst of her frantic search, she called Mrs. Edwards at work.

"I really hate to bother you at work but Rashon has gone *crazy*!" Gertie was out of breath. Her adrenaline was really pumping.

"Oh lord what happened?"

"For starters he locked me in the bathroom and turned on the gas on the stove. I had to kick a whole in your bathroom door to get out." Gertie said talking fast. "When I was on my way to the kitchen to turn off the gas I saw blood on the floor. It looks like he might have cut himself because he wrote on the front door with blood!"

"He wrote on the door?"

"Yes! He wrote in all caps *DEVIL*." Gertie reported getting more and more excited as she spoke. "And now he's gone. I'm going to call the police."

"No! Please don't. I don't want them to hurt him." Mrs. Edwards screamed. "Please just wait until I get there. Please!" She begged. "I'm leaving work now."

"Ok I'll meet you in front of the house. I'll be sitting in my car. *Please* hurry." She yelled into the phone.

Gertie was driving back to the house when she saw Rashon in the distance, down the street from his house. He had on only a pair of black boxer shorts, no shirt or shoes. He was wielding a butcher's knife and blood was dripping from both of his wrists. She broke down and cried as she frantically drove back to the payphone to call 9-1-1. She couldn't wait for Mrs. Edwards to arrive. She told the operator she was an off-duty police officer and reported that her *boyfriend* had cut his wrist in an attempt to commit suicide. Gertie gave the operator the last location where she saw him but she purposely did not report that he tried to blow her up in the house. She really wanted the situation to be regarded as a mental health issue versus a criminal incident so he could get some help.

Gertie was worn out from this nightmare of a relationship that was spinning more and more out of control each day. After calling the cops she parked her car near the house and sat there and watched him pacing up and down the street in his underwear with the knife dangling from his bloody hand. The Paramedics arrived before the police however, when they spotted Rashon in the street with the knife they refused to treat him until the police got there. Gertie heard the police sirens blaring as they got closer and closer. When the first police unit arrived she bolted from her car and flagged them down. She identified herself and quickly briefed them on the situation while keeping an eye on Rashon. When he saw the cops pull up, he quickly dropped the knife. *Thank God!* Gertie thought. She didn't want him to get shot.

Officers slowly approached Rashon and called him by his name. He looked confused and dazed, like a scared kid. He ran away towards a nearby church, which was directly across the street from his house. Gertie backed away since she seemed to be the object of his aggression. She didn't know why he thought *she* was the *DEVIL*.

The church was surrounded by an eight-foot chain link fence, which Rashon jumped over with no problem. He was so crazed he didn't even see the open gate on the other side of the building in plain sight. Officers started yelling commands in unison; *'Stop!' 'Put your hands up!' 'Get down on your knees!' 'Turn around'!*

"Can only one person give him orders, please?" Gertie yelled to officers while watching the confused look on Rashon's face.

"Ma'am, you called *us* so please step back and let *us* handle this." The Sergeant on scene advised waving his hand directing her to go back across the street away from the action.

Gertie backed away stumbling over the curb then went to stand in front of the house watching in amazement as more and more officers arrived on scene. Paramedics were still standing by waiting for officers to gain control of Rashon. As they shouted commands, he started singing a church song. The louder the officers got the louder he sang. *'Holy, Holy, Holy, Lord God Almighty'*. Rashon chanted right on key.

Gertie stood off to the side as instructed when she saw an officer she recognized in her peripheral vision. She turned slightly away from him hoping he didn't notice her standing there. *Oh God, I can't believe this! Shit! Damn! Ugh!* She thought as she paced back and forth watching Rashon acting out. Her private life was being exposed in ways she couldn't have ever imagined.

All of a sudden, Rashon dropped to the ground with his legs spread wide and his arms dangling by his side. He was finally giving up just as his mother arrived on the scene.

"I thought you would *never* get here!" Gertie said stomping one foot. "I'm so glad I didn't wait for you to arrive before I called the police!" She said scolding Mrs. Edwards. "I am out here embarrassed as hell in front of my peers trying to help *your* son."

"I'm sorry but I got here as fast as I could!" Mrs. Edwards exclaimed. "I came all the way from Riverside." When Mrs. Edwards saw officers run in to handcuff Rashon she tried to run towards him.

"No. No. No! You don't want to do that!" Gertie warned as she pulled Mrs. Edwards back by her arm. "This nightmare is finally over." Gertie said as she breathed a sigh of relief while still holding on to Mrs. Edwards's arm. Officers lifted Rashon up from his kneeling position, dusted him off and started to walk him towards the RA unit, which was parked directly across from where Gertie and Mrs. Edwards were standing.

"It's gonna be okay baby!" Mrs. Edwards yelled to Rashon. "Just do what the nice police men tell you to do and everything is going to be alright!" Rashon turned his head in Gertie's direction and yelled "You sucked my dick last night! That devil right there sucked my dick!"

Gertie stood there stunned staring back at Rashon. *Where did that come from and why would he say that to officers?* She thought. *That boy knows I didn't suck his dick last night.* She said to herself. Everyone, including Mrs. Edwards looked at her. They were mortified for her.

"Oh, Lord please just get him out of here. I can't handle much more of this." Gertie said to the Sergeant, who walked over to talk to her and Mrs. Edwards.

"We are trying our best young lady." The Sergeant responded.

"Sir, are you taking him to jail or to the hospital?" Mrs. Edwards asked.

"Ma'am I need to get some information from the two of you and then we can decide what action we are going to take. Once we assess him we will take him to the appropriate place based on that assessment. Either way, we will let you know *exactly* what our intentions are." The Sergeant advised.

After interviewing Gertie and Mrs. Edwards quickly, the Sergeant explained that Rashon was being placed on a 5150 hold for 72 hours at County USC Medical Center. After he briefed them Gertie and Mrs. Edwards returned to the house so Gertie could find her phone and Mrs. Edwards could secure the house. They hurried so they could follow the ambulance to the hospital. They drove separately so Gertie could go straight home from the hospital.

Rashon's initial diagnosis was that he had so much stress that it resulted in him having a *manic* episode. He was prescribed Lithium that the doctor said he would probably have to take for the rest of his life. It was a blessing in disguise that Mrs. Edwards's mother had passed on, as she had no idea that she would have to also care for her adult son and his mental illness. She would not have been able to care for the two of them.

Gertie felt like she had been in a knock down drag out fight for her life all day long.

"I hope you will visit him." Mrs. Edwards said with tears running down her face as she followed Gertie out of the waiting room.

"Oh I don't know. This whole situation has been a bit much for me. I mean it's been a crazy, crazy weekend." She said feeling herself slowly giving in the longer she talked to Mrs. Edwards. "Ok. Ok. I'll *try* to visit when I can so that Rashon won't feel like I abandoned him."

"Oh thank you so much baby. I know he will really appreciate that." Mrs. Edwards said wiping the tears from her face. "Thank you so much."

"You're welcome."

After leaving Rashon in the doctor's care, Gertie hugged and kissed Mrs. Edwards goodbye and walked to her car. She was glad to be going home. She sat in her car in the parking lot for a good 20 minutes gathering her thoughts and trying to calm her nerves. She was trying to make sense of the nightmare she had just experienced. It was getting late and she needed to get home.

"Hey daddy. I'm so sorry." Gertie said holding her cell phone in her shaky hand. "I'm on my way now to get Marcus."

"Hey baby girl. No problem. I was getting a little worried because I have not heard from you all day. Are you ok? You sound tired."

"Yeah I'm good *now.*" She was exasperated. "Daddy, Rashon is crazy for real."

"No shit? What happened?"

"It's way too much to recap over the phone." Gertie said shaking her head as she slowly pulled out of the parking lot. "I'll tell you all about it when I get there."

"Ok girl. I can't wait to hear all about it."

When Gertie got to her dad's house Robert and Clara were getting ready to eat dinner. Marcus was happy to see his mommy. He told her all about his T-Ball game and about the upcoming birthday party he was invited to.

"Are you hungry?" Robert asked as Gertie sat at the table next to Marcus.

"Oh yeah. I am famished." She said looking at Clara. "Can you please give me some of those greens and just half a Cornish Hen? Man, it's been a crazy day."

"So, what happened? You look a hot mess." Clara said caught off guard by her disheveled appearance.

"I don't even know where to start. I'll just say this. Rashon had a nervous breakdown and is hospitalized right now on a 72-hour hold." She said with her head down diving into the mound of greens on her plate.

"Oh wow." Clara said. "Poor baby."

"That nigga looked crazy to me when I first saw him up there singing in the choir with that big ass wide ass grin plastered across his face." Robert said trying to lighten the mood.

"Daddy you are so stupid." Gertie laughed hysterically at her dad's commentary.

"I can't believe he tried to blow up his mama's house with me in it!" Gertie said looking at her dad.

"Oh hell naw!" Robert dropped his fork on his plate. "Oh I think it's best that you leave that brotha alone and give him some time to heal." Robert said picking up his fork again.

"I agree. But I say leave him alone point blank period." Clara looked shocked.

"I know you ain't going to tell your mama about this are you?" Robert asked.

"What *you* think daddy?"

"Hell NO!" Robert and Gertie remarked in unison as they broke out laughing.

"Ya'll both crazy." Clara said as she joined them in laughter.

Gertie finished dinner and grabbed Marcus and went home. She needed to rest up so she could totally recover from the weekend drama. As soon as she got home she remembered that she wanted to call Karisma and update her but she needed to bathe Marcus first.

"C'mon baby let's get a bath so you can get ready for bed." Gertie said.

"I already had a bath at Papa's." He said.

"Did you wash yourself good?" Gertie asked as she continued to help him undress.

"Yup. I washed my balls good just like Papa told me to." Marcus said squirming out of his T-shirt.

"Papa told you that?" Gertie asked trying to stifle her laugh when she saw how serious he was. "Well ok then." She said as she bent down to smell his underarms. "You did pretty good son. You smell like good old fashioned soap!" Gertie said tickling his belly as he giggled. They finished putting on his pajamas then he scurried off to bed. "Nighty night." Gertie tucked him in and kissed his forehead.

"Good night mama-bear." Marcus said as Gertie backed away towards the door.

"I love you. Baby bear." She said turning on the nightlight.

"I love you too."

———◆———

Gertie showered and washed her hair. She had missed her weekly Saturday appointment messing around with Rashon's ass. She got settled in the den with a big glass of wine before dialing Karisma's number.

"Hey girl. It's me. How are you?" Gertie didn't talk to Karisma as frequently while she was dating Rashon.

"Hey. What's been going on? You don't call a bitch no more." Karisma said jokingly.

"You got time to talk? I need to catch you up."

"Yeah. Morgan is with the donor this weekend so I'm just sitting here watching TV."

"At least the *donor* ain't in prison like my baby's daddy. Oh yeah, and congratulations on passing the Detective's Exam." Gertie was genuinely happy for Karisma. "I have to tell you about *sexy chocolate*. Girl we are *done*."

"Whaaaat? Get out of here. What happened? I just knew that was your *husband*. Ain't that what you said when you reconnected with him?" Karisma was being facetious.

"I was too embarrassed to call you. I feel so over-whelmed right now."

"Oh no." Karisma said realizing that Gertie was getting emotional. "What the hell happened?"

"I *thought* I was dating a man who I believed to be my soul-mate but Rashon suffers from a mental illness that is beyond his control. He is so broken Karisma. I don't even want to talk about *everything* that happened but today he had a major manic episode and I had to call the police."

"What police?"

"LAPD girl."

"Oh shit." Karisma exclaimed.

"This fool was running around the neighborhood like a mad man with a butcher knife cutting his wrist and shit, so I *had* to call!"

"What the hell!"

"Girl yes! Then when the police and paramedics came he started telling them I was the *devil* and that I sucked his dick!" Gertie had regained her composure. "I think I saw red, I know I felt lightheaded and dizzy like I wanted to faint. Girl I wanted to hide because his mama was standing right there next to me and police officers were all around."

"Why would he think you were the devil and why would he tell *them* you sucked his dick?" Karisma asked trying to follow the story.

"Girl I don't know. I mean I did suck his dick but not that night." Gertie retorted. "It's over but it's so hard to let go."

"What's so hard about letting go of a crazy man?" Karisma was confused by Gertie's ambivalence.

"Because I *loved* this man and I know he loved me too." She declared. "Everybody ain't as cold and flighty as you Karisma."

"Whoa...don't take your frustration out on me. I'm just trying to get clarification." Karisma snapped back.

"I'm not *frustrated*...I'm *devastated*. How could all this happen?" Gertie began to cry. "Anyway, I need to get my life together. That's all." She swiftly dried her tears.

"I'm so sorry Gertie. You are such a sweet person and you deserve so much better. You just need to take some time to get over this loss; focus on you and Marcus and study and pass that Detective Exam." Karisma subtly tried to help her prioritize in that moment.

"I know right?" Gertie asked rhetorically. The two women laughed ending their call.

Gertie requested to take several days off from work so she could decompress. Lieutenant Lane and Marisol asked her a few questions and then granted her the time off.

CHAPTER 13

"Can't Get Right"

———◆———

GERTIE WAS WELL RESTED WHEN she returned to work after her devastating weekend with Rashon. She had come to terms with letting him go. She wished she could sever ties with Jaxon too but they had a child in common so that was going to be more challenging. This was a perfect time for her to focus on her son, and on her work she thought. It was imperative that she study for Detective.

PJ was the first to welcome Gertie back to work. He hadn't seen her in a few days and she was surprised that he noticed she was off.

"Where have you been?" PJ took a seat at the empty desk next to her at the Sex Table. "Marisol is off for the next few days so she wanted me to review the Search Warrant you are writing for your suspect's last known address."

"Ok. It's almost done." She said stirring her instant oatmeal.

"Well chop chop then!" PJ said clapping his hands and laughing. "I'll be at my desk when you are done." He got a kick out of messing with Gertie. He thought she was a good sport.

"Yes sir!" Gertie said laughing at his animated verbiage.

"I'm going to have the gang officers help serve your warrant so you don't have to request Patrol resources in your Game Plan ok?"

"Ok cool." Gertie was excited to be back at work hitting the ground running.

———◆———

Moses and Deanna didn't hear from Gertie as much after Jaxon was convicted. They consistently requested that she bring Marcus to visit them but Gertie didn't want to take him. She knew they despised the fact that she was still a cop for the very agency that they believed failed Jaxon. When they offered to babysit. She was not willing to accept their help because she was afraid they would take Marcus to the prison to see Jaxon against her wishes.

"Gertie, Jaxon has a right to see his son."

"Deanna, you know I love and respect you and Moses but I just can't allow my son to be in that place. We have enough of our black men *in* the prison system and I don't want Marcus to grow up thinking that is an ok place to be." She said with conviction. "It's not a safe place for any child."

"I understand exactly how you feel *but* Jaxon really wants to see his son." Deanna said tearing up. "And he still has rights as a father." Her voice was quivering.

"Just like Jaxon has a right to know *who* his father is and you never told *him*. So that's hypocritical." Gertie fired back.

"You don't know nothing about Jaxon's daddy, or why I chose not to have him in Jaxon's life. That's none of yo damn business." Deanna yelled into the phone.

"Deanna you are absolutely right *and* that's my point exactly, it's none of *your* damn business how I choose to raise my son." She said firmly.

"*I* also have a right to see my grandson." Deanna declared as a last minute appeal.

"Well I am his parent, and as long as you keep pushing the issue of taking him to see Jaxon *you* will *never* see him." Gertie proclaimed calmly. "I need to get back to work." Gertie was tired of going back and forth with Deanna.

Gertie returned to the squad room a little shaken by her first adversarial conversation with Deanna. She didn't like the tone of the conversation but figured she would give it some time and everything would work out the way it was supposed to.

After Gertie returned to her desk she submitted her Game Plan to PJ for his review and approval. She was happy that he and the gang unit were going to help with her Search Warrant. She was sure to learn from them.

"Where's your hospital information and did you notify the Watch Commander in Southeast Area about our plan to be in their division?" PJ asked.

"Oh no. I'll do that right now." She said grabbing the report from his loose grasp.

"That's why yo ass didn't pass the damn Detective test. You have to pay attention to detail. *Mija.*"

"Whatever!" Gertie snapped back waving the incomplete Game Plan in the air. "I can't stand your ass." She said under her breath as she walked away.

"You say something?" PJ did not understand her last comment.

"Nope. I ain't say nothin'." She said laughing hard to herself glad that he didn't hear her flippant comment.

"Here." PJ said walking towards her handing her a piece of paper. "Here are the names of the gang officers assigned to the warrant detail."

"Ok thanks." She said as she sat down and fired up her computer. "Is Loren going with us too?"

"Maybe. Why?" PJ responded without looking up.

"Just asking so I know whether to add him to the Game Plan or not *and* he's nice to me unlike some people I know."

"What you sayin'? I'm not *nice* to you?" PJ quickly looked up in her direction. "Girl you lucky I even talk to you damn rookie."

"See! That's what I'm talking about." Gertie laughed heartily. PJ kept her laughing and she needed that levity in her life.

Gertie and PJ went back and forth for a little while until she finished correcting the Game Plan and resubmitted it for his approval.

"All looks good now." PJ said as he reviewed the final version of the Plan. "I'm going to need you to come to roll call this afternoon and brief the gang officers on the operation. Go have Gina make enough copies for everyone and I will see you at 6. I'll approve your overtime."

"Thanks but who is Gina?" Gertie looked around the room.

"She's the new Senior Clerk Typist." PJ pointed to Gina across the room. "She sits right outside of Lane's office.

"Oh ok. I didn't know her name. Will do."

———◆———

Gertie had not heard from Karisma since their conversation about her break up with Rashon. Although their call ended on a good note Gertie was still embarrassed about the whole ordeal so she was slow to reach out to her following their last conversation. Karisma was a more seasoned Investigator than Gertie, as she had been a Trainee for a little bit longer. Gertie envied the fact that Karisma was about to be a full-fledged Detective since *she* passed the Detective's Exam and on her first attempt.

"Hey girl!" Karisma exclaimed.

"Aren't you chipper?" Gertie quipped. "You must have gotten some last night."

"Of course I got some. That's what I do." Karisma said.

"What's up with you my sista?"

"Not much. I was just calling to tell you I'm about to serve *my* first Search Warrant. I wrote the Warrant and Game Plan"

"That's so cool. I'm happy for you. You are going to be so far ahead of the game when you do finally make Detective. That's so awesome."

"Yes. I'm really excited. Do you have any last minute advice for me?"

"No. As long as you follow your Game Plan you should be good. Who is serving the warrant with you?"

"Detective PJ and the Gang Unit because Marisol is off." Gertie said.

"Oh shit. You mean PJ Martin?"

"Yes. Why?" Gertie didn't know what to make of Karisma's response.

"He's crazy as hell but in a good way. He teaches at Homicide School and the guys in my class loved his ass. He is easy on the eyes too but he's too old for me to fuck with. Besides, he's married." Karisma recalled.

"You are funny. Ain't nothing wrong with having a *Sugar Daddy*." Gertie said laughing. "But PJ ain't that sugar daddy type."

"What you know about that? The only sugar daddy you know *is* your daddy." Karisma said laughing hysterically.

"You better leave my daddy alone. Anyway, girl if you think of anything I might need to know hit me up if it's not too late ok? I gotta get up bright and early in the morning."

"Ok. But I think you are in pretty good hands with PJ." Karisma said in earnest.

"Yeah you're right. Ok. I'll talk at you later." Gertie said ending the call.

Gertie followed PJ's lead in roll call that evening. He introduced her to the room full of raucous young gang officers who were eager to hear all about the detail. She took her time and went over the Game Plan thoroughly. She appeared calm but she was intimidated by all of the eyes staring back at her. Even still she stayed focused on the task. Her briefing was impressive.

"Great job Bellamy." PJ said following her from roll call back into the Detective squad room.

"Thanks sir."

"Don't call me that sir shit. I'm serious." PJ reminded her.

"Yeah. I forgot. I'm brainwashed."

"Make sure that you give me your overtime report before you leave." PJ directed.

"Ok. I'll do it right now."

"You know your secret admirer is still alive and well." PJ said when Gertie handed him her overtime slip.

"Nope and I don't want to know." She said turning her nose up. "We are not in high school so if my *secret admirer* has something to say to me he needs to be a man about it and just talk to me directly."

"Damn girl you are hard." PJ said. "It's that Booker dude. Do you know who I'm talking about?"

"Mmm hmm. I know exactly who you are talking about and I'm not interested."

"Why not? I thought you were divorced."

"Look at you all up in my business." Gertie said cocking her head to the side looking down at PJ. "I just got out of a crazy relationship so I'm not trying to get with *anybody* else right now. I mean he is fine though." Gertie added under her breath.

"Understood." PJ said relenting. "I hear he's a real good cop. But you may want to watch out for guys like him because I have heard some not so good things about him and yeah he might be *fine* as you put it; yeah I heard you, but everything that shines ain't always gold. So I'm gonna go back to minding my own damn business."

"Ok. You are funny as hell with them old ass sayings." Gertie walked back to her desk to prepare to leave for the day. "First you try to set me up then you tell me to watch out for him. I'm good. I'll see you in the morning." She grabbed her things and walked towards the door.

"Get some sleep." PJ yelled across the room. "And don't be late!"

Gertie got home just in time to shower and turn in for the night. She had already arranged for her dad to keep Marcus overnight and take him to school the next morning. She couldn't go to sleep right away because she was nervous about oversleeping. She eventually fell off to sleep at just past midnight. When her alarm clock went off at 3AM she was startled and sat up in bed in a panic thinking that she had overslept. She took another quick shower to help her wake up, and she got dressed in a hurry. She texted her dad and let him know that she was on her way to work and asked him to kiss Marcus for her.

When she arrived at work she saw the gang officers by the gas pumps loading up their vehicles and putting on their gear. She was carrying her gear as she walked towards the back door. She felt someone staring at her.

"Good morning." Gertie said as she passed the gang officers' vehicles carrying her gear.

"Hey how you doin' Bellamy?" Booker asked. He was louder than anyone else. "You get some sleep last night?"

"Yes. I slept well. Thank you very much." She responded cheerfully. She felt a sense of camaraderie, as all the officers were very friendly towards her, which allowed her to let down her guard.

"Tell PJ we will be inside in a few minutes." Booker yelled as Gertie entered the building with the Velcro straps on her bulletproof vest dragging on the ground.

"Sure thing." Gertie yelled back as the heavy door slammed closed behind her.

PJ was putting on his vest when Gertie entered the squad room. It was only 3:45 AM so the room was pretty empty except for the Search Warrant team milling around. Lt. Lane appeared from her office dressed in a dark pants suit, and ready to accompany them to the Search Warrant location.

"I didn't know the L.T. was going with us." Gertie whispered to PJ.

"That's because you don't know shit." He whispered back jokingly.

"Yeah you're right." It was early and she was not in the mood for his bluntness.

"I'm just fuckin' with you girl." He said when he saw the look on her face. "We *have* to have a Lieutenant present at *all* search warrants remember and since she's *our* boss *she* has to go." He explained.

"Oh ok. That's cool I guess." She was happy to know that PJ wasn't being mean spirited after all.

"No the fuck it ain't cool. She's just gonna get in the way." He said as Lane walked up behind him.

"Hey PJ." Lane startled him. "Hi Bellamy. Are you guys ready?" She asked as she walked around to face PJ and Gertie.

"Yes ma'am. We are ready." Gertie responded.

"Very good. Well then let's roll." Lane walked away putting on her RAID jacket.

Gertie jumped in the car with PJ and rode to Watts, where the DNA suspect last resided. It was 6:10 AM when they pulled up at the location and strategically parked. Uniformed officers immediately approached and door knocked the location with Gertie and PJ right on their heels. An older black woman slowly opened the door totally surprised by the officers' presence.

"Ma'am we have a warrant to search your residence. Is there anyone here with you?" PJ asked as officers prepared to enter the residence and clear the location.

"No. There ain't nobody here but me." The elderly woman answered backing away from the door as officers entered. "What ya'll lookin' for?"

"Ma'am here is a copy of the warrant." Gertie handed her a copy of the folded document. "It will tell you all that you need to know. Who lives here with you?" Gertie asked.

"My son stay here sometimes." Ms. Collins said as she continued to back away into the living room.

"Ma'am I'm gonna need you to have a seat." PJ said in an authoritative tone. "We have a search warrant so it's best you cooperate so we can do what we came here to do, and get out of your hair as quickly as possible." He said looking down at the messy wig sitting atop the woman's head.

"Ma'am what's your son's name?" Gertie asked.

"Terrence. But he not here I told you." Ms. Collins sat on the edge of the couch. "What do ya'll want with him?" She asked.

"Ma'am, where is Terrence right now?" Gertie was being very patient with the elderly woman.

"What...Do...Y'all... Want... With... Him!" She yelled stomping her big crusty barefoot.

"Ma'am, we need to *talk* to him. Do you know *where* we can contact him?" Gertie asked politely.

"He *should* be at work." Ms. Collins surmised.

"Where does he work?"

"He's a mechanic somewhere in Downtown L.A. I got his cell phone number." She said rattling off the number as one of the officers quickly recorded it in his Field Officers Notebook.

"What kind of car does he drive?" Gertie asked.

"I don't know." Ms. Collins said. "He got a few clunkers he use."

PJ assigned officers to monitor Ms. Collins as he and Gertie searched. Within minutes Gertie walked out from the back bedroom in the tiny two-bedroom house. She approached PJ in the hallway where he was searching a cluttered cabinet. She was waving a piece of paper in the air.

"It looks like Mr. Terrence *is* a mechanic alright for the City of Los Angeles. Can you believe that?" Gertie reported to PJ. "Here's his pay stub."

"No shit." PJ said as he walked towards Gertie. "Well, I'll be damn. Call Gina and have her call down to Personnel and find out where in the hell this clown works."

"Ok will do." Gertie stepped outside to make the call.

"Ma'am. We will be out of your hair in a few minutes." PJ said as he walked into the living room to continue his search.

"Good, because I'm missing my damn shows." Ms. Collins said folding her arms and pouting with the TV on mute.

Gertie poked her head into the door a few minutes later and motioned for PJ to join her out on the porch.

"Where does this asshole work?" PJ asked as soon as he cleared the threshold.

"For the Department of Building and Safety at their downtown facility on Main Street." Gertie advised. "Gina gave me the address and phone number."

"Ok. I need you to call and see if he's working today, and I'll send a unit to hook his ass up." PJ said.

"Ok I'll call right now." She said walking away from the door as PJ re-entered the house.

PJ continued searching the living room and kitchen occasionally providing direction to the officers and answering Ms. Collins's angry questions. Gertie poked her head into the house and summonsed PJ to step outside again.

"He *is* scheduled to work today according to someone in HR. So I called for Loren to go hook him up because I don't want a Patrol unit to go. They may unknowingly violate his rights and we can't afford to lose this case on a technicality." Gertie offered.

"Oh shit. Look at you thinkin' like a true Detective." PJ was pleasantly surprised at her attention to detail.

"I *do* pay attention man. Come on give me some credit." She said squinting at him.

"I'm pretty much done inside so as soon as we get word that your guy is in custody we will head back to the barn." PJ said.

"*Barn?*"

"The office, Bellamy. The office." He said shaking his head as he walked back into the house.

"Oh yeah. One more thing." Gertie said as she waved PJ back to her. "I told Loren to make sure and identify what kind of vehicle he drives so we can get a Search Warrant for his vehicle since his mama allegedly don't know what he drives."

"Good call." PJ said as his phone rang. "Hey Loren what's up?"

"He works here but he called in sick today and they don't know what kind of car he drives." Loren reported.

"Damn? Ok." PJ said disappointed that Terrence was not at work. "I'm gonna have an undercover unit sit here on this location in case he returns home."

"Ok. I told his supervisor to contact us if and when he returns to work." Loren said. "They only have the phone number to his mom's residence but no cell phone number for him."

"No worries we have his cell number. We got it from his mama. We are going to head back to the office." PJ hung up the phone and looked down at Gertie, who was still standing close by. "Well missy, it looks like your suspect has absconded. I will have the watch commander assign a plain-clothes unit to remain Code 5 here at the house and when Marisol returns I will let her decide what she wants to do after that.

"Man I just knew we had him." Gertie said. "Since I have his cell number I'll write a Search Warrant for his cell phone records. Hopefully I can get somewhere with that." PJ notified Lane they were done. She took photos of the location and they cleared the scene.

Booker wasted no time in trying to forge a friendship with Gertie. He had already asked PJ a series of questions about her so his interest was piqued when he found out she was no longer married but he didn't know if she was dating anyone exclusively. Every time Booker saw Gertie he flirted with her and that annoyed her, because she was still not completely over Rashon.

"So I take it that you are my *secret admirer* huh?" Gertie asked late one afternoon when Booker passed through the squad room getting his flirt on. "Leaving those notes on my car."

"Why you say that?" Booker asked. "Let me see the notes." He said playfully.

"Boy bye." Gertie exclaimed. "I threw that shit away. I'm not here to play childish games. I'm a grown ass woman."

"Ok. Yeah it's me." Booker relented. "I was just trying to get your attention. Ain't nothing wrong with a man acknowledging beauty is it?" Booker added.

"Oh *jeesh*. Is that all you got?" Gertie asked blushing. "I heard you are a pretty good cop." She said quickly changing the subject as he sat down in the chair next to her.

"I'm alright." Booker said smiling. "I just love what I do ya know?"

Within a few weeks after serving the Search Warrant Gertie and Booker had developed a lightweight friendship only at work. She wasn't really interested in a *relationship* with him but she was coming around and definitely open to a new friendship. Booker had the gift of gab and was very charismatic. He knew how to handle himself around his peers and higher ups and he treated everyone with respect, which Gertie came to admire. He challenged her by testing her observation skills and he always gave her good information whenever she asked him for advice. He helped her see criminal activity that she was oblivious to whenever they were out in the field at the same time. She was eager to learn and appreciated his willingness to teach her. All the while he kept trying to *date* her.

"Dude really, you need to stop flirting because I am starting to feel uncomfortable." She warned while out in the field with the Gang Unit one day conducting *due diligence* on Terrence Collins. "You just don't take *no* for an answer." She was riding shotgun in Booker's assigned police vehicle.

"PJ said you were hard and I didn't believe him." He removed his sunglasses and turned to look Gertie in the eye. "You know I got Moselle's Detective Trainee spot so

I'm gonna be working back in Detectives full time with you guys starting next month."

"Whoa, where did Moselle go?"

"She transferred to Pacific Division. I heard she was mad that you took her spot on the Sex Table and although she got to move to another table of her choice she didn't want to work at Northeast anymore after all."

"Where have I been? I mean I haven't seen her in a while but I didn't realize she transferred out. She didn't like me so I avoided that little hateful heffa like the plague. I guess I need to pay attention to what's going on around me."

"Uh... ya think?" Booker retorted.

"Well good for you and good riddance to her. Welcome to the good life." Gertie said. "Are you going to miss working Gangs?"

"Nah. I'm timed out so this was the best option for me. Lt. Lane encouraged me to apply for the spot so I did. Aren't you happy?" Booker burst into laughter. He knew he was starting to really get on her nerves.

"I'm happy for *you*." Gertie said as they walked back into the squad room after completing their field investigations, searching for Terrence.

Several months after Booker was assigned to Detectives the flirting continued nonstop. Gertie would see him in the squad room dressed like he was a GQ model and they laughed and talked as time permitted otherwise they were hard at work.

———◆———

Gertie wasn't ready to date exclusively but she was open to the idea of meeting someone new. She hadn't had much luck with her relationships but she wasn't giving up on the idea of finding a true and lasting love.

———————

"So are we going to Little John's this weekend or not? I need to get back out there. I'm ready."

"Is that code for *I'm horny*?" Karisma asked teasing Gertie.

"Why is your mind always in the gutter?" Gertie laughed. "I might be horny but that has nothing to do with going out for an evening on the town with my girlfriend."

"What's happening with your *secret admirer*?" Karisma asked.

"Ain't *nothing* happening. He is so damn annoying but the brother sure can wear a suit. He looks fine as hell all dressed up." She said reflecting on seeing Booker in the squad room over the previous few weeks.

"Girl if he's that fine and dresses that good and he ain't married or spoken for then something is wrong with his ass." Karisma noted.

"We have never discussed his personal life. He flirts like he's single and he doesn't wear a ring but that's all I know. I'm not interested so I haven't inquired." Gertie said.

"Shit he might be good for a booty call ery now and again. I'm just sayin'" Karisma said.

"You know what. I can't with you."

"I mean if he looks that damn good then he must smell good so why the fuck not? No strings attached. Like Mary Mary says, '*Go get it, go get it, go get that blessing*'!"

"Oh my God! We are definitely going to Little John's this weekend so get a baby sitter." Gertie said ending the call.

Before the weekend hit Booker invited Gertie out for drinks. She felt comfortable hanging out with him at work but she hadn't thought about an actual *date* with him.

"Change of plans." Gertie said when Karisma picked up the phone that Friday evening. "Old boy just invited *us* out for a drink." Gertie said. "He said he works off duty sometimes on the weekends at *The Red Onion* on Wilshire, and that he can get us an off duty job there if we can use some extra money."

"Oh so he invited *us* out for drinks huh? And said he can get *us* a job if *we* need the money huh?" Karisma asked.

"Well he said *me* but I told him my girl was the one looking for work so honey I told him *we* are a package deal. You said you could use some extra cash right?"

"Yeah. I did."

"Well then this may be a good thing for *you* if it pans out. He said if we come to the restaurant he will introduce us to the manager and show us the ropes for the off duty job."

"Sounds good because I have not been successful finding a decent off duty gig on my own so it sounds promising. Let's go see what he's talking about. I can't stay out long tonight because I have to pick up Morgan from her dad later on tonight."

"Ok well I will let him know *we* are on to meet him."

Gertie hadn't asked Robert and Clara to babysit on a weekend in a long time so they were more than willing to keep Marcus overnight so she could go and hang out. Karisma called Gertie as soon as she was off work and later picked her up so they could ride together to *The Red Onion*.

The club part of the restaurant was dimly lit when the ladies walked in. Gertie was wearing a cute sundress showing her big legs with her freshly painted toenails showing through her peep toe sandals. Karisma was wearing a form fitting jumpsuit with lace up booties on her cute little feet. Gertie's hair was down and flowing past her shoulders and her make-up was pure perfection and Karisma's pixie haircut was lying just right. The ladies were looking fly. They were ready to meet the restaurant manager and land an off-duty job for Karisma. Booker was sitting at the bar but didn't see them walk in.

"Is this seat taken?" Gertie asked when she approached Booker with Karisma by her side.

"Damn is that you Bellamy?" Booker turned sharply to look at her. He was shocked to see her looking so gorgeous. "You clean up good girl!"

"Oh thanks." Gertie said blushing. "This is my friend Karisma who I told you is interested in off duty work."

"For sure." Booker said turning to Karisma. "Nice to meet you *Karima.*"

"It's Ka-ris-ma." She said rolling her eyes. Her first impression was she didn't like Booker.

"I'm sorry. *Ka-ris-ma.*" Booker said slowly as he stood to his feet. "I have lots of connections for off duty gigs and not just here at the restaurant. So I got you ladies. Me and some of my buddies work security at The Oakridge Apartment complex in Culver City and in return they let us live there rent free so if you want a hook up like that I can help you get in there too, and I also have an in for security jobs working for several celebrities. Just tell me what you want and I'll do my best to hook you up." Booker was bragging.

"It sounds like you do have the hook up." Karisma said nodding in acceptance of his information. "I don't need an apartment. What I need is *work* so I can save up for a down payment on a house, so the other security opportunities here at the restaurant and for the celebrities sound doable for me. What kind of celebrities are you talking about?" Karisma asked.

"Like the heiress to the Arm and Hammer Brand fortune and the wife of a Grammy winning recording artist. I don't want to say her name. But Ms. Arm and Hammer has 24 hour security to guard her millions and her estate in Brentwood." Booker said with a chuckle. "And she prefers female officers so that may be a good option for you."

"Really? Ok cool. I want in." Karisma was really interested.

"Yeah. Yeah. Yeah. Enough shop talk. We can't stay long tonight. I just wanted to stop by for a little bit. My girl has to get home *and* I need to go spend some time with my son as well." Gertie explained as Karisma nodded in agreement.

"The restaurant owner had to leave early tonight so if you are interested in working *here* I will set up a meeting for you next weekend. Ok?"

"Ok. Thanks." Karisma said as she and Gertie turned to leave.

"I'll catch you later Bellamy." Booker said as the ladies walked away.

"Thank you girl for remembering that I couldn't stay long."

"No worries. So what you think?" Gertie asked.

"That nigga is a slickster sis. You need to watch out for him."

"Girl I already know. You have to admit the nigga is fine though. Right?" Gertie asked. "But, I'm not fucking around with him." She said. She was trying to sound convincing.

———◆———

After working in Detectives with Booker for a while Gertie found him to be *very* charming. He had a good sense of humor and made her laugh. She felt comfortable with him after getting to know him so they finally exchanged phone numbers.

Gertie's primary goal was to make Detective in the near future so she took advantage of Booker's knowledge and experience. He mentored her and shared his plan on how *he* was also going to study and prepare for the test. He provided her with insight on how to tackle oral questions and directed her to the right sections of the various Department Manuals for the best information. Gertie appreciated his help and thought he was genuine in his quest to help her promote. She really felt he had her best interest at heart. She and Booker finally got to a point where they talked about their personal lives, which is when Gertie realized that he knew a lot more about *her* life than she knew about his.

"So how's the Stockbroker doing?" Booker asked while he and Gertie were at lunch one day.

"What?" She was not sure she heard him correctly.

"Don't you date a Stockbroker?" He asked boldly.

"For your information I don't, but who have *you* been talking to about *me*?" Gertie pursed her lips. She didn't appreciate his prying. "Did PJ tell you that?"

"Hell no." Booker answered quickly. "I got mad love for PJ because when I asked him about you a while ago he refused to give up any info and that showed me he really respects you so I never asked him again. I have *other* sources though." He said. "I know you grew up in New York or Jersey; you went to USC where your daddy works; you have a son and your ex husband was a cop before he was convicted for Rape. Actually I met him once when he was working at Southwest. I thought he was a cool brother."

"Wow...that's crazy and scary at the same time. You are something else." Gertie said shaking her head while picking at her food. "Your source is fairly accurate. Since you seem to know so much about me why don't you tell me about *you?*"

"Can I call you tonight?" Booker asked. "We gotta get back to work."

"Sure. I don't like that you know so much about me and I know *nothing* about you." Gertie said as they got up to leave the break room.

In spite of Booker's prying a little too much into Gertie's personal life, she still found herself drawn to him. The two talked on the phone later that evening just as Booker requested and on a regular basis after that. During those conversations Booker told Gertie that he was single, he lived alone in Culver City, and he shared custody of his 8-year-old son with his ex girlfriend/baby mama.

"I never married my child's mom because she couldn't seem to leave her ex boyfriends in the past." Booker offered. "I had to demand a paternity test to make sure the boy was mine. Luckily we have an amicable relationship for our son's sake."

"Oh ok. Well that's good at least your son has you in his life. My poor baby has no father figure since my sorry ass ex is locked up for the next few years. I thank God for my daddy being there for us though." Gertie said.

"Maybe we can change that..." Booker started.

"No. Don't even go there. We are just *friends.*" Gertie blurted out.

"No girl I meant maybe I can pick your son up sometimes when I have my son and he can hang out with us."

Booker offered. "I love sports and my son plays little league baseball."

"Oh. Ok. That sounds nice. My son is playing T-Ball right now so maybe he can learn from watching the older boys play." Gertie felt a sense of comfort believing that Booker's intentions were good after all.

"You know I play on the Department's Men's basketball team right?"

"For real? I played basketball growing up and in college." Gertie said.

"Yeah I know. At USC right?" Booker said as he broke out into a hearty laugh.

"Oh you got jokes with your nosey ass." Gertie laughed along with him.

"I also love water sports, camping, riding motorcycles, and traveling." Booker rattled off.

"Dang! So do I. I love doing some of those things as well so it looks like we have more in common than I thought."

———◆———

Karisma had been working security at *The Red Onion* for a few months but she still didn't like Booker any better. He kept trying to get Gertie to work off duty as well.

"No thank you." She said once again turning down the opportunity to work off duty. "I was mainly helping my friend get work. I'm not trying to work off duty anywhere. So I will respectfully decline again. But I do appreciate the fact that you are a man of your word. Thanks for hooking up my home girl. You know everybody." Gertie complimented Booker.

On occasion when their schedules allowed Gertie and Karisma met up at different police functions or events and Booker seemed to be at every single event. He was a social butterfly. He and Gertie socialized in those environments and he always bought her drinks and paid her special attention. They clearly weren't coupled up at those times but it wasn't long before he asked her out on an actual date and to his surprise she accepted.

Booker and Gertie hung out often and thoroughly enjoyed each other's company with and without their kids. They spent countless hours laughing and talking about any and everything. She was still in love with Rashon and often thought of him even when she was with Booker and she wondered if by some miracle, Rashon would come back to normalcy. Ultimately she knew it was impossible so she abandoned those thoughts and over time her feelings for Rashon diminished. Booker's timing was impeccable in that he was there when she needed her spirits lifted. He made her smile again.

On one Friday night Gertie went to Little John's with Karisma to unwind. She needed a break from Booker but as it turned out he was also there as it was one of his favorite hangouts too. They acknowledged each other, but he acted like he didn't really want her to be there. He seemed to have an attitude when he saw her dancing and having a great time with some of her classmates.

"Hey what's wrong with Booker?" Karisma asked. "When you were dancing he was staring at you like a damn stalker."

"I don't think anything is wrong. We are just *friends* and he knows that." Gertie assured Karisma while sipping slowly on her Long Island Ice Tea.

"Well, he's gawking at you like a jealous boyfriend and I don't like that."

"I'm just glad he is not in my face because I don't want everyone all up in my business asking a bunch of questions about me and him. So let his ass stay over there and gawk all he wants from a distance." Gertie said as she pulled one of her male classmates onto the dance floor.

———◆———

Gertie had not heard from Taylor in a while but she figured she was getting more and more into rebuilding her relationship with Cassie. Taylor finally got around to talking to Sergeant Alese about joining the women's basketball team.

"Hey Gertie you know we have the World Games coming up in a few months so Sergeant Alese asked me to reach out to you to see if you want to play on our *5 on 5 team.*"

"Oh yeah, that's right you're at Training Division now. I have been so wrapped up in my drama I haven't talked to you but I do remember seeing your name on the Transfer Order a couple of months ago. How do you like it there?"

"I *love* it at Training. Sergeant Alese is hella cool *and* she has my back." Taylor happily reported. "I needed to get out of Patrol at Southwest because it's just too crazy over there so when Sergeant Alese transferred out she asked me if I was interested in working Training Division and I jumped at the opportunity. I'm working Human Relations." Taylor said.

"That's cool, and yes I would love to play in the World Games. Where are the games being held this year?"

"At the Convention Center in Downtown L.A."

"I am so out of shape it's ridiculous." Gertie reported.

"We have practice on Saturday mornings here at the Academy so you need to come and practice with us." Taylor was glad it was an easy sell on Gertie. "How have you and Marcus been?"

"Marcus is amazing. He's playing T-Ball and doing well in school. As for me, I'm just trying to get my groove back. Dating a little bit." Out of respect for Taylor and Jaxon's close friendship Gertie didn't share the details of her dating life after Jaxon.

"So, have you heard from Jaxon or his mom?" Taylor asked.

"Nope sure haven't heard from Jaxon, and Deanna is talking about suing me under some Grandparents Rights Bill." Gertie shared.

"What the hell?" Taylor asked in disbelief. "How is she gonna sue you to see *your* child? She crazy."

"No, she's not crazy Tay. I honestly feel bad for her *and* Moses and I understand how she feels but I am just afraid that if I let her keep Marcus she's gonna take him to see Jaxon and I'm dead set against that as you already know."

"Yeah I remember you said you don't want that, and I get it but maybe you can take Marcus to visit them and you stay with him during the visit." Taylor reasoned. "I know they love Marcus and they want to see him especially now that Jaxon is going to be gone for a while."

"You know that's actually a good idea." Gertie exclaimed. "Maybe I will call Deanna even though our last contact didn't end so well. Marcus needs to have a relationship with them just as he has with my family. Ok. Thanks Tay I'm so glad you called. Don't forget to tell Sergeant Alese that I'm in. I'll see you on Saturday."

———◆———

Gertie enjoyed hanging out with Karisma at Little Johns. She was a little put off by Booker's attitude the last time she saw him there but she just figured it was typical jealousy because she knew he longed to be in a monogamous relationship with her. He was fine at work. It was business as usual.

"Mija, I need an update on suspect Terrence Collins. Have you any info for me?" Marisol asked.

"Yes ma'am. You know the day we served the warrant we discovered he works for the City as a Mechanic. Well when I checked with his supervisor yesterday they told me he has not been back to work since he called in sick on the day we served the warrant. They have been showing him as *Absent Without Leave* but the funny thing is he has not even returned to pick up his last two pay checks either."

"I wonder if he's dead." Marisol remarked. She was being facetious.

"It *is* like he dropped off the face of the earth." Gertie responded. "There haven't been any new rapes so I'll just keep conducting due diligence and exhausting all leads that come up."

"Switching reels. Have you been studying for the upcoming Detective Exam?" Marisol asked.

"Yes ma'am I'm in a study group and I have been attending the training seminars at the Bureau."

"That's good because you *have* to pass this next test or you will be back out in Patrol."

"I know but that's not happening ma'am." She said shaking her head vigorously.

———◆———

Gertie tried her best to steer clear of Booker as much as possible in the office as she didn't want anyone to know they were hanging out so much. Even though their relationship was still strictly platonic he took her to nice restaurants, jazz concerts, comedy clubs, and weekend excursions to Las Vegas. She was still not ready to take their relationship to the next level but to her surprise, he told her he was falling in love with her. She didn't take him serious at first because she figured he was just trying to get her into bed.

One evening Booker and Gertie were hanging out and stopped at Tito's Tacos for a quick bite to eat. Since they were in the area Booker decided to stop by his apartment there in Culver City for a few minutes before taking her back home. The grounds at the Apartment complex were immaculate, however once inside Booker's apartment Gertie noted that it was a straight up bachelor's pad, which struck her as odd. She thought to herself *a brother with his style and finances should be able to afford a nicer place.* He drove a Porsche 911 and a Lincoln Navigator SUV, but he was living like a bum.

After hanging out with him for about a year as friends Gertie entered into a dating relationship with him. When she had sex with him the first time she was shocked to see that he was uncircumcised which kind of turned her off but she was so horny she didn't care. Besides, she thought he had *mad skills in the oral sex arena* so she gave him a pass for not being circumcised. She made sure that she kept condoms in her possession at all times after that night to make the feel of his penis more inviting whenever they hooked up. Gertie thought about PJ's admonition that *everything that shines ain't always gold.* That saying rang true in this case with Booker, Gertie thought after having sex with him.

As Booker and Gertie got deeper into a relationship he started to describe the rules they were going to play by, which made her immediately regret taking their relationship to the next level.

"I'm a very private person." He warned. "I don't like people knowing my business, especially people on the Department."

"You weren't that *private* when you were asking everybody and they mama about *me*, so what is really going on here Booker? I mean we have been *everywhere* together so I'm *really* confused."

"Well, I just want to keep our *relationship* out of public scrutiny because anyone who may have animosity against *me* may try to take it out on *you* and vice versa."

"Hold up a minute. Why are you all of a sudden concerned about *my* welfare?" Gertie asked in an angry tone.

"Why are you getting mad?" He was trying to placate Gertie. "Hear me out. The Department is full of racist and sexist cops who would love to see *us* fail and I want to protect you at any cost."

"Ok you are killing me with your concerns and rules." Gertie said studying his face trying to figure out what was really going on. When he was hounding her he didn't mind being seen with her. She didn't like that.

Of course, being fairly new to the Department what Booker said made sense to her so she kept their relationship out of the public eye but she finally told Karisma that she and Booker were actually *dating*.

"Are you serious?" Karisma asked. "I do not like that man but if you like his ass I guess I'll have to get used to him being around. I just don't trust him."

"I don't trust half the niggas you hang out with either but I don't say anything because you don't keep them around that long." Gertie quipped.

"Girl I am not offended by your recall because guess what? It's all about the *D* with me. I don't need to *trust* they ass. I hit it and quit it, so now what?" Karisma commented as they laughed at each other.

"I took Booker to meet my daddy, *and* I met his parents. They live in Northeast Division in Silver Lake so I give them extra patrol whenever I'm out in the field." Gertie said proudly.

"What did your daddy say about him?"

"My dad and Clara think he is charming and good for me and Marcus."

"You think they are just glad that you didn't go back to crazy Rashon? So basically anybody sane will do?" Karisma asked.

"Oh you are funny as hell. No, they are glad that I am finally *happy*. Thank you very much."

After the staycations in and near California early on in their relationship Booker took Gertie to Acapulco, Cancun, Hawaii, and on boating trips in Lake Havasu. He treated her like a queen. He repeatedly told her he loved her and she fell for him hard.

One summer weekend Booker and his friends planned a boating trip to Lake Havasu and he invited Gertie to go with him.

"Wait a minute. Are you sure you want to expose our relationship to your cop buddies?" Gertie asked.

"These guys are cool babe. Plus they already know about your fine ass." Booker boasted.

"What? How? I thought we were keeping our *relationship* out of public scrutiny? I'm really confused by you."

"Just let it go and let's just have some fun. You think too much."

Booker picked Gertie up in his Navigator, which had a newer model jet ski in tow. She had never jet skied before so she was super excited to try it. When she got to their two story cabin at the Topock Marina, 25 miles up the river from Havasu they checked in and later went to the bar to meet Booker's friends. Gertie recognized several of the officers from around the Department and Booker formally introduced her to all of them.

Gertie knew that two of Booker's friends were definitely married but the women they were with were *not* their wives. That made her uncomfortable because she *knew* their wives, who were also female officers who she liked and respected. Gertie could not wait to get back to their room.

"So, Booker what's up with your friends hanging out with these random women?" Gertie asked.

"Aww girl it ain't no big deal *and* it ain't any of our business." He laughed it off casually.

"I agree it's not my business but I don't like being put in this situation." Gertie felt nervous about the weekend.

"Look, can we just have a good relaxing weekend? Please?" Booker pleaded.

The weekend was off to an uncomfortable start however Gertie thought she would try to make the best of it. They spent all day Saturday taking turns on the Jet Skis and eating and drinking on the boat one of Booker's friends brought to the lake. They were supposed to stay at the lake until Sunday afternoon but Booker received an emergency call late Saturday evening after they returned to their cabin from a day on the lake.

"Hey." Booker said nudging Gertie, who had fallen asleep. "We gotta go. My dad is sick."

"Ok. What's wrong with him? Where is your mom?" Gertie asked. She was groggy.

"I don't know what's going on all I know is he's sick and we need to go so I can check on him and make sure my mom is ok too." Booker said as he washed his face and brushed his teeth in a hurry. "Girl, get up!"

"Ok damn." Gertie said throwing the covers off of her naked body. "I have to get dressed and pack my shit."

"Ok but hurry up." He said. She noticed that he was suddenly in a foul mood.

Booker loaded up the suitcases on the back seat and made sure the Jet Ski was secured to the back of the SUV. He called his friends and told them he was cutting out early and then he drove home quickly, dropped Gertie off at her dad's house and sped off in a hurry. He later called and told her they took his dad to the hospital where he was admitted for *observation.*

"I will keep him in prayer." Gertie said genuinely concerned about his father.

"Please do. But I'm sure he will be ok."

"I'll stop by the hospital tomorrow to see him." Gertie said.

"Please don't do that. My son's mother will be there so it may be awkward for you to be there too."

"Oh ok...no problem." Gertie said.

The next day, Booker called Gertie and said his father was released from the hospital and he was home resting. He had high blood pressure and hadn't taken his medicine as directed so he was dizzy and lightheaded when they took him to the emergency room. But all was well.

———◆———

That whole next week was hectic at work with Marisol on Gertie's case about everything. They were shorthanded and Terrence Collins was still roaming around free to commit more rapes. Gertie was glad that Friday had finally arrived. She needed to unwind so she agreed to meet Karisma at Little John's after she got Marcus in bed at her dad's house.

There were several folks at Little John's from Gertie's office that night and everyone was having a good time partying. Gertie hit the dance floor as soon as she got there. She bypassed her usual Long Island Ice tea and just ordered a glass of White Zinfandel. After tearing up the dance floor for a little while she returned to the table where Karisma was guarding their purses. Karisma was talking to a woman Gertie didn't know. Karisma introduced the woman to Gertie as Officer Ramona Fletcher, who worked Pacific Division.

"Nice to meet you Ramona." Gertie said casually sipping on her wine and watching what was going on on the dance floor.

"Are you the *Gertie* who's seeing Corey Booker?" Ramona asked.

"Who?" Gertie furtively looked around the crowded room.

"*Corey Booker.*" Ramona repeated. "I heard he was seeing a girl name Gertie, who works Northeast."

"Well I do work Northeast and my name is Gertie."

"Oh well do you know that Booker is married, and his wife *just* had a baby this past weekend?"

"What?" Gertie asked. She was stunned; paralyzed by the news. Absolutely shocked but tried not to show it.

"You might wanna close your legs to married men." Ramona said as she chuckled and abruptly turned and walked away.

"Hey! Hey. What the hell is your problem?" Karisma asked as he scurried out of the booth.

"Bitch. Fuck you! You don't know me." Gertie said trying to keep her voice down as Karisma grabbed her by the arm to keep her from following Ramona into the crowd.

"Get your shit and let's go!" Karisma said as she pulled Gertie back towards the booth. Gertie grabbed her purse with one hand and her glass of wine with the other. She guzzled the remainder of her wine and set the glass down just in time for Karisma to yank her towards the door. Gertie shook her head in disbelief as she stomped out of the location. She felt like she had been kicked in the gut by big foot. Her head was spinning and it was *not* from the wine.

"This is *not* possible!" She said as Karisma guided her out of the club.

"Who the fuck is this bitch and *why* is she gossiping with someone else about *me?*"

"I just met her tonight." Karisma explained as they walked towards Karisma's car in a nearby parking lot.

"She has it all wrong! I was with Booker this past weekend so I know damn well he didn't have a baby. She obviously has shit all fucked up." Gertie ranted as she and Karisma stood outside of Karisma's car. Gertie then looked up and saw Ramona walking at a fast pace towards her and Karisma in the parking lot.

"Hey!" Karisma shouted to Ramona while standing in front of Gertie to shield her. "You need to stay your ratchet ass over there. We are grown ass women and *not* trying to fuck with you. What do you want? This is ridiculous."

"I'm not trying to start anything. I just want to apologize." Ramona said slowing her pace with her hands up. She explained that she acted impulsively with Gertie and knew immediately that she needed to apologize to avoid any future drama since they were both on the job.

"When I heard your name I just had to say something because my sister used to date Booker before he started dating you that's how I found out about you. He's such a womanizer and he pretends to be single. When my sister found out he was married she dumped him. But she was heartbroken because she was pregnant with his child and he made her have an abortion. He was playing her big time then he moved on with you." Ramona said.

"Well I'm not seeing anyone." That's all Gertie was willing to say. She wasn't confirming anything about her personal life with that chick.

"Well. I just thought you should know what's being said. I apologize for coming at you wrong like I did." Ramona said.

"No problem." Gertie said looking over Karisma's shoulder.

"Lord Jesus, please let this be *another* Corey Booker she's talking about." Gertie whispered to Karisma as Ramona walked away. Karisma turned and looked at Gertie, and Gertie looked back at her. "I have to find out what is really going on with Mr. Booker."

"Just calm down." Karisma warned. "It's probably *not* true. Her sister is a woman scorned so they trying to hurt you thinking you took him from her. We don't know if he's really married."

Gertie cursed to herself all the way home. Something told her there was some truth to what Ratchet Ramona was saying. Reflecting back on the previous weekend Gertie recalled that they did leave the Lake abruptly. She wondered if Booker's dad was really sick and if it was really the reason they had to leave. She had met Booker's parents for Christ's sake. *How could he be so manipulative?* She asked herself.

She and Booker went on trips together, spent nights together, spent weekends, weekdays and holidays together so she could not understand how any woman would allow her husband to be away from home *that much.* No way. There had to be a good explanation. A major red flag was that Gertie had been to his apartment and she saw how bare it was with hardly any furniture, like he didn't really live there. She chose to change that red flag to green. Her head was pounding as it was filled with a million questions she had for him. She couldn't focus. She needed desperately to talk to him.

She called him as soon as she got home that night because she didn't want to talk to him while she was driving. She needed to get her thoughts together first. Booker didn't answer his phone so she paged him *9-1-1*, which was an emergency code they used when they needed to speak to each other right away. He called her back within 15 minutes.

"Are you married?" Gertie went right in.

"Who told you that?" Booker asked.

"That was not the answer I was expecting. Damn it. Answer *my* question. Are you fucking married?"

"Yes!" Booker said after a moment of silence on the phone. "But I'm *separated.*"

Gertie's heart sank. She couldn't believe what she was hearing. Ratchet Ramona was telling the truth.

"You are such a fucking liar!" Gertie yelled into the phone. "You lied to me big time. So, so, so, did your wife, who you are supposedly *separated* from, have a baby this past weekend? And don't fucking lie to me!" She demanded to know.

"*Who* told you this? *Who* have you been talking to?" Booker's response was clearly a diversion tactic. "Didn't I tell you that people on the Department are nosey and always in peoples personal business?"

"Will you please just answer my fucking question? Did your *wife* have a baby this past weekend? That's all I want to know is if your wife had a fucking baby! Just tell me the truth."

"Yes!" He finally screamed into the phone. "My *daughter was* born Sunday evening."

"Oh...my...God. So it's true?" Gertie asked as she sank to the floor in her living room. "All this time I have been lied to, duped, bamboozled, hoodwinked and deceived to the nth degree! I've been played for the biggest fool in the world. No wonder your married cop friends don't mind me knowing about *their* girlfriends on the side because *I* was your fucking girlfriend on the side. Go fuck yourself you uncircumcised piece of shit!" She said as she slammed the phone down. She cried all night.

Gertie was devastated once again but she didn't want to call her parents and she was sorry that Karisma was up close and personal when the drama unfolded. She hoped that her split from Booker did not interfere with Karisma's off duty job he got for her but she couldn't remain friends with him. Karisma called Gertie bright and early on the next morning. She needed to check on her friend.

"Good morning sis." Karisma said tentatively.

"I'm devastated." Gertie said whimpering. "I have been sick to my stomach all night knowing that I fell in love with a married man and didn't even realize after all the time we spent together that he was married. How could he be so dishonest and cruel? He was certainly good at hiding his family life that's for sure. I thought he loved me, but instead he used me."

"Do not blame yourself. You had no way of knowing he was a total fraud. You are such a loving person and you love so hard maybe sometimes you're blinded by these rotten crazy motherfuckers."

"But how did I not know this shit. I should've stayed my ass at home the first time he invited me out to *The Red Onion*."

It turned out that Booker had been married for 12 years to a woman who had his 2 children and they lived in a brand-new housing development in an exclusive area of the San Fernando Valley called Porter Ranch. Booker's shabby apartment was a crash pad for him and other officers to use while they worked security at the apartment complex. He never *lived* there. He was a predator; a member of a police officer's fraternity group of guys who went after newer female police officers with a vengeance and Gertie was one of his victims.

CHAPTER 14

"SHE DID IT"

———◆———

"Hi mom…" Gertie said. She wasn't her usual bubbly self.

"What's wrong baby?" Celeste asked.

"I'm just tired of making the same dumb ass decisions mom. Every relationship I have had has ended horribly and *I'm* the common denominator."

"Nope. You stop that shit right now." Celeste gripped the phone tightly. "You need to tell me what's going on. Did you and Booker break up or something?"

"Yes we sure did." Gertie sounded angry. "I just found out that he's married with children!"

"You have got to be kidding me." Celeste was surprised. "But you guys dated for a long time."

"Yes and I *trusted* him. He really deceived me mom. He made a fool out of me. I should have followed my first mind and stayed away from him but instead I let my guard down."

"Gertie you are such a smart woman. Didn't you see *any* red flags?" Celeste asked.

"Yes I saw red flags. But when I expressed my concerns about various things that came up he explained *everything* away. I should have trusted my gut. I really thought he loved me."

"You did nothing wrong but give of yourself, and the asshole took advantage." Celeste said trying to comfort her. "I know you have your dad there but do you want me to come and hang out with you for a couple of weeks?"

"I would love that mom." Gertie said perking up a bit. "Marcus is getting so big and you really need to see him."

"Ok let me make some arrangements for someone to cover for me at work and I'll call Ms. Wanda and have her book my flights. I will let you know when my travel plans are made ok?"

"Yay!" Gertie squealed. "Thanks mom. So, how's Michelle?"

"Oh she is fine. Her club team has a tournament coming up in the DMV area so maybe I'll come visit you when she's gone to that." Celeste said.

"Ok cool because I really want your undivided attention and if Michelle comes we won't be able to spend any real quality time together." Gertie said.

"You sound like Bea. You know she still can't stand Michelle." Celeste said.

"Well I like Michelle but I want to spend time with *you* alone mother." Gertie explained. "I hope that you don't let Michelle totally ruin your relationship with Aunt Bea." She was happy to change the subject from Booker. "Bea has been your ride or die for many years."

"I agree and that's why *I* have been spending more time with *her*. Actually Michelle has encouraged me to spend more time with Bea so everything will work its way out I'm sure of it."

"Ok mom. I'm about to turn in. I have to work in the morning."

"Please be safe out there ok? Keep your head up and kiss my baby for me. I love you lots."

———◆———

GERTIE SPENT THE NEXT FEW months working sex cases and trying her best to locate Terrence Collins the sexual predator. There were no new crimes committed at the Gentlemen's clubs and no new leads developed to locate him.

Gertie cringed every time she saw Booker in the squad room. She kept her head down and prayed daily that he would transfer out of the division. He on the other hand took every opportunity to engage her in conversation in front of others making it difficult for her to ignore him. He thought his charm could win her over again.

"Hey Bellamy. You guys find your rape suspect yet?" Booker asked in passing early one morning when there weren't many in the office yet.

"When are you going out on Bonding Leave?" Gertie asked in return loud enough for others to hear. "I heard your wife had a baby. Congratulations!"

"Aww man. I didn't know you had a new baby." PJ said. "Congratulations man. Where the cigars at?" PJ asked. "Oh you don't know anything about that protocol huh? I didn't know you were married." PJ said walking towards Booker to shake his hand.

"Me either." Gertie said under her breath cutting a side eye at Booker as he nervously walked away without answering PJ or shaking his hand.

"What's that niggas problem?" PJ asked Gertie after Booker slithered away.

"Oh he has a lot of problems but I ain't one to gossip." Gertie said.

"Ok then." PJ looked down at Gertie then turned to look at Booker still walking away. He suspected that something was going on with them but he decided not to inquire. PJ had barely sat down when two patrol officers approached his desk.

"Detective Martin?" The young officer was tentative in his approach.

"Yeah that's me. What you need?" PJ studied the faces of the two young officers.

"We are here to make a notification." The senior officer advised.

"Ok. I'm listening. What ya got?"

"Sir there was an Assault with a Deadly Weapon behind the Gentlemen's Club over on Fletcher Drive and the victim was transported to County USC Medical Center. She's not expected to live so the Watch Commander told us to notify you. They also believe she might have been sexually assaulted."

"Ok. We'll roll out. Thanks guys." PJ said as he stood to his feet and looked around the room for Loren. When he didn't see him he asked Gina to page him. He then went to talk to Marisol.

"Hey your serial rape suspect may have struck again." He reported.

"Why did they notify you instead of me?" She asked looking up at PJ's imposing figure standing over her.

"I guess because the victim is *circling the drain*. Apparently the call came out as an ADW that occurred at the Gentlemen's Club but it might turn into a homicide." PJ was annoyed by Marisol's attitude. "Isn't that the same place your suspect has been capering *Mija*?"

"Yeah *Puto!*" She responded realizing he was mocking her.

"Look damn it I know you weren't notified but you still may want to roll with us or better yet send somebody because I'm sure you have some smoke breaks left to take before you go home." PJ said. "Anyway the victim was possibly sexually assaulted so you can see if the MO matches your suspect's M-O." PJ turned sharply and walked away.

"Bellamy!" Marisol yelled across the room.

"Yes ma'am. Be there in a minute." She responded as she finished making copies of a report.

"Mija." Marisol yelled. "I need you to roll out with Homicide. It appears we have an ADW/Sexual Assault incident at the strip club on Fletcher."

"So why is Homicide rolling?" Gertie asked when she got back to her desk.

"Because the victim might die from the assault." PJ interrupted as he walked toward Gertie putting on his jacket. "Get your shit and let's go." He said. "I'm going to teach you some real police work."

"What's that supposed to mean PJ?" Marisol took offense to his snide remark.

"You heard me." He said looking at Marisol. "Let's go so I can teach you *some real police work*." He repeated diverting his attention to Gertie. "I didn't stutter." He nodded for Gertie to follow him as he walked towards the door with one of his favorite Goorin Brothers hat cocked to one side and his leather notepad case tucked under his arm.

"Hey PJ." Gina yelled from across the room. "Loren is at an autopsy."

"Oh yeah I forgot about that. My *all timers* is acting up again." He said laughing.

"I can help out if you need me." Booker said from across the room.

"Hell no." Gertie said under her breath looking at PJ.

"Naw man." PJ saw the look on Gertie's face. "We good. Thanks."

"What in the hell is going on with you and Booker?" PJ asked as he and Gertie hurriedly walked to the car. "Y'all were bosom buddies a little while ago and now you throwing darts and shutting him down at every turn."

"There's *nothing* going on. That's for sure." Gertie said nonchalantly.

"Are y'all fuckin'?" PJ asked bluntly.

"No... Well... not anymore."

"Oh ok I got it. Ya'll *were* fuckin' and now you are not so now shit is awkward."

"No. We were in a *relationship*!" Gertie emphasized. "And then I found out his ass was married. I swear PJ I have the worst luck with men. My husband is in prison for raping prostitutes; my boyfriend after that went fucking psycho on me and then I dated *this* asshole for a while only to find out that he's been married for 12 years and has two kids! What in the hell is wrong with *me?*" She was fighting back tears.

"Whoa...are you ok?" PJ asked abruptly pulling his car to the curb.

"I'm sorry. I'm sorry." She said as tears starting streaming down her face. "Keep going please. I'll pull myself together before we get to the hospital."

"No. That victim isn't going anywhere. I'm sorry. I don't mean to be insensitive but right now what's going on with *you* is more important to me. Talk to me." PJ turned towards Gertie. He was really concerned. He liked her.

Gertie cried uncontrollably for a good 3-4 minutes while trying to explain how she was feeling. PJ could not understand a word she said. He sat patiently and waited for her to regain her composure.

"I don't want to talk about it." Gertie finally proclaimed as she sat up and looked straight ahead without blinking.

"This seatbelt is choking the shit out of me." She said as she yanked on it.

"My bad. It locked in place when I pulled over so abruptly. You good?"

"I don't want to talk about it right now. For real."

"Really?" PJ looked at her sitting stoically staring straight ahead. "Ok. Well, I'm not going to force you to talk. Just know I'm here if you want to talk." He said slowly pulling away from the curb.

———————————

By the time they arrived at County Hospital the victim had died. The young stripper had only been in the City of Angels for two weeks from Missouri. Officers were still standing by to brief Detectives when they arrived. PJ went to talk to them and Gertie went directly to the victim's body, which was still in the emergency room covered with a bed sheet.

"Sir the victim's purse with her ID is missing, but the club has tentatively identified her as Ms. Shana Lovelace. At least that's the name she gave them when she applied for employment there." The young officer reported. "She was pretty much dead by the time paramedics arrived at the hospital but they put her on a respirator because they felt a faint pulse. When we arrived on scene we canvassed the area and found a witness. The wit who works at a restaurant next to the strip club said he was about to go out to empty the trash when he heard the commotion in the alley. He thought it was just a boyfriend girlfriend scuffle because the victim was not screaming so he backed away into the doorway of the restaurant and that's when he saw the man hold the woman down with his knee on her throat while he put on a condom and that's when he realized the man was raping the woman. He then saw the suspect place his forearm on the victim's neck to hold her down while he had sex with her. The wit was scared to intervene so he just ran back inside and called 9-1-1 at that point. When he returned to the alley he saw the suspect running away from the nearby dumpster, which is when the wit ran to the victim to check on her."

"Damn. So there may not be any DNA evidence." PJ commented.

"Not true sir. We were checking the area of the dumpster for her purse when we found a freshly used condom. The suspect probably tried to throw it away but missed the bin and didn't realize it."

"Ok cool. Great job guys. You got good info on the witness right?" PJ asked.

"Yes sir we have a full written statement from him."

"Ok that's great." PJ said shaking the officers hands.

———————

Gertie slowly peeled back the corner of the sheet revealing the victim's pretty young face. She was standing over the body studying it closely when PJ walked through the opening of the closed curtain that surrounded the victim's bed.

"I wonder *how* she died because she doesn't look battered." Gertie uttered looking at PJ.

"We will get answers about the cause of death at the autopsy." He said. "In the meantime you need to request to have the condom that officers recovered analyzed to see if this incident is connected to your suspect Collins."

"Ok. I didn't know *what* evidence officers recovered." Gertie said shaken by the dead body lying there.

"You ok?" PJ asked.

"Yeah. It's just so sad that some asshole killed this girl. She's so young."

"Yeah. It's always sad when I see an innocent person like her killed. It just makes me want to solve the case that much more and arrest the bastard responsible." PJ stepped out of the room to give officers some last minute direction. Gertie slowly pulled the sheet back over the victim's face and followed right behind him. The dead body lying there all of a sudden spooked her.

"Let's try to confirm her identity and get the next of kin information and contact the law enforcement agency in Missouri so they can make the Death Notification."

"Ok. I'll get all the the reports from the officers." Gertie said.

PJ and Gertie returned to the office to find Lt. Lane in the squad room laughing and talking with Marisol. PJ walked past them purposely ignoring them. Marisol and Lane looked at him as he passed and then back at each other and then shrugged their shoulders. Lane knew PJ and Marisol didn't get along so she wasn't too surprised by the snub. Gertie went to the ladies and immediately briefed them.

"Hey PJ." Marisol called out in his direction.

"What *Mija?*" PJ looked up and saw her and Lane staring at him. "*What?*" He asked again at a higher octave. They could tell he was annoyed. "I just heard Bellamy brief you so what you need from me?"

"Marisol and I were just talking and I'm thinking that if this case ends up being related to the serial rape case, maybe I will move Bellamy to Homicide and *you guys* can work the serial rape case too along with the murder from today. That's *if* they are related."

"Whatever you wanna do L.T. you're the boss." PJ said turning towards Loren.

"So, how did the autopsy go today?"

"It's *Undetermined*." Loren said about the elderly man found dead in his car on the side of the 105 Freeway. "So what happened at the strip club?"

"A 19 year old blond here for only 2 weeks from Missouri was raped in the alley behind the club and later died at the hospital. I guess we will know more about the cause of death at the autopsy."

"So what do you think PJ?" Lane asked as she walked towards PJ and Loren.

"About what L.T." He was still annoyed by her and Marisol's impromptu meeting that he walked in on. Marisol was always bartering behind his back so he figured they were up to something.

"About moving Bellamy to Homicide and you guys take on the Rape case as well since the MO sounds so similar."

"Oh that. Yeah. Yeah. Yeah. I think it's a good idea." PJ said nonchalantly.

"I bet you do. It's a good idea because *you* get another body." Marisol said walking towards PJ's desk. She was in agreement with the L.T. to have homicide handle the case but she didn't want to lose the help from her table.

"Mind ya business Detective. Mind ya business." He said waving her back to her desk. "L.T. knows the case will get *solved* if I take it from your ass."

"Yeah. Mind ya business *Mija!*" Loren echoed as the men laughed heartily.

"Let's do it L.T." PJ said smirking at Marisol as she walked back to her desk. "Bellamy is sure to learn something under *my* leadership. We will be happy to take on the stripper case."

"Yeah right! Whatever PJ." Marisol quipped as she sat back down. "Mija you may as well get your things together and get set up in Homicide because you will be working with them ok?"

"Ok ma'am. Wow. Really?"

"Yes. Really."

"Ok. Thank you so much for everything. I'll start moving my things right away." Gertie was beaming on the inside. Although she looked forward to working Homicide she knew that PJ was going to be on her case about passing the Detective's Exam and that's just what she needed. "I'm still going to be picking your brain for the upcoming test."

"For sure Mija. Anything you need. All jokes aside." Marisol whispered. "You will learn a lot from that old bastard. PJ does know his shit."

"I don't see why you guys don't get along. You are both so awesome." Gertie said boxing up some small items from her desk

"Because he's an asshole that's why." Marisol said as the two laughed out loud causing PJ to look up in their direction. He rolled his eyes and then went back to what he was doing. He didn't care to ask what they were laughing about. He didn't give a shit.

———◆———

Gertie was beaming when she left work that evening. She was excited about working with PJ and Loren full time. That was just what she needed to take her mind off of Booker. Karisma was the first person she told about her move to Homicide. She was genuinely happy for Gertie. Gertie had avoided talking to her dad and Clara at length because she didn't want Booker's name to come up forcing her to talk about their break up. They really liked the Booker they thought they knew. Gertie broke down and told Robert her good news.

"Daddy, remember the rape case I was telling you I have been working on?"

"Yeah." Robert was half asleep in his easy chair.

"Well I'm going to be working Homicide now because one of the strippers was killed and they want me to work the murder case along with the rape cases with the Homicide Unit."

"Uh huh." Robert uttered.

"Daddy, are you asleep?"

"Yeah baby girl. I'm tired. Clara had me running around after work today, way after my bedtime." He said yawning. "Where's Marcus?"

"He's asleep. I love it when I am able to pick him up from school. I appreciate you guys so much but *I* want to pick him up as much as possible since you guys take care of him most of the time." Gertie said. "Anyway go on back to sleep. I'll talk to you tomorrow."

"Ok girl. Goodnight." He said hanging up the phone.

———◆———

Gertie was hurting but was keeping up a brave face in front of her dad and Marcus, which was the hardest thing ever. She wasn't as strong when she was at home alone. At those times she gave into her emotions and cried at the drop of a hat. Booker's faulty game of deception left her with a major void in her life.

She felt good when her mom came out and spent some good quality time with her and Marcus but it was a Band-Aid solution since she couldn't stay to offer ongoing moral support. Gertie had purposely not told her dad, Clara or Savannah the *real* reason she and Booker broke up when they asked because she was just too damn embarrassed. They had witnessed the fall out from the other two relationships and she just could not bring them into the latest drama. She had to deal with it on her own terms.

———◆———

Gertie couldn't get the image of the dead girl's face out of her mind so she sure wasn't looking forward to attending the autopsy.

"As soon as you finish getting settled in I need you to roll with me to the Coroner's Office. They are performing the stripper's autopsy first thing this morning."

"Ok. I'm almost done." Gertie instantly felt butterflies fluttering around in her stomach. "So, what is *our* role at the autopsy?" Gertie asked as she stuffed her handgun into her shoulder holster.

"We need to be present to find out the *cause of death* and other contributing factors early on in our investigation so we know if we have a murder or just a death investigation. It helps us determine the appropriate charges to file if we have a crime.

"Oh. Got it. I'm ready to roll when you are." She said as she put her jacket on.

PJ and Gertie took the short ride to the Coroner's office east of Downtown L.A. When they pulled up in the parking lot at the rear of the building there were several white County Coroner's vans backed into parking stalls close to the building, and the double doors to the building were wide open.

"Here." PJ said handing Gertie a small open jar of Vicks Vapo Rub before they exited the car. "Put some of this in your nostrils *and* under your nose."

"What does this do?" Gertie asked holding the jar high up in her hand to read the label.

"It helps to mask the odor of formaldehyde." PJ explained. "I know it might fuck up your little make up situation you got going on but trust me you're going to need it."

Just as Gertie laced her nostrils with the menthol salve she got out of the car and followed PJ through the back doors into the hallway of the Morgue. She immediately gagged and turned and ran back outside at the sight of the dead bodies on gurneys lining the hallway. There were too many to count. PJ continued to walk a short distance before he realized she was no longer following him. He turned and briskly walked back to the door and looked outside quickly scanning the area when he spotted her bent over and throwing up in a nearby trashcan.

"What in the hell are you doing?" He asked as he quickly walked towards her. "What is your problem?" He asked as he started to chuckle under his breath.

"Man. This is some freaky shit." Gertie said as she stood up straight wiping the corners of her mouth with a napkin. "It's not funny."

"I know *it's* not funny but what in the hell did you expect? It's the *Morgue* damn it. Dead people live here shit." PJ continued to chuckle. "I can't believe you are over here throwing up like a little bitch. Girl you better put your big girl panties on if you are going to work Homicide. Can you handle it or not?" PJ asked after allowing her to get herself together for a couple of minutes.

"I don't know."

"What do you mean you don't fucking know? Either you go in with me or you take yo ass back and wait in the car until I'm done." He said walking away from her and back into the building.

Gertie quickly refreshed her nostrils with a fresh coat of Vapo Rub, popped a mint in her mouth and sprinted back into the building at a fast pace to catch up with PJ.

"Oh I see you found your big girl panties." PJ said when he realized she was back on his heels. They paused for a few minutes in the holding area where he directed her to put on her protective gear; a paper jumpsuit, paper booties to cover her shoes and a protective mask.

"*Why* are all of these bodies in the hallway though?" Gertie asked as she grimaced and followed PJ down the hallway towards their final destination. Her eyes were focused straight ahead as she tried not to look at the rigid corpses lining the walls.

"They are in intake so to speak. They just recently arrived here from all over the County." PJ explained. "Eventually each body will end up at its proper location. Some will be released directly to mortuaries without undergoing autopsies; some to crematoriums, some in the freezer as John or Jane Does and others will end up on the table for autopsies for various reasons. I understand it can be overwhelming your first time here so don't feel bad about the little purging you just did outside." PJ acknowledged. "I was laughing because I remember my first trip to the Morgue many years ago. I acted like a bitch just like you."

"Oh wow. I just never thought about having to attend an actual autopsy as an integral part of working homicide." Gertie said trying to adjust to the strong odor permeating through the Vapo Rub and her mask.

"Yep they sure are, so get used to it. Well that's if you plan on being a *real* Homicide Detective." PJ said opening the door to the examination room.

Gertie followed him into the room. She looked around the room and saw *more* dead bodies sprawled out on metal tables; and

Coroner's examiners scattered about performing autopsies on all of them. Gertie and PJ located their victim's corpse and stepped to the table where the once healthy blond lay naked as blood from her lifeless body drained through a tube into a bucket beneath the table.

"Good morning Chuck." PJ said greeting the Coroner, Charles "Chuck" Mahoney, M.D.

"You are just in time. I'm about to get started." He advised. "I see you changed partners. This one is a lot prettier than Loren. Where is *he*?"

"He's the designated Detective Watch Commander today so he doesn't get to come out and play." PJ responded. "Officer Bellamy here is new to our Homicide Unit so you will be seeing her around. I'm trying to get her trained up."

"Welcome Detective." Chuck said winking at Gertie as he pushed up the sleeves of his paper jumpsuit with his gloved hands. "Are we waiting on anyone else?"

"No. It's just us today." PJ responded.

"No Lorenzo?"

"Nah."

"I like that young man. He's so bright and inquisitive." Chuck commented.

"Yeah Lorenzo has gone off to college at UNLV so we probably won't be seeing him much over the next few years."

"Oh ok. Well good for him. I hope he can stay focused there in Vegas. Bellamy are you ready for this?" Chuck asked.

"Yes sir. I think I am."

All of a sudden Gertie's anxieties about being there, mysteriously left her body. She stood up straight and hovered over the body as Chuck started slicing and dicing. She was ready for the journey. After all was said and done Chuck proclaimed that the cause of death was due to *asphyxia by strangulation* and *facial congestion* based on the presence of the petechial hemorrhages in the victim's eyes. The Coroner's findings confirmed PJ's initial thoughts, which fit the rapist's MO. Luckily none of the other victims died from their injuries. Gertie vowed that she would find Mr. Terrence Collins and stop his reign of terror.

———◆———

Gertie had not heard from Ryan in years so when he tracked her down she thought it was odd but she was still happy to hear from him.

"Hey Ryan. Yes, I got your message." She said sitting at her desk.

"How have you been?" Ryan was happy to hear her voice.

"I have been great. How about you?"

"I am working like a slave but other than that I'm really good. I heard you are a big time city Detective now. I never knew you wanted to be a cop when you were growing up."

"Neither did I but when the opportunity presented itself I went for it and I'm glad I did." She proclaimed. "Are you still in Atlanta?"

"Oh no. I moved to DC when I graduated from Law School and now I am a U.S. Attorney here in DC." Ryan proudly reported. "Hopefully we can catch up more later but the reason for my call is to give you a heads up.

"*Heads up?*" Gertie asked. "About what?"

"There was a murder that occurred on campus when Michelle and I were Grad Students and roommates at Sarah Lawrence." Ryan said choosing his words carefully. "Anyway, back then the case was not solved and for whatever reason now they have reopened it as a cold case and they determined that Michelle and I might be key witnesses or *persons of interest.*"

"Oh really?" He had Gertie's full attention.

"Yes really. Is Michelle still living with your mom?"

"Yes. They are still living together. Actually they have been in a *dating* relationship now for a few years." Gertie reported.

"*What?* Like with each other? That's interesting." Ryan said shocked by that revelation. "I'm speechless child. If I had pearls I'd clutch them. I had no idea your mom was a lesbian. Wow."

"Oh so you knew *Michelle* was?" Gertie asked.

"Yes. I sure did. Remember we were *roommates* before we moved in with you and your mom." Ryan said. "So of course I knew. Anyway, listen. The authorities interviewed me and I was cleared as a *person of interest.* They didn't tell me much more than I already knew about the case from back when it happened but they asked a lot of questions about Michelle, who is still considered a *person of interest.* I just want *you* to be aware of what's going on so you can make sure that your mom is ok since Michelle is still living with her. I'm really glad I got a hold of you and didn't call your mom at the house. I don't want to spook Michelle and possibly compromise the investigation."

"Oh my God. Do you think Michelle was involved?" Gertie asked. "You really have me scared."

"No please don't be scared. Michelle is just like I was before they interviewed and cleared me." Ryan interjected. "Just be *aware.* Please, whatever you do don't say anything to your mom about this. Ok?"

"Ok. I promise I won't say anything." Gertie reluctantly agreed. "But only if *you* promise me that you will keep me posted if you find out anything about the investigation moving forward."

"For sure. I'll keep in touch. I promise you little mama." Ryan assured her.

You have my number. Save it and call me if you need to ok?"

As soon as Gertie hung up the phone she grabbed her keys and went to her car to call Bea. She needed some privacy. Gertie told Bea about her conversation with Ryan and asked her to *please* watch out for her mom.

"I sure will baby doll." Bea promised. "I have been telling your mother for a while now that there is something wrong with that woman. I never trusted her but your mom is totally in love so she doesn't listen to me anymore especially when it comes to Michelle. "

"I love my mom and I care about Michelle. I just hope whatever is going on with this *case* does not affect my mom if Michelle *is* involved in any way."

"I remember when that murder happened on campus. I just hope that the cops are wrong about Michelle being a *person of interest*. I remember it had something to do with a love triangle or something like that. I will keep my eyes and ears open for sure so don't you worry ok? Your mama is too mean to let Michelle do anything to her. I got this boo." Bea said trying to sound cool. "Isn't that what you young folks say to each other? *Boo*?"

"You are so funny." Gertie laughed at Bea. "I'll check in with you again soon. Gotta get back to work. I love you."

"I love you too." Bea said. "Don't worry. I'm close and I will suck it up and go around more often so I can keep an eye open for *anything* weird."

Gertie was so fed up with her poor choice in men that she decided she would be celibate until she found *the* right mate. Sex always had a way of clouding her common sense resulting in her changing those bright red flags that shone early in her relationships, to green. When she told Karisma about her decision to abstain from sex Karisma offered to get her a big black strong vibrator with a batch of fresh batteries to keep on deck. Karisma promised it would be rejuvenating and definitely cheaper than repeatedly buying condoms for the worthless pieces of shit she had encountered.

Gertie spent many evenings hanging out at home spending quality time with Marcus and studying for Detective. PJ had developed a seminar for the officers at Northeast to help them study but he and Loren were Gertie's *personal* tutors. Whenever she went in the field with either of them they quizzed her relentlessly about everything.

Booker was still walking around the squad room like he owned the place. He took every opportunity to get Gertie's attention when they were both in the room but she was no longer fazed by his sly antics. She had heard through the grapevine that he was looking for a new assignment at another division and she prayed that he would move on. Although Gertie had purposely avoided talking about him to her folks she vented often to Savannah. At least *that* relationship was working.

When the Detective test rolled around again Gertie was just about a year away from timing out in the Trainee assignment. She had one test and 3 years under her belt so she *had* to pass the test. She showed up extra early on test day and sat in her car in the parking lot at Fairfax High School after a hearty breakfast at Canter's Deli down the street. She rummaged through some Special Orders and Flash Cards that cluttered the floorboard in front of her passenger seat trying to get some last minute studying in. She was about to get out of the car to go stand on line when she saw Booker walk up to the end of the line. He stopped at a young female officer and gave her a hug before engaging her in a brief conversation. Gertie stayed in her car a little while longer to allow the line to grow a little bit more in order to put distance between her and Booker when she got in line. She did not want to end up in the same classroom with him so she waited.

Finally when the line started to move Gertie ran to get in line. She felt confident going into the test because she had studied well since she no longer had the distraction of a relationship *but* she was still nervous because there was a lot riding on passing the damn test. Most of all she did not want to face PJ if she failed it again. The test appeared to be straightforward enough but Gertie still suspected it wasn't as easy as it appeared.

"So how do you *think* you did?" Karisma asked.

"Girl I don't know how to feel. I'm just glad it's over. I studied my ass off I just hope I studied the right stuff. You know how it is. These tests can be tricky." Gertie said talking to Karisma on the phone while walking back to her car.

"I got my fingers crossed because I don't want you to have to go back to Patrol." Karisma said. She really hoped that Gertie passed.

"I definitely don't want to go back to the field. Working Homicide has been a real shot in the arm for me."

"Yes." Karisma said interrupting Gertie. "We both lucked out getting to Homicide early in our careers so I know you got this!" Karisma said cheering Gertie on.

"And guess who was there lurking in line probably looking for his next victim?"

"Oh lord." Karisma remarked rolling her eyes. "Who? Booker's ass?"

"Yup. Oh he's so annoying. I hope he passes the test and ends up high on the list so he can hurry up and transfer out. I heard he is looking for a new assignment so I hope he gets whatever he is looking for because I'm tired of looking at him."

"Fuck *him.* I really hope *you* passed." Karisma said turning her lip up in disgust at Gertie's well wishing spirit albeit for selfish reasons.

A few weeks passed when Gertie received notification that she passed her test. She couldn't wait to tell PJ before he heard it through the grapevine.

"It's about damn time. You should have passed it the first time." He said.

"Why can't you just say *congratulations*? How does your wife put up with you?" Gertie asked jokingly.

"Don't you worry about my wife and me. Anyway I *am* proud of you. You are sharp and shoulda passed the first time that's all the hell I'm sayin'." PJ said in a softer tone.

"Thanks for your vote of confidence but you know I had a lot of shit going on."

"Yeah. Yeah. Yeah. But I didn't know nothing about that shit when it was happening." PJ said. "So I was judging you."

"I know but you know *now* and that's why you shouldn't be fussing *now* about me failing the first time."

"You right." PJ conceded. "You better not fuck up your oral interview though. That test was just pass/fail and the oral is gonna separate the boys from the men or rather the girls from the women."

"Ok well I'm gonna count on *you* to help me get ready for it."

"You got it." He said. "Switching reels. Have you followed up with the Department of Building and Safety to see if Collins ever picked up his last payroll checks?"

"According to Loren, his supervisor was supposed to contact *us* if he returned for his checks."

"Yeah but they don't always follow through so *we* have to be vigilant and call *them* back." PJ advised while Gertie listened intently.

"Ok I'll go call right now." She followed direction well. After a few weeks the final Detective list was published and Gertie was at the top with an overall score of 101%. She was excited and shared the good news with Robert and Clara who were extremely proud of her accomplishment. She also called her mom to tell *her* the good news.

"Everything is fine honey." Celeste said. She seemed to be in a great mood.

"That's good." Gertie was surprised by her mom's cheerful nature. "Thanks so much for dropping everything and coming out here to spend time with Marcus and me. I really miss you mom." Gertie said.

"I miss you all too. What's going on doll face?" Celeste asked.

"I was calling to tell you that I finally passed the Detective Exam."

"Woo hoo! That's wonderful. I can't wait to tell Michelle." Celeste said.

"Speaking of Michelle where is she?" Gertie asked.

"She's holding a late evening basketball clinic over at the YMCA. But as soon as she gets here I will tell her the great news."

"Mom, how are you and Bea getting along these days? Have things gotten better between the two of you?"

"Bea and I are fine. So yes things are a lot better. For some odd reason she's been coming around a lot more and hanging out with Michelle and I. I guess she is trying to be more accepting of my relationship with Michelle. So all is well." Celeste offered.

"That's really good. I'm so happy to hear that." Gertie said reflecting on her last conversation with Bea. She was true to her word. "I will keep you posted about my Badge Ceremony. I hope that you will be able to come out again. I'll even buy your plane ticket."

"You will do no such thing. I will gladly come out and I'm sure Michelle would love to come too." Celeste said.

"Oh ok. Looking forward to it. Love you."

"I love you more." Celeste said smiling as she hung up the phone.

It had been a few months since the Detective list was published and Gertie was due to be promoted within a few weeks. As the time drew near she was sent to the Department's month long Basic Detective School to prepare her for her impending promotion. She was ecstatic but PJ wasn't so happy as she was going to be gone for an entire month.

"You came out so high on the list you are gonna make it very soon. I'm really proud of you." PJ said. "I have already talked to Lt. Lane about keeping you here at Northeast because I need you to help me with this damn rape and murder case that we have been working on."

"What did she say?" Gertie asked excitedly.

"She's good with it so she is going to convince the powers to be to allow you to remain here at Northeast. I'll keep you posted if we get word while you are in training."

CHAPTER 15

"Hello Detective"

GERTIE WAS IN DETECTIVE SCHOOL for about 3 weeks when all of her 34 classmates received word that they were being promoted to Detective within days of completing their Basic Detective Course. Excitement filled the classroom until they realized that Gertie, who ranked higher than all of them, was not on the Transfer Order for promotion.

"PJ." Gertie was talking fast.

"Hey girl what's up? How's School?"

"Not good. Listen. I just found out that *everyone* in my class, except me, is being promoted to Detective. They all came up on this Transfer Order. Can you please check with the L.T. and see if *she* knows why *I* am being passed over for promotion?"

"Oh damn. Ok let me check. Call me back on your next break." PJ hung up the phone and headed for Lane's office. "Hey L.T. I just got a call from Bellamy."

"Where is she?" Lane interrupted.

"She's still in Detective School. Anyway she said they made 34 Detectives on this Transfer and she was supposed to be promoted as well but for some reason she was passed over and she doesn't know why."

"Hold on a minute." Lane said rifling through her inbox. "Gina gave me the Transfer Order this morning but I didn't look at it." Lane acknowledged as she retrieved the 4-page document from her inbox and flipped through it. "Nope she sure isn't on here. Let me make a few calls and find out what's going on."

"Ok. She says she is not the subject of an Administrative Complaint or anything else that would interfere with her being promoted." PJ shrugged his shoulders. "So I don't know what it could be."

"Well she sure didn't have any complaints a couple of weeks ago when I signed her Work Verification Form and returned it to Personnel Division. I'll get to the bottom of it." Lane promised.

"Ok. I'll be at my desk."

Lane immediately called Personnel and after speaking with a few people she was finally put in touch with someone at the Inspector General's Office.

"Yes Lieutenant you're right. Officer Bellamy was removed from the list. Apparently a Chennelle Booker has filed a lawsuit against the City of L.A. in which she is alleging serious misconduct against Bellamy. Bellamy's alleged activity is administrative in nature and has been categorized as *Conduct Unbecoming an Officer* versus criminal allegations." The IG's representative reported. "You should have received notification from Internal Affairs last week when we notified them and Personnel Division about the filing of the lawsuit."

"Oh ok. I'll call Internal Affairs and get the details. Thank you so much." Lane said as she hung up the phone. She stepped out of her office and had Gina page PJ via the intercom system when she didn't see him at his desk.

"What you find out?" PJ asked rushing into Lane's office.

"Close the door." Lane leaned back against her desk with her arms folded across her chest. "She *does* have a complaint."

"No shit." PJ said. He was surprised.

"No shit." Lane responded. "It stems from a lawsuit filed by Chennelle Booker. I called IA and they say she's Officer Booker's wife. She is accusing Bellamy of fornicating with her husband for the better part of two years."

"And what about them fucking around justifies a lawsuit against the Department?" PJ asked.

"She's suing the Department because they have deeper pockets than Bellamy I guess. Anyway she's citing that because of Bellamy there was *Alienation of Affection* by her husband *and* she's saying that Bellamy accepted *gratuities* from an apartment owner. Supposedly she lives at an apartment for free in Culver City, in exchange for some *fake* security services that she does not provide and she has no Work Permit on file. I don't know what all of that is about but I'm sure it will all be addressed by the City."

"What the fuck? Well she does live in Fox Hills, which *is* in or close to Culver City but she never mentioned that she works off duty anywhere. Oh well, you want me to tell her what's going on or you want to tell her?" PJ asked.

"I'll let you have that conversation with her since she's working for you right now and in the meantime I'm going to call Mr. Booker in and tell him about the complaint. He's also an accused and obviously there is a relationship going on that has gone sideways and I can't have this drama up in here so since he was the last one in I will strongly suggest that *he* find another assignment to avoid conflict with Bellamy in the workplace." Lane advised as she followed PJ to the door.

Gertie called PJ on her break just as she said she would but he was not in the office and he wasn't answering his cell phone so she returned to the classroom and finished the day. She was in a funk. While walking to her car that afternoon she noticed PJ standing next to his city car, which was parked right next to her car in the lower parking lot at the Academy. He was on his phone.

"Hey man let me call you back." PJ said to the person on the phone when Gertie walked up. "Hey you."

"What are you doing here?" Gertie asked walking towards PJ. "I called you back but you didn't answer."

427

"Yeah I decided to come here instead of talking about this shit on the phone." PJ put his phone away and looked down at her. "I know I asked you this before but what in the hell is really going on with you and Booker?"

"Like I told you before *nothing* is going on with me and Booker."

"That's some bullshit and you know it."

"Well not anymore." Gertie said cutting PJ off. "Remember when we were on the way to the hospital and I had the mini breakdown?"

"Yeah but you didn't tell me shit because you were so choked up."

"That's because I didn't want to talk about it then."

"Talk about *what?* That *something* happened between you and Booker?" PJ asked.

"Yes. We were in a *relationship* and then I found out his ass was married. That's *all* that happened. Is there something else that I need to know? And does it have anything to do with why I'm not making Detective?" Gertie asked.

"It sure as fuck does have *everything* to do with why you are not making Detective. It looks like Booker's *wife Ms. Chennelle* has filed a lawsuit against the City accusing you of *Alienation of Affection,* which resulted in a personnel complaint, and *that* my dear is why you were removed from the promotional list."

"Oh my God!" Gertie exclaimed. "That's so fucked up! I didn't know the lying asshole was married and I damn sure didn't intend to interfere with their fake ass *happy* marriage." Gertie started crying tears of anger. "This motherfucker has literally ruined my life."

"Get it together. You are out here in public right now. So, what's this about you providing *fake security* services at an apartment in Culver City in exchange for free rent which she is alleging is a *gratuity*."

"*Whaaaat?* I don't work anywhere but here. What the hell are *you* talking about?" Gertie asked aggressively drying her tears.

"Well that's what *Ms. Chennelle* is also accusing you of." PJ said. "This complaint could hold up your promotion for a while.

"Fuck. Fuck. Fuck me!" Gertie said as the angry tears started to flow again.

"Girl pull yourself together. This shit ain't going any where." PJ said. "The Department don't give a shit about who you are fucking around with unless it is a superior officer in your chain of command and you don't work for Booker's dumb ass, *and* you can easily prove that you don't get free rent from the apartment right? Lastly, that damn ancient ass *Alienation of Affection* law has specific elements that have to be met. *Ms. Chennelle* and Booker's ass have to prove there was *genuine love and affection* in their marriage *and* you have to have known that fool was married. With his track record of infidelity I doubt they can prove *genuine love and affection* in that piece of shit marriage."

"Wow. I like the way you broke all that shit down." Gertie said perking up. "By the way, it's *Booker* who works at the Oakwood Apartments in Culver City in exchange for free rent. It's *his* crash pad that I found out about when our shit fell apart. Then I *later* found out that he was married *and* his wife was pregnant. He ain't nothin' nice." Gertie said pacing back and forth in front of PJ.

"Well just so you know Lt. Lane is trying to ship him out of Northeast because she doesn't want the drama with his wife to cause a problem with you and him in the workplace."

"I'm so embarrassed on so many levels." Gertie said feeling a little better after talking to PJ. "This whole ordeal has been a huge eye opener for me."

"Well lucky for you we are all in your corner because you are an amazing worker and person. Do not let this sideline you or your goals. Lt. Lane is no joke. She will make sure that your promotion is not held up for too long if at all." PJ said with conviction. "I need to get out of here. Lane and I figured I should be the one to talk to you. I thought it best to meet you in person so here I am and now I gotta go."

"Awww thanks PJ." Gertie said extending her hand for a handshake but he gave her dap instead.

"You got this." He said as he got in his car. Gertie stood there and watched him drive off then she walked to her car feeling enlightened by PJ's insight.

Gertie had a week left in Detective School. During that week PJ told her that Booker was moved out of Detectives just as suggested. He wasn't due to make Detective any time soon because his standing on the list was not as high as hers so he had nothing to lose by the untimeliness of the complaint investigation. Turned out the allegations his wife made also accusing him of accepting gratuities at the apartment complex, were no violation as the free rent was his *salary* in exchange for his actual security services. There was nothing fake about the arrangement. She was angry when she found out he had a crash pad at the complex.

Once Lane got Internal Affairs involved, I.A. jumped on the case and scheduled Gertie for an interview right away. Once again she reached out to the League and secured a Rep. This time she was afforded an Attorney since there was a lawsuit attached and she was the actual accused. The interview was quick down and dirty. The I.A. investigator assured her that she would be cleared of any wrong doing since they confirmed that she did not work off duty at the apartment complex and the *Alienation of Affection* allegation was considered a *civil matter* so the Department sent a letter advising Ms. Booker that the City didn't give a shit about that issue.

It took 2 months for the investigation to be completed and closed out during which time Gertie continued to work tirelessly in the Homicide Unit. She never let the investigation distract her from her work, which her bosses appreciated.

"Ok Bellamy you have been restored on the Detective's list for promotion." Lt. Lane advised. "Congratulations. You should make it in the next month or two after the Chief reviews and signs off on the investigation."

"Whew." Gertie said breathing a sigh of relief. "Thank you so much ma'am." These last few months have been pure hell."

"I still have you flagged to stay here at Northeast due to the ongoing critical investigations you're working on. Are you ok with that?"

"Yes ma'am, especially now that Booker is gone."

"I don't know all that went on between you and him but he left willingly because he felt responsible for what occurred between you and his wife." Lane said.

"Ma'am *nothing* occurred between me and Booker's *wife*. Booker and *I* were in a dating relationship and I didn't know he was married the entire time we dated. Maybe I should have been more diligent in figuring it out but he was very convincing. I apologize for causing this drama here at Northeast. It won't happen again."

"No worries. I get it. Girl my ex husband was on the job but he couldn't let go of some of his bad habits and old friends. When I objected to him smoking weed with those knucklehead friends from his past he got mad and put hands on me. I had to call the police and it turned into a huge complaint. It was quite embarrassing so I understand what you are going through." Lane shared with Gertie.

"Oh wow. Thanks. I appreciate you for sharing that with me. I guess everyone has a story." She said as she got up to leave Lane's office.

January 2010 When Gertie saw her name on the Transfer Order a few weeks later she was elated beyond belief. She was on cloud nine. She told her dad and Clara, Savannah and her Aunt Jocelyn about her upcoming Badge Ceremony and she called her mom who immediately made travel plans so she could attend. Gertie tried to pay for the trip and Celeste would not allow it just as she had warned when the topic of the impending promotion first came up. Robert was beaming with pride when Gertie told him she wanted *him* to pin her new badge during the ceremony.

"But your mama is coming all the way from across the Country so I think she should have the honor of pinning your badge." Robert offered.

"Daddy. You have been here for me since day one. Mom didn't even want me to be a cop. In fact she called cops *bottom feeders,* which didn't sit well with me so, *no* she can just come and enjoy the festivities. I appreciate the fact that she is coming but you are my biggest supporter and I'd be honored if you would do that for me."

"Well alright then. I will be honored to pin your badge." Robert said proudly.

Gertie had been in touch with Deanna and Moses and they had worked out a visitation schedule, which included Gertie being present during the visits. They were actually ok spending time with her too. They loved her. Deanna and Moses even visited at Gertie's house sometimes and joined Robert and Clara when they took Marcus to Disneyland and LEGOLAND. Regardless of Jaxon's change of address they were all still family. The Department was a sore spot for Deanna and Moses so Gertie didn't dare invite them to her Badge Ceremony. Actually she never discussed her work with them at all.

Celeste arrived in Los Angeles on a Red Eye flight the night before the ceremony. She rented a car and went right to Gertie's house instead of staying at a hotel because Gertie insisted she stay with her and Marcus. Gertie had a spare bedroom since Savannah had moved out.

"Surprise. Surprise!" Bea said as Gertie approached the passenger side of the rental car.

"Auntie Bea what are you doing here?" Gertie squealed bouncing around the outside of the car on her tippy toes.

"Oh you're not happy to see me?" Bea asked as the two embraced.

"Of course I am *boo*! Hey! Where's Michelle?" Gertie asked as she peered furtively into the car and then at Celeste who was walking around the back of the car and then towards her and Bea.

"Hi baby!" Celeste said hugging Gertie tighter than ever. "Michelle can't travel right now." She said as she released her grasp.

"What do you mean she can't travel *right now*?" Gertie asked as she quickly looked at Bea who was staring back at her over Celeste's shoulder.

"I'll explain when we go inside." Celeste said grabbing her and Bea's suitcases from the trunk.

Once inside, the women put their things down and tiptoed in to see Marcus who was fast sleep in his bed. They backed out of the room and went to their respective sleeping quarters, showered and then met in the den for a nightcap. After chatting for a little bit Bea went to her room and Celeste crawled up in the bed with Gertie so they could talk privately.

"So what did you mean Michelle *can't travel right now.*" Gertie asked.

"It's a long story but the short version is that a few years ago a girl was murdered on campus at Sarah Lawrence and the case was never solved. Now the cops have reopened the investigation due to some DNA evidence they discovered. They contacted Michelle and Ryan because they were friends with the girl so they are considered *persons of interest.* As a result she and Ryan are not allowed to leave town." Celeste explained. "She really wanted to be here. So when I told Bea that Michelle couldn't come she agreed to come with me."

"Oh wow. Mom are you scared about this investigation since Michelle lives with you now?"

"No. Michelle had nothing to do with that crime. It's just a matter of routine I guess until they rule her and Ryan out as possibly being involved."

"Yes it is a *matter of routine* but how do you know they don't *suspect* Michelle as the perpetrator?" Gertie asked.

"Well how do you know they are not suspecting Ryan?" Celeste sat straight up in bed and stared down at Gertie lying beside her.

"I'm not concerned about Ryan as much because he doesn't live with you anymore. I'm only asking about Michelle because she lives with you and that's huge if she is involved in this crime in any way." Gertie didn't share with her mom that she knew Ryan was no longer a *person of interest*. She had no idea he and Gertie had spoken.

"Well she's not and we will just have to wait and see what happens." Celeste said reaching over to kiss Gertie goodnight. "It's late and we need to go to sleep. We have a big day tomorrow."

"Ok. Well I'll trust your instinct. Goodnight."

———◆———

Karisma and Taylor arrived early at Deaton Hall to save seats for the entire family. Gertie was anxiously awaiting everyone's arrival as she milled around outside in front of Parker Center. She needed to introduce Bea to Clara and Savannah before the ceremony started. Celeste had forgiven Clara for sleeping with Robert while they were married. The two had a heart to heart talk several years after the divorce when Celeste realized how special Clara was to Gertie and Marcus. Gertie was happy to see the two embrace when the family arrived at PAB. Celeste was somewhat star struck by Savannah knowing that she was a news Reporter and she thought she was gorgeous. Once the greetings and introductions were done Gertie ushered everyone into the auditorium. She could not wait to introduce everyone to PJ. She had told them all about how crazy he was.

Celeste totally understood when Gertie told her that Robert was pinning her badge. When the Detectives were called to the stage one by one, their family members joined them. Robert proudly pinned Gertie's badge as Clara, Jocelyn, Celeste, Bea, and Savannah stood by on stage watching. Gertie held Marcus's hand as he stood by her side looking up adoringly at his mommy. It was a proud moment for all of them; even Celeste.

Robert and Clara agreed to keep Marcus so that Gertie could join her peers for celebratory drinks at Clancy's Bar and Grill in Glendale later that afternoon. She had invited several Detectives from the Division, and Savannah, Celeste and Bea looked forward to experiencing the *Buy Out* tradition that occurred after LAPD promotions. Jocelyn headed right back home to Mississippi after the ceremony. She got home just in time to pick up Stevie and Ricky from school. They had been with their paternal grandmother while she was in California. Gertie and her peers, who also promoted, pooled their funds and put money on the bar to cover drinks and finger foods for everyone to enjoy for several hours, as was tradition with the *Buy Outs*.

PJ and Loren were at Clancy's when Gertie arrived that afternoon. They were already drinking and were in rare form *shootin' the shit* with some old timer's at the bar. They were loud as hell.

"It's about damn time you got here." PJ said as he walked towards Gertie with Celeste and Bea standing close behind her. One Detective, who recognized Savannah as the *pretty Reporter* from the Channel 5 news, stopped her and talked to her for a little bit before she was able to catch up to Gertie, Celeste and Bea.

"Hey PJ, Loren, I want you to meet my family. This is my mother Celeste, my Aunt Bea and my sister Savannah." Gertie said pulling Celeste and Bea by the arm in front of her and then locking arms with Savannah next to them.

"Nice to meet you ladies." PJ said. "How long are you all staying?"

"Nice to meet you as well Detective." Celeste and Bea said in unison.

"We leave on Sunday." Celeste said.

"I live here." Savannah said making flirty eyes at PJ.

"Nice. Nice. Well you ladies enjoy your visit here in the Los Angeles and *you* enjoy yourself tonight *Channel 5.*" PJ said smirking at Savannah.

"Come on ladies. I want to get you all a drink." Loren said.

"Thanks so much." Celeste said as she and Bea followed him to the bar where they sat and watched the festivities all around them. Loren kept them occupied for about an hour before he moved on. Savannah made *her* rounds in the room talking to some of her fans. She was enjoying the attention.

Loren met back up with PJ and Gertie to chat for a minute when Gertie spotted a female Detective who she recognized, walk in to Clancy's.

"What's *she* doing here?" Gertie asked just as the woman looked in their direction and smiled. "Oh snap! That's the Internal Affairs investigator who interviewed me a couple of years ago on Jaxon's case."

"PJ!" The Detective called out as she continued in their direction.

"Hey baby." He said waving her over to him.

"*Baby?*" Gertie remarked as she turned to look at PJ and then back at the woman.

"That's my wife fool." He said looking at Gertie.

"Oh. Damn. *Detective Martin and Detective Martin.*" Gertie said to herself as the woman reached their location and kissed PJ on the lips.

"Hi ma'am." Gertie said right away admiringly.

"Gertie meet my wife Terri." PJ said proudly looking her up and down.

"Hi Officer Bellamy." Terri said. "It's nice to see you again. How are you?"

"So you remember me?"

"Of course I remember you. I don't forget a pretty face and it ain't that many of *us* around here you know?"

"Look at my baby. She looks good don't she?" PJ commented.

"Yes she looks amazing." Gertie was surprised at how nice Terri was to her.

"We are here celebrating Gertie's promotion." PJ said. "So, I don't want to hear about no past IA interview shit or no other work shit."

"Congratulations Bellamy." Terri said rolling her eyes at PJ. "How do you put up with him?" She asked looking at Gertie and laughing. "You gotta love him."

"Put up with *me*? Shit she's lucky I even talk to her ass." He said lovingly wrapping his forearm around Terri's neck. "You drinking today?"

"Hell yeah I'm drinking." Terri said as she rotated out of PJ's hug to face him. "Can you get me a Long Island Ice Tea, please honey?"

"Oh that's my favorite drink too!" Gertie exclaimed.

"You got it." PJ said heading for the bar. "I'll get you one too rookie."

"That's why we are gonna get along just fine." Terri said reaching in to hug Gertie.

Gertie saw a different side of PJ, a softer side, on that evening. He and Terri seemed to have a cool chemistry when they interacted. Gertie stayed there talking with Terri for a little bit when Savannah walked back up. Terri excused herself and walked towards the bar to retrieve her Long Island potion from PJ.

"Who is that?" Savannah asked turning to look at Terri walk away. "I've seen her before. Oh that's right she was at Jaxon's Press Conference when he was arrested huh?"

"Yup she was the lead investigator on that case." Gertie acknowledged. "I just found out she's PJ's wife. She's very nice."

"Oh really. *He's* so handsome." Savannah said looking off towards the bar area where PJ and Terri were talking to Celeste and Bea."

"*He* who?"

"Detective PJ."

"Well he's totally in love with his boo thang Ms. Terri so don't even try it missy."

"Girl I was just making an observation." Savannah said with her eyes stayed on PJ.

Celeste and Bea were enjoying their night out with the boys and girls in blue when they saw Loren walk back to the bar area.

"Hey man I just got a call from the Watch Commander and they want us to roll out on a call."

"I didn't get a call from the Watch Commander." PJ responded very annoyed. He hated when they didn't follow the chain of command.

"Well he said you didn't answer your phone man. So he called *me*." Loren explained.

"Bullshit. I don't have a missed call." PJ said squinting at the dim light on his phone. "Who called you?"

"That new Lieutenant I was telling you can't find his ass with both hands." Loren said shaking his head. "Anyway apparently officers responded to an ADW radio call in Highland Park where a shooting occurred at an intersection. A 35 year-old male victim, a Carlton Riggs was shot in the head. He's been transported to Huntington Memorial Hospital." Loren said referring to the notes in his field officer's notebook.

"So he's not dead yet?" PJ asked.

"Not yet. But he *was* shot in the forehead and was pronounced *brain dead* after they worked on him. They are going to keep him on life support until his organs can be harvested for transplant. Patrol officers and the night watch Detective already processed the scene so I guess we can really follow up on Monday." Loren suggested.

"Yup we sure as hell can. No need to go in tonight since the scene was already processed and he's not pronounced dead yet." PJ agreed. "Dang girl you were spared tonight." PJ said to Gertie who had joined them at the bar. "We almost had a call out." He said handing her the Long Island Ice Tea he promised her.

"Oh really? That's cool we *almost* had a call out." Gertie said smiling. "So do I have your permission to get my drink on since we are not rolling?"

"Gone ahead and enjoy yourself. We will follow up on the case on Monday." PJ said as he and Gertie lifted their glasses and toasted.

Gertie enjoyed the rest of the evening and weekend with her mom and Bea. She kissed them goodbye at the airport on Sunday afternoon and then headed back home to get ready for the week. She was a big time Detective and happy that something was finally going her way.

She explained to Robert and Clara how her new role was going to change in that she would be subjected to off-hour call outs on designated weekends but she might also on occasion catch an impromptu case mid week. Robert and Clara assured her that they would continue to support her and Marcus however they could. She thanked her lucky stars that she had such a wonderful support system. She felt so blessed, which is why she continued to attend First Baptist every Sunday even though it brought back sad memories of her relationship with Rashon.

———◆———

Gertie and Loren met with PJ bright and early on Monday morning following her badge ceremony and discussed the incident from the weekend.

"I'm going to need you to complete a crime report for Murder *and* a Death Investigation Report." PJ advised as he scoured over the mound of reports from the weekend.

"Ok." Gertie agreed. "I have the evidence that the Night Watch Detective and officers collected from the scene."

"What evidence was collected?" Loren asked.

"There is a spent casing; and officers checked with the businesses in the area and found that the Sparklett's Water business nearby recorded the incident so they recovered the DVD, as well as a VHS tape from Bart's liquor store across the street from Sparklett's."

"Oh damn. Ok. Well package and book the items as evidence and then we need to go review the recorded footage."

"I attempted to view the digital videodisc (DVD) from Sparklett's on our digital recorder here at the station but the machine could not read the disc."

"I swear. LAPD has the raggediest damn equipment I have ever seen in my fucking life. How do they expect us to do anything with all of this outdated ass shit?" PJ was annoyed.

"I contacted the Operations Manager at Sparklett's to see if *their* recording was still available for me to review on their machine but their office is closed today due to the Martin Luther King holiday so I will check back with them tomorrow. I guess we are the only ones working on this here black people holiday." Gertie joked.

"You got a problem with that black girl?" PJ asked.

"Nope, not at all. Because black people need to work." Gertie responded.

"Good because working Homicide, your time is not your own anymore." He warned. "Holiday or not we will be working."

"I think I know what I signed up for." Gertie said labeling the coin envelope for the spent casing. She was being silly.

"Ok smart ass. Look, as soon as you are done booking the evidence we need to go out in the field; canvass the area ourselves and search for additional evidence and additional locations that could have recorded the incident from other angles." PJ said.

"Ok. I'm almost ready." She replied.

When she was done packaging the evidence PJ called ahead and they went to the victim's home to meet with his spouse to get background information on the victim.

"Ma'am. I'm so sorry for your loss." Gertie said as Mrs. Riggs led them to the dining room table. She was expecting them. "Is this a good time to talk to you?" She asked gently.

"Of course. I guess it's as good a time as any." She said solemnly. She looked understandably distraught.

"We need you to take us through the events prior to your husband leaving home on the day of the shooting." PJ requested as soon as they sat down.

"Yesterday morning at about 10 AM I went to Target to buy some things that Carlton needed for an upcoming out of town business trip. He was still asleep when I left." Mrs. Riggs said waving for her mom to join them at the table.

"When was he due to fly out?" PJ asked.

"He had a flight scheduled for tomorrow; Tuesday to fly to San Francisco." She recalled.

"Ok. Then what happened?"

"I returned home from Target at about 11AM and I saw that Carlton was up and about, and he appeared to be very happy. He was drinking a Bloody Mary cocktail and when I teased him about drinking so early in the day he said *it's 5'0 clock somewhere* and made me one too." She explained as she stopped to wipe the tears rolling down her cheeks. "He is very silly. Well, he *was* silly. So, we listened to music and we danced around in the kitchen and then he made us some breakfast. After breakfast he wanted to smoke but didn't have any cigarettes. He was an *occasional* smoker and usually walked to the liquor store for cigarettes and then he would walk in the neighborhood afterwards to smoke. He usually went to Bart's liquor store to buy his alcohol and cigarettes."

"Did you think it was odd for him to walk through the neighborhood just to smoke?" Gertie asked.

"He wouldn't smoke in the house because the smoke really bothered *me* so I was so glad he was outside smoking that I didn't give it another thought." Mrs. Riggs said with a nervous giggle. "He had a lot of weird habits when it came to his smoking. Anyway he asked me for some cash to buy the cigarettes and I gave him $5.50. He then told me that he was going to walk to the corner liquor store to buy cigarettes. Sometimes he'd go to the corner and sit on that wall by the Sparklett's Water business and just smoke and talk to people from the neighborhood. He enjoyed *that* location to smoke because it was a private little area off the main drag."

"Did he have beef with anyone in the neighborhood that you know of?" Gertie asked.

"Oh no. I don't believe so." She said. "Anyway after I gave him the money we walked out of the house together and I got into my car to drive to the gym for a quick workout while he walked to the store. After I drove off I changed my mind and decided to just run other errands instead of going to the gym. At about 1PM I returned home when I saw fire trucks at the corner. I drove by slowly and saw a man down on the ground but I thought that the paramedics were working on a drunk. Then I took a closer look and saw the man on the ground was wearing a blue Dodgers sweatshirt, which is when I realized it was my husband." Mrs. Riggs broke down and started sobbing.

"Do you need to take a break ma'am?" PJ asked lightly touching her shoulder.

"No. I'm so sorry." She said as she tried to regain her composure.

"Don't be sorry." Gertie interjected. "We understand this is a hard time for you. We can take a break if you would like."

"No. It's ok. I need to tell you what you need to know so you can solve my husband's murder." Mrs. Riggs said as she ran her fingers through her thick curly mane. "When I recognized the sweatshirt I parked my car and ran towards my husband. He was moving slightly but he didn't speak. Then I saw an injury to his forehead and brain matter was coming from the hole in his head. I stood by while they worked on him for a few minutes and I identified him for the paramedics then I followed the ambulance to the hospital."

"Thank you for that information." PJ said. "I tell you what. We are going to let you rest for a bit while we go conduct a few more follow-ups. You have painted a pretty good picture of what occurred on yesterday morning before the incident and that's going to help us tremendously. We will call you if we need anything else from you otherwise we will just keep you apprised of what's going on with the investigation ok?" PJ advised.

"Thank you so much." Mrs. Riggs said as she walked them to the door.

"One more thing before we go." Gertie commented. "I really hate to ask you this but it's necessary. Did your husband have any gang ties?"

"Absolutely not. Not recently. Not ever." She responded.

It was a long day and Gertie was mentally exhausted from the day's events especially sitting through the interview with Mrs. Riggs. She found herself getting emotional at times. She needed to get home and rescue her dad and Clara from Marcus. He had just turned 7 and was in the second grade. He was rather rambunctious and was actually starting to act out a little bit in school. Robert tried to fill the void caused by Jaxon's incarceration but his patience was worn thin rather quickly whenever he dealt with Marcus. He was tired on most days from dealing with his *adult* students at USC and their demanding parents, so Marcus wore him the rest of the way out on the days he kept him. Clara just babied him and offered no discipline at all. When Gertie shared with Moses and Deanna that Marcus was acting out in school Deanna felt it proved her point that he needed his dad in his life.

"I agree he *needs* his dad." Gertie said. "But Jaxon can't be an effective parent while he is in prison."

"Yeah but he needs to know that he *has* a father and that his father cares about him." Deanna said. "You got him around all of your *boyfriends* and that's why the boy is frustrated and acting out in school. He needs to see *his* father. He needs to know who *his* daddy is."

"I beg your pardon." Gertie was caught off guard by Deanna's sudden hostility. "First of all you don't know anything about what goes on in my life. Yes. I date. But I don't have random men around my child. It's unfortunate that I chose to marry some wretched nigga who decided to use his dick as a weapon landing him in prison! I'm not going to stop living my life." She said angrily. "It is obvious Jaxon's daddy, whoever *he* is, didn't provide a good example for him so you are one to talk." Gertie said gripping the phone tightly.

"Who in the hell do you think you are talking to me that way?" Deanna asked sitting on the edge of her couch with Moses sitting close by in his easy chair. His ears perked up when he heard the change in Deanna's tone. "You don't know nothin' about Jaxon's daddy."

"Yeah and obviously he doesn't know about his daddy either so maybe that's why *he's frustrated.*" Gertie said as she hung up the phone. She was trembling after that exchange. She was sorry she had called to check in with her.

———◆———

Gertie had made it a point to make all of the parent teacher conferences and all of Marcus's school events to try to get a grip on what was going on with him. She also signed him up for Tae Kwon Do hoping it would help teach him some form of discipline. She made sure that his classes were on the weekends so *she* could be there with him at every class and every tournament event instead of having her dad and Clara take the lead. Gertie hoped that she could nip his errant behavior in the bud.

———◆———

Gertie hadn't talked to Karisma since her Badge Ceremony. Karisma wasn't able to go to the *Buy Out* afterwards because she had to go to Morgan's dance recital at school. Gertie couldn't wait to tell her about the murder case she was working on and couldn't wait to tell her about her and Deanna's latest blow up.

Taylor was very happy working Training Division. She enjoyed training the new recruits and most of all she loved working out and running with them during physical training. Taylor was Sergeant Alese's *go to* person especially when she needed someone to work overtime to lead the evening workout classes for police candidates. That was right up Taylor's alley. She hadn't seen much of Gertie since they competed in the World Games. The women's team took home the Gold and Gertie and Taylor were the one two punch the team needed for their successful outcome.

———————

PJ waited anxiously for Gertie to show up to work that next day. He had a message on his desk from the Coroner's office notifying him that Riggs's autopsy was scheduled for 9AM that Tuesday morning.

"Are you ready?" PJ asked when Gertie walked in.

"Ready for what?" Gertie sat her coffee cup down, and placed all of her personal belongings on her desk. "Where are we going?"

"To your favorite place for Riggs's Autopsy." PJ stood by watching her unload all of her shit onto her desk.

"Of course I'm ready. Can I please catch my breath?" She asked huffing and puffing. "I had to park all the way up on the roof of the parking structure today. Are we max deployed?"

"No. People just showed up to work today. Now look heffa. You need to get your mind right before we get to the damn Coroner's Office. I'm not holding yo damn Yaki phony tail while you earl all over the place."

"Excuse you but this is my *real* hair." She declared tugging at her long flat-ironed ponytail.

"Well the shit looks fake but whatever." PJ said laughing. "You need to get it together before we get to the Morgue. I know that much."

"Ok let's go. I'm good." Gertie responded.

PJ drove to the Coroner's Office where they met Chuck, their favorite Medical Examiner.

"Most of his organs and bones have been harvested and several skin grafts have been removed." Chuck advised PJ and Gertie after he assessed Riggs's body. "He sustained a single gunshot wound to the center of his forehead." Chuck slightly touched the wound with his gloved fingertip. "The projectile traveled from front to back, with a right to left trajectory. The projectile fractured the front of his skull and traveled through his brain. It also fractured the rear of his skull but remained inside his head.

"So no exit wound huh?" PJ asked.

"Nope. It did not penetrate the victim's scalp as it exited his skull. I recovered a deformed, medium caliber, jacketed projectile between the left occipital skull and scalp from the victim and I also removed a projectile fragment from the left side frontal lobe of his brain." Chuck said as he held out his hand displaying the items.

"I'll take that." Gertie said taking custody of the evidence from Chuck.

"Ok looks like we have confirmed how the victim died. That was simple." PJ said turning to Gertie as Chuck continued to clean his work space, and package Riggs's organs.

"I'll see ya soon." PJ said tossing his gloves in the trash as he walked out of the examination room.

"Later Detectives." Chuck said.

PJ and Gertie met with Mr. Abbott the owner at Bart's Liquor Store and reviewed the VHS tape. They saw Riggs on the video walking towards the store; and then saw him enter the store. They also noted a *male Hispanic* park a silver 2004-2008 Honda minivan in the lot adjacent to the store. The male Hispanic then entered the store right after Riggs, selected an item and then stood next to Riggs at the counter while Riggs paid for his cigarettes. The male Hispanic then paid for *his* item and followed Riggs outside. He then returned to the minivan in the adjacent lot.

"That guy and his vehicle in the video matched the description of the suspect and suspect's vehicle as seen on the Sparklett's Water video." Gertie pointed out to PJ.

"Yup. He sure does."

They then saw Riggs on the video walking through the parking lot and out of sight. The suspect was also seen at about that same time driving away from the store and out of sight in the minivan.

"The guy in the video who bought the cigarettes was one of my regular customers and I don't know of any problems he might have had with the male Hispanic who was also in the video." Abbott said looking over PJ's shoulder at the monitor.

"Do you recognize the male Hispanic as a regular patron?" Gertie asked.

"I don't remember ever seeing that guy in the store before." Abbott responded.

"Ok. Thanks for letting us view the video." PJ said as they left Abbott's office at the back of the store.

"We will be in touch if we need anything else." Gertie said to Mr. Abbott as she and PJ walked out of the store.

"When we get back to the station I need you to go to roll call and get a hold of the gang unit and Criminal Apprehension Team (CAT), foot beat officers, and Senior Lead Officers; let them view the digital still photographs from the shooting, and request their assistance in trying to identify the suspect and/or the vehicle used in this murder." PJ directed.

"Slow down man." Gertie said. "So you want me to get all of these folks together *today*?"

"Do what you can. But yes get *all* of them involved if you can." PJ said.

Later that night after Gertie went to roll call Detective T. Samuels from the CAT Team contacted PJ at home.

"PJ what's up man?" Samuels asked. "I might have some good info for you."

"Hey man. How are you? What you got for me?" PJ asked.

"One of my units conducted an undercover surveillance of the neighborhood around the crime scene where your murder occurred and they saw a silver Honda minivan with Arizona plates drive into a driveway on Avenue 26. The vehicle parked to the rear of the main house and a male Hispanic exited the vehicle and entered a back house at that location. Officers did not get a good look at the driver's face but his general description along with the vehicle matches the info Detective Bellamy put out at roll call about the possible suspect."

"Ok. That's good stuff." PJ responded.

"Due to lighting, weather, and tactical considerations, I told my officers not to contact the occupants at the residence without direction from you, but I had them remain Code 5 on the house and vehicle. Is that cool?" Samuels asked.

"Absolutely. Let me know if the vehicle moves or any other suspicious activity."

"Sure thing."

"Thanks man." PJ said.

———————

Gertie had been working so much she hadn't spent any time with Karisma or Taylor. Her first priority was Marcus who seemed to be doing better in school but now he was starting to ask a lot of questions about his daddy. Gertie didn't want to lie to him but she didn't have the heart to tell him that his dad was in prison for raping women.

"Girl you are going to have to tell that boy something." Robert said when the topic came up at Sunday dinner. "How about we sit him down and try to explain to him about being punished when we do things wrong and how prison is for adults like *time out* or *detention* is in school for kids."

"I like that daddy. So, do you think I should take him to see Jaxon?" She asked reluctantly.

"Hell no. I don't think *you* or Marcus need to be in that environment." Robert said sternly. "Jaxon made his bed and the bottom line is that part of his consequences include him missing out on his son's life for 6 years. Don't you feel guilty about this boy not seeing his father. I'll just have to do more to provide a father figure for him. Taking him to a prison will do more harm than good. That's my two cents." Robert said.

"Whew. That was a mouth full but you make me feel better. I was having second thoughts about taking him to see his dad." Gertie said walking to the door to call for Marcus to come inside so they could leave. "I need to get him home and get ready for work." She said hugging Robert goodbye.

"Clara will get Marcus from school everyday this week so I can take him to the batting cages." Robert said following Gertie to the door. "I'll keep him busy. He can get to know his daddy when he gets released. Goodnight baby girl."

"Goodnight daddy."

Gertie arrived at work bright and early on that Monday morning. It had been a week since Riggs's murder so she was juggling cases with the serial rape investigation and the strip club murder all still underway. She had received information from the gang unit that they saw someone matching Collins's description down the street from his mother's home where they served the Search Warrant. By the time the officers made the block the person was gone and they didn't see where he went.

Gertie and Loren conducted a follow up to Mrs. Collins's house on the next morning and she swore that she had not seen her son since they served the Search Warrant at her residence. PJ was at his desk when Gertie and Loren returned from the field. He was briefing Lane on the two homicides they were working on. He hated telling her that they had no new leads on Collins's whereabouts, but he felt confident Riggs's murder was going to be solved real soon.

"Loren I need you all to contact the Crime Analysis Detail Unit and request that a 187 PC Murder/Wanted Crime Alert Notification be published with the suspect and vehicle description on Riggs's case. I have four digital still images from the surveillance footage they can use." PJ said. Just as Loren and Gertie traipsed off to the Crime Analysis Detail Unit the Watch Commander walked up to PJ's desk.

"Detective Martin?" The Watch Commander searched PJ's desk looking for a nameplate for confirmation.

"Yeah that's me." PJ said looking up from the report he was reading. "I have two officers who are in the area where your murder occurred and they just saw the possible suspect vehicle drive out from the home on Avenue 26. The vehicle did not have a front license plate affixed to it. So they conducted a traffic stop and identified the driver of the vehicle as Joel Ruiz. Ruiz said that he was from Henderson, Colorado and that the registered owner of the vehicle was his stepson Herbert Salcedo. Ruiz did not match the physical description of the suspect on the still photographs so he was released with a warning for no front plate."

"Ok that's good to know. Thank the officers for their due diligence." PJ said.

Once Gertie and Loren were done requesting the crime alert PJ commandeered an undercover vehicle from vice and he and Gertie headed out to conduct surveillance in the area of the crime scene hoping to locate the possible suspect and possible registered owner of the van Ruiz was driving that matched the description of the van from the video footage.

While traveling south on Avenue 26 Gertie observed a male Hispanic who more closely matched the description of the suspect than Jocl Ruiz, walking north on Avenue 26 from the residence where the Van was seen on previous occasions. Gertie noted that the male Hispanic appeared very similar to the photograph of the possible suspect. As he approached the street from the residence they stopped him and identified him as Herbert Salcedo.

During a pat-down search PJ felt a hard object resembling a handgun in the left front waistband area. PJ lifted Salcedo's sweatshirt and saw a black pistol protruding from his waistband. He removed the handgun and handed it to Gertie.

Gertie carefully removed the magazine and observed that it was fully loaded. She then locked the slide to the rear and captured a live round that was in the chamber. She requested a black and white unit to transport Salcedo to the station for questioning. They followed the unit to Northeast Station where they interviewed Salcedo regarding his possible involvement in Riggs's murder.

"How long have you been in Los Angeles?" PJ asked.

"I have been here for about one month and I have been living on Avenue 26, in the back house on my aunt's property." Salcedo said.

"Do you know why you have been detained?" PJ asked.

"Si, because of the gun I had when you stopped me."

"Where did you get the gun?" Gertie asked.

"I just *found* it right before you arrested me. I found it on Lincoln Avenue on some grass by a tree. The gun was already loaded and I was just taking it home to throw it away." Salcedo explained.

"Really? You were taking a loaded gun home to throw it away?" PJ asked. "Tell me about the silver van parked at your house and do not lie to me."

"That van belongs to my stepfather." Salcedo said nervously backing away from PJ.

"What's his name?" PJ asked.

"Joel Ruiz... sir."

"You are full of shit. I already know the van is registered to you asshole. When is the last time you drove the van?" Gertie asked.

"Like on a Wednesday or Thursday when I went to do laundry and then I went to the liquor store to buy some chips."

"We will come back to the liquor store." PJ said. "Have you heard about a shooting near your house?"

"Uh..." Salcedo pondered the question for a moment. "Yeah on the day of the shooting. That was the same day I drove the van." Salcedo recalled. "After I went to the store and bought the chips I went back to the van and drove on Avenue 26 and then I stopped at the curb by the Sparklett's Water building. While I was sitting in the car I heard a gunshot behind me by the corner at Avenue 26 and Lincoln Avenue. I got scared and drove back home.

"Ok…Did you see *who* got shot?" PJ asked.

"Not really. But when I was…when I was driving through the intersection I seen a man wearing red shorts. He was just standing at the corner and I remembered him because he was the same man I seen inside the liquor store when I was buying my chips. So it might be him who got shot." Salcedo said avoiding eye contact with PJ and Gertie.

"Ok. Did you see anyone else around?" Gertie asked.

"Nope. I didn't notice nobody else in the area when I heard the gunshot."

"I'm going to show you some photographs taken at the liquor store and you tell me if the person you saw in the intersection is in the photographs." PJ said.

"That's him." Salcedo said immediately pointing to Riggs on the photo. "That's the man wearing the red shorts who was on the corner." Salcedo then identified himself in the photograph and the vehicle as the van *he* was driving on the day of the shooting.

"You know man. I believe *you* shot that man with the gun you had in your waistband. Didn't you?" PJ stood up and leaned over the table into Salcedo's face.

"No man. I didn't shoot nobody." He responded backing his face away from PJ.

"You're a lying sack of shit and I'm going to prove it!" PJ said. Gertie sat there with her eyes wide-open watching PJ break the suspect down. "We are going to be here all night. So you better tell me something. Why did you kill him?"

"I was scared!" Salcedo blurted out after a few moments of silence. "I…I…I thought he was going to *rape* me."

"What in the hell are to you talking about man?" PJ was totally shocked by his emerging confession. "You thought he was going to *rape* you? That makes no fucking sense. Are you on drugs?"

"When I was inside the store we didn't talk or nothing but he *smiled* at me…man he smiled at me." Salcedo said as he started to cry.

"So wait a minute. There was no conflict with this man?"

"No. Not really."

"That's *yes* or *no*." Gertie said.

"No. He didn't say nothing to me. But… but…but after I left the store I was sitting in my car when I saw him walk past my car and I believe he *mouthed* the word *rape* and then he licked his lips. He was scary." Salcedo said as he continued to cry.

"So he *mouthed* the word *rape*, but didn't say anything?" PJ was perplexed.

"Yeah and then he walked away from the liquor store. And then…and then I started to drive away from the store and as I drove toward Lincoln Avenue, I saw him walking along Avenue 26 and he crossed the street right in front of my car and when he walked in front of my car, he didn't look at me, he just kept walking until he reached the corner. That's when I drove through the intersection and stopped about one block past where he was and I waited in my car for about 40 seconds and then I got out of my car and I walked up to him and I shot him with the gun I had in my pants, then I drove home after that." Salcedo said shaking his head.

"You have got to be kidding me. You're kidding me right? Answer me damn it!" PJ demanded.

"I was *scared* of him and if I didn't shoot him, he would eventually rape me. So, I needed to shoot him." Salcedo yelled aggressively drying his tears with the sleeve of his sweatshirt.

"If you were that *scared* why didn't you just call the police?" Gertie asked in disbelief after hearing his ridiculous story.

"I coulda called the police but I thought the police would not believe me."

"So, prior to the shooting, did the man display any weapons or say anything at all to you?" Gertie asked.

"No."

"This is *unbelievable!*" PJ said shaking his head. "Did you take any medications or did another person, or voices in your damn head tell you to shoot this man?" PJ asked.

"No."

"What did you do after you shot the man?"

"I went home." Salcedo said coldly.

"Did you tell anyone about this?" Gertie asked.

"No. I didn't tell nobody."

"I'm going to ask you again. Where did you get the gun?" PJ asked.

"I brought the gun with me from my house in Henderson, Colorado."

"So you didn't find the gun by a tree?" Gertie asked.

"No. I brought it with me from my old house in Colorado where my brother Leonardo had it buried in the backyard. I don't know where my brother got the gun from but when we moved here I kept it in my suitcase in the house where I'm staying. Whenever I leave the house I always take it with me because I don't want my little brothers to find it and hurt themselves. I have more bullets for the gun in a red suitcase at my house. I know I was wrong for shooting the man but I had no choice." Salcedo said rambling.

"That just makes me sick. Makes absolutely no sense at all." PJ was incensed by the senselessness of the crime. "What made you think this man was going to *rape* you?"

"Because he smiled at me and licked his lips." Salcedo answered.

"But you were in a car and he was walking so how could he be a threat to you? I'm tired of talking to you. You disgust me. I'm booking your ass for Murder. Get up!" PJ reached for Salcedo's arm to unhook his wrist from the table. Gertie then walked up behind him and handcuffed both of his hands behind his back once PJ freed his wrists from the table. "Let's go." PJ said looking at Gertie. "You got a babysitter for your son?"

"Yeah why?" Gertie asked caught off guard by the question.

"You better call them and let them know you gonna be a while."

Gertie followed PJ and Salcedo out of the interview room and they transported him to Jail Division.

Gertie and PJ took the expended bullet, and the handgun recovered from Salcedo, to Scientific Investigation Division/ Firearms Analysis Unit where the gun was test fired.

Gertie took a moment and called her dad to let him know that she was going to be extremely late. PJ directed Loren to get a hold of the on-call Judge so they could get a Search Warrant for Salcedo's residence and the van. PJ had rolled up his sleeves, removed his tie and loosened his collar. He was prepared for an *all nighter.*

———◆———

Within minutes of entering the small back house on Avenue 26, where the suspect lived, Loren recovered two boxes of ammunition from a red suitcase and two video games depicting violent acts from the residence. The vehicle was searched but no evidence was recovered that was related to the murder. After the warrant was served PJ and Gertie went immediately and met with Mrs. Riggs to advise her of Salcedo's arrest.

"God bless you." Mrs. Riggs said reaching out to embrace PJ.

"The suspect confessed ma'am but we will still have a trial unless he is offered and accepts a plea deal." Gertie explained. "The court process can be very daunting for the family. We will be with you every step of the way should it end up in a trial ok?"

"Thank you so much. The memorial is tomorrow so I can at least go *there* knowing that we have some type of closure. Did the guy who did this say why? Why he killed my husband?" Mrs. Riggs asked.

"It's hard to really understand *why* he did what he did because the reason he gave was so way off base." PJ explained. "I need to ask you something based on what the man said."

"Sure. Please ask me especially if I can help make sense of this tragedy."

"Do you have any knowledge or belief that your husband may have been gay or bi-sexual?"

"To my knowledge my husband was neither homosexual nor bi-sexual." She said looking puzzled.

"It doesn't mean anything in terms of justification for the murder, but the suspect, for whatever reason, thought your husband was going to sexually assault him simply because of the way your husband *looked* at him. There's clearly some mental illness or episode going on with this suspect. Again, I'm so very sorry for your loss." Gertie offered.

It was after midnight by the time PJ and Gertie returned to the station. Loren was there coordinating information and packaging evidence secured from the residence.

"Go on home." PJ said to Gertie. "You need to be back here early in the morning so we can go file this case at the DA's office."

"Are you sure you don't need me to stay?" Gertie asked. She was beat so she hoped he meant it.

"You better go before he changes his mind." Loren said. "We will be right behind you. We're pretty much done here anyway."

"Ok. Well, goodnight." Gertie said as she gathered her things.

Gertie texted her dad when she left the office, to let him know she was on her way home. He thanked her for keeping him updated and told her Marcus was asleep so she went on home. It was late.

It seemed like Gertie had barely fallen off to sleep when her alarm clock went off. She got up and showered. She was still tired but she was loving her new gig in Homicide. She walked into the squad room looking refreshed and perky. She was ready to take on the day.

"Good morning." She said to everyone she passed on her way to her desk.

"You looking pretty good for three hours of sleep." PJ looked up at Gertie as she hung her suit jacket on the back of her chair.

"Thanks PJ. You don't look so bad yourself." She replied.

"Here's a fax from SID." Gina said. "It's the Analyzed Evidence Report."

"Oh let me see that." Gertie said taking the report from Gina.

"What does it say?" PJ asked.

"Looks like the criminalist test fired the gun that was recovered from Salcedo and she found that the bullet casing she recovered from the test fire and the casing that was recovered from the crime scene matched. They were fired from the same gun. Bingo!" Gertie exclaimed. She was excited. "Guess what else? I just got off the phone with Colorado Metropolitan Police Department and they are faxing me a copy of a Burglary report from 2 years ago, which documents the theft of the handgun that was used in our murder. I spoke with the victim of the Burglary, Mr. James Costello, and *he* said he was dating our suspect Salcedo's mother Connie, and that approximately two weeks prior to the Burglary of his house, he had ended the relationship with her. Connie lived in Henderson, Colorado with her boys but Costello never met the boys. He always felt that Connie's boys had something to do with the burglary of his residence and the only item taken was his handgun, which ended up involved in our murder."

"Damn. They should have stayed their asses in Colorado instead of coming here ruining people's lives." PJ said.

Lt. Lane and PJ held a Press Conference in front of the station announcing the arrest of Salcedo, after which time Gertie and PJ headed to the DA's office where they filed Murder charges against Salcedo. Gertie impressed upon the DA that the gun recovered was fully loaded with a bullet in the chamber and it had a full magazine, which indicated that he reloaded his gun *following* the shooting of Riggs indicating *presence of mind*. Gertie also explained that the suspect was very familiar with the operation of the weapon. She wanted to make sure he didn't use a *diminished capacity* defense. At the preliminary hearing Herbert Alejandro Salcedo was *Held To Answer* on the multiple charges that were filed against him.

"How does it feel solving your first homicide so soon after making Detective?" PJ asked.

"It was a major team effort." Gertie said reflecting back over the previous couple of weeks. "We could not have done it without the CAT team and Patrol resources." Gertie said.

"I'm glad that you realize that. We are not an island and as soon as you start thinking you can do it all yourself you will never accomplish anything. Where are you going on your vacation?"

"I'm going to take my baby and we are going to meet my mama and my Aunt Bea in Cabo San Lucas! After this past year I am long overdue for a vacation and what better place to hang out than on Medano Beach in downtown Cabo? I'll see you in a month! Gertie exclaimed grabbing her jacket and briefcase and saluting PJ on her way out the door. Later!

T. M. Morris

Tia M. Morris is a retired Los Angeles Police Captain and Author of the best selling book Mama's Curse-*A Memoir*. Tia's desire is to tell a good story whether it be her own true story or fictional drama. Tia is a realist and wants the reader to see real people dealing with real life issues in challenging arenas for women and most notably women of color. Tia's 33-year law enforcement career has made her a credible Consultant for TV shows and Security Companies as part of her role with The Morris Legacy Group. Tia is also the Chief Financial Officer at Vintage City Entertainment; where she is a Producer of films and Stage Plays, and she is a highly sought after Set Designer. Tia is a breast cancer survivor and State Advocate for Victim's of Domestic Violence and a Motivational Speaker who shares her story of struggle and survival and overcoming adversities. She is a survivor!

To schedule Tia for a speaking engagement or book club meeting, contact Brit Morris at morrislegacygroup@gmail.com. Please visit website at www.vintagecityent.com. Be sure to pick up Mama's Curse-*A Memoir* available at Amazon.com, BarnesandNoble.com and other booksellers.

ACKNOWLEDGEMENTS

PJAI, MY ROCK AND MY inspiration and best damn Homicide Detective on the planet, thanks for sharing your stories with me. They are sure to make Gertrude Bellamy's journey believable or maybe even UNbelievable! I thank God for making you just the way you are. You are funny, loving, and caring and you are brutally honest and unapologetically so. Thank you for loving me so much and for believing in me. I love our *Tea Time*. It keeps me current. I couldn't have published this book without you... Loving you always and forever.

Pjai

Britt where do I start with you? Thank you for taking such good care of me and for always protecting my Brand and me. You are an amazing scholar, leader, business-woman, and Manager/Publicist extraordinaire. You make me a better person and stretch my abilities to the max. Thanks for pushing me to be *great*. The sky is the limit for you, for us... Sarg! Let's go **M**orris **L**egacy **G**roup.

Brit

Natalia-"Tai French" Edwards your talent is out of this world! There is truly nothing you can't do! Your business savvy and brilliant writing has truly inspired me. Thanks for teaching me all about character development and showing me effective ways to *kill my darlings* for a more succinct product. Lord knows I can be wordy. Your professional feedback has been right on point. Thanks for your AMAZING graphics and photos. Thanks for allowing TiaMPublishing to be a part of your Vintage City

Brand. Please never stop making me laugh. Let's go **V**intage **C**ity **E**ntertainment and Face By Frenchie!

Natalia

Michael "Mike" Eddie Thanks for helping to bring balance to our estrogen charged family. You and Pops keep us Morris girls grounded. God truly sent me an Angel for a Son-In-Love; the man with the golden voice. Keep being the loving and kind spirit that you are.

Mike

Special Thanks to my sis LAPD Detective **Cheryl Nalls** (Retired) for allowing me to use your beautiful image for this Series and most importantly for your support and encouragement. I am so proud to have Gertrude Bellamy in your likeness. You are beautiful on the inside and out. Our candid talks helped me add dimensions to Gertrude Bellamy in bringing her to life! I am forever grateful.

Cheryl

Special Thanks to two of the most beautiful twins I know; **Precious McGill** and **Lady Gray** for your amazing insight. Because of you **Precious**, Gertrude Bellamy became a *Series...* you truly inspired me to bring this *Series* to fruition. **Lady** thanks for always keeping it real and for always inspiring me to operate in greatness. #Naptapestry

Special Thanks to **Parenthysis Gardner** for giving me confirmation that Gertrude Bellamy truly exists. Your Aunt and my Mom planned this. I'm convinced. RIH our Angels.

Special Thanks to my fur baby **Harlee** for keeping me company when I was burning the midnight oil in the wee hours of the morning writing and refining this story. Your snoring kept me awake old lady!

Thanks to my Facebook Family, especially those of you who *Liked* and *Followed* my Gertrude Bellamy Page. Your comments and feedback from my posted excerpts truly inspired me to write a story that is rich in character.

Thanks to the LAPD for the 33 years of experience and the stories…oh the stories…and the drama of it all!

Lastly, God bless those families who have lost loved ones to violence in our communities.

Don't forget to pick up your copy of *Mama's Curse-A Memoir*
By T. M. Morris
Available at Amazon.com and other booksellers!